Reviewers Are ⎡
Sweeter Th

"...a lovely, imaginative idyll...evokes
the wine country... [with] a perfect wo
her next novel."
—*Contra-Costa County Times*

"...stylish... the characterizations are finely drawn and sympathetic...
will enchant fans of historical romance who like something a bit
unusual...
—*The Romance Reader*

"...a stirring tale of love, lies, and atonement. *"*
—*Under The Covers*

"...exceptional... should be read by all lovers of good books...will keep
you turning the pages, faster and faster, reluctant to put the book down.
Make a point of reading this one!"
—*Romance Reviews*

"...my pick for historical novel of the year....It was with a profound
sense of regret that I turned the last page, but the aftertaste lingers long
and sweet on the tongue and in the memory."
— *Romance Communications*

"...a grand story built around passionate characters... Siegfried and
Alice, with their fears, desires, courage, and compassionate hearts...
carry the reader through the pages."
—*The Romance Reviewer*

"...warm and sensuous as the sun-drenched vineyards of its setting,
mingling golden lyricism with an earthy reality to create two special
lovers to touch your heart. A wonderful debut filled with tenderness and
tears, passion and joy."
— Gayle Feyrer, author of *The Thief's Mistress*

"...excellently plotted... unusual and as refreshing as a new, heady
wine... a rich-full-bodied story with just a taste of suspense..."
— *Affaire de Coeur*

SWEETER THAN WINE

Michaela August

Neighborhood Press
Middleburg, Florida

ACKNOWLEDGEMENTS

This book is dedicated to the memories of Elisabeth Dorette Hüschens, beloved *Candy-Oma*, and Raymond and Margaret Huntsman, loving parents.
You are missed.

The Author gratefully acknowledges the help of the following people and organizations in writing this novel:

- David Gibbons for his unfailing support, encouragement, and Sunday morning waffles;

- Fritz Welss for giving Siegfried such colorful invective when dealing with automobiles;

- Elke Welss Crabbe, Esq. for legal advice on inheritance and property laws above and beyond the call of sisterly duty;

- the late Robert McSheehy for information about American Catholicism as practiced in California earlier this century;

- Virginia Feeney for help on restaurant etiquette for nice young ladies;

- Barbara Welss and the late Elisabeth Hüschens for help with German grammar and various wonderful little tidbits of family history shamelessly appropriated for Siegfried;

- Samantha Hassler of Karlsruhe, Germany, for proofing and correcting the German passages, and sending photos of Alsace;

- Friedrich Hüschens for the details of the *Richtsfest*;

- Jim Bundschu and the tasting room staff at the Gundlach Bundschu Winery;

- Tom Martini and the staff of Martini & Prati Winery, for giving a special tour of their winery;

- Jason Breaw and the Sebastiani family at the Sebastiani Winery;

- Marcia Kunde Mickelson and staff of the Kunde Estate Winery;

- Mr. James B. Alexander, Mrs. Florence Oddie, and Mrs. Kay Hartman of the Sonoma County Historical Depot Museum for very helpful minutiae and keeping alive the history of Sonoma County;

- Roxane Wilson at the Historical Annex of the Sonoma County Library;
- the library staff at the Healdsburg Wine Library;
- Duncan Stuart, Western Region Sales Manager at the Alderbrook Winery in Healdsburg, Calif;
- Rich Thomas of the Santa Rosa Junior College Agricultural Dept. for information about crop yields;
- Bill Levinton for sharing his Model-T knowledge;
- Sally Norton for help on period clothing, jewelery, and etiquette;
- all the beta readers, who provided invaluable fine-tuning assistance;
- the always helpful and supportive members of the RW-L, RWALINK, and WWI-L listservs;
- the Spellbinders for cross-genre critiquing
- Mary Elizabeth Sperry, Publishing and Promotion Services of the US Catholic Conference, for corrections to the manuscript and permission to reprint excerpts from *The Roman Missal.*

Let him kiss me with the kisses of his mouth:
for thy love is better than wine!
The Song of Solomon, 1.2

Sélestat, Alsace, France
(formerly Schlettstat, Elsaß, a Reichsland of the German Empire)
Wednesday, April 2, 1919

Siegfried dozed, his cheek pressed against the cold, damp window of a jolting railway carriage, dreaming of food the way poor men dream of riches.

He feasted on salad dressed with mustard vinaigrette, garnished with tomatoes and Gruyere cheese; heaping plates of sauerkraut and thick smoked pork chops, fat-dripping bratwurst and bacon; a glass of Pinot Blanc; real coffee with a dash of cherry brandy; almond-and-raisin Kugelhopf cake, crowned with powdered sugar...

As the train squealed to a halt, he started awake, blinking and squinting through the fog on the inside of the windows. Raindrops marched like weary soldiers down the outside of the glass.

He buttoned his wool greatcoat and stood up cautiously, testing his leg to see if it would bear his weight. It did, but it took most of his strength to haul his knapsack down from the metal shelf above his seat and wait patiently for the aisle to clear. He had not eaten for two days, not since that last meager breakfast of toast and thin tea at the military hospital near Heidelberg.

It seemed as if he had been hungry forever. Food had been sometimes scarce or horrible at the Front. In Germany, since the Allies had begun a blockade in order to force the chaotic, newly democratic government to sign the surrender, it had been in short supply for everyone.

But it should not have taken two whole days to travel the short distance. He had been stopped for over a day at the border. Before the Great War, there had been no border between Germany and Alsace.

I will be home soon. I will be warm and dry. My Vater *will feed me.*

He had sustained himself on such promises for years. He could survive fifteen more minutes.

He walked a little unsteadily onto the station platform, wincing at the twinges of pain in his thigh. The chilly air, fresh after the train's thick atmosphere of wet wool, unwashed bodies, and coal smoke, revived him a bit.

An old man jostled him and began to apologize, then recognized Siegfried's field gray uniform and scowled before muttering darkly and turning away.

The space around Siegfried grew steadily wider as the other passengers greeted family and walked briskly into town. In a few minutes, he was completely alone. Across the wide cobbled square of the *Bahnhofplatz*, red-roofed, half-timbered houses closed their shutters against the dying storm. Gray misty rain blurred all the edges, but he knew every line, every detail.

He was home, at last, after four-and-a-half years in Hell.

His knapsack became too heavy to hold. He lowered it to the clean-swept platform, leaning it against a tub planted with geraniums. Siegfried averted his gaze from the scarlet blossoms scattered like splashes of blood among the patterned green leaves. He must not think of what it had been like. He was home. There was no blood here. But the smell of the trenches returned to him, the ripe odors of violated earth, decomposing flesh, sulfur, and cigarette smoke.

His stomach made a low, pained sound, not fierce enough to be called a growl. Fifteen minutes passed, then twenty. Father and his beloved Daimler never appeared. Had he not received the telegram? Sending it had taken Siegfried's last few *Marks*.

If Father didn't come to pick him up, then Siegfried would have to walk home on an empty stomach. He checked his pockets, but no coins had miraculously appeared. He couldn't even afford to buy himself a bread roll. He swayed at the thought, turning the motion into a stiff bow as an old woman and a little girl in a *schlumpkapf* walked by. The grandmother's silver hair was tucked securely under a close-fitting hat, her black umbrella held at a precise angle. She ignored him utterly and he flinched, knowing how he must appear to her, skinny and ragged in the uniform of the defeated Enemy.

At least his comrades, the ones who had not deserted to the French, had fallen honorably before they could be considered traitors by their neighbors. Siegfried envied them their peaceful rest, secure in the knowledge they had defended their *Heimat*, their homeland, with their lives. He had come home to find it a different country. French territory.

The cathedral bell tolled one o'clock, the deep, mellow sound echoing from the walls of the town's close-packed houses. Siegfried shifted uneasily, watching as the rain changed from a sullen trickle to a hard downpour.

It's only four miles, he cheered himself. *You used to be able to walk to Schlettstat and back in an afternoon.*

He set off through the cramped, winding streets, heading for the western gate, trying to ignore the garlicky scent of frying *bratwurst* wafting from the cafEs, trying to stifle his resentment. French Alsace did not want for food like Germany did.

He heard his name called as he neared the Gothic bulk of the Cathedral of Saint George. Startled, he saw a neighbor waving at him from the entrance of a nearby *Winstub.*

"*Grüß Gott, Herr* Rodernwiller!" old Johann Bauer greeted him warmly. "When did you return?"

Siegfried limped quickly over to stand in the doorway, grateful to be out of the rain. "Just now, *Herr* Bauer." He dropped his soaking knapsack with a sigh. He shook the older man's hand. "How are you? And *Frau* Bauer?"

"She was very sick with the influenza. But she is well now, thank God, not like—" Bauer's face fell. "We were so sorry when your dear mother passed away. She was such a good neighbor, for an American." He patted Siegfried's wrist with clumsy sympathy.

A sudden unwelcome stab of tears ambushed Siegfried. *Mutti.* He had not even known she was ill until the black-bordered letter arrived at the hospital.

Bauer released his hand and, after an embarrassed cough, added, "We were grateful for your letter about J,rgen. He was so proud to serve. Not like those Frog-lovers, dancing in the streets because—"

"Jürgen was a brave soldier. He did his duty with honor," he said, suppressing grief and guilt. At least Jürgen had died before seeing his sacrifice rendered futile. "I wish he could have been here instead of me."

"No, no, *Herr* Rodernwiller," Bauer protested, shocked. "Please, may I buy you a cup of wine?" At Siegfried's hesitation he said, "Please. I insist!"

Siegfried followed the old farmer into the tavern, giddy from the scents of spilled beer, onions, and bacon, almost thick enough to chew. Almost... The plump barmaid brushed past, and Siegfried had to wrestle down a powerful impulse to seize the plate of fried potatoes she carried and cram them into his mouth. Perhaps Herr Bauer would...?

No. Siegfried could not, would not, beg a meal from a man whose son he had so miserably failed.

Once they were seated on benches at a long wooden table, the barmaid came by with a blue-glazed pottery wine pitcher and two matching cups. As she placed them on the table she gave Siegfried a long, cold stare. Unsmiling, she accepted Bauer's payment.

Siegfried poured for them both, inhaled the fragrance of fresh greenish-gold Sylvaner, and raised his cup in a toast. "To the Fatherland," he said ironically, and drank, floating on the taste of sweet summer fruit. The wine warmed his belly, masking the emptiness there. "What will become of us?"

"We will learn to be Frenchmen, and drink to *La Belle Patrie*," replied Bauer. Then he spat on the immaculate floor.

Bauer's farm wagon was old, and drawn by an even older horse, but Siegfried gratefully accepted a ride. The horse plodded along the cobbled streets under graceful wrought-iron signs advertising bakeries, tailor shops, and hotels.

Siegfried nervously eyed the multitude of shuttered windows, shoulders tensed against the threat of sniper fire. He told himself firmly, *I am home now.* It was a relief to broach the Western Gate and head out on a muddy road into the open countryside, leaving the rough stones of the ancient Witches' Tower looming behind, its square top lost in the lowering clouds.

Siegfried thrust his hands deeply into his greatcoat pockets, regretting the lost warmth of the *Winstub*. The faint odor of onions clung to the damp wool like the perfume of an unfaithful lover. After another half-mile the rain lessened to a drizzle and Siegfried ventured a remark on the weather.

"Ach, Gott! I hope we have a good, hot summer! The last vintage was so poor," Bauer replied, shaking his head. "I'll be glad when the rest of the young men come home from the army. It was hard to harvest with only women and children."

"Not many will be coming home." Of his patriotic friends from Rodern— Franz, Jürgen, Karsten, and Helmut— only Siegfried had lived to endure this shameful surrender.

"No," agreed Bauer sadly. "Your father, he will be glad to see you."

Then why didn't he come to pick me up?

Siegfried's imagination leaped to paint the scene with his father's anger and disappointment: "*I sent you to defend the Fatherland, or die trying. You are a coward to come home, defeated yet alive.*"

Siegfried shook himself. *Had* he tried hard enough? He was whole when so many others were maimed or dead. In the slowly passing vineyard, leafless trunks stood in rows like cemetery crosses.

"You've seen my father more than I, Herr Bauer. He...rarely wrote to me. How is he?"

"Unhappy, Herr Rodernwiller." Bauer clucked at the old nag, whose speed did not increase. "I'm sorry to say it. He gave his all for the war effort..." He thought for a while. "Maybe you can get him to come back to church. We have all been worried about him."

Siegfried was oddly relieved. That was one thing they would not fight about. He never wanted to set foot in a church again. The war had proved to Siegfried that God was deaf, or dead.

They passed the village of St. Hyppolyte in silence. Siegfried's spirits rose a bit when the red-tiled roofs of Rodern's houses appeared. Almost home!

Bauer stopped his wagon on the outskirts of the village at the entrance to Rodernwiller Vineyards.

The climb down from the high hard wagon seat was painful, and his knapsack was heavier than ever. Siegfried paused at the bottom of the drive and waved his thanks.

Bauer nodded, flicked his horse's reins, and slowly pulled away.

The gravel of the drive crunched under his worn boots as Siegfried limped toward the house. He looked eagerly ahead, but only the sharply triangular peak of the tiled roof was visible through the veiling branches of the garden trees.

He slowed as he approached, passed under the trees, and saw what was left. All the windows were boarded-over. The east wing of the house, where his bedroom and Ernst's had been, was roofless. The white-plastered walls bore ugly shrapnel gouges from the shelling at the beginning of the War, from the attack that had changed everything, forever.

No smoke issued from the kitchen chimney, and Father's Daimler was missing from its usual place of honor in the middle of the cobbled courtyard. The rain dripped quietly from the surrounding trees and a superstitious shiver threaded down his spine.

We must have missed each other at the train station. Any minute now, he would see the Daimler's headlights approaching from the road. But why hadn't Father caught up with Bauer's wagon? Was he still in Schlettstat?

Siegfried's stomach cramped as he saw a black-ribboned pine wreath, gray and brittle now, lying where it had fallen on the doorstep. He imagined Father fastening it on the door after *Mutti*'s death. It was unlike him to leave rubbish lying about. What had happened?

The front door opened at his touch. Siegfried's boots squeaked on the checkered parquet floor, and he stood still, drawing his coat around him more tightly. It was hardly warmer in the house than outside, and there was a musty smell of disuse and abandonment. No lights shone anywhere.

"*Vater!*" he called into the silence of the house. No one answered.

He dropped his knapsack by the side table near the door and found a kerosene lamp and matches. He lit the lamp, thankful for the warm glow. As he lowered the clear glass chimney, two envelopes on the table caught his eye. The first was unopened, bearing a San Francisco postmark and addressed to Father in his grandmother Tati's unmistakable handwriting.

He frowned at the second, clearly opened, envelope. It was the telegram he had sent, listing his arrival date and time.

Where was Father? Why had his telegram been ignored?

The light wavered as he picked up the lamp and ascended the stairs. The walls were bare, and large unfaded squares of antique wallpaper attested to the places where portraits of his ancestors had hung. Had they been put away for safekeeping during the War?

Siegfried arrived on the second floor, where a dirty expanse of bare hardwood stretched down the hall. The long Persian carpet— the furniture— the gilded rococo mirrors — bronze gaslights— all gone.

He walked quietly towards his father's study. Very slowly, he pushed open the door that guarded his father's sacred precinct. The glow of the lamplight fell first on empty bookshelves, mahogany expanses once crowded with rare volumes. What in God's name was going on here? His father loved his books almost as much as he loved his wine.

Father put them away, Siegfried reassured himself, but the back of his neck and his arms were prickling. He knew this feeling from a thousand terrified moments spent awaiting the order to advance into a deadly rain of enemy bullets.

Siegfried saw his father, slumped forward over the massive desk, head pillowed on his arm. *He fell asleep! That's why he missed the train.* For an instant, he was glad.

"*Vater? Ich bin zu haus'.*"

The figure did not stir. The lamplight touched silver-blond hair and gleamed from the barrel of a pistol, held loosely in the slack fingers of his father's right hand. On the gilt-edged leather blotter, a thick brown stain congealed. Blood.

"Oh, God, no." The lamp shook violently as Siegfried very carefully placed it on the corner of the desk.

He knew I was coming home today.

He had known. He had *known*, and had done this monstrous thing.

Siegfried's stomach heaved. Sour wine stung the back of his throat, then subsided. Shadows fluttered as he steeled himself to view his father's corpse.

Heinrich Wilhelm August Rodernwiller was dressed in his best suit, dark blood staining the stiff collar of his shirt. His left hand curled over a folded paper.

Siegfried tugged the document out from beneath cool flesh, gingerly avoiding further contact. He slowly unfolded the page, tipping it toward the lamp.

It was a foreclosure notice, advising *Herr* Rodernwiller that the house and property known as Rodernwiller, its contents, demesne, and chattel were now the property of the *Allgemeine Landesbank Schlettstat, Elsaß,* and that *Herr* Rodernwiller should be prepared to vacate immediately. 'Schlettstat, Elsaß' had been crossed out and 'Sélestat, Alsace, France' hand-written in above.

Siegfried let the paper fall. There was another envelope, weighted down by his father's gold signet ring, on the far right corner of the desk. It was addressed to Siegfried. He opened it and tried to read, but the meaning of the words escaped him.

Mein lieber Sohn!

Ich wünschte, daß ich Dir diese Enttäuschung ersparen könnte. Ohne mein Weingut oder meine geliebte Gattin bin ich so verzweifelt, daß ich leider keinen Ausweg finden kann. Mein Leben ist nichts mehr wert. Hoffentlich verstehst Du meine endgültige Entscheidung und kannst mir dafür vergeben.

— Dein Dich liebender Vater

He had to read it again and again before he could comprehend.

My dear son:

I wish I could spare you this disappointment. But— without my vineyard, without my dear wife— I am in such despair that I can see no way out. My life is no longer worth anything. I hope you will understand my final decision, and forgive me for it.

Your loving father

Black patches spotted Siegfried's vision and the world tilted. He caught himself on the edge of the desk. The wood was sticky, and he realized dully that he had put his hand squarely into his father's blood. The smell of violent death was sickeningly familiar. He had not left it behind in the trenches. He staggered back, staring at his tainted palm.

The naked bookshelves served to hold Siegfried up as he

waited for his dizziness to pass.

After a long while, he straightened. The pain was still with him, but he could act again. Trying not to look at his father, Siegfried picked up the gold signet ring— his only patrimony now— and tucked it into his greatcoat pocket, where it nestled against his military discharge papers.

He needed to notify the authorities. Someone would have to... dispose of the body. He should write to his father's sister, *Tante* Hilde. At least she would grieve. Siegfried had nothing left for a father who had committed the ultimate betrayal.

Now who is the coward? You have run away, and left me to deal with the ruins.

Siegfried left the study and stumbled downstairs, his body disconnected from his mind, the house, once so beloved, strange and unreal. It was no longer his home.

He thought about having to deal with the bank officials regarding the foreclosure, and a spark of rage ignited, but it had no fuel to feed on. He had nothing left. His hands trembled, and he missed the last step. He fell heavily to his knees and the lamp flew from his hand, shattering against the parquet floor. Kerosene splashed in fiery tendrils against the wall and vines of flame blossomed upward.

Siegfried watched in disbelief as the fire spread. *At least it is finally warm.* But warmth turned to searing pain an instant later, bringing him back to reality as sparks attacked his hands and face.

He had to get out!

He could not get to his feet, so he crawled toward the door. The crackling sound swelled to a roar. He looked over his shoulder. Flames devoured the wall his ancestors had graced.

He grabbed his knapsack and the letter from *Oma* Tati, pulled himself up the doorjamb, then hobbled down the drive to the road leading toward *Herr* Bauer's farm.

He did not look back as his father's house burned, a funeral pyre for all his dreams.

CHAPTER

1

Healdsburg, California
Tuesday, May 13, 1919

"Alice, you've got to make up your mind. Either sell Montclair to me, or tear out the vines and plant prunes." Hugh Roye said, his high forehead wrinkling with exaggerated concern. "This is not the best time to run a winery. Even Lake County voted dry!"

"I loathe prunes." Alice Roye set down her fork, unable to take another bite of the tough chicken her brother-in-law was serving for lunch. His cluttered, dusty dining room seemed suddenly close despite the window opened to the early afternoon air. The sharp smell of chicken manure came from the yard outside, and she fought an unladylike urge to sneeze.

"I wish I knew why you were being so stubborn. I can't imagine why someone like you— a city girl, I mean." He slanted a look at her, then smiled charmingly as if he hadn't meant that comment at all, "—would want to sully her hands with such work anyway. I'd give you a fair price. You could reestablish yourself in San Francisco, and perhaps— marry again."

"It's too soon." Alice shook her head, patting her lips with the linen napkin, her heartbeat quickening until she could feel each heavy beat in the tips of her fingers against the cloth. She didn't care about being married again, but she did *not* want to return to San Francisco. And she would die before she revealed to anyone in Sonoma County the reason why.

"It's been over a year since Bill—" Hugh's mouth set in a stubborn line, an expression she had seen only occasionally on her young husband's face. Bill had always smiled and joked to fend off any unpleasantness. Sometimes she wondered, when she couldn't help herself, if Bill's good humor had survived the rigors of the Western Front, if he had been smiling and jesting with his men, until—

Alice bit her lip, and Hugh, obviously realizing he had pushed too hard, relented in his attack. He poured gracefully from the bottle of wine she had brought to serve with lunch and remained silent as they both sipped at the delicate Gundlach-Bundschu Traminer.

The wine was delicious, dry and fragrant, but Alice grimaced inwardly, remembering the failures of this last year. Bill had only been the first loss. Montclair's vintner, hired by

Bill's grandfather at the winery's inception, had succumbed to the Spanish Influenza before they finished crush last fall. Alice had done the best she could, but the Traminer had all spoiled in transit to the East Coast. Park and Tilford, her distributors, had refused to pay for the vintage, and had, in fact, billed her for shipping costs and damages.

She hoped that her new vintner would know how to avoid spoilage this year. She *had* to turn a profit. She just had to hang on until harvest.

Truce over, Hugh set his glass down, and leaned forward. "I worry about you, all alone out there. You can't take care of that property with only field hands."

"Surely you're not calling Mrs. Verdacchia a *fieldhand*, Hugh," Alice laughed, determined to dispel the adversarial mood. "You never refuse an invitation to dinner if Maria's cooking! Really, it's good of you to be interested, but I believe I have a buyer for this year's wine."

"Montclair's profits were always in champagne, but you won't make champagne, will you, dear?"

"It's too much effort," Alice protested. "And I don't want to make wines just for the liquor trade—"

Hugh pushed his chair away from the table. "You don't seriously believe you could obtain a sacramental wine license, Alice! *You*?" Hugh laughed unkindly. "So, the Archbishop is a family friend?"

"I'm sorry, but I really must return to Sonoma." Alice spoke through gritted teeth as she stood up. She picked up her long-handled suede handbag and said with imitation cheerfulness. "Oh, I almost forgot to tell you. I won't be quite alone this summer. Your cousin has arrived from Europe and I promised your grandmother I would hire him."

"What cousin? You don't mean Siegfried? Coming here? He's got some gall." Hugh's long face turned an ugly red. "It was bad enough that Aunt Betty married that foreigner—"

"I thought your grandparents were happy to be connected with an established European winemaking family," Alice reproved gently.

"That was before the Huns killed Bill."

Alice winced, smoothed her gloves on, and buttoned them. "Your grandmother says Siegfried is an experienced vintner."

"You don't need Tati's kind of help," Hugh said bitterly. "It'll be useless after Prohibition, anyway. Promise me you'll reconsider my offer!"

"I will." Alice pinned her straw hat securely to her neatly

coiled hair. *If Prohibition goes into effect at all.*

Hugh rose belatedly from his chair. "Let me see you out to your car."

They left his white clapboard house and walked towards a battered Model-T truck parked in the dusty driveway.

The early-morning fog had burned off, leaving bright summer sunshine and warmth. The smell of chickens, although much stronger out here, was mitigated by the pleasantly biting fragrance of the eucalyptus trees planted for shade. Incessant clucking and an occasional squawk came from the poultry houses that climbed the gentle slope of the hill behind the house.

Hugh paused in front of the Model-T and rolled up his shirtsleeves. He raised an eyebrow as she opened the door for herself. "How do you start this thing when you don't have a man around?"

"I manage well enough." Alice slipped into the long linen coat that protected her blue-and-white summer frock from the dust of the road and settled herself behind the steering wheel. "I've learned to take my gloves off first." She smiled at her own dry joke.

"You shouldn't have sold Bill's— *car.*" Hugh's voice was punctuated by the effort of turning the crank. The Model-T's engine started with its usual belch and rumble.

"I do miss the electric starter, but the Buick wasn't very practical at Montclair," Alice said. The sale of the car had paid this year's wages for Peter and Maria Verdacchia, and she had gotten the truck in trade— a bargain for which she was still congratulating herself. She wouldn't have to rent a team of horses this season for the harvest wagon. She put the truck into gear and prepared to release the brake. "Thank you for lunch, Hugh."

Hugh's wave good-bye was desultory. She caught a last glimpse of him before the drive curved abruptly south onto Chalk Hill Road. He stood, arms akimbo, clearly disappointed that she hadn't accepted his offer.

Alice sighed as she negotiated the twists and turns of the bumpy road heading towards Santa Rosa. Since Bill had been gone, she had come to depend on his older brother's help and advice, but every visit now Hugh grew more and more insistent about buying her vineyard, and skirting closer to voicing his unspoken opinion that she didn't deserve to own Montclair.

She didn't like to agree with Hugh, but he was right: she had no excuse for loving her land except that she had found unexpected delight in being Mrs. William Roye, of Montclair, and not Alice O'Reilly of brazen San Francisco, city of miserable rainy winters, cold foggy summers, and questionable morals.

The Ford bounced over a rough patch in the road and Alice gripped the steering wheel tightly. She understood, even sympathized, with Hugh's position. He wanted Montclair as much as she did.

The first time she had seen the property, in the autumn of 1914, she had been newly-graduated from St. Rose High School. Her father had brought her along on his yearly trip to inspect the new vintages. As he drove through orderly acres, the lanes between the trellised vines had opened straight every way she looked, forming mystical geometric patterns which surrounded her with peace and a sense of homecoming. She had fallen in love.

Bill Roye's bright blue eyes and merry smile had welcomed her into his home. He had married her and she had enthusiastically thrown herself into the life of a country wife. If only it could have lasted longer.

The dust—— it must have been the dust thrown up by the tires—— made her throat tight.

The breeze from the truck's speed fanned against the sheen of perspiration on her face, and she stopped for a moment to release the buttons on her driving coat. The warm day had suddenly turned hot, the air spiced with bay laurel and wild fennel. Red-trunked manzanita bushes raked dry elongated leaves along the side of her truck. Over the rattle of the engine, a meadowlark's piercing melody lifted her heart, reminding her she was far from the City.

She tried very hard to drive straight through Santa Rosa, but there was a shaded place to park right by the entrance to the White House department store and temptation got the better of her. Feeling guilty and delighted at the same time, Alice went in to admire the new shipment of clothing on display.

She wished she could afford to buy some long hobbled skirts and loosely belted jackets, and at least one summer hat trimmed with flowers and feathers. Alice admired all the beautiful things she couldn't have today. *Maybe next year....* She lingered by the perfume counter, seduced by the fragrances.

"Can I help you with something, ma'am?" asked the young shopgirl, flyaway hair tousled around an apathetic moon face.

"I believe the young lady over there was ahead of me," Alice nodded in the direction of the shirtwaist display, where a dark-haired woman was holding one of the blouses against herself to measure its arm length.

The shopgirl wrinkled her nose. "Oh, *her*," she said. "She's no lady. She can wait while decent folks get served."

"I beg your pardon?" Alice's suspicions were confirmed with the shopgirl's next words.

"She's from one of *those* houses on Sonoma Avenue. Don't know why she insists on coming here and offending our respectable customers. In fact, if she's causing you any trouble, I'll call the manager and he'll put her out on the street where she belongs."

Alice burned in silent shame and horrified sympathy for the girl. She had grown up in one of *those* houses, and had many times experienced the same scorn when Mama dared to venture to stores outside the free-wheeling Barbary Coast. "No... no, that won't be necessary."

"Well, all right," said the shopgirl, disappointed. "Now, how may I help you, ma'am?"

"I need some middies." She studied the young prostitute covertly while the shopgirl went to fill Alice's order. A heavy coating of rice powder covered the thin, pretty face. *Probably hiding a bruise*, Alice thought sympathetically.

Two matrons entered the shop, noticed the girl's bare hands and scarlet-painted nails, and gave loud, condemning sniffs. The girl's lips thinned, but she kept her gaze focused on the pretty lace shirtwaist she was examining as the matrons carefully walked around her, holding their purses away as if she might contaminate them.

Alice remembered her own youthful determination to hide how much that kind of disapproval hurt. And if her current friends and neighbors ever found out about her past, Alice knew she would be treated no differently. At that moment, the prostitute looked up and met Alice's gaze, her expression one of weary defiance.

Alice bit her lip and turned quickly away. She reminded herself that she had put her past behind her. She was respectable now, a war-hero's widow. There was nothing left of the little girl who had been fussed over by the working girls in her mother's parlor house, who had sat listening to the stories of their adventures and their precarious lives, who knew too much about what happened to women who weren't ladies. She wasn't standing in that young woman's shoes, forced to earn her living on her back because she had no other choice.

But she might be, if this harvest failed, or if the law made winemaking illegal without a license.

Forcing down her fears, Alice handed over four dollars and accepted the neatly wrapped package of middies in return, trying hard to feel satisfied. The modest cotton sailor-blouses were comfortable to work in, and would last. Out of the corner of her eye, Alice saw the dark-haired girl, her chin raised proudly, bring her lovely acquisition to the shopgirl.

Alice escaped outside, tossing her sensible purchase onto the seat of the truck. She took off her gloves with a pang, then bent awkwardly in her high heels and strained at the Ford's crank. The first quarter-turn was always easy, but the half-turn that followed took all of her strength as she battled increasing resistance. Perspiration trickled down her forehead and neck. If she let go now, the kickback could break her wrist. She hoped no one was watching— the engine shuddered to life as the crank slid into the last quarter turn.

She hurriedly pulled her gloves on over her reddened palms, donned her coat, and sat behind the wheel, collecting herself.

The dark-haired girl came out just then, jauntily carrying her parcel. She looked neither right nor left as she departed down the sidewalk, hips rolling in blatant advertisement. Male heads swiveled to watch her while every female turned away.

Alice clutched her steering wheel. *It's not my business. It has nothing to do with me.*

Driving rapidly away from the store, Alice shoved away thoughts of the past by speculating on what the afternoon mail might bring. Maybe a response from Archbishop Hanna? He might not be a family friend, but as a good Catholic winemaker, she had as much right as anyone to petition him for a sacramental wine license.

And Montclair's wines were more than worthy of his consideration. They would be her financial salvation as well as her offering to God, even if the sins she hoped to atone for were not her own.

The memory of her mother's practiced laugh mocked her thoughts. Deliberately, she filled her mind with the beauty of the scenery: dairy pastures, walnut orchards, plum orchards, hayfields, vineyards, high rock palisades, and long stretches of empty, rolling golden California countryside. She had spent her entire adult life proving to herself that she was nothing like Mama. She would not stop now.

Two hot hours later she turned onto West Spain Street, and quickly maneuvered through the light traffic around Sonoma's picturesque Central Plaza. She rejoiced when she finally reached Lovell Valley Road, because it led directly to Montclair, nestled in the curve of the Sonoma-Napa hills. Her vineyard was situated north of Gundlach Bundschu's four-hundred-acre Rhine Farm, south of Carl Dresel's much smaller vine-bearing property, and east of colorful Agoston Haraszthy's now-deserted Buena Vista.

She left her engine running by the wrought-iron front gate at the bottom of the hill, and went eagerly to open the mailbox. Pulling out a sheaf of mail, she scanned it, looking for official stationery. *Nothing today.* Alice sighed, and tossed the packet of bills and circulars next to her practical purchase on the seat before negotiating the gate and the drive up to the house.

Alice heard the telephone shrilling as she slammed the truck's door. "Wait! Wait! I'm coming." She hurried up the walkway and threw open the front screen door, running down the hall to the base of the staircase, grabbing the conical receiver. Panting, she bent toward the mouthpiece hanging on the wall. "H-Hello?"

"Hello, Mrs. Roye. This is Gertrude. You have a call from San Francisco," announced the local operator. "I'm connecting you now."

A horrible apprehension struck Alice. "Who is it?" she demanded, but Gertie Breitenbach was already gone.

"Goodness, child. Did I catch you at a bad time?" a vibrant voice asked with a laugh. "Shall I ring you back?"

Alice patted her chest and took a deep breath, reprieved. "No, Grandmother Tati! It's always good to hear from you."

"How are you?"

"I'm well. I just returned from Santa Rosa— shopping and lunch with Hugh."

"I see," Tati's voice was abruptly cool. "And how are things at Montclair?"

Alice had never understood the hostility between Tati and her oldest grandson, so she decided not to mention Hugh's latest offer to buy Montclair. "Peter says the vines are doing very well. He and Maria will be going to her brother's wedding in San Jose this weekend. I'm glad that they're finally getting out again, after all the dreadfulness last winter. And we're excited that you've found us a vintner."

"Speaking of Siegfried, I would like you to meet him. Do come tomorrow. We'll have high tea at the St. Francis."

"But—" Alice hesitated, caught a little off-balance. "I don't know if I can leave again so soon. We're in the middle of dusting the vines. And he *is* coming up here next week."

"It will be good for you to meet first," Tati said firmly. "To make sure that you will get along. I was so sorry that I couldn't help you with Montclair after Bill—" The old woman's voice thickened, and she coughed to clear it before she continued. "You've worked so hard at Montclair to preserve my dear husband's legacy, and it means a great deal to me that you've considered taking Siegfried on, Alice dear. Do say you'll come tomorrow."

Alice hated going in to the City, but she could not refuse Tati. Bill's grandmother had welcomed Alice into the Roye family and treated her with never-failing politeness, almost like a real daughter. She had earned Alice's eternal gratitude, because although she must be aware of Alice's circumstances, she had never once mentioned them out loud, or allowed her awareness of Alice's origins to show in word or inflection. Tatiana Feyodorovna Roye was exactly the kind of lady Alice aspired to be. "All right. I'll come."

"I'll expect you on the one o'clock ferry. I know it's a long trip from Sonoma, dear, but I do so look forward to seeing you again."

They rang off, leaving Alice standing in the shadowed hallway, studying the carved ball on the newel post. Tati's husband William Roye, silver baron and amateur vintner, had built the house, the vineyard, and Montclair's reputation. Alice hoped that things would indeed work out with Bill's cousin Siegfried. She badly needed a skilled winemaker. Another shipment of spoiled wines would seal Montclair's doom— and hers.

San Francisco
Wednesday, May 14, 1919

The cold air rushed up from the Bay's gray-green water, flinging drops of spray over the ferry's deck. Alice clutched the handrail, watching as San Francisco drew nearer. The Ferry Building with its huge clock shone white above the harbor crowded with steam and sailing ships of every description. Grandmother Tati and Cousin Siegfried would probably already be waiting for her.

Alice vainly tried to tuck wayward strands of hair, faintly damp with salt spray, back under her hat. The ferry would dock in a few minutes. She should have known better than to stand on deck, but the cabin had been crowded and she had felt the urge to escape into the fresh air. She gave her hair a final despairing pat, then sighed and gave up the struggle. After all, it didn't matter what she looked like to her vintner.

"—Alice is almost like a granddaughter to me now, even though I was so surprised when Billy married her. She's worked hard to keep Montclair going since Billy enlisted, but it's too much for her. She needs someone to take care of things *properly*, especially after that debacle with last year's Traminer—"

Wondering vaguely why his normally serene grandmother was chattering so volubly, Siegfried let his gaze drift past the Ferry Building, down the endless-seeming row of immense white piers that marched along the Embarcadero to Fisherman's Wharf. In the gaps between the buildings, he saw distant hills crowding up against the opposite shore of the Bay. Their winter coats of green were already dulled in anticipation of the long summer drought.

His thoughts flew home to Alsace, where the first velvet buds were probably just now appearing on the vines. He would never again see them furl into tender leaf, never again walk the rows with Father, inspecting the tiny sprays of greenish grape blossoms, never again experience the anticipation of the young berries' maturation to sweet, full ripeness on Rodernwiller's prized Pinot Noir vines.

Don't live in the past, he chided himself, as he had a hundred times a day, each day of his long, tedious journey into exile. *I must learn to be an American now. I* will *have a vineyard of my own, someday. I swear it.* He jammed his hands into the pockets of a suit jacket that had once belonged to his grandfather, and wrinkled his nose. The jacket had been stored for a long time, and smelled strongly of camphor.

The pause in Tati's monologue alerted him.

"Of course, *Oma* Tati," he said with grave politeness, since she was looking at him expectantly. He suppressed his homesickness, his grief. "I will do my best to assist Cousin Ahlees. Alice." He did his best to pronounce her name the way his grandmother had, with short, impatient American syllables.

"Does she sound... compatible?" Tati pulled her dark coat tighter around her in the brisk breeze blowing off the water.

Siegfried forced himself to smile a little. "You describe a paragon. But I am only her vintner. I am not going to marry her."

"Actually, I hope that you will," Tati said seriously.

"Marry?" Siegfried, asked, aghast. "I have not even met your Alice!"

"Now, Siegfried," Tati said, looking suspiciously sweet and frail. "Don't make up your mind until you've heard me out. I must admit that I've been trying to find a way to bring up this subject gracefully. Now—" she raised a black-gloved hand to ward off his automatic protest. "Alice really *is* in dire straits, up there all alone. I suspect Hugh is pressuring her to sell, and you know how I feel about *that.*"

Siegfried felt sorry for his cousin, deprived of his

expected patrimony. But *Oma* Tati's words, tearless and harsh after the reading of *Opa* Roye's will, came back to him. *He doesn't deserve Montclair. He doesn't have a heart. He can't have ours.*

"So, if you and Alice could come to an... arrangement, it would benefit everyone."

Siegfried had heard of such marriages for the sake of property in Europe, but that sort of union was generally confined to the nobility.

But hadn't Frau Schliessig, who owned the dairy in Rodern, married her head milker after her husband died? And if Alice was as determined as Tati to keep Montclair out of Hugh's hands, then she might be willing to marry a man she had never met, for the good of the estate. Siegfried wondered if he would have been willing to do the same for Rodernwiller.

Of course, if I could have saved Father from... But he wasn't going to think about that.

Tati's voice broke into his thoughts. "It would be so wonderful to see a Roye at Montclair again. It was your grandfather's pride and joy, after all, and he would have wanted you to have it now."

Siegfried recognized that his grandmother would not relent in her efforts until he had thrown her some sort of a sop. "I will consider your idea," he said, carefully. "But I think it will be best if I work as her vintner first, to see if we suit."

Tati made an annoyed sound, not quite a snort. "Really, Siegfried! Your grandfather would roll over in his grave if he knew that you were working as a hired hand at Montclair!"

Stung by his grandmother's scorn, Siegfried remembered his father's final message: *Without my vineyard...my life is no longer worth anything.* Tati was right. If Alice were willing to marry him, he would be a fool to turn down this opportunity for a new start.

But something in him rebelled at being pushed. He dug in his heels. "Of course Montclair should remain in our family," he said, keeping his tone deferential toward his aged grandmother. "But a marriage— that is not a matter for hasty decision. At least let me meet her first!" He glanced out towards Treasure Island and saw a wide-bowed ship approaching. "The ferry is coming."

People began to stream around them, filing toward the Ferry Building hall. Siegfried would have joined the crowd but Tati narrowed her eyes and stood with her chin raised, clearly unwilling to move until she had secured his concession. He glared back, letting her know that he could be just as stubborn as she. They had played this game more than once during his boyhood summers in California.

Siegfried sensed a reprieve when the corner of Tati's mouth began to twitch with an incipient smile, but his grandmother was not yet ready to concede defeat. She straightened her coat, slipped her arm through his, and flowed with the others, saying conversationally, "I hope that you can come to an agreement with Alice, but if not, dear, of course you're welcome to stay with me as long as you like. However," she sighed deeply as they emerged onto the broad space before the dock, "you know my resources aren't what they used to be..." Seemingly intent on watching the men wheel the gangplank up to the edge of the now-docked ferry, she did not meet Siegfried's eyes. "Oh, look, there she is!"

Siegfried's pride chafed at the implication that he was a burden on his grandmother's charity as she began waving her handkerchief. It was an unfair accusation. He had planned to earn his future meals fairly with hard work. Tati might be piqued that she could not have her way, but he had spent four years taking orders from officers who remained warm and dry while he slogged through the mud and snow, and he was sick of making sacrifices for someone else's good.

He would *not* let his grandmother bully him.

The ferry bumped into the pier and tied up. Alice cautiously tapped down the gangplank in her high louis-heeled shoes. She spotted Tati, waving.

Bill's grandmother was stylish as ever in a three-quarter length black ponyskin coat with a large fox-fur collar. Her narrow black hat brim was trimmed in the same fox fur and bore an insouciant black ostrich plume.

Alice returned Tati's wave, quickening her step. Then she noticed the tall man standing next to Tati.

An invisible hand closed painfully around her heart, and she came to a full stop, gasping for breath.

The early afternoon sunshine haloed the man's short blond hair. An old-fashioned dark suit hung loosely from his wide shoulders, and his face was gaunt, the cheekbones sharply defined.

It was her husband, back from the dead.

Why hadn't Tati told her? Why had the government lied, sending that damned telegram?

"Bill," she said, in a strangled whisper. Another deep breath, and her voice returned. "Oh, my God— Bill!" Tears blurred her vision. Blinded, she ran the last few yards separating them. "You're alive! How did you—?"

Alice realized her terrible mistake the instant before she flung herself in his arms. *Not Bill!*

She tried to pull up short, but stumbled into him, causing them both to stagger like drunkards. Against her breasts, for an instant, she felt his heart, beating frantically fast. She pushed herself away in a startled recoil, but his steadying hands on her shoulders held her near.

"I'm so sorry!" Alice gulped, mortified. "I'm all right now. You can let go."

He did, and Alice clasped her gloved hands together, unable to look into that dear, familiar face, worn by a stranger. "You look so much like—"

"Alice, this is my *other* grandson, Siegfried Rodernwiller." Tati presented her lined cheek to Alice for a kiss.

Alice obeyed, her own face flaming, then awkwardly offered her hand to Siegfried. "I'm pleased to meet you. Mr. Ro-Rotenviller." As she stared at his neatly knotted tie, she caught his unexpectedly sweet, slightly embarrassed smile from the corner of her eye.

"For your sake, I wish it had truly been my cousin here to meet you, Cousin Alice," Siegfried said, in fluent but slightly accented English. His ears turned red. He clicked his heels together, straightened sharply, and gave her a jerky nod. "Please accept my condolences on your loss." His fingers closed around hers, their warmth penetrating through her thin gloves, and he stared intently down at her with eyes that were sapphire rather than Bill's sky-blue.

Alice let him keep her shaking hand and he led her and Tati through the Ferry Building and out onto the broad Embarcadero.

He's not Bill.

She had almost gotten over missing her young husband, his jolly laugh, and the lightness of heart that carried him over every obstacle but the last.

"May I?" Siegfried stood at the door of a waiting taxi, ready to hand her in. Tati was already seated inside.

Alice ducked into the car by herself. She could not bear it if he touched her again.

Letting habit guide him, Siegfried opened the taxi door for his grandmother and ushered her in while he stole glimpses of Alice's trim figure and slim ankles.

Dazed, he remembered taking her hand, speaking to her,

acting as if nothing had happened, as if the ground had not teetered beneath his feet when she flung herself into his arms. He had reeled at her touch, as if an earthquake had struck that only he could feel.

His chest still held the impression of Alice's bosom soft against him. He longed to kiss that sweetly curved mouth, to trace her features, Celtic-fair with a sprinkling of freckles, with his fingers and his lips.

The incredulous joy in Alice's hazel eyes upon seeing him had been meant for another man, but he wanted it for his own. Insanely and completely, he wanted her as he had never wanted anyone else. At that moment Siegfried realized he was going to agree to his grandmother's crazy scheme.

As the taxi crawled through the busy lunchtime traffic of vehicles and people on Market Street, Grandmother Tati chattered brightly. Squeezed beside Siegfried, Alice was morbidly aware of the texture of his wool suit where his arm and thigh pressed against her. She responded to Tati's questions at intervals, but Siegfried sat silently during the short journey, apparently absorbed in studying the flowers sold in profusion on the sidewalks. His gaze jerked away from hers whenever she caught him looking at her.

Trying to draw him into the conversation, Tati pointed out a bank building that she said was new since Siegfried's last visit.

"I hate banks," he said flatly.

So did Alice, but she didn't go around talking about it. Bill would have—

No. He wasn't Bill. On the worst day of their married life, when they discovered his entire fortune had been embezzled, her husband had joked that it was God's way of telling him to join the Army.

She wished for the gift of his laughter now.

When the taxi had delivered them to the St. Francis Hotel, Alice followed Tati and Siegfried into the enormous foyer of the hotel, intimidated by the huge marble columns, polychrome floors, and enormous urns of fresh flowers. She always felt out of place amidst such magnificence. The opulence of the Mural Room with its carved Oriental screens and cushion-heaped divans was worse, because it was more intimate.

The maitre d' knew very well Tati's exact standing in San Francisco society. He knew Alice by sight also, and professed himself overjoyed to meet Monsieur Rodernwiller. He led them to a spot five tables from the door. It was a better place than he would have offered to a casual customer off the street, but not as good as one he would have offered to the cream of San Francisco society, like Miss DeYoung or Mrs. Cameron.

A pot of fragrant tea accompanied by plates of finger sandwiches and scones with jam and Devonshire cream appeared on the lacquered table. Siegfried, possibly prompted by Tati's pointed toe tapping peremptorily on his foot, addressed Alice. "*Oma* Tati tells me that you are a native of the city."

"Why—- ah, yes. I was born here. But I prefer living at Montclair." She stopped speaking, aware how flustered she sounded. "*Oma* Tati?"

"It means 'grandmother' in German, dear," Tati explained. "I always loved it when you and Ernst called me that," she said to Siegfried.

"German? I thought you said he was Alsatian," Alice asked, suspiciously.

"He is," Tati answered hastily, shooting Siegfried a quick glance. "But Alsace was occupied by Germany for many years, and they prohibited the teaching of French. Poor Siegfried doesn't even know his native tongue."

"So should I call you Grandmère from now on? Or would you prefer 'babushka'?"

Alice thought Siegfried's tone was a bit sharp.

Tati hastily changed the subject. "Bill and Alice, when they married, bought new acreage and expanded the vineyard. It's up to one hundred sixty-five acres now. Alice, tell Siegfried about the grapes you planted."

So it was to be school recitations, was it? "We put in Grenache and some more Pinot Noir. Bill thought they would do well." Alice's throat constricted, so she took a sip of tea. "We had our first crop last year."

"How you must regret that he never got a chance to see it," Siegfried said gently.

"The harvest was good. We averaged two and three-quarter tons per acre." Alice did *not* want to discuss Bill with him.

"That's an excellent yield for young vines," Siegfried said, respecting her change of topic. He wiped jam from his fingers with one of the stiffly starched linen napkins.

"We got a good price for the crop." The sale of the Pinot Noir grapes to Inglenook in Napa Valley had saved Alice from ruin after the Traminer vintage spoiled.

She noticed that Siegfried had cleaned off his plate to the last crumb and passed him her untouched plate of *petit fours*. He thanked her with a self-conscious smile. Alice, trying to divert the conversation away from herself, asked, "And how was your journey from Europe? Did you take the transcontinental railroad, Mr. R-Rodernwiller?" She stumbled again over the pronunciation of his name.

"Please call me Siegfried. It will be much easier," Siegfried said to Alice, as he refilled his own cup and Tati's. "Actually, I traveled by steamer through the Panama Canal. It was a very interesting journey."

"I'm sure it must have been." Alice nodded politely as she took a tiny nibble from her cucumber sandwich. She hoped he wouldn't go into raptures about the technical achievements of the new canal. She'd seen the model at the Pan Pacific Exhibition in '15. "Did you have a chance to disembark anywhere?"

"Panama City, where I made the mistake of bringing on board a large bunch of bananas, about so wide." He spread his hands two feet apart, grinning at her, and his resemblance to Bill made Alice's heart leap. "I had read about them in Mr. Haggard's African adventure books, and I was very eager to try one. I was attempting to twist a banana from the main stalk when a tarantula crawled from the bunch and ran across my hand. I am not sure which of us was the more startled: the eight-legged stowaway, or I. The Captain was convinced that I was being set upon by ruffians—" Siegfried used his napkin to pantomime his attempts to stalk the spider around the steamer cabin with a rolled newspaper held carefully at arms' length.

Alice laughed. "Did you ever get to eat any of your bananas?"

Siegfried nodded in dreamy recollection. "They were very good. Almost like a custard pudding in texture but much sweeter."

"He has a sweet tooth, like his grandfather. I planted the plum trees behind the house at Montclair years ago, because my William was so fond of jam," Tati remarked, her gaze lingering on Siegfried.

Siegfried nodded at his grandmother, as if giving some sort of signal, and relaxed.

Tati raised her eyebrows, looking both surprised and pleased. She smiled fondly at Alice, put aside her napkin, and began to rise. "Would you join me, Alice?"

Siegfried hastily stood and pulled back his grandmother's chair, an unaccountably furious blush rising up from the celluloid collar pinching his throat.

Alice, mystified, let Siegfried pull her chair out, too, then followed Tati into the brocaded grandeur of the ladies' room.

Their footsteps echoed on the marble floors, and their figures reflected in the large gilt-framed mirror hung over the washbasins.

Tati leaned forward to check her flawless complexion. She had once been one of the most beautiful women in San Francisco, and even now, in her seventies, her blue eyes were as luminous as ever, although the hair under her dashing hat had transmuted from gold to silver. She turned from the mirror to Alice. "My dear," she said earnestly, "I have an immense favor to ask of you."

"You know I would do anything for you, Grandmother Tati." *What could she want?*

Tati smiled sweetly. "I'm so glad to hear you say that. It's about Siegfried."

"He'll be perfectly fine as my vintner."

Tati rubbed at the age spots on the back of her hand with her thumb. "It's slightly more complicated than that."

Alice felt a velvet trap close around her, but she forced herself to stillness. "Oh?"

Tati said coolly, "I want you to marry him."

San Francisco, California
Wednesday, May 14, 1919

Alice almost laughed at the joke, nearly as good as one of Bill's best. But then she looked at Tati and realized the old woman was serious. It was like receiving the news of her father's death— or Bill's— that instant of disbelief, and then the urge to scream.

Tati waited patiently for her reply.

Alice stole a moment to think, tucking wisps of hair back into her chignon. She recalled Hugh's recent offer to buy her out. Was this another attempt to dispossess her? *No*. After all Tati's kindness to her, she had to dismiss the ugly notion. She straightened one eyebrow with her little finger. But stalling wasn't doing any good. She couldn't think of anything else to say except: "Why on earth should I marry him?"

"I know it's an imposition." Tati smoothed her bare fingers as if they were too-tight gloves. "His father lost everything: his estate, their fortune, everything! in the War. Then he killed himself. Siegfried almost starved to death."

A surge of compassion left Alice uncertain. She'd read the newspaper stories about war-ravaged Europe, and Siegfried was gaunt enough, but— "Grandmother Tati, this is absurd! I'm perfectly willing to hire Siegfried, but I can't marry him. I just met him!"

"You didn't know Bill much better when you married *him*. And you were happy together. Weren't you?" Tati's blue eyes were wide, searching for signs of weakness, bringing to the surface things they had never spoken of before.

"I loved Bill—"

"And now you own Montclair," Tati said grimly. "I have *never* asked you for a thing, Alice. I am asking you for this." She must have seen Alice wavering, because she continued pitilessly, "You know I never believed you were in any way like your mother, but it would be a shame if people— I think you know the ones I mean— found out about your unfortunate connections, and came to the— shall I say?— wrong conclusions..."

In a flash, Alice's thoughts crystallized. If Tati made public what she knew, there would be no more friendly tea parties with the ladies from church, and no altar wine license for a woman of low character. Without the license.... Alice clutched the edge of the marble counter and her reflection in the mirror stared back, a scattering of freckles harshly distinct against bloodless cheeks. *Out on the street where she belongs...*

"All right. I'll do it. I'll marry him." Even though she would regret this moment for the rest of her life.

Tatiana Roye opened and closed her pocketbook with a snap. She gave a pleased smile that made Alice feel slightly nauseous. "I knew I could count on you, dear. Let's go back now, shall we?"

At their return, Siegfried leapt to his feet, almost knocking over the table. At his grandmother's satisfied smile and nod, he took Alice's hand, bowed over it, and said all in a rush, "I-hope-you-will-do-me-the-honor-of-becoming-my-wife."

All that was visible of him was cornsilk hair and ears red as ripe tomatoes. She said breathlessly, swallowing indignation, "I accept your proposal." *Tati left me no choice.*

Siegfried stayed where he was. "Thank you."

Alice stole her hand back from his grasp, then Siegfried straightened. He had the look of a man reprieved from a death sentence.

"You've made me very happy, children," Tati said, peering at the watch pinned to her jacket. "Oh, dear. We have to be there in twenty minutes."

Alice turned to her, newly alarmed. "*Where* do we have to be?"

"City Hall," Tati said, a shade too brightly. "Judge Reynolds, bless him, promised to wait until four o'clock for us."

Alice gasped. "You arranged all of this in *advance*?" She glared at Siegfried, but he was gaping at Tati, seemingly as astonished as she.

The corners of Tati's mouth quirked as she patted her watch back into place. "Only if you said 'yes.'"

The ostrich feather trimming Tati's elegant hat bobbed as she ascended the shallow granite steps toward the huge, neo-Classical City Hall.

This is utterly ridiculous. I've agreed to marry a man I met less than three hours ago. What in God's green earth am I doing? Alice wobbled dangerously as she fought the impulse to dash down the stairs and hail a taxi back to the Ferry Building.

"Are you all right ...Alice?" Siegfried's hand gently cupped her elbow, supporting her, cutting off her retreat.

"I'm— I'm fine," she murmured. She allowed Siegfried to tuck her arm in his, and escort her up the steps and into the building, but her heart pounded, and her stomach fluttered with hysterical laughter. *This can't be happening to me!*

Judge Reynolds was a bald, rather rotund contemporary of Tati's, and, as his greeting made obvious, an admirer of hers as well. He welcomed them into his book-lined chambers. Quiet dignity was provided by a patterned Turkish carpet, brass lamps, and massive mahogany furniture.

Alice scarcely blinked when Tati, with terrifying efficiency, produced a marriage license from her handbag. The only detail lacking was a wedding ring, but Alice still wore Bill's ring, and they all politely agreed that it would serve.

They recruited a second witness for the marriage when a clerk rapped on the door to inquire if the judge needed anything. Then, all of the simple arrangements completed, Alice and Siegfried stood side-by-side as the judge spoke: "William Roye was a fine man, and I was privileged to call him my friend. Now, I'm equally honored to be able to preside over the wedding of his grandson." He paused as Tati smiled at Siegfried, her eyes shiny.

Alice turned her head to observe the man who had taken Bill's place, measuring him against Bill's memory, as Judge Reynolds continued: "Siegfried Heinrich Wilhelm Rodernwiller, do you take this woman to be your lawfully wedded wife, to love and to honor, in sickness and in health, for better and for worse, until death do you part?"

A fresh wave of scarlet tinted Siegfried's fair skin. "I—" He coughed, and cleared his throat, as nervous as if this were a real wedding, and not a hastily-arranged ceremony of convenience. "I do."

The judge addressed her, but she only heard: "Alice Mary O'Reilly Roye... until death do you part?"

"I do." Alice lied, amazed at her own assumed tranquillity. She wondered what Bill must feel, if he were indeed watching them from Heaven. He had known everything there was to know about her, and still loved her. What was Siegfried thinking?

"By the authority vested in me by the City and County of San Francisco, I declare you man and wife." Judge Reynolds beamed at them. "Congratulations! Mr. Rodernwiller, you may kiss the new Mrs. Rodernwiller."

Rodernwiller. It was an ugly, unpronounceable, *foreign* name. *Mrs. Siegfried Rodernwiller.* How awful that sounded!

Siegfried captured her hand in his cold fingers, and bent towards her. There was a awkward pause as both of them hesitated, then Alice turned her face slightly. His lips were gentle as they pressed against her cheek. "Thank you, dear Alice," he whispered.

"You'd better be a *good* vintner!" she whispered back.

"No, Tati, I'm sorry, I should have left hours ago," Alice said, hands shaking so badly her hatpin grazed scalp along with hair. She winced. The hat stayed put.

"You are not dining with us?" Siegfried's expression turned thunderous as he shifted his attention to Tati as if to say, *Can't you change her mind?*

"It's your wedding supper, dear," Tati coaxed, but Alice was in no mood to listen to her. She wanted to go home so badly she almost missed Tati's next statement.

"Siegfried won't be joining you until this weekend. I had hoped you would use this time to get to know one another better."

"He's not coming with me?" Alice blinked in astonishment. All this trouble for nothing?

"He must sign some papers," Tati said, carefully avoiding Siegfried's gaze. "But my friend in the Immigration Department said there shouldn't be any problem."

"Well, perhaps that's for the best. I'm very tired and I need time to think. This has been *quite* a day." She darted a glance in Siegfried's direction. He remained focused on Tati.

"I know you have a long journey back to Sonoma, dear. But I wish——" Tati pressed her lips together. "I cannot tell you how grateful I am to you for helping Siegfried."

"That means a great deal to me." *A very great deal*. She'd traded her freedom for Tati's goodwill and silence. Alice bent and kissed the proffered cheek. "How long before he does arrive?"

"A few days, perhaps. I will telephone when all the arrangements have been made. Good-bye, Alice."

Siegfried had hailed a taxi passing on Grove Street. He opened the door for her and kissed her hand with formal correctness before handing her into the car. He began to shut the door, then stopped. "When you declined our dinner invitation, I felt that perhaps——" He cleared his throat awkwardly. "Well. Oma Tati *did* tell you we could get an annulment, if you decide we do not suit?"

She searched his expression for some clue that he understood how Tati had coerced her into this farce. He didn't seem like a devious man. Surely if he knew anything at all about her he would show it in some way, by a sidelong glance, or a significant pause before he spoke. But his eyes— a deep blue, darker than Bill's eyes— held only concern, as if he actually craved her good opinion.

Alice realized with an odd sense of relief that Siegfried

had not been party to his grandmother's blackmail, otherwise he would know that Tati would never let Alice obtain an annulment. He was trying to make amends because he sensed something wrong.

"Then you'll agree to separate bedrooms?" she asked, adding hastily, "for now, I mean." One thing she had learned from Mama: always leave hope in a man's heart.

"Of course," he said without hesitation. "I would not expect you to, ah— I mean..." He flushed and cleared his throat again. "I would not impose on you."

She found herself smiling at him. *Alice, don't be more of a fool than you have to. He just wants your land.* But he was so sweet, with a natural charm more potent than Bill's cultivated variety. "I'll see you in Sonoma, then," she said, when the pause grew awkward.

He gave a stiff bow and she settled herself in the seat as her new husband firmly waved the taxi off. They sped down Market Street, where the pale clock tower of the Ferry Building loomed like a beacon in the late afternoon sunshine.

Saturday, May 17, 1919

Siegfried put down his valise with a hollow thump. He stood on the narrow platform of the ochre-painted Sonoma train station, searching hopefully for Alice's trim figure and trying to quell his dismay. Against his will, he remembered another railroad station, glistening with rain and decorated with tubs of spring flowers. Now, as then, no one came to greet him.

His stomach cramped slightly. The foreign-yet-familiar landscape made him nervous. Rugged California hills surrounded Sonoma, a few resolute wildflowers making a last yellow and white stand before summer's gold swallowed them up.

He wondered what awaited him at Montclair. What sort of a woman was Alice? Why had she agreed to marry him? Tati had been vague when he questioned her after the wedding.

He could not afford to fail, as his father had failed. Siegfried scrubbed the palm of his free hand vigorously against the wool of his trousers, trying to dispel the memory of his father's desk, sticky with blood.

He would succeed here. He must. He would make the marriage work, and make this sun-browned place his new home.

He heard the rattle and roar of an automobile engine approaching from the Plaza, and eagerly picked up his valise, but the sound faded as the car passed the station and continued down the street.

Where was Alice?

Finally, he walked down the platform to the door of the stationmaster's office.

Behind a rolltop desk, an older man with mutton-chop side whiskers wearing a gold-braided black cap and uniform jacket scowled at a logbook spread open before him. He put down a chewed fountain pen to say, "May I help you?" when Siegfried entered.

"May I use your telephone? Someone from Montclair Vineyard was supposed to meet me here, but..." He half-shrugged towards the door and the deserted platform beyond.

"It's broken."

As Siegfried wondered what to do next, the stationmaster squinted at him and asked suspiciously, "Are you German?"

"I am Alsatian! Montclair's new vintner."

"Well, uh, the Depot Hotel, just across the street, has a 'phone. If anyone comes for you in the meantime, I'll let them know where you've gone, Mister, er—"

"Rodernwiller."

"Road and villa?"

Siegfried bit his tongue at the mangling of his name, but before he could correct him, the stationmaster jerked at the loud jangling of the telephone on the wall next to the desk. He jumped up to answer it, avoiding Siegfried's gaze and his lethally courteous thanks.

As Siegfried left the stationmaster's office, he heard a low-voiced curse: "Damn foreigners."

Four blocks away, Alice traced an impatient pattern against the red linoleum floor with the toe of her shoe. Mrs. Springer was complaining to the butcher in excruciating detail about her arthritis, and Alice, in politeness, could not interrupt, although she was anxiously aware that she was very late.

She had driven into town a half-hour early, hoping to quickly buy extra supplies of coffee and sugar, as well as some meat for dinner. She had been delayed by chatty Mr. Duhring at his hardware and grocery store on the Plaza. And it was taking Ralph Cummings forever to wrap up an order of lamb chops. Finally Mrs. Springer left with long farewells.

Alice stepped up to the counter and spoke hurriedly. "I'd like two sirloin steaks, please."

"Certainly, Mrs. Roye, and congratulations on your marriage! Although I guess I should be calling you Mrs. Rodernwiller now?"

Alice's heart stopped momentarily, then pounded

furiously. "How— how did you know?"

The butcher reached unerringly into his cabinet for a slab of meat and began slicing it. "Saw the announcement in the *San Francisco Chronicle*." Creases in Mr. Cummings' jowls extended his generous smile.

"Er, thank you," She should have remembered there were no secrets in a small town. How long would it take before *everyone* in Sonoma knew about her hasty marriage?

"How did you two meet?" Mr. Cummings sounded ready to hold a detailed conversation as he trimmed the fat from the thick edge of the first steak.

How could she explain? "Bill's grandmother introduced us. Siegfried is Bill's cousin, from Europe."

"Aha! I thought the name sounded familiar. He visited here a couple of times when he was just a lad—"

Alice checked the little gold watch pinned to her blouse. "I don't mean to be rude," she interrupted, as she accepted the wrapped meat, "but I really must go. I'm already late in meeting my— my husband's train."

"Don't let me keep you, then," the butcher drawled as he took her coins. "See you next time." He waved, and she departed, rushing across the street to her truck. She put the steaks in the back with her other purchases, grateful she had found a spot to park under the shade of the Plaza trees, grateful that she had escaped relatively easily.

Should she drive or walk the short distance to the station? The thought of promenading back through town with her brand new husband made the decision simple.

Worry gave her the strength to turn the crank handle smoothly. It might not be as easy as she had first hoped to dissolve her marriage, consummated or not. Afterwards, there would be gossip of the same type that attached itself to a divorcée. Everyone had been so kind since Bill's death. Would her neighbors treat her respectfully after an annulment? Or would she be the scandal of the county?

The dusty black Ford coughed to life. She let the engine turn over a few extra times before she found the courage to put it in gear.

The sun was hot on his dark wool suit as Siegfried walked across the street. The sign announced "Depot Hotel - Est. 1870," on a building of rough-cut gray fieldstone stuccoed with pale rose-colored plaster on the second story. The wooden shutters on the windows were freshly painted, and seeing them gave him a pang.

He pulled open a door decorated with a lion's-head knocker. Strong sunlight streamed through a wide-open doorway straight ahead, setting the haze of cigar smoke in the saloon aglow. Several splintered pieces of wood lay on the waxed flagstones near the feet of a large man wearing a carpenter's apron. He gave Siegfried a quick glance, then went back to fitting new louver slats into the broken patio door.

Two rough laborers sitting at the mirror-backed bar sipped their beers and eyed Siegfried with bleary interest. The room to the right, under gilded-brass gas chandeliers, was a dining room redolent of garlic and tomato sauce, with tables covered by red-checked cloths.

Siegfried addressed the genial bartender. "Good afternoon. May I use here the telephone?" He was uncomfortably aware that his normally faint accent had grown stronger in the aftermath of the stationmaster's rudeness.

The bartender's expression changed. No longer friendly, he jerked his chin towards the dining room. "It's in there."

"Hey, Joe, the Hun wants to use the 'phone," the taller of the two drinkers complained.

"Guess he got tired of murdering Belgian babies, George," the other replied. He wiped his forehead with a red bandanna and stuffed it into the pocket of his dusty jeans.

Siegfried clenched the handle of his valise tightly. This was not the welcome to Sonoma he had imagined, however, he had no desire to trade futile insults with drunkards, so he deliberately turned his back and took a step towards the dining room.

The scrape of a barstool against the stone floor was as loud as a sniper shot. "Hey, Hun, we don't want you dirtying up this hotel!"

"Take it outside, boys," warned the bartender, watching them closely. "Mr. Behrens here hasn't fixed the damage from last night yet."

"Yessir! Come on, George, let's take it outside!"

From the corner of his eye, Siegfried saw Joe draw back his fist. He ducked under the blow and drove his valise into the other's middle in the same smooth motion. Joe folded, groaning loudly.

"You filthy German bastard!" yelled George, knocking over his barstool with a crash as he jumped from his seat. "My brother died Over There!"

"Hey! Cut it out!" the bartender shouted, unheeded.

Siegfried sidestepped the first of George's flailing punches with the same twist used to counter bayonet thrusts, but a second roundhouse caught him squarely on the cheekbone. He reeled, his vision clouded with black motes and bright sparkles, then he landed a hard right to George's jaw. He would have delivered another one except that his arms were grasped from behind. A powerful reek of stale sweat and beer emanated from his captor.

"Got 'im, George!" Joe's voice rasped in Siegfried's ear, just before Siegfried whipped his head back, trying to avoid the full force of the blow on his mouth. His lips went hot and tingling at the same time that the back of his skull connected with Joe's face in a satisfying crunch.

Joe gave a muffled moan and clutched his nose, releasing Siegfried. Bright red blood seeped between his fingers.

Siegfried twisted away from George's next punch. He heard his pulse drumming in his ears, and sucked in great draughts of air. "I am not German," he insisted, but it made no difference.

George grabbed one of the barstools, and swung it. Siegfried dodged to one side but lost his balance on the slippery floor, falling flat on his back. He watched George reverse the barstool's swing. Time froze as the unwieldy weapon poised at the top of its arc, aimed at directly at his head.

Parked under the acacias at the train station, Alice wasted another few minutes composing internal apologies for her lateness, even as she sat in the driver's seat, frozen in place despite the dry heat of the afternoon. She teetered on the verge of running away, but, recalling Tati's threat, Alice knew she had nowhere to run. Montclair's success was her only hope. And Montclair needed Siegfried's skills as a vintner.

She forced herself to climb out of the truck.

The train was long gone. Gravel shifted under her feet as she hurried as fast as ladylike propriety would allow. She came around the corner and saw the empty platform.

Alice considered what to do next. Siegfried might have gone for a brief walk to stretch his legs or stepped into the nearby hotel for a drink. Perhaps if she just waited for a few minutes, he might return to the depot and find her. For one bright instant she hoped that Siegfried had despaired of her arrival and departed with the train.

"Excuse me, ma'am? Oh, Mrs. Roye. How are you?"

Alice turned, and saw Mr. Myers standing in the doorway of the his office. "I'm fine, thank you. My new— vintner was supposed to be on the 3:25 train from the Tiburon Ferry. Have you seen a tall, blond man?"

"Oh, yes, ma'am. The foreigner? He went over to the Depot Hotel. Said something about wanting to use their 'phone."

"Yes, that's he. Thank you," Alice said, guiltily. How long had he waited before he decided to call her?

She walked slowly back to her truck, feeling the heat radiating from the black paint. The still air smelled of dust, eucalyptus, and sun-warmed wooden buildings. Cicadas clicked randomly. Alice took off her linen driving coat and folded it neatly on the driver's seat. She reached up to touch her wide-brimmed straw hat, making certain that it was pinned firmly in place. Then she took a deep breath and started across the quiet street.

As she drew close, Alice heard a commotion, and she recognized the sounds instantly. There was a fight going on in the saloon.

She stood outside the saloon, dithering. A respectable woman would never be caught dead in this sort of establishment at any time, much less in the midst of a brawl! But Siegfried was in there, and it was her fault because she was late.

In the next moment she heard Siegfried's protest: "I am Alsatian!" A pained grunt accompanied a crash against the door, which flew open toward her violently.

CHAPTER
3

The door slammed into Alice, knocking her down to the sidewalk. Before she could feel anything except disbelief, a man dressed in shabby field hand's clothes sprawled next to her, a barstool flying loose from his hand to bounce into the street. She locked startled gazes with him.

"Mrs. Roye?" he croaked.

Her disbelief vanished in horrified embarrassment. She knew this man! He had been part of the crew who put in her new vines. Abruptly she realized that her knees were exposed, and her bottom hurt. Abruptly, she shoved down her pleated skirt. Her right arm awoke from numbness and began to throb with a dull pain.

Siegfried appeared in the doorway, a large reddened patch marring his cheek. He gave her a quick assessing glance, then stared, astonished, as he recognized her. "Ah-lees! Are you all right?"

"I'm fine," she said, hastily. *How dare Siegfried make a spectacle of himself— and me!* As she tried to get back on her feet, Siegfried stepped toward her, hand extended to help.

The workman next to her scuttled to his feet and interposed himself. "Don't worry, Mrs. Roye," he declared, shoulders hunched menacingly. "I'll protect you from that Hun."

"My wife needs no protection from you!" Siegfried growled.

"She ain't your wife," sneered the workman. "She's Corporal Bill Roye's widow." He brought up his fisted hands, and held them waveringly at chest-level like a woozy prizefighter.

"That's enough," said the man in the carpenter's apron as he stepped out of the hotel, rolled-up sleeves revealing massive biceps. "You watch your manners around the lady, George."

George took exception to the familiarity. "You stay out of this, Behrens." But his fists lowered, and he took a step backwards.

Alice climbed shakily to her feet, disdaining Siegfried's outstretched hand. She tried frantically to think of the proper response to being caught like this. Should she flee, faint, or brazen it out? Damn Siegfried anyway for putting her in this predicament! What sort of ruffian had Tati foisted on her?

"We dod't deed his kide aroud here." A second man, from his clothing evidently George's companion, staggered out of the saloon. Fresh blood stained the handkerchief he held against his nose. Alice groaned inwardly. More witnesses to her humiliation!

"We don't need *your* kind around here!" Behrens interjected. "You'd better take yourselves off before someone calls Sheriff Albertson!"

"But what about Mrs. Roye?" George protested, standing protectively near her.

"She is no longer Mrs. Roye. She is my wife now," Siegfried pronounced.

George and Joe looked to Alice for confirmation, disappointment and dismay clear on their battered features, waiting for her to speak. "It's true— Mr. Roder— This gentleman is my husband," Alice managed to choke out. "He's Montclair's new vintner."

There was a long pause punctuated by shuffling while George digested this information.

"And you will apologize to my wife for knocking her down," Siegfried demanded.

"Aw, hell," George mumbled, lowering his gaze. "Beggin' your pardon, ma'am. We didn't realize that he was— that is— look, Joe, Mrs. Roye wouldn't marry a *Hun*."

"Appears we bade a bistake," Joe said, grudgingly. He examined his blotched handkerchief, then looked sideways at Siegfried's implacable scowl.

"Sorry, ma'am." George chimed in, hastily, as Siegfried cleared his throat. "C'mon, Joe." He pushed Joe back inside the bar, the lion-knocker door slamming closed behind them.

"It is very kind of you to help a stranger," Siegfried said to Behrens, tugging his jacket back into place. "I am Siegfried Rodernwiller."

The carpenter nodded politely. "Good afternoon, Mr. Rodernwiller." He pronounced the name effortlessly, and offered a meaty hand to Siegfried. "I'm Henry Behrens, from Glen Ellen."

"So pleased to meet you," Siegfried murmured, shaking Behren's hand vigorously. "Thank you for your assistance."

Alice gave Behrens a stiff smile and a small nod, trying unobtrusively to pat the dust from her long skirt, hoping it wasn't torn. She studied Siegfried. Had he been drinking?

Henry Behren's next comment allayed some of her fears. "Troublemakers," he commented, hooking a thumb through his belt. "I thought I was going to have make some extra repairs in there. It's a shame anti-German sentiments are still running so high in the county. Those boys ought to know better."

Siegfried shrugged. "I hope that they have now learned."

Alice noticed, irritated, that he stood a little straighter, squaring his shoulders. At least Siegfried hadn't started the fight— not if she could believe the implications of Mr. Behrens' words.

"I'd better finish up inside. Good day, Mrs. Rodernwiller." Mr. Behrens nodded at her. "And— welcome to Sonoma, Mr. Rodernwiller. Call on me if you need help with anything."

Siegfried smiled and sketched a salute.

"I'm so sorry I was late," Alice said when Behrens had gone. She was simultaneously guilt-stricken and resentful. "I needed to buy some things for dinner. If I hadn't been late—"

"It is nothing." Siegfried smiled although his lips were bloody.

"Your mouth!" Alice found her handkerchief in her skirt pocket. What if they encountered someone she knew? She raised herself on tip-toes, and dabbed at the blood beading from Siegfried's swollen lower lip. Siegfried closed his eyes but didn't flinch from her ministrations.

"That's a little better." Giving up the battle against the drying blood on his chin as futile without water, she tucked her stained handkerchief away. "Do you need a doctor?"

"I have lived through worse without one," Siegfried said, firmly. His bruised cheek flushed purple.

"But—" Alice protested.

"The touch of a pretty woman is better than any doctor," Siegfried opened his eyes wide and winked at her.

"My automobile is in front of the station," Alice informed him. Her cheeks were hot. The nerve of him!

Siegfried picked up his valise, took her arm, and together they walked across the street to her truck.

Alice hurried to keep up with him, comparing him to Bill. To begin with, Bill would never have fought in a common bar brawl. A quick flash of Siegfried poised for combat in the hotel bar translated itself into an image of Bill with bayonet raised. Had Bill's mouth bled? She would never know more than what had been written in the brief, dry words of the telegram. *Regret to inform you... missing in action... ultimate sacrifice... St. Mihiel Salient.*

"Allow me." Siegfried was holding open the truck's door for her.

Alice blinked and the moment of intense sadness dissipated. She started to pull on her coat, and Siegfried helped her with that too.

She bore his courtesies and seated herself cautiously behind the wheel, reminded anew of the indignities she had suffered. He stowed his valise in the truck bed next to the groceries and man-handled the crank until the Ford grumbled to life.

When he settled himself on the passenger's side, she thanked him without looking at him and stepped on the left floor pedal. After putting the car in first gear, she moved the gas lever on the steering column, and drove cautiously away from the train station, through the neighborhood of pretty houses on the outskirts of town.

Fifteen miles an hour seemed too fast as the Model-T jounced, each pothole and rut in the eucalyptus-lined road reminding Alice of her abused nether region. As they passed the turn-off to the neglected Buena Vista winery, the truck emerged from shade into a vista of gold-green pastures. Siegfried was silent, staring at the landscape. Alice saw the beauty, too: the pinkish-white creeper blossoms climbing over the wire fences and a scattering of shocking-orange poppies left over from springtime's great flowering.

When they arrived at the entrance to Montclair Siegfried jumped out, unlatched the gate, opened it so she could drive through, and closed it again afterward. He stood for a moment, looking upwards, before returning to the truck.

Alice followed his gaze, remembering her own first sight of Montclair, and what it had meant to her. The narrow graveled road leading through the main vineyard rose gently towards a cluster of buildings perched halfway up the gentle hillside. The centerpiece was a tall square house trimmed in gingerbread with a wraparound porch. A line of dark-green fruit trees nearly hid the modest foreman's cottage and other outbuildings further up the hill behind the house. The whitewashed stone winery was set at the top of the drive, just at the point where the line of northerly hills curved around to the west.

"We're home," she said when he returned to the truck, unable to keep the note of pride from her voice.

"It looks just the same," Siegfried said wonderingly.

"What are you doing?" Siegfried asked. He held on to the edge of the door to stay in his seat because Alice performed a three-point turn, put the Model-T into gear, and lurched—

backward— up the hill.

"The truck has a gravity fuel feed." Alice craned her head out the window to see behind the vehicle.

"So?" The truck jounced and he held on tighter.

"The first time I drove it straight up the hill, it stalled well before I reached the house. Peter had to help me turn it around."

"Peter Verdacchia?"

"Yes." She glanced at Siegfried for an instant before returning to her driving. "He's never let me live it down."

Siegfried was relieved that she seemed willing to talk with him again. He had been so angry with himself— and those rowdies— for offering her an injury. How protective of her he felt, even on such short acquaintance. And now at the mention of Peter's scolding her, he felt that way again. "He has not changed at all!"

"He's been an excellent foreman. I don't know what I would have done without him these last few months," Alice said, twisting the steering wheel for the last turn. "He mentioned that you had been friends."

He seized the opportunity to remind her that he was not a complete stranger to Montclair. "When we were boys, he and Bill and Ernst and I played forts and castles in the wine caves. We used to get into terrible trouble together. Once, *Opa* Roye forbade us to eat any of his ripe pears— he wanted them for *schnaps*— so Peter suggested that we climb the tree and take a single bite out of each hanging fruit. We would have gotten away with it, but Ernst fell and broke his collarbone, so we were discovered. Peter never forgave Ernst for the whipping we older boys received."

"Ernst? Grandmother Tati mentioned him, too."

"My younger brother. He died at the beginning of the War." The five intervening years had burned away the rage, and he had locked away the grief so that he could remember happier times.

"I'm sorry." Alice parked the truck in the level area in front of the house, setting the parking brake with a determined yank. Her look was filled with sympathy and the shadow of losses of her own.

"It is all in the past now." Siegfried, said, sorry he had brought the subject of the War to her attention. He needed a distraction. "As for Peter, I would keep an eye on your pears," he forced himself to joke.

"If I notice any bite marks this visit, I'll know who to blame." Alice rejoined with a smile that flashed, then vanished.

Siegfried smiled his own appreciation, then, irresistibly,

the house captured his attention. He gazed beyond the two Fortune Palm trees standing like giant sentries by the opening in the short picket fence. Sunlight sparkled from the curved panes in the north-corner oriel and illuminated the bunches of fat amethyst grapes and emerald vines in the stained glass above the front door. He had never seen anything so beautiful.

The clicking sound of the driver's side door opening woke him up. *Where were his manners?* He scrambled quickly around the truck to help Alice down.

"Thank you." The curve of her lips emerged from the shadow cast by the broad brim of her hat. She took off her driving coat, folded it neatly, and laid it on the driver's seat. Then she picked up a large parcel from the back of the truck and passed between the palm trees, walking across the short flagstone walkway and up the four painted wooden steps to open the unlocked front door.

She turned, waiting by the open door. "It's okay. You can come on in," she offered.

Siegfried roused himself to shoulder a ten-pound sack he found in the truck bed. The aroma of coffee beans—- *real* coffee—-surrounded him like incense. How often had he choked down the thin dandelion-root substitute at the Front? Not often enough to forget the taste of the real thing.

At the doorway he asked, "Shall I put this in the pantry?"

Alice turned, amazed, from where she was unpinning her hat in front of a mahogany-framed foyer mirror.

Had she expected him to leave her to unload the truck alone? The thought fired Siegfried with impatience to prove himself, to win her admiration— and her heart.

After a brief hesitation, Alice hung her straw boater with its wide dark-blue silk ribbon on the brass hat rack. "Yes, thank you. The kitchen is through the last door on the left and the pantry is to your right."

Siegfried nodded. "I know." The bag rested against his cheek like a pillow filled with frankincense and myrrh. Eyes half-closed in blissful anticipation, his feet remembered the way down the hall bisecting the house. Rooms opened up on either side: a small study behind the first door on his left; the parlor on his right; then an oak-banistered stairway leading upstairs to the left. The family rooms opposite the kitchen and dining room had been shut up after *Opa* Roye's death, when *Oma* Tati had found it too painful to remain at Montclair.

At the end of the hallway a screened door led out to the porch. A wraith of wind bore scents from the vegetable garden. A wide, finely molded archway opened between the hall and the kitchen. In the afternoon light, buttercup-yellow cupboards and crystal knobs brightened the room. Copper-bottomed pans hung like shields over the modern, spindly-legged stove. Gray icebox by the stove, plain table along the hall wall, cupboard toward the dining room— Alice had not changed a thing. Joy surged up in him.

This house had escaped the War unscathed.

In the pantry, Siegfried lowered the coffee sack next to a nearly depleted twin sagging in a corner. He spent a moment worshipping the bounty stored in the closet-like chamber with its clean linoleum floor and tiled counters. Mason jars on the shelves gleamed with peaches, plums, apricots, raspberries, tomatoes, pickles, and carrots like polished gems. Jars of dark honey glowed like a king's ransom in Baltic amber. The spicy perfume of cloves, cinnamon, ginger, and nutmeg wafted from small ceramic bins fastened to the wall above bulging sacks of sugar, rice, and potatoes.

His stomach growled, reminding him of the long hours since the sandwich eaten on the ferry from San Francisco. Siegfried forced himself to leave the pantry and go back outside to finish unloading the remainder of Alice's supplies from the truck.

But before he picked up the next sack, the breeze brought a faint, heady whiff of wine and oak from the square stone building about a hundred feet up the hill.

Tati had said Alice had nearly ruined Montclair, but he had seen no sign of that yet. Perhaps his grandmother had been mistaken.

On his next trip past the kitchen, he saw that Alice had tied on a large apron. Steam was beginning to rise from a pot of water on the gas stove. Thick pale-ivory quarters of peeled potato tumbled into a bowl after each definitive thunk of her broad-bladed knife against the cutting board.

"Peter and his wife Maria— our cook— are away at a family wedding, but I think I can manage supper for the two of us," Alice said. "It's the least I can do for making you work before dinner."

"Work? This is nothing," Siegfried assured her, depositing his burden in the pantry. He made two more trips out to the truck to fetch the remaining items and his valise, which he set at the foot of the stairs.

When he returned to the kitchen, the potatoes were boiling and a wooden bowl filled with bright green asparagus sat next to the stove. He felt a rush of homesickness. Asparagus in Alsace was white, but he wasn't in Alsace anymore. He set down the last armful of Alice's purchases and looked for her.

She was in the adjoining dining room, positioning plain white dishes and ornate silverware on a spotless tablecloth. A cluster of heavy-headed pink roses in a crystal vase at the center of the table filled the room with fragrance. Siegfried stood by the swinging door, just watching.

He remembered how his mother had loved her rosebushes. In the summer months, every vase and bowl in their house had overflowed with pink, white, red, and yellow blossoms. He wondered if Rodernwiller's new owners would take proper care of the gardens, and if the rosebushes would bloom for them with the same abundance.

The thought gave him a chill, raising prickles between his shoulder blades. He shrugged uncomfortably. It did no good to dwell on something now forever beyond his reach.

"Oh," said Alice, hastily putting down the linen napkin she had been folding. "I didn't see you."

"I did not mean to startle you." Siegfried apologized, hoping she would speak more. Her voice was like good cognac: smooth as velvet or honey, with a bite of spirit underneath.

"Let me show you to your room," Alice offered after an awkward moment. "Dinner will be ready in a half-hour or so, and I'm sure that you would like a chance to wash up and unpack your things."

Alice led Siegfried up the carpeted staircase and opened the third door down from the landing. "This will be your bedroom. I hope that it's to your liking— if there is anything you need, please let me know."

Her tone and manner were those of a hostess to a guest, not of a wife with her husband. When Siegfried smiled at her, his split lip smarted. He hoped that she would not hold the unfortunate circumstance of the fight against him. He had only been defending himself, after all.

As Alice preceded him, drawing back the drapes and opening the window to let in the freshening late afternoon breeze, Siegfried stepped into the guest bedroom. He had slept here during his apprenticeship with Opa Roye, and the room looked just the same.

It was furnished with a heavy walnut wardrobe, a chest of drawers, and a writing table with chair. A narrow stencil of roses marched around the walls just under the plaster moldings, matching the dark-green rug patterned with pink cabbage roses. Near the window, an armchair upholstered in dark green leather overlooked the vineyards.

No, there was one difference. The old gaslight hanging

from the ceiling had been transformed into an electric chandelier, and a small electric lamp stood on a night table next to the walnut bedstead.

The bed, plump with goosedown pillows and a quilted comforter, looked like heaven to a man accustomed to the bedroll of a soldier. "This will do wonderfully."

"I couldn't make you sleep in a wine barrel," she said, roses blooming in her cheeks. She backed away, smoothing down the front of her apron, and left him in possession of his new quarters.

Dropping his valise onto the bed, Siegfried removed his jacket and hung it precisely in the empty wardrobe. He extracted his shaving kit, then rolled up his shirtsleeves and walked down the hall to wash his bruised face and hands with soap and warm water. Drawing a wet comb through his hair, he scowled at the face in the mirror. He must appear the perfect villain to Bill's pretty little widow. He would have to work very hard to change her impression of him.

He returned to his bedroom and unpacked his few belongings— underclothes, socks, some clean shirts, an extra suit cut down from one of Opa Roye's, and two pairs of work trousers— no, *jeans*, he corrected himself— that Oma Tati had bought him from Levi-Strauss.

The last item he took from the valise was a photograph. He set it down on the night table, and twisted his father's gold signet ring around on his finger as he studied it. Taken just before the War started, Mother, Father, *Tante* Hilde, Ernst, and a painfully young Siegfried sat formally posed among the leafy vines and fat grape clusters of midsummer. Despite the warm sun, all of them were dressed in their best dark clothes. He remembered the heavy heat and the naive resentment he had felt at the prospect of returning to classes in Heidelberg that fall.

Now, of all the people in the portrait, Siegfried and *Tante* Hilde were the only survivors. He had a chance for a new life if he could convince Alice to forgo her plans for an annulment. He *would* make a new life for himself at Montclair.

As he stored the empty valise in the wardrobe, the divine scent of broiling meat drifted up the stairs, redolent with the promise of tender brown flesh and rich drippings. The smell brought a rush of juices to his mouth. Oma Tati's charity meals had failed to take the edge off his hunger, but here at Montclair, he would be expected to work for his supper. He could eat his fill with a good conscience.

After what seemed eternity, he heard Alice's voice calling him to dinner. He came down before the echoes of her voice died, and was greeted by an angelic vision: a beautiful woman presiding at a bountiful table. There were platters and bowls of cooked food, as well as a silver filigree basket with a loaf of sourdough bread, a ceramic crock mounded with butter, and a crystal decanter of garnet-red wine.

Alice took in his rapturous expression. "Good. You're hungry. Please sit down and eat."

He pulled out her chair for her. "This looks delicious," he said. Was he so transparently famished? He must try not to look too eager.

As she sat, a bit stiffly, he lifted the decanter and filled first her glass, then his own. The wine had good legs. It might be potent, or sweet. He mustn't drink it too fast on an empty stomach. He needed a clear head.

He moved to his chair at what he hoped was an unhurried pace,   and sat down, dropping his napkin to his lap with painstaking correctness. He raised his wineglass to her. "To the hospitality of a generous hostess," he saluted, then took a sip. Instantly, he regretted it. There was a faint but distinct hint of mercaptan in the bouquet of the Cabernet Sauvignon, and the finish proved it, bitter and astringent.

He sniffed the wine incredulously. Montclair Cabernet— mellow flavors of oak and blackberry, overlaid by a hint of vanilla— sullied by the unmistakable odor of *poultry manure*? God, yes. It was definitely there, the most grievous of winemaking sins. He studied Alice, wondering if she had noticed at all.

She was swirling the wine gently in her glass and breathing deeply. A tiny frown marred the serenity of her expression.

"Bill made this, yes?" Siegfried inquired, not needing to ask.

"This was his last vintage," Alice answered. "He was so proud of it. I don't— that is, do you smell... something odd?"

"Too much hydrogen sulfide."

"Ah," said Alice, as if that explained all, and went a long way toward repairing the fault. She took a sip, and instantly grimaced. "I can't understand it!" she exclaimed. "I remember when he bottled this; it was a little tannic then, but nothing like..."

Siegfried ran through the possibilities in his mind. "Which sort of fungicide are you using?"

"Bordeaux mixture."

"So it wasn't for lack of copper on the grapes," Siegfried mused, half to himself. "Did Bill change the brass piping?"

"No," she said uncertainly.

"Then he used too much sulfur while disinfecting the barrels, although I am surprised that Signor Verdacchia overlooked it."

Alice shook her head. "Bill insisted on doing everything his own way that year. He tried to get Mr. Verdacchia to retire." Remoteness overtook her. "I'm so sorry. I want you to enjoy your meal. Let me find something else." She stood up before he could speak, and headed for the kitchen.

Siegfried knew he ought to wait for her to return and say grace, but he could not allow this magnificent food to grow cold. He served himself a portion of the beefsteak and potatoes, then took a generous serving of the asparagus. He closed his eyes in ecstasy as he chewed the first, tender bite of steak, its salty liqueur banishing the foul taste of Bill's wine. The sourdough bread was fresh and crusty, the butter smooth and sweet as a benediction, and the asparagus, although the wrong color, was superbly tender.

Alice watched Siegfried from the shadows of the kitchen, noting the determined set of his mouth, his dark blue eyes— so serious, not like Bill's eyes at all, although Siegfried's hair was the same shade, gold as summer grass. She wasn't sure what to make of him. He seemed very gentlemanly and certainly eager to help her. But the afternoon's events had left her wary. Was he like some men she had known, hard-working and industrious during the week, hard-drinking hell-raisers on the weekend? Time would tell.

In the meanwhile, she needed a minute— at least— to recover her composure and allow a wave of disconcerting sympathy to ebb. Tati's fears for her grandson's future had become horrifyingly real. He *had* been starving.

She recollected herself, got fresh glasses, and opened a new bottle of Cabernet from a different vintage. As Siegfried poured, she served herself a modest portion of steak and potatoes, and then passed Siegfried the platter for a second helping. He accepted it with a grateful smile.

When he finished eating, he laid his cutlery across a polished plate and poured them both another glass of wine. He savored it, then set the empty glass down. "Thank you. That was the finest meal I have ever eaten."

"You're welcome." She couldn't help adding a light rejoinder. "I'm glad you enjoyed it. But wait until you've tasted Maria's cooking."

"I am sure I will not enjoy it half as much. Your mother

taught you well." His face was rosy now from the effects of food and wine.

Alice's heart began to pound heavily. Her chest became a reverberating drum, and her temples throbbed with the force of her pulse. Had Tati told him after all?

"She must be very proud of you." Siegfried continued, busily pouring himself a third glass, and indifferent to her fear. "More wine?"

Alice released the fold of skirt she had been clenching. It was just an innocent remark. She hastily changed the subject. "I hope you left room for dessert."

"Dessert," he echoed. "With coffee? Port?" He sounded like a child offered his choice of the presents under a Christmas tree.

It was a good thing to know: if the subject of her mother came up again, his attention could be easily diverted by food. She smiled deliberately: "Both. If you like."

He nodded eagerly, then rose to help her clear the table. Alice quelled her momentary gratitude. Siegfried was obviously just trying to make a good impression.

But I like it, whispered a traitorous little voice. Bill had never shown the least inclination to help her. On Maria's days off, he used to sit talking through the open doorway while Alice washed up by herself.

Brusquely, Alice directed Siegfried to place a glass bowl under the spout of the brass and walnut grinder fastened to the counter edge. While a kettle of water heated, Alice scooped coffee beans and Siegfried turned the long crank, watching with deep concentration as the dark grains rained down.

Fetching a pitcher of cream from the icebox, Alice poured some into a creamer and the rest into a large bowl, adding a teaspoon of vanilla extract and several spoons of sugar. As she spun the handle of the eggbeater and whipped the cream into froth, she studied Siegfried.

He opened up the grinder to clean out every speck, as if each particle of coffee were as precious as diamonds. He transferred the ground coffee into the china filter on top of the coffee pot and then sighed, as if he had accomplished some great mission.

The kettle whistled and she let the eggbeater settle into the thickening cream, shaking her wrist— still sore from the impact with the hotel's door— to loosen up her muscles. She poured boiling water through the coffee filter, checked that the porcelain coffee service held sugar as well as cream, and handed a willing Siegfried the tray. "I'll be finished in a moment," she promised, shooing him out.

When Alice emerged from the kitchen a few minutes later, she had a dusty bottle of well-aged port tucked under her arm and was balancing plates of fluffy shortcake heaped high with strawberries from the garden and topped with whipped cream. Siegfried sat at the head of the table, waiting expectantly.

She handed him a dessert plate and poured out cups of coffee and small glasses of deep-red port before sitting down opposite him. "Can you tell me a bit more about your winemaking skills?" she asked after his plate was clean.

"I used to make— that is, I used to help my father make wines at Rodernwiller, and I apprenticed here under *Opa* Roye and *Signor* Verdacchia," Siegfried replied. Absently, he fingered the rim of the plate as if searching for nicks, or crumbs. "I know he lived a good long life, but I was very sorry to hear that he had passed away, and I shall miss him. My grandfather was a great vintner— when he could take the time from his business concerns— but he depended on *Signor* Verdacchia to take care of all the day-to-day tasks which must be done to achieve a good wine."

"We all miss him," Alice said, eyes stinging. Last winter had been a nightmare. Everyone at Montclair had come down with the Spanish Influenza one after the other, and both Peter's father and his young son had perished. Maria still grieved for little Mario in silence, but she had begun to recover her ability to take joy in the simple things of daily life. It had taken the foreman a long time to regain his balance, and Alice was not entirely sure he had achieved it yet.

"I'm surprised that you learned much from *Signor* Verdacchia," she said, a bit off-balance herself. "He would never talk to me."

An involuntary smile tugged at Siegfried's lips. "Not even his lecture on 'Winemaking, Man's Work?' He gave it to me, forcefully, several times."

"So that's why he never let me into the winery alone!" Alice exclaimed. "Bill always had to come with me, before he— left." She hated the catch in her voice, and the thought of getting swept up in those memories again. She focused on the lesser pain. "I paid attention during crush, and listened to Peter and *Signor* Verdacchia argue about sugar and length of fermentation, but I can't say that I know very much yet."

And she needed to know everything. Someday, if she could figure out a way to annul this travesty of a marriage without bringing Tati's vengeance down upon her, she would run Montclair alone. She took a sip of port, its complex, sweetly perfumed taste a memory of crisp autumn days. She said, raising her glass, "I want Montclair to produce the finest wines."

"Why?" Siegfried asked intently. "There are many ways to make a profit from a vineyard, and from what I have learned since I arrived in this country, this 'Prohibition' will make winemaking illegal."

"There's a hope that wine and beer will be exempted. But, even if it isn't generally allowed, wine will have to be made for the Church." She held her breath, waiting for Siegfried's disdain to echo Hugh's.

"That is true." Siegfried wasn't laughing at her yet. "But I am certain every winemaker and his brother will wish to——" He searched her face, apparently finding confirmation there. "You have planned for this! Excellent! The Church is a good market. And they accept only the best, which I can provide." He sat back swirling his glass and inhaling the bouquet. He allowed a few drops to trickle onto his tongue, exhaling with satisfaction. "Montclair has always had the most modern equipment, and the best combination of grapes and *terroir.*"

"I don't know how good our equipment is now. You heard about the Traminer?" Alice gulped the remaining port in her glass with embarrassment.

"Oma Tati mentioned that you had a failed vintage last year." Siegfried said with a sympathetic grimace. "It can happen to the best of vintners. The transformation of grapes into wine is as close to magic as we mortals get."

"I guess I don't have the magic touch." Alice put down her empty glass.

"Do not worry, Alice. I do."

Alice blinked, wondering if he were actually that arrogant, then she saw the twinkle in his eyes.

"If you give me complete command, I will produce great wines for you," Siegfried continued. "But you must agree never to interfere."

"*You* would bar me from the winery too?" Alice asked, bitterly. Not here even a day and he already planned to take over!

"No, Alice!" Siegfried exclaimed. "I only meant that I alone will manage the winery operations. My decisions will be final. The grapes cannot serve two masters." He watched her patiently, awaiting her agreement.

She pushed her empty glass away, and reined in her temper. "I agree. Your decisions will be final. However, I want to learn how to make wine so I know your decisions are the best for the winery." She waited for Siegfried to turn her down, bracing herself for an argument.

"You want to learn?" Siegfried's twinkle turned into a beam of joy. "I will be happy to teach you anything you wish."

"You will?" The wind was knocked out of her sails; far from wanting to fight about this, he looked happy at the prospect. "Well, good," she managed. "We'll tour the winery tomorrow morning."

"That would be excellent." Siegfried suppressed a yawn, then stood and helped her out of her chair.

"It's gotten late. I'll wash up these dishes."

"Let me help, Alice. I am not tired—" Another yawn slipped out.

"Of course not," Alice said. Her lips twitched. He was so improbably earnest about his offer to help. "All right. If you must."

Together they cleared the dessert dishes away. Using hot water from the kettle, she filled the dishpan and washed the dishes. Siegfried toweled them dry, handling each plate like a baby.

Then he followed her upstairs, pausing at the top of the landing. "Thank you again for the marvelous dinner, Alice." His next yawn nearly cracked his jaw.

"You're welcome," she replied, forcing herself to remember that she was annoyed at him. "Goodnight." She walked past his bedroom, entered hers, and closed the door firmly.

Siegfried stood in the hallway a few moments longer, wondering why on earth Bill had *enlisted*. With a wife like that, Siegfried thought enviously, only an invasion would have torn him from Montclair.

Montclair
Sunday, May 18

Lost in the middle of a maze-like vineyard, she ran down rows that were endless one moment, crazily turning inward the next. She was following a voice, the memory of laughter, a ghostly whisper. Bill...

Alice awoke, her pillow damp with tears. Seeking to reassure herself, she turned over automatically and reached out a hand to touch Bill's side of the bed.

Empty.

She smacked his untouched pillow and threw back the bedcovers. *Why did you leave me alone?* But there wasn't any answer to that. She slipped from the bed, and raising the window shade, blinked at the morning light filling the room, banishing dreams.

While she combed out her nighttime braid with her fingers, she leaned out the window, never tired of this view of Bill's last gift to her. Sunlight on the tender leaves of the vines colored them the essence of green against the tawny earth. As far as she could see, the land was hers.

With a sudden jolt she remembered she wasn't alone in the house. She wasn't the sole owner of Montclair anymore.

She tugged the last twining of her braid apart and checked the clock. It was later than she thought. She had to hurry through her toilette, or she would be late.

A little while later, she knocked tentatively on Siegfried's door.

"Yes?" His voice came muffled and sleepy.

"I'm going to nine o'clock Mass. Would you like to join me?" Alice called.

"No." Siegfried said definitely.

"Are you ill?" Alice asked in alarm. Had Siegfried been more grievously injured in his fight yesterday than they had thought?

"You can say I am."

He sounded healthy. What was wrong? "I'm sorry I didn't tell you Mass was so early. I forget we're such a small town— there isn't a later one."

"I do not go."

Although rebuffed and shocked, thinking, *It's a mortal*

sin! Alice responded with automatic politeness, "I'll leave the coffee pot warming on the stove. Please help yourself. I'll cook breakfast when I return."

"Thank you."

Shaking her head, Alice walked down the stairs, feeling the pull of her strained muscles at every step. *He doesn't go to Church? What have I gotten myself into?*

Siegfried despised himself for not rising to help her start the truck, but he had no time to dress, and he could hardly go downstairs naked. And he was so comfortable here, warm, surrounded by softness. He could easily fall back asleep. He didn't want to move. He couldn't remember the last time he had felt so good, not hungry, and the sheets were so smooth...

Drowsily, he listened to the truck depart, thinking about Alice: the delicious color of her flushed skin, her small, competent hands. He wondered if her unbound hair was long enough to brush the curve of her hips, and imagined the texture of it, sliding through his fingers.

He opened his eyes wide, staring at the white pillowcase, stained by a seeping dot of blood from his cut lip, and rose, stifling an involuntary groan as yesterday's contusions and bruises assailed him. A fiery claw of pain swiped at the muscles of his right leg when he planted his feet on the carpet and tried to rise from the rumpled bed. Siegfried swayed, glaring angrily at the raised pale-pink furrow plowed down the length of his thigh by shrapnel. After a moment, the pain loosened its hold, and he thought he might be able to walk without toppling over.

At least he still had a leg, he told himself, repeating the litany he had chanted during the long weeks of healing and recovery in the hospital. Each visit of the soft-voiced surgeon, frowning down upon the infected wound, had brought terror. What if he should return with chloroform— and a saw?

In the end, Siegfried had been more fortunate than many other soldiers. He took a determined step forward, wincing as he moved to the bedroom door and opened it a crack. Good. The hallway was deserted. He did not trust his leg to support him yet, which meant putting on his underwear must wait.

A hobbled dash got him to the bathroom. The wood-framed mirror showed his eye was now puffed up and black. He probed gently at the scabbed cut on his lower lip and thought that Alice should be glad he had not accompanied her to church looking like a common barroom brawler. He avoided the mirror as he bathed, shaved, and combed his hair. The hot water relieved his many aches, and his leg was feeling almost normal by the time he crept back to his room and dressed.

He found the coffee Alice had promised, and poured himself a cup, sitting down at the table against the wall to enjoy it.

After only a few sips, he carried his half-finished cup of coffee to the screen door. Outside, wisps of translucent fog clung to the hills. He moved to the porch and breathed crisp, shining air.

Nothing had changed. The palm trees shushed gently in a breeze he could barely feel. A flock of finches chirped and cheeped their nonsense music in the bushes beside the house. Sparrows searched for crumbs of food near the gravel path, while a blackbird surveyed him suspiciously from the flat top of the vegetable garden's corner fence post. Siegfried stayed very still, but the bird flourished its brilliant red-patched wings at him and flew away.

He leaned on the porch railing, entranced by peace. There were no bomb craters pocking wounded earth, no thunder-rolls of artillery, no staccato bursts of rifle fire. There was no smell of death here, only the sweet fragrance of the roses planted at the end of each row of vines marching almost up to the house.

The vines drew Siegfried. Leaving his cup on the porch, he walked the rows. They were planted further apart than in Alsace, but even so, the shoulder-high, densely curling tendrils reaching towards each other almost blocked his passage. He brushed them aside gently, pausing occasionally to lift a cluster of pale yellowish-green grape blossoms, to examine the underside of a broad, trefoil leaf.

At the crest of the hill, Siegfried paused and inhaled the scents of Montclair: vines, roses, bay laurel, fennel, and eucalyptus. He raised his arms to the serene blue sky, filled with unlooked-for triumph. He was alive! He had only to convince Alice to become his wife in fact as well as name, and Montclair was his.

Alice genuflected, crossed herself, and slid into the pew, grateful to be late. She was thus spared the chit-chat indulged in by the ladies of the parish who invariably gathered outside the church before the service.

Usually she enjoyed being welcomed as part of this small society. Today she felt like an impostor. What could she say if they disapproved of her hasty marriage? Would they turn their back on her? Would she suddenly become invisible to her neighbors?

She bent her head and folded her hands as if in prayer, but she was too keyed-up and nervous to actually bother God with her troubles. The hard pad of the kneeler and the satiny finish of the next pew's back helped to calm the chaos in her mind.

She loved this church. It was her favorite spot in Sonoma, next to Montclair. Painted simple white, plain dark rafters and thick square columns held up the high-pitched ceiling. The gilded altar gleamed, bright with candles. Sunlight jeweled the high stained-glass windows, memorials to the faithful departed.

There was only the wail of a new baby crying and the rustling of clothing as the other worshippers knelt and prayed for their own private concerns before sitting down to wait for the service to begin. The scent of incense mingled with store-bought perfumes and the homely smell of soap, cigars, and some dairyman's dirty boots, probably old man LaFranchi's, if this was anything like a normal Sunday.

Everyone sat in their accustomed places. Just ahead of her were the spinster housekeeper sisters, Adele and Margaret Livernash, and to her left, Mrs. Mary Ricci, who had worked so hard to build up her own laundry. The Sebastiani family across the aisle, and Susannah Kennedy, who, like Alice, struggled alone to keep her farm in Schellville going. The Breitenbachs— if she didn't look, she wouldn't have to acknowledge Gertrude, a stout matron in her forties with artificially black hair marcelled into stiff waves under her dashing hat. Gertrude Breitenbach, who knew everything anybody said into a telephone...

Why had she come? How much did Mrs. Breitenbach really know about Alice's past? She wouldn't be able to stand it if they pointed at her, and whispered. She trembled, ready to leap and run—

On the balcony above the back of the church, the organist started to play the *introit*.

She couldn't leave now.

Alice stood with the congregation to welcome the priest, and looked again as an unfamiliar young man appeared from the sacristy door, led by altar boys in their spotless surplices.

Adele Livernash, who didn't see too well these days, hissed loudly to her slightly younger sister, "Who's that?"

Margaret was a little deaf. Her return whisper was more than loud enough for Alice and the rest of the back of the church, as well as her sister, to hear. "That's Father McGrattan from Saint Rose, assisting here while poor Father Moran's in Mary's Help."

Adele crossed herself. "God save him, the poor sick man. When's he coming home?"

"I don't know. We could ask Gertie Breitenbach—" Margaret shushed herself as Father McGrattan began to pray in sonorous Latin.

Alice let the beautiful sounds wash through her as she tried to quell a burgeoning sense of relief. She shouldn't rejoice that Father Moran was ill, but his misfortune meant she might escape unscathed, today.

Father McGrattan wouldn't know the local gossip, so he probably wouldn't chastise her for marrying in a civil ceremony, nor would he badger her to rectify the situation with a proper sacramental marriage. He didn't know *her* the way Father Moran did, her petty current sins, and her old, old stains of guilt.

Eventually she'd wind up paying penances. After Confession, Father Moran used to assign her twenty Hail Marys for her unchaste thoughts. What would she have to pay for marrying Siegfried? Belatedly she began whispering the *Credo* with the rest of the congregation.

She submerged into the beauty and the sadness of the ceremony. "*Domine, non sum dignus*," she murmured at the consecration. "Lord, I am not worthy; but only say the word, and I shall be healed." If He could forgive Mary Magdalen, maybe He could forgive Alice, too.

She slipped out the large double doors just before the very end of Mass, clear hot sunlight almost a tangible force after the candlelit dimness of the church.

Her neighbor Carl Dresel, enjoying a cigar on the front steps, waved with mild friendliness and said, "Heard you caught yourself a vintner. Wonderful news!"

She smiled tentatively at him, still hoping to make good her retreat, but Gertrude Breitenbach called from the steps behind her. "Oh, Mrs. Roye! Don't go yet! We heard the news, dear. Did you *really* get married?"

Alice slowly turned around, pasting an artificial smile on her face. "Uh, yes."

"Well, *she* didn't believe it," said Adele Livernash, emerging from the shadow, pointing to her younger sister.

"I heard that! I did too believe it," contradicted Margaret. "I saw it in the paper. Isn't your new husband Billy's cousin from Alsace?"

"I suppose we shouldn't call you Mrs. Roye anymore," Gertrude said. She seemed a little disgruntled that she wasn't the first with the news. "How did you two meet?"

"Let us through, please," someone said from the dark

interior of the church. "You're blocking the steps."

"Oh—" Alice seized on this chance. "Excuse me, ladies. I must go home and cook breakfast." She moved away as the crowd streamed down the steps.

Gertrude followed determinedly, cutting off Alice's departure. "So where is this husband of yours? Why didn't he come with you?"

"He's—" Alice pulled on her gloves, buying a little time. "He's— not feeling well."

"I remember when he was here as a boy," said Margaret, her lips pursed to disguise a smile. "He and Billy brought frogs in their pockets to Mass! And tried to get them to sing with the choir. You watch out. That young man was quite a prankster."

"Come to think of it," Adele twittered. "He·would be just the type to elope. How romantic!"

"Well,·I hope he feels better soon. You tell him we want to see him again," Gertrude ordered.

"I will," mumbled Alice, feeling even more like a stranger in this town where everybody knew everyone— and everything. Even Siegfried had a history here. If only her own past were not so full of secrets and lies...

Siegfried studied the pruning and training of the vines until he heard the rattling cough of Alice's Ford coming backwards up the drive.

Limping down the hill, Siegfried arrived just as she parked the Model-T. He felt absurdly pleased to open the car door for her.

Alice rewarded him with a word of thanks as she took the hand he offered her and allowed him to assist her out. She unbuttoned her driving coat, revealing her Sunday best. The ivory silk dress had a square neckline embellished with a wide band of dark green embroidery, and over it she wore a long, open tunic in dark green. The peach-golden skin over her throat and collarbones and the gentle curves of her breasts under the layers of silk made Siegfried's blood pound.

He looked down. Her narrow hobble skirt ended at mid-calf, revealing shapely ankles clad in ivory stockings. All of his earlier fantasies about her returned full force, and he did not, for decency's sake, dare to immediately follow her into the house.

"The misses Livernash said to tell you hello." Alice was determined to be polite over a substantial brunch of fried eggs, ham, coffee, and toast with fresh butter and plum jam. "And Gertrude Breitenbach wants to see you again. I had no idea you had so many acquaintances here."

Siegfried grunted, apparently concentrating on devouring his food.

Alice poured herself a cup of coffee and nibbled on a piece of toast. "Did you *really* bring frogs to church?" she asked into the silence a few minutes later.

Siegfried had the grace to look embarrassed. He swallowed a huge mouthful. "The choir was very bad that summer. And it made Bill laugh, so I counted it quite successful." He slathered jam on his toast. "Is that what people remember about me?"

"Margaret Livernash," Alice corrected.

"I hope she and her sister are both well. They were very kind. Have they grown into wild old ladies?" Siegfried grinned, folded a piece of toast, and took the whole piece in one gulp.

"I only know them from church," Alice said primly. "They wondered why you weren't there."

Siegfried's eyes darkened. He finished his coffee and laid his napkin on the table. "I have not been in the habit of going— I will try to look up the Livernashes some time when I am in town. This morning I walked the Cabernet vines near the house. I must say the canopy trimming was nicely balanced, and all of the clusters appear to be receiving adequate light."

"Peter's crew does excellent work," Alice said. She rose and began clearing plates from the table.

"I was pleased there were no visible infestations. Have you any black rot?"

"No. We've been lucky. Peter is spraying the Traminer vines in the north vineyard with Bordeaux mixture against oidium. The Dresels had some, so we're taking preventative measures."

"Has there been any recurrence of Phylloxera?" he asked anxiously, trailing her into the kitchen.

Alice, rinsing off the dishes, said without thinking, "Not since before the W—" She stopped, appalled at her automatic dating; there was life "Before the War" and life "After the War." She could just as easily have said, 'Before I came to Montclair' or 'Since I've lived here.' Jerkily, she set the dishes in the sink to drain, and untied her apron. She dried her hands and hung the apron on a wooden peg.

Siegfried's expression was troubled.

Alice said softly, "I'm sorry I brought up the subject. It must be painful for you. I know how I would feel if I lost

Montclair." She touched him lightly to convey her compassion. His arm was thin under her fingers, and tense, with a current of vitality that surprised her. He was suddenly more real than anything else in the kitchen, poignantly alive and male in a room where Bill had never intruded.

He looked back at her, his eyelids half-drooping, his eyes intensely blue, the pulse leaping in his throat. His expression at that moment held nothing of nostalgia, or sadness, just an elemental need so intense that it shook her.

She retreated, self-consciously tucking wayward strands of hair back into her coil of braid with quick motions. Her fingers trembled, but not with nervousness.

"I have to go— upstairs— to change into something more appropriate— for the tour. I should only be a moment."

She fled.

Siegfried leaned his forehead against the cool cupboard. The faint scent of her eau-de-cologne lingered. He had wanted very badly to take her in his arms, and lower her to the shiny linoleum. In his mind's eye he saw the ivory silk of her skirt bunched up to her waist as he buried himself in her softness...

He had to get himself under control. He would need to court her gently, gradually, not like some contemptible fortune hunter trying to seduce Montclair away from her.

He had promised *Oma* Tati that he would help Bill's widow. He *would* be calm. He *would* be a gentleman.

Siegfried looked down at his shirtsleeves and smiled wryly. Father had always come into the winery wearing a coat and tie, befitting his lofty status. Montclair's newest vintner could do no less. He went upstairs, took *Opa* Roye's jacket and a tie out of the wardrobe, and put them on.

True to her word, Alice came downstairs again very shortly. The stylish silk dress and stockings had been replaced by a long, gray skirt and a shirtwaist, its lace trim limp from repeated washing. Sturdy black leather boots laced up past her ankles. Her hands were ungloved, and she clutched a bunch of large iron keys and a rather battered-looking straw hat. She looked every inch a farmwife.

He wanted to make love to her more than he had ever wanted anything.

"Shall we?" She walked briskly towards the front door.

He followed her in silence up the hill. A slight breeze carried the rich scent of wood steeped for years in wine. He took a deep, savoring breath, adjuring himself to pay attention to business. He loved this air, laden with the mysteries of winemaking.

And he loved this building, tradition embodied in wood and whitewashed stone. The outside had changed very little since Siegfried's summer visits here. *Opa* Roye had cut a carriage-way high into the hillside to provide upper-story access for wagonloads of grapes at harvest time. They were unloaded and crushed in the wooden basket press on the third floor, syrupy juice pouring to several huge fermenters below, then delivered through brass pipes to the huge redwood vats on the concrete ground floor for aging.

Alice clucked her tongue at the sacks of Bordeaux mixture leaning against the door frame as she unlocked the door. "These should have been put away before now. I guess Peter forgot, in all the to-do before the wedding." She shrugged and ushered Siegfried in.

Then Alice turned on the electric lights, and Siegfried gasped as if he'd taken a bayonet in the gut. The floors and gutters were dirty, cobwebs and dust everywhere. The exteriors of the eleven-hundred-gallon redwood tanks were shrouded with a thick, velvety layer of gray mold. He did not want to imagine the interiors. The hoses, where there were any left, were cracked and rotten.

Upstairs was just as bad. The fermenters were layered in debris; some even contained small animal bones. The basket press at least had been rinsed off after its last use, but some of the slats had been gnawed by rats or mice, and the screw was rusted. Under the high wooden roof, birds' nests clogged the vents.

In appalled silence, he surveyed it all.

Alice turned to him, her eyes shining. "Well? What do you think?" She sounded proud, and shy, as if totally unaware of the ruin surrounding them.

And perhaps she was. She was certainly ignorant enough not to recognize mercaptan. Siegfried controlled his voice. "I see now why your wine spoiled."

"You do? I'm thrilled! That means we'll have a good vintage this year. Do you want to see the wine cave now?" She stopped, as if she'd just caught a glimpse of his face. "What's wrong?"

"No. I could not bear— No, thank you, Alice. Not now." He touched a piece of moldy cooperage reeking of vinegar, and clenched his fist. "No good wine can come from *this*."

His loathing at squalor must have shown, for Alice jerked away from him as if he'd slapped her. But she squared her shoulders and said defiantly, "Bill made perfectly good wine here. And you said the equipment was—"

"You have not had it cleaned since Bill left. Pasteur would have wept!"

Alice's expression became stony. "Old Mr. Verdacchia told me— and Bill, too— 'Don't touch anything!'"

She was trying to explain her failure! Militant contempt filled him to overflowing. "Your wine spoiled because of filth!" He gestured emphatically at the brass fittings and spouts, layered with bright green corrosion. He rapped his knuckles against the dark stains of spilled wine and tartrate deposit, furry with the generations of mold that jacketed the huge redwood tanks. "Would you cook in a kitchen like this?"

"I— no—" Alice turned away from him, her arms folded tightly across her stomach.

Siegfried realized with a shock that she thought he was angry at *her*. And capable of acting on that anger physically.

He took a step back, mastered his emotions, and shrugged in the fashion his old drill sergeant repeatedly damned as "too French." He shook his head as futility replaced fury. "You do not need my help here, Alice. You need a *miracle*!"

CHAPTER 5

Alice escaped into the kitchen after that.

Siegfried let her go, feeling as guilty for telling her truth about the conditions inside the winery as if he had actually man-handled her. He stayed out of her way, walking the verdant rows of vines, until it was time to eat.

Throughout the Sunday supper of tender pork roast, home-canned vegetables, mashed potatoes, and a crisp, fruity Riesling, Siegfried was painfully aware of the crushed expression in Alice's eyes as she made polite conversation. It destroyed all his pleasure in the meal.

And her silence left him too much time to think. He had to do something with his life. He couldn't stay at Montclair and expect Alice to feed him for nothing. The fields gave promise of an abundant harvest. They might sell the crop to another winery, but he longed to make his own wine, to participate in the magic of that transformation. Yet how could he practice his art in a ruin?

His mind began to enumerate the tasks that needed to be done, the manpower required, and the expense to make the winery operable. He had faced similar situations before, during the War, when he had been asked to perform the impossible with too few men, and all of them dispirited. Then, he had succeeded against the odds. Could he do it again?

As Siegfried continued to eat his dinner, he began to look at each part of the disaster in the winery separately, to divide the gigantic whole into tasks that were merely daunting. He could see each step, and he began to hope. It would be difficult. But maybe it could be done. And for a man who wanted to make wine here—his own wine— it would have to be done.

He took a second helping of roast pork and ate it with gusto. When he had cleaned his plate, he refilled Alice's glass, and then his own. "I have been thinking, Alice," he announced. "I think we can do it. I think we can be prepared in time for this year's crush."

Alice looked at him blankly. "Excuse me? I thought you said-"

"A complete renovation will be necessary," he interrupted, eager to convince her, and ticked off the points on his fingers. "The winery floors must be swept and washed. We must scrape all of the mold and tartrate deposits from the inside and outside of the redwood and oak tanks, and scrub them with soda ash and potassium permanganate. That will be a hard, dirty task, and I will need men to help me."

Alice eyes narrowed during his enthusiastic recital. "I see. And how *many* men will you need for this housecleaning project?"

"At least five," Siegfried replied, ignoring the suspicion in her voice.

"For how long?"

"Until crush. Three months, perhaps a little more. Also, the crusher and pumps are in dire need of cleaning and maintenance. We will have to remove as much of the rust and corrosion as we can from the pipes and fittings. I saw only a single crusher, and a very small one at that. A second crusher, much larger, is needed. The bottling equipment is inadequate as well. We must replace all of the pumps and pipes with nickel-plated—"

Alice fixed him with a cold stare. There was nothing in her face now of the solicitous angel who had fed him or of the vulnerable girl whose treasure had tarnished in her keeping. "Your grandfather made perfectly good wine with that equipment. You said so yourself last night. With barely three months to go before the harvest, I cannot possibly tear out machinery that's in working order."

"I cannot guarantee good results with the existing equipment."

She shook her head. "An hour ago, you said it couldn't be done at all!"

"Ah-lees," Siegfried, said, his accent slipping, "I have thought this over. We *can* do it. We can make wine at Montclair."

"Great wine?" she asked, and bit her lower lip uncertainly.

Could she be wavering? "The best." He *had* to convince her.

The shrill vibration of the phone intruded. "I'll get that!" Alice sprang to her feet and rushed into the hallway.

"Hello?" Siegfried heard her say, cautiously. Then her voice changed. "Oh, Grandmother Tati— how nice to hear from you. Siegfried and I were just finishing supper."

A silence, then Alice said, a little stiffly, "Certainly. I'll ask him to come to the phone. Siegfried!"

He left the dining room, took the small receiver from her, and spoke down into the cone-shaped mouthpiece. "Hallo, *Oma?*"

"Oh, Friddy— but I mustn't call you that anymore. You're all grown up now. Siegfried. I just wanted to find out how things were going."

"They are going well," Siegfried slanted a glance at Alice's back. She had returned to the dining room and was stacking the plates. "Alice is a wonderful cook, and she has made me feel very welcome."

"That's good," Tati said, and immediately asked, "Have you had a chance to look over the winery yet?"

"Well, it's all very... dusty." Siegfried saw Alice stop, and her back become rigid. "But the vineyards are in the best order, and everything else will be fine by crush."

"Oh, I'm so glad to hear that, dear!" Tati said. "Please let me know if you need anything. I want so much to help you. And do let me know how you're getting along with Alice. I know that Montclair will be all right, now that you're there."

"Alice has been taking very good care of Montclair," Siegfried said, quickly. Alice knocked over a glass, and it rang against the edge of a plate. The sound stopped as she snatched it up. "You need not have worried. We shall get along very well together."

They rang off, and Siegfried went into the dining room. Alice had disappeared, so he picked up a serving platter and joined her in the kitchen.

"Why didn't you tell her the truth?" Alice asked, stooped defensively over the dishpan. "That I've ruined everything!"

"Because you have not," Siegfried replied, surprised by his desire to put a comforting arm around her. "You have taken very good care of the house and the vineyard. It was not your fault that no one explained to you how to care for the winery."

The gratitude in her eyes made him feel heroic. And besides, he decided, he had not really lied to *Oma*. He *would* have everything in order by crush— or he would die trying.

They spent the afternoon in the winery, doing a thorough inspection and inventory, and all evening in Alice's office, compiling a complete listing of the necessary tasks.

When Alice retired to her room after supper and cleanup, Siegfried grabbed *Grape Culture, Wines, and Wine-making,* one of his favorite books from *Opa* Roye's library, then undressed and went to bed. He turned the pages of Haraszthy's European adventure until his eyes crossed, then switched off the light. But sleep was slow in coming. He was keyed-up and conscious of the hours slipping by. Harvest would come too soon!

When he finally did drift off, he dreamed of Rodernwiller.

... the house was dark, cold, and deserted. Siegfried climbed the stairs, knowing what awaited him in his father's study.

He steeled himself to touch the corpse. The dead fingers twitched as Siegfried pulled the signet ring from the cold hand. They reached up blindly towards him, grasping, as Siegfried tried to make his suddenly heavy limbs dodge out of the way.

Father's shoulders tensed and the dark-stained head struggled to rise from the pool of dried blood on the gilt-stamped blotter. Siegfried whimpered with terror as he scrabbled at the doorknob. He did not want to look at that shattered face.

He ran down the hallway, clutching the gold ring he had looted from the dead, the heavy metal weighing him down as if he were running chest-deep in a flooded trench.

Down the dark staircase with its stained wallpaper, towards the beckoning square of the front door... behind him he could hear an irregular shuffle, growing ever closer. Dread gripped Siegfried's stomach at the thought of those cold fingers grabbing him. Out— he had to get outside!

Enemy artillery fell, a rain of deadly fire, screaming with the lost voice of his little brother.

There was a faint whoosh *as the curtains ignited, then a wave of heat that dissolved the sticky bonds weighing down his limbs.*

Siegfried looked over his shoulder to see fire flowing like water across the parquet floor towards him. His father's corpse, now a flaming torch, stood at the foot of the stairs.

"Bring the buckets, son, and fight to the death!" *rasped the thing.* "Bring water!"

"Water?" *Siegfried managed to force a whisper around the fear strangling his voice.* ""But there is no water, Father. No water!"

Alice awoke abruptly as she heard Siegfried cry out.

A terrible fear squeezed her chest. Before she could think, she jumped out of bed and ran down the hallway.

Siegfried had not drawn his bedroom curtains before retiring. In the faint moonlight coming though the window, she saw that he was asleep, moving restlessly under the coverlet, captive to some disturbing dream.

Her anger at his arrogant and belittling remarks about the winery had faded in the face of his plan to save Montclair. And he had been gallant, defending her to Tati.

Alice started as he spoke suddenly, his voice low, harsh: "Wasser? Aber da ist kein Wasser, Vater. Kein Wasser!"

She sat down on the edge of the bed. "Hush," she whispered, as if to a child. "Hush. It's all right now." She gently stroked his face to comfort him. His cheek was faintly rough with stubble— and wet.

He was crying in his sleep.

She stopped, unwilling to experience such a feeling of communion with this stranger, her husband. He did not wake, but her touch had already soothed him. His jaw muscles relaxed and he turned towards her, one arm reaching over her lap, his face nestling against her thigh. "Mutti," he mumbled, drawing her close.

She knew that much German, at least. He had mistaken her for his mother. Feeling oddly tender, she rested her hand in his rumpled hair. "It's all right. You're safe here."

Even though she wished with all her heart that he had never come, she felt sorry for him now. No one should have to wake up to a damp pillow, alone.

Alice sat there a few minutes longer, until Siegfried fell into deeper sleep, then she carefully removed his hand from her waist, and went silently out of his room.

Back in her own lonely bed, she still felt the warmth of his arm across her lap.

He woke to the sound of a man's voice, cursing, then retching repeatedly. Sitting up, reaching for a rifle, it took Siegfried a moment to recognize where he was in the gray gloom. Four intact walls and a floral carpet. *Montclair. California. Safe.*

He relaxed onto his pillow, feeling sympathy for the sufferer, and sweet guilt for the extra minute of rest before he extricated himself from the delightful bed with its clean dry sheets.

He ignored the aching in his leg as he dressed swiftly and limped downstairs. When he reached the archway to the kitchen he straightened, steadied himself with one hand on the jamb, and came around the corner.

A young woman was setting the kitchen table. She was slightly plump, a smooth olive complexion and dark hair combed into a neat bun. Her fine features showed strain in a smudge of indigo beneath soft brown eyes. Full lips, pursed in concentration, opened in surprise as she looked up at him. Her "Good morning," died in her throat as a fork clattered to the floor.

"Good morning?" Siegfried's greeting turned into a question.

"Peter said you— but I didn't expect you to— Oh, my. You look just like Bill. Like Mr. Roye did, I mean. But your poor face." She closed her mouth and nervously bent to pick up the fork.

When she stood facing him again, Siegfried gave her a half-bow. "You must be... Maria? Peter is a lucky man."

As if in response to his name being spoken, Peter Verdacchia banged open the screen door and came inside. His sturdy trousers and shirt, along with a battered Stetson, already showed the effects of several hours of work.

He was a handsome man in his mid-twenties, with a full head of blue-black curly hair, but his sun-weathered face was rather green this morning, as if he had a miserable hang-over.

Seeing Siegfried, Peter exclaimed, "Crimeny, but you're tall, Sig— almost taller than Mr. Roye was!"

"No one could ever be that tall," Siegfried answered with a slow smile. "It is good to see you again, Peter." He put his hand out, remembering the sun-drenched days and easy camaraderie of his apprenticeship.

The three of them, he and Peter and Bill, had shared their dreams that summer. Bill, in his first year at Berkeley, had been army-mad. Siegfried had wanted nothing more than to be a vintner. Peter had been ardently in love and pursuing a shy young thing still in school.

She was now whispering furiously out of the side of her mouth into her husband's ear. "Why didn't you tell me he's as good as the ghost of Bill Roye? I nearly lost a year's growth!"

Peter gave a rusty chuckle and murmured disparagingly: "It's just because he's so skinny. You fatten him up and there won't be any resemblance at all."

Maria turned and said with a hasty smile, "Welcome to Montclair, Mr. Roderrn... Mr. Roddenwell... Is it all right if I call you Mr. 'R.'?"

Siegfried realized he had missed his opportunity to shake hands with Peter. He stuck his thumb through a belt loop and considered Maria's question. "I will not mind if my wife does not."

"Your wife?" In confusion, Maria turned to Peter again. "I don't remember hearing about a wife. Oh, dear. I hope I've made enough for breakfast."

Before Siegfried could say anything, the screen door creaked and Alice entered from the garden, carrying an armful of pink and white roses.

"Good morning." The door slammed behind her. "I see you've met Maria and Peter." She eyed the tableau in the kitchen warily.

"He's just come down, Mrs. Roye," Maria said, busying herself at the stove. Bacon sizzled, sending its tempting odors into the air with spits and spats. "Eggs'll be ready in a minute. Hope you're all hungry! But I do wish you'd told me there'd be another person for breakfast!"

Siegfried raised his eyebrows at Alice. *Mrs. Roye?* he mouthed. She hadn't told Peter and Maria about their marriage?

"There will only be four for breakfast," Alice said guardedly. She tumbled the roses into the sink and continued, "Won't you be seated? Coffee?" She stripped thorns and leaves from the lower stems, then slipped the roses into a large vase half-filled with water.

Siegfried sat at the table, refusing to wince as his leg resisted bending. Alice placed the bouquet on the table, poured and served him a cup of coffee, then sat down.

"Thank you," Siegfried said, enticed by the coffee. Did heaven smell this good?

Peter hung his hat on the chair back and sat, too. He flinched and his mouth twisted as Maria passed a platter of creamy yellow scrambled eggs swathed with bacon too close to his nose before setting it on the table. "I hope you've made me something I can eat!"

"Don't worry! You get oatmeal to settle your stomach. Too much wedding celebration!" Maria said to Alice as she patted Peter's shoulder and placed a full bowl quickly before him. Peter flung his arm toward her as if he might like to hug her, or hit her, but she deftly avoided him. Out of reach, she clicked her tongue at him and shook her finger. "Try it before you throw it back at me!"

Siegfried hoped Maria would sit down soon, so he could begin eating. He swallowed heavily as she set down golden pancakes and a jar of raspberry syrup. His mouth went dry when she carried another place setting to the table and asked, "But when will Mrs. R want to eat?"

"Who?" Alice looked up guiltily.

"Mr. R's wife," Maria explained.

It was gratifying to see the cherry-red blush spread across Alice's fair, freckled skin and down past the open neck of her sailor blouse. When she didn't speak, Siegfried announced for them both: "Alice has done me the honor of becoming my wife."

Maria dropped the plate she was holding. It fell two inches and the good porcelain rang on the oak table top. "So *that's* what Mrs. Duhring meant by—"

Peter straightened, frowning fiercely, thick eyebrows nearly meeting in a dark bar across his livid face. "Mrs. Roye said you were coming to be the new vintner. But you *married* her?"

Siegfried nodded.

Peter stood up, slammed his hat onto his head and stormed out of the kitchen without another word.

"Oh, dear." Maria said uncertainly. "Congratulations."

Siegfried eyed the plate before him. There was so much food that the pattern of pale blue flowers around the rim of the platter was nearly eclipsed. He stood up resentfully. "I had better go talk to him. I do not think he was pleased by your *news*, Alice." He could not believe that she had failed to tell her closest employees about their marriage.

Alice ignored him, fiddling with the arrangement of the roses in their humble vase.

She would not take care of things? So be it. He would.

As Siegfried pushed through the door onto the porch, he heard Maria demanding of Alice: "Did you *really* marry him, Mrs. Roye?"

The door banged shut as he cleared the steps. Siegfried set off after Peter, whose hat was just visible above the vines, making good speed into the heart of the vineyard. Siegfried cursed his leg and the rest of his bruises, and followed as fast as he could.

It was a foggy morning. Green rows of vines disappeared, swallowed by mist, and the sky was a lowering gray bowl. Even the tips of the palm trees seemed indistinct, yet it was not cold. The damp air held only a hint of chill; the kiss of the deep ocean, not its embrace.

Siegfried's stomach growled. He thought of his beautiful breakfast, growing cold on the kitchen table.

"Peter! Wait!" he called. He ignored the pulling of his scars as he forced himself to run. Peter did not stop but he slowed down. Siegfried caught up with him, although he had no breath left for conversation. They walked together, almost companionably, for another hundred yards, over the crest of the hill, and out of sight of the house.

Peter stopped as if to examine one of the vine shoots splayed out from a gnarled trunk. "When?" he demanded, not looking at Siegfried.

"Last week, when she came to have tea with *Oma* Tati in San Francisco." Siegfried did not pretend to misunderstand Peter's question.

"Why didn't she tell me— us?" Peter snatched his

battered hat from his head, fanning himself.

"You know her better than I," Siegfried confessed.

Peter's cheek twitched. "And you're *married*?"

"It *was* very sudden," Siegfried admitted. "I expected to become the vintner, but my grandmother..."

"Tatiana Roye." Peter muttered her name with a mixture of frustration and grudging admiration and returned his hat to his head. "That explains most of it. But how did she get you to come to California? Oh, damn! Mrs. Roye— that is, Alice — did say that your father passed away. I'm sorry. I know what that feels like," Peter said, putting his hand out in condolence.

In the gray-wool world of fog, they might have been the only two men on earth. Siegfried accepted the handclasp, but he could not take the sympathy. "My father left me nothing. Your father's loss is the greater for both of us. He was a good man, and a fine vintner."

Peter did not move, but he seemed to go away inside himself. Then he took his hand back and said, "Life is funny, isn't it, Sig? It never turns out the way you expect."

"No," agreed Siegfried. He took a hard breath. "For one thing, I never expected that a winery in your charge would ever look like Montclair does today. What *happened*?"

"There's nothing wrong with these vines!" Peter protested, seizing a whip-supple cane and shoving it in Siegfried's face. "They're bearing better than they ever have."

"But the equipment! How could you neglect it so? If your father knew, it would break his heart."

"Too late," Peter said wearily, then he mustered a defense. "Alice never wants to part with a penny. I can't hire enough men to do everything! She tries her best, I'll give her that, but she doesn't know any more how to run a vineyard than a day-old chick does."

Siegfried glanced at him sidelong. "I do not know her well, yet, but she does not seem ineducable."

Peter colored again. "My father..."

Siegfried shook his head in rueful understanding. "Was it so hard for him to work for a woman? Oh, Peter." They took a few more steps in silence. "What about you?"

"Me?" Peter scuffed his boots into the beige dirt. "I don't mind. She's a hard worker, for a city girl. Of course, she does run back to the City every once in a while."

"Tell me more about her," Siegfried prompted. "*Oma* Tati was not forthcoming. How did she and Bill come to meet?"

Peter's mouth twisted. "She doesn't talk much about herself, does she?" He looked away over the fields. "Her daddy introduced her to Bill. Patrick O'Reilly was a real dandy. He wore checkered suits, and his long hair was redder than hers." He smiled slyly. "And he *never* let his shoes get dirty. But you wanted to know about Alice."

Siegfried nodded.

"From what I hear, she finished high school, St. Rose's in the City, like a good Catholic girl. I dunno whether the nuns found her 'ineducable' or not." He paused, waiting for Siegfried to fill in the blank.

"But she does not talk about herself," Siegfried responded obligingly.

"That's right."

"Why did Bill leave her?"

"Sig, 1915 was a bad year."

Siegfried nodded. For him, too. He refused to remember the stench of blood-soaked, corpse-sown mud.

"Bill wasn't near as good with the wines as you were. He took some to the Exposition in the City— the one Mr. Roye was going to help with before he passed on." Peter coughed. "Bill didn't win any prizes at all. You know how he was. That made him feel littler than a root louse. That fall, prices fell out the bottom— some farmers couldn't *give* grapes away. So after Christmas, Bill up and joined the Army.

"He wound up serving under Black Jack Pershing in Mexico and sent his pay home to us. The '16 prices went through the roof, but he was bound for two years, and they sent him over to Europe." Peter scuffed the hardened dirt clods. "He didn't want to go. He knew you'd be there, somewhere, after Ernst—" He broke off. "Poor squirt. I'm sorry. And your mama too— Sig, it's been a bad five years all around."

Siegfried nodded. "Alice mentioned you also suffered another loss. I am sorry about your son." Siegfried meant to offer sympathy, but Peter's face became a strained, white mask, rigidly holding at bay emotions too strong for expression.

"I can't—" Peter grated, blinking desperately, staring into the fog. "I can't talk about it."

Siegfried averted his gaze until Peter coughed, a thick, wet sound, and spat richly onto the dry earth. They walked to the end of a row of vines, then, by unspoken consent, turned their steps back to the house.

Overhead the fog thinned, revealing a streak of blue.

Before they reached the porch, Siegfried stopped Peter gently, hand on his arm. He understood better now why the winery was so neglected. It was not really Peter's fault. But he hoped for a bit more information. "You said that you knew

Alice's father?"

Back in control, Peter gave a half-smile. "Oh, yeah. Didn't I mention it? He was Montclair's wine broker. Bought all your grandpa's champagne for his wife's establishment in San Francisco." He seemed to wait for a reaction, but when Siegfried only nodded, he hitched up his jeans and turned toward the door. "Guess breakfast's waiting."

Siegfried let him enter first. He had no wish to share the revelation so forcefully washing away the puzzlement he had felt about Alice: why her manners were so formal, and why she might be willing to pledge herself to a marriage of convenience to a penniless bridegroom to save her land.

Only gentlemen brokered wine in Europe. Alice's family must have been very good, indeed.

Pleased hunger woke in him as he came through the squeaky kitchen door. He smiled. There was still plenty of food left.

The door to the huge stone winery slid open. Siegfried winced at the reek: vinegar, yeast, and spilled wine. The floor was nearly in darkness. Huge redwood tanks blocked the diffuse light from the small windows near the roof. His foot splashed in a scummed puddle on the uneven concrete and in the gloom something scuttled away.

He had told Alice that the winery must be cleaned, and in the absence of a crew, he would have to do it alone.

He found a doorstop and fixed the door open, battering the gloom with a shaft of sunlight, revealing the scabrous growths on the tanks. He could almost sense the malignancy of the mold, feeding on the seepage through the old black wood of French oak aging barrels, oval ends rising to twice his height. He knew the texture of that mold, as soft as fur or rotten velvet. Just one touch left his fingers dark gray.

Opa Roye had loved this cooperage, had cared for it like a violinist for his Stradivarius. *Grapes grow every year, but fine cooperage can last for generations*, had been one of *Opa*'s favorite sayings. *Take care of your wood, and your wine will take care of itself*, had been another. *Opa* had told him stories about the great wooden barrels other winemaking families had brought with them from Europe: the Beringers, with their ornate heirlooms crafted in France before the Revolution; Etienne Thée's Bordeaux casks 'brought round the Horn' in use at Almaden.

Siegfried   remembered   the   echoing   winery   at

Rodernwiller on the hideous day he had walked the property with the official from the Landesbank. Only splinters had remained; but whether his father had sold the casks or used them for firewood, no one had been able to discover.

At least he might be able to save these masterpieces of the cooper's art. He would free them from their sticky shrouds of spilled wine and silver-gray mold, using hot water and soda ash to banish the ghost of Bill's mercaptan-tainted vintages. And he would get rid of the spiders and birds' nests layered thickly in the corners and under the vats.

The smell of spoiled wine pained him as he hurried through the tunnel formed by the tanks with their catwalks and overhanging pipes, to the stairs that led to the upper story.

He opened a door and, because overgrown cypresses shaded the dust-splattered windows outside, pulled a frayed cord to turn on the electric lamp.

His grandfather's distilling room was crowded with relics of the past. A small hand crusher rusting in the corner under years of dust was attached to the wall by dark gray spider webs and surrounded by the husks of countless sacrificed insects. Tools and chemical equipment lay jumbled next to a small still on a long wooden table. A fourteen-foot ladder leaned protectively over a large-scale still. Behind the ancient roll-top desk, which held bits and pieces of yellowed correspondence, a battered wooden swivel chair sat slightly canted.

Siegfried moved toward the desk in a daze. He stroked the cracked dark green leather on the arm of the chair and bumped his fingers across the brass studs that held the padded leather in place. For a moment he smelled his grandfather's scent, mingled Bay Rum and pipe tobacco.

Another breath, and he was reminded of mold, and rotting wood, and blood. His fingers trailed meaningless marks through seven years of dust. He grabbed a broom, reining in a surge of outrage, gripping the handle tightly as his hands remembered the heft and thickness of a rifle balanced by the weight of a bayonet.

He cleaned out the room. Then he wore blisters into his hands awkwardly sweeping up piles of old dried leaves and cobwebby dirt from the dark corners and gutters of the winery. The smell of wine-soaked wood and mildew teased his every breath.

He pushed the broom against the floor left-right, left-right. The silence in the old building unnerved him after a while so that, once, when he heard a sudden creak, he found himself aiming the broom into the dark. He chided himself for foolishness. No enemy used the giant tanks as cover to creep up on him. There was no enemy here, in Sonoma.

Alice never came.

He tried to stop himself from thinking about her, about the beautiful curve of her neck, the soft roundness of her bosom, her eau-de-cologne.

He decided, after he had thoroughly cleaned out the corner behind the huge barrel closest to the door, that he had been harsh, and she had, rightfully, reacted badly. He regretted his stern words to her for an hour, sweeping between the barrels. Then, when she still did not appear, he began to feel more and more ill-used. She should be here, helping him! The vastness of the winery multiplied into infinity. It was far too much work for only one man.

The day drew on toward noon. Siegfried tried to divert his resentment by imagining how hot the day was, outside the winery's thick stone walls.

"Sig?" Peter called from the entrance.

Siegfried stopped sweeping, and walked from behind the third tank into the aisle.

"Time for dinner," the foreman announced. "Maria's made pot roast."

Siegfried's stomach growled, demanding its due, and he joined his friend. Together they walked back toward the house.

The fog had utterly burned away, leaving a pure cloudless sky. It was hot enough to make his sweat feel cool.

"Spraying's going okay," Peter reported. "Cleanup?"

"It is slow, with only one," Siegfried said.

The field workers were already seated at the long trestle table set up outside near the kitchen. Maria was setting out just-baked biscuits and pitchers of fresh milk. Siegfried hardly waited for Peter to mumble grace before smashing one of the biscuits into the pot roast's brown gravy. He carried it, broken and dripping, to his mouth.

Siegfried was nearly finished with his dinner before he realized that the only woman present was Maria.

He looked up at Peter, who said, "Mrs. R. usually shares dinner with us."

Chewing methodically, Siegfried swallowed and cleared his throat. "Where is she?"

"She went to the City." Maria's voice was heavy with disapproval. "Left about ten. Dressed," she sniffed, "for shopping."

Siegfried felt the stomach-dropping sensation of betrayal. Like receiving orders to go over the top with poorly trained, inexperienced recruits. Like finding out the last horses had been eaten. Like hearing that an unbeaten army was to surrender...

He put his fork down into gravy gone gelid. He stood, and bowed slightly to Peter and his wife. "I'll be in the winery, then, if she comes back."

Montclair
Monday, May 19

When the ruddy sunset stole the light in the winery, Siegfried set aside his broom and had supper in the yellow kitchen with the Verdacchias. He ate in silence despite Maria's efforts to draw him into conversation, his palms burning from the unaccustomed manual labor as if he bathed his hands in acid. He had grown soft since his long hospital stay, and he welcomed the prospect of honest work to build his strength.

After dinner, he went into Alice's downstairs office, and invaded it, rooting in the drawers for blank paper and a pencil. To his surprise, as he was rummaging around, he also found a dusty bottle of tawny port hidden in the bottom drawer of the filing cabinet.

He sat down at the large rosewood desk and poured himself a glass. He smiled in appreciation as he swallowed. It was *good* port, the flavors of raisins and peaches lingering on his palate in a smooth finish. As the sweet liqueur numbed the back of his throat, he found himself almost ready to let go of his ire towards Alice.

But not quite. She was not home yet.

He seated himself behind the big, polished-wood desk and started making projections: how large a harvest? Did they have enough tank capacity for the whole fermentation? How many man-hours to clean a tank? How many additional hands were needed? At a dollar a day, what was the cost of labor?

His dismay at the figures grew. He had told Alice she needed a miracle. Not only that, she needed a rich man for a husband.

Opa Roye had often joked that the best way to make a small fortune in the wine business was to start with a large fortune. *Opa* had had one to spend, made from the lucky purchase of shares in a Nevada silver mine. But Siegfried had no such luck.

He considered asking Tati for a loan, but he had seen the reduced way she was living in San Francisco. She lived without ostentation in her own home, her fortune now in the fact that she was still alive at her age. And still charming and completely unstoppable. She had wanted Siegfried at Montclair, and here he was.

He took another sip of the exquisitely aged port and

gazed out the window. Twilight lingered. The air was soft and gently warm, and the sky glowed preternaturally blue above the mountains.

No sign of Alice.

He bent to his paper, sketching another set of possibilities. What if the harvest did not reach the quantity he had first estimated? *Not two, but only one and a half tons per acre... sixty-five acres in white grapes, one hundred acres in black...*

He refused to look at the clock, because then he would only wonder where Alice might be, and whether she was safe. When would she deign to come home?

He took another sip of port, swallowing the anger that burned in him. She had run away.

Only cowards run.

In the distance, finally, the clattering rumble of a Model T fell to a shallow idle. Siegfried charted the three-point turn by the rise and fall of noise, and then Alice started backing the truck up the hill.

Siegfried put away the port, then hurried to the porch, turning the light on and slipping back inside before the truck came up over the last steep rise of the driveway. He settled back into the chair in Alice's office, pretending to be absorbed into his notes. He refused to show any concern for her to her face. He was furious about her desertion.

He watched her through the window as she climbed wearily out of the truck, folded her driving coat, and walked toward the house. She carried no shopping bags.

What had she been doing all day, then?

Through the half-opened front door, Alice saw Siegfried in the office, behind her desk. She clutched her heavy purse tightly to her chest, and shifted the coat she carried over her arm.

Was he waiting for her? She was acutely aware of his disapproval, and jumped when he spoke.

"Welcome home." His voice was flat.

"I didn't expect—-" She paused in the doorway to the office, lies tumbling on the tip of her tongue. Resolutely, she swallowed them. There was no need to explain herself to him. "You shouldn't have waited up for me."

"I did not. I am," he waved a much-penciled paper, "making plans for renovation. Did you enjoy your outing to the City?"

She made herself smile and throw down her coat with casual flair. "I had a lovely time," she lied, repressing her conscience. "I just love all the flower stalls on Market Street."

"I swept out the winery today." He did not add, *alone*, but the word vibrated between them.

Alice pressed her lips firmly together, suppressing an automatic apology. He was supposed to work. That was why he was here. She clenched her fingers around the purse handle. "I thought about what you said, about needing more crew. I'll speak to Peter in the morning. You'll have your cleaning men tomorrow." Her pearl necklace had been a wedding gift from Bill. Pawning it in the City had felt like the worst kind of betrayal. But she had nothing else she was willing to sell for the money they needed.

The silence lengthened. Siegfried said at last, both his tone and his expression guarded. "That's good then. We'll get an early start."

She nodded. They did not say another word all the way upstairs.

Siegfried, unwilling to face another night of evil dreams, slept badly and woke late. He was out of sorts and cross with himself as he hurried downstairs, gobbled a cooling breakfast from the empty kitchen, and stumbled outside looking for Alice or Peter.

They were conferring by Alice's truck.

Peter, shaking his head, must have caught sight of Siegfried's approach because he said, loud enough to be heard, "I thought Sig was going to do the cleanup all by himself."

"We have decided to renovate extensively. Therefore we need workers. This morning." Alice said, her words clipped with irritation.

Siegfried suppressed his limp as he closed with them. No weaknesses must show!

"That right, Sig?" Peter asked him directly, over Alice's glare. "You're the vintner now. We're hiring?"

"As soon as possible."

"Well, it's all right with me," Peter shrugged and looked inquiringly at Alice. "— if we can make the payroll?"

She nodded. Her face appeared composed but Siegfried was aware, somehow, of her tightly controlled anger. Was she angry at Peter, or at him? She asked Peter, "How soon can you have more workmen here, ready to start?"

Peter looked at the sky, measuring the time. "Oh, by about dinner time."

"Fine. Send them to me in the winery as they arrive,"

Siegfried ordered, cutting short anything else Alice might have been about to say.

Peter tugged on his hat in acknowledgment and sauntered toward the house.

Alice crossed her arms and scowled. It made her look twelve years old, and Siegfried hastily hid a smile as she turned her wrath on him. "Why didn't you tell him we wanted the workers here sooner? Don't we have too much to do to waste a morning?" She started walking up the hill and he went with her.

"We have far too much to do. However, the job will never be finished with the wrong crew."

"The job will never be finished if we don't start soon," she said grimly, drawing on cotton gardening gloves. As he reached the winery door he noticed, belatedly, that she was wearing over-large faded coveralls and a baggy shirt that must once have belonged to Bill.

"You should not do this work!" he protested. "You will ruin your pretty hands."

Alice snorted. "I'm the one responsible for the mess in the winery, so I'll help clean it up. Besides, we'll be short-handed, even with the extra workers."

Siegfried considered. She spoke the truth, and he felt grudging admiration that she admitted it. "Very well."

He handed her the broom with a brusque nod, and directed her behind a nearby tank. She began to sweep debris together with long competent strokes.

Seemingly intent on her task, she never glanced up as he cleaned and sharpened the flat blades of scrapers, and interviewed the men Peter sent them sporadically throughout the morning. Siegfried could not tell whether she was abashed by the ruinous conditions around them, or annoyed at Peter's blatant deference to Siegfried's opinion. In any case, her efforts were energetic. When he returned from the tool room with more scrapers, he saw she had swept together quite a pile already.

By noon there were seven of them at work: skinny Bernard, who wanted to save up money for his wedding; gruff Tony, who continually mopped his face with a fine linen handkerchief; apologetic, clumsy Julio; weather-beaten Johnny; giant Herculio who lived up to his name; Siegfried; and Alice.

Siegfried handed them all brooms, and the building was free of leaves and cobwebs by the time Maria rang the dinner bell.

They joined the vineyard crew at the long trestle tables set up under the fruit trees near the kitchen. In contrast to the loud Italian banter of the workers who had spent their morning in the

sun and fresh air, Alice and the new winery crew sat silently at
their end of the table, eating with gloomy concentration. Siegfried
recognized the signs of men intimidated by the magnitude of the
task that awaited them. *Well*, he thought wryly, *It could be worse.
At least no one is shooting at us. And we are not eating the
horses.*

That thought cheering him, Siegfried tore off a large
chunk from one of Maria's freshly baked loaves, and began to
shovel down spoonfuls of beef stew, scalding his tongue even as
he burned with impatience to return to work.

Back inside the odorous dim cavern of the winery, they
all started scraping the fungus off the tanks. Siegfried quickly fell
into the rhythm of scrape-pull-throw, breathing mold dust
through the red kerchief tied over his mouth and nose as he bared
four-inch wide swathes of redwood dark as blood. The loosened
mold fell in gray shrouds to the newly-swept floor.

Faster! The thought spurred him with every square meter
of filthy wood scraped clean. There was so much left to do before
they could make wine in these tanks.

Time passed; another hour, perhaps two. Siegfried
paused momentarily to roll his shoulders in an attempt to loosen
tight muscles.

He glanced over at Alice. She had traded places with
Johnny, and was shoveling chunks of loosened mold into a
wheelbarrow while the wiry Italian peeled off great strips of the
stuff from tank number two. Her oversized clothes hid the
appealing curves of her waist and bosom, but her tight chignon
left the back of her neck delightfully exposed, and Siegfried
wondered what it would feel like to kiss her nape.

As he watched, she put down the shovel for a moment,
kneeling next to the tank to help Johnny with something. When
she picked up the shovel again, gingerly, Siegfried saw the dark
stains on the palms of her cotton gardening gloves.

His own blistered palms, securely shielded now in thick
leather work gloves, gave a sympathetic twinge.

He was beside her in an instant, taking her elbow
roughly. "Why did you not say anything?" He gave her arm a
shake, and she curled her hands shut, hiding the betraying reddish
blotches. "You will come with me now. To the house."

"It's nothing. They don't even hurt," Alice asserted,
trying to pull away from him. "You don't have to—"

"Yes, I do, because you will not do it for yourself," he
said, irrationally incensed at the thought of her beautiful white
hands bleeding inside those filthy, inadequate gloves. He should
have known better than to allow her to perform manual labor!

"What if they become infected?" The thought of her hands, rotting with gangrene, was too terrible to consider. Siegfried forced his voice to a calmer tone. "Please, Alice. Allow me."

"All right." She gave a noisy huff, but allowed him to steer her out of the winery, and down the gentle slope to the house.

As they climbed the porch stairs, the late afternoon sunlight gilded her hair, sparking auburn and red beneath the veil of dust, warming her hazel eyes to golden-brown. Siegfried fought the temptation to stare, open-mouthed, at her sudden transformation into a creature of fire and amber. "Where do you keep your bandages?" he asked.

"Upstairs. In the bathroom." She gave that noisy sigh again, and stopped on the top step. "You don't have to pamper me, you know."

"This is selfish necessity." Siegfried was acutely aware that her elbow was cupped in the curve of his hand like a fragile egg. He forced himself to continue coolly, "I find we need your assistance in the winery after all."

The inside of the house was shadowy. As they walked up to the second floor, the muffled thunk-thunk of Maria chopping vegetables in the kitchen was the only sound.

A pale wash of light greeted them in the bathroom, the immaculate white-tiled floor and walls glowing as if illuminated. Alice stood hesitantly in the middle of the large room while Siegfried gathered clean towels, ointments, and bandages, and filled the washbasin with warm water.

She caught sight of herself in the medicine cabinet mirror. "Oh, goodness, I look a fright. Maybe I should just—"

"Your hands come first," Siegfried said firmly, leading her over to the washbasin and deftly rolling up her shirtsleeves. The skin on her arms was every bit as soft as he had imagined. He fought the distraction. "You can wash your face afterwards if you use a cloth."

She dipped her hands into the hot water, sucked air between her teeth, and pulled her hands back so quickly that droplets sprayed over the mirror.

"I know it stings, but you must be stoic," Siegfried advised, lathering up a washcloth with soap. "It is best if you soak them for a little while." He kept his own expression carefully blank, concentrating on the white foam spilling over his fingers.

After a moment, she cautiously put her hands back in the water and kept them there, catching her lower lip between her teeth. She ventured in a small voice, "The winery is bigger job than I thought."

Siegfried nodded, the bar of soap making tight circles against the cloth in his hand. "I have been thinking the same thing. We must find a way to work more quickly, or we shall not be finished before crush."

"I was afraid of that. Do— do you have any ideas?"

"Sometimes it can help to make the work a little more interesting." His hands stilled as Siegfried relived memories of a half-finished trench and the discouraged faces of his men, weary with what seemed pointless digging. He returned to the present with a start. "I have found that offering small prizes for progress often spurs the men along."

Unexpectedly, Alice nodded, sending a ripple of water through the washbasin. "Something like a contest?"

"Yes, exactly. Perhaps we might offer as a prize something that Maria has baked, or..." He paused, considering. "Have we the funds for a bonus?"

He expected Alice to immediately dismiss the notion, but she surprised him. "If it's a small one. What did you have in mind?"

"Nothing, yet." Siegfried reached into the water, and picked up her unresisting hand. "This will also sting," he warned her, before tenderly dabbing at her raw palm with the soapy cloth. She gasped and stiffened, but suffered his attentions without complaint as he finished gently cleansing one hand, and started on the other.

He patted them both dry with a clean cloth, then directed her to seat herself on the closed lid of the commode.

Siegfried knelt before her like a supplicant, the bathroom tiles cool and hard under his knees as he smeared her palms thickly with Vaseline. She gave a tiny twitch. "That tickles!"

"*Halt still,*" he said, automatically, and remembered with surprised pleasure his mother's efforts to doctor him after some mishap when he was a boy. He had been perched on the old wooden stool in the kitchen, squirming uncomfortably while *Mutti* dabbed something on his scraped knees that stung horribly. "Hold still, Friddy," she had said, repeating it in her American-accented German. "*Halt still.*"

"*Halt still, Ah-lees,*" Siegfried whispered to the soft hands lying so trustingly in his.

"I beg your pardon?"

"Nothing," he mumbled, hastily wiping the excess Vaseline from his fingers. Then he reached for a roll of gauze and wound a long strip around her hand. Not too tight, or the circulation in her fingers might be impaired; not too loosely, or the bandages would be worse than useless, trapping dirt and infection against her broken skin.

"You should have been a doctor," Alice commented.

"No, I am a vintner, but also somewhat of an expert," he said, ruefully showing Alice his own bandaged palms, "when it comes to blisters."

She smiled fleetingly, and he finished tying off the bandage ends.

He held her hands for a long moment after finishing, studying the bluish-green branching of veins in her slender wrists. He rubbed his thumb unconsciously over her pulse. Her skin was so tender there, like a baby's... On impulse he bent his head and kissed her bandaged palms.

Alice inhaled sharply, and he realized what he had done. His face grew hot. "To help them heal, my mother always—" He hastily let go, and tried to make his tone matter-of-fact. "You must wear thick gloves like mine until your hands heal."

"It's all right." Alice said, addressing his embarrassment, and coloring as well. Her white-wrapped hands briefly rose to touch his hair. "Thank you, Siegfried." She stood up quickly. "Let's get back to it."

"I believe that went well," Siegfried said in an undertone as Julio, Tony, and Johnny went back into the winery with a noticeably brisker step. He and Alice stood at the winery entrance, where she had just announced that the best worker would be awarded a daily bonus. Herculio trotted past them, and disappeared into the blinding sunlight outside.

A loud scraping sound startled them, and they turned towards the doorway, leaning out into the daylight.

Herculio reappeared, dragging something large around the corner of the winery.

"It's about time to start scrubbing down the outside of the first tank. Where do you want this, Mr. R?" he puffed. *This* was the remnant of an old aging barrel, long since sawn in half to form a deep vat.

"As near the winery doors as possible," Siegfried answered, his heart lightening at the young man's initiative. "And we will need a great quantity of fresh water. Do you think you might find somewhere a pump and a hose long enough to reach here from the pond?"

"Sure. I saw some in the back. Coming right up!" Herculio disappeared in a rush.

Alice grinned wryly. "Well, they certainly seemed to like the idea of the extra money."

Siegfried smiled back at Alice. "With the *right* crew, anything is possible."

"Who wants chocolate cake?" Maria called from the winery entrance. Tools dropped with a clatter, and the men crowded eagerly around her, avid for a treat in the middle of a Friday afternoon.

Alice put down her long-handled scrub brush, and followed the rest of the crew outside.

It was the fourth day of cleaning the winery, and Siegfried's suggestion had already worked miracles. Yesterday, Herculio had walked away proudly with a nickel when the day ended, because his pile of filth outside the winery was nearly twice the size of anyone else's. And the outside of the first row of tanks was nearly finished.

Only ten more to go, Alice thought. *We might finish before harvest, after all!*

She spotted Siegfried's telltale blond hair and wandered over to him. "Why wasn't there a contest today?"

"Oh, but there *was* a contest," Siegfried assured her around a mouthful of cake, with the same sunny smile Bill had always used when evading the truth.

"Oh yeah?" Johnny asked, overhearing. "I didn't hear nothing about no contest."

"Today's contest was: who can get the dirtiest?" Siegfried announced. "Mrs. Verdacchia, you must be our judge. Who among us wins the prize?" His blue eyes were bright with mischief in a face darkened by smears of grime.

As the winery crew hastily formed a ragged inspection line, Maria shifted her empty tray, resting it on her hip. Smiling broadly, she peered at the assembled crew, checking over each man in turn before giving a tiny shake of her head and moving on to the next.

Alice, intentionally standing at the far end of the line, frantically fished in the pocket of Bill's old Levis for one of his large handkerchiefs. The jeans were very baggy on her— she had needed to punch a new hole in one of Bill's belts this morning so that they would stay up.

As Maria pursed her lips and rejected yet another candidate, Alice scrubbed at her face and neck. She had spent the day *inside* tank number one, ankle-deep in a sticky mess that reeked of mold and vinegar. Only she and Bernard had been able to fit through the tiny round openings at the bottom of the aging tanks— and he had his own tank to clean. It had been dark, and lonely, with her scraper, a scrub brush, and a portable electric lamp for company, and she had found herself missing the now-constant banter between Siegfried and the crew.

"Mrs. R.!" Maria said, pointing, a dimple indenting the corner of her mouth.

Alice hurriedly stuffed the kerchief back in her pocket. "Yes?"

"You win the contest!" Siegfried called gleefully from the other end of the line.

"What's my prize?" Alice asked, suspiciously. She didn't like the impish grin on Siegfried's face as he advanced towards her.

"A bath!"

"Oh, no... no!" Alice backed away.

Maria clapped a hand over her mouth in a vain attempt to restrain her laughter.

"No— definitely not— Siegfried, don't you dare— no! Don't! Aaaaaaaah!" Alice's protests were ignored as Siegfried bent, pushed his shoulder against her middle, and easily scooped her up over his shoulder. "Let me go! Please!" She hung upside-down against his back as he strode forward, his arms pinioning her thighs. As she pounded ineffectually at his back, Herculio's deep laugh boomed out, followed by a chorus of masculine chuckles.

"Oh yeah, Mr. R. You show her who the husband!" Bernard called out in his reedy voice. "She don' give you no trouble then."

"Siegfried!" Alice wriggled madly and tried to clutch handfuls of his shirt. But to no avail. He was headed for the large rinsing vat standing nearby. He bent forward as he came up to the rim of the vat, and sent her backwards into the cool water with an enormous splash.

"Noooooo—" Her shriek turned into a splutter. As she sat up and cleared the water out of her eyes, she saw Siegfried clinging to the side of the vat, convulsed with laughter.

You beast! she thought, hot for revenge. She brought her hands together in the special way that Bill had taught her during their too-brief honeymoon at the Sutro Baths in San Francisco.

She was amply rewarded by Siegfried's started recoil when a long jet of water hit him in the face. As he stood there, looking silly and wet and startled momentarily out of laughter, she squirted him again. He shook his head in a spray of droplets, and his smile returned, even brighter.

Alice carefully took aim at Herculio. "I think," she said, as Herculio jumped and shouted. "We could all use a bath." She splashed the water invitingly. "Care to join me in Montclair's luxury swimming pool?"

Siegfried tried unsuccessfully to pull his brows together and school his mouth to sternness. "This is a winery, not a spa, young wom— pfaugh!"

Alice squirted him one more time for good measure, catching him squarely in the mouth. She giggled, then hid her mouth with her hand. Had that joyous noise come from her? She had not laughed like that in over a year.

"All right, all right, the slaves must return to work," she pretended to grumble, rising on her knees and reaching for the rim of the vat to pull herself upright.

To her astonishment, Siegfried immediately shoved her back down into the water. "You cannot get out like *that*!" he whispered.

She followed his fascinated glance downward. Bill's cotton shirt, sopping now, was nearly transparent, revealing the lacy edge of her silk camisole and— she sank lower in the water with mortification. The cold water had left absolutely nothing to the imagination.

Hers *or* Siegfried's.

She saw Siegfried swallow heavily, and the tips of his ears glowed crimson. "Um, perhaps you will just stay there for a minute— for a while?" he said, finally tearing his attention away from her breasts and fixing his gaze determinedly at a point somewhere over her left shoulder. He shivered, despite the summer heat. "No, the water is too cold," he said to himself, and started to unbutton his own shirt. "Please take mine."

"Siegfried!" Alice reproached him, wondering what the rest of the crew must be thinking. But he stripped off his shirt, anyway. He was far too thin, muscles sharply corded under the pale skin of his arms and every rib showing through his white undershirt. His broad shoulders must have once been as generously muscled as Bill's. Perhaps with more of Maria's good cooking, Siegfried might... Alice broke off her train of thought. How could she even contemplate such a thing?

"You must take it," Siegfried insisted, holding his shirt out to her. "I will not shame you in front of the men."

"Couldn't we just ask them to turn their backs?" Alice asked, half-jokingly as she climbed out of the vat, water pouring in streams from her shirt and her heavy, sodden jeans. Her sturdy shoes squelched in their own little puddles.

"No, they would peek," Siegfried replied, a smile creasing the corners of his eyes. As he wrapped his shirt around her shoulders, he bent close and whispered, "I know I would."

Montclair
Sunday, May 25

A tap on her door awakened Alice. She wriggled out of the tangle of sheets and turned on the lamp, squinting at the alarm clock. *What time is it?*

Her head hit the pillow. It was far too early. Still dark outside.

"Alice?" That was Siegfried's disembodied voice, echoing in the high-ceilinged hall.

She blinked hard, trying to open her eyes. "What's wrong?"

"Nothing. I thought you might want to walk the vineyard with me this morning, and learn a little about the grapes. As you asked."

She *had* asked. Alice kicked the covers off. She strangled a yawn, and said with her best semblance of enthusiasm, "Oh, yes, please! I'll be down in a moment." She tied back the strands of hair that had slipped out of her braid and began struggling into her work shirt and trousers. At least Siegfried had remembered his promise to teach her.

He met her in the kitchen and handed her a cup of coffee strong enough to dissolve the crystal cupboard knobs. She thanked him with a smile and forced it down, waking up more with every sip. Siegfried drank standing, gazing through the window overlooking the vegetable garden. The black mirror of the window above the sink reflected his unguarded expression.

Alice emptied her cup. She wasn't awake enough to think yet, but she saw what Siegfried felt as he focused on the slope of vines rising up out of sight.

Longing.

The world outside lightened by gray degrees, dissolving his image in the glass. Her cup clinked into its saucer when Siegfried said, "Shall we go?"

They left their cups in the sink and went outside. The low-lying fog made Alice fancy she was walking inside an enormous pearl, luminous with the increasing light of dawn. Simply breathing the cool moist vapor was a pleasure.

And somehow, even though he was an interloper foisted on her by Bill's scheming grandmother, it was pleasure, too, to be among the vines with someone who loved them as much as she did.

They walked steadily up the hill, Alice hurrying to keep up with Siegfried's long, uneven strides, then turned into the Pinot Noir section.

Siegfried stopped part-way down a row in front of one of the four-year-old vines. He pointed out the large number of grape clusters hanging from the slender canes like pendants of tiny, hard green beads.

Alice estimated the size of the harvest, if all the plants produced like this. "This is wonderful," she breathed. She had visions of solvency. Her heart pounded and she wanted to dance.

"We should thin them out," Siegfried said, pulling a pair of shears from his overall pocket. The sound of snipping was like money being torn in half.

"Why? What's the matter with them?" She gave an anguished cry and picked up the fallen cluster to inspect it closely. "It looks fine to me. There's no fungus, or insects. There's nothing the matter with it! It's perfect! Why cut it?"

Siegfried waited for her to calm down before he spoke. "This vine is too young. It is overburdened, trying to ripen such a heavy crop. When you thin out the clusters like this," he left only two or three bunches hanging from the branch, "then the plant can focus all of its energy on the remaining grapes. The flavor of the wine will be concentrated."

Alice fingered a soft green leaf, trying to understand.

"I also hate to do this," Siegfried said aloud what she was thinking. "For each cluster we prune, it is like pouring a glass of wine into the dirt. But it must be done if you want Montclair's wine for the Church."

So much potential income wasted! It was absurd. She wouldn't listen to him.

The damp air turned clammy and she shivered, running the cluster of hard little grapes through her fingers, almost like a rosary. *If you listen to him, there's no going back,* said one portion of her mind. *You already decided,* she told herself. *You said you were going to make wine for the Church.* A memory of her spoiled Traminer firmed her resolve. *Do what your vintner says, that's why you—* she threw the cluster down. *Married him.* "All right," she said unhappily.

He only nodded. He had expected no other response. He started walking again.

"How long do we have until harvest?" she asked after a few yards.

"The grapes seem to be ripening very slowly this year. Perhaps another three or four months."

That surprised her. "Won't that be too late? We started crush in mid-September last year."

He shrugged. "I will know when the grapes are sweet enough. And the— the... balance must also be there."

"Balance? What's that?" Alice remembered abruptly that Bill had always laughed off her questions. *Don't worry your pretty head about that*, he would grin. *I'll make the wine and you make the babies*. Neither of them had been any good at— She steeled herself against Siegfried's scorn. It never came.

Siegfried frowned, but he was only searching for the correct words. "Balance is the promise of the wine, an intensity." He waved his arm, frustrated. "Sweetness is not everything. The soil, the weather, and the variety of grape, all impart subtle tones to the wine's flavor. You could make wine from table grapes, but it would not have *depth*. Balance is something that is there in the grape that you can still taste after a count of ten."

"Like finish in a wine?"

"Yes, that is exactly what 'balance' will become." He smiled brilliantly. "If you taste it in the grape, you will taste it in the wine." He paused, then said as if compelled, "*If* your equipment is scrupulously clean. Which ours will be."

"Yes. It will." She agreed wholeheartedly, and they continued to stroll comfortably together through the cool morning.

Siegfried's willingness to answer more of her questions warmed Alice until they returned to the house some while later. She smiled as she heard Siegfried's stomach rumbling in tune with hers. "Maria will cook us a good breakfast when we return from Mass."

Siegfried halted on the first step of the back porch. As she stood on the next step up, their eyes were level and she saw the pain he immediately shuttered away. He groped for words and finally settled on a defiant: "I am not going to church with you."

"Siegfried, you're not sick now!" Alice said, shocked. His bruises had healed nicely over the course of the last week.

"No, I am quite well, thank you."

"Are you worried what people will think?" Alice pressed. "I mean— about us? Don't be. Everyone is expecting to see you, especially the Livernash sisters."

Siegfried shook his head, and studied his shoes. "I do not attend Mass at all. Anymore."

Alice felt a cold chill that had nothing to do with the weather. *You'll go to Hell!* A nightmare vision of Siegfried, burning in torment, shocked her even more. She hated the thought of him in pain, even if was self-inflicted. "You should go."

"God abandoned me during the War," Siegfried retorted. "I have no cause to praise Him." He withdrew from the porch and stood staring at the fruit trees. "You do not know. You cannot know—"

"I know what it was like to be here, when Bill was gone," Alice said forcefully. "If God abandoned anybody, it was *Bill*." She started to walk back to the house. "But I suppose I can't drag you to church if you don't want to go. There's bread in the breadbox. Make yourself some toast if you feel like it. I have to get dressed now." She quickened her pace, and climbed the porch steps, putting as much space between them as she could.

"I will be in the winery, cleaning, when you get—"

The slamming door cut off the rest of his words.

Siegfried put his back into the hard work. He ached all over, sweat streaming from his skin even in the artificial coolness gathered between the thick stone walls. Scrape, pull, throw. Scratch a dusty itch at elbow or cheek—careful not to rub your eyes— and do it all again. It seemed as though he had been cleaning the tanks forever, not for less than a week.

He paused and blotted sweat from his forehead on the blue cotton sleeve rolled over his upper arm. From the corner of his eye, Siegfried saw Alice, back from church, come in dressed in her work clothes. She picked up a shovel and manhandled a wheelbarrow nearby, then started removing the pile of mold he had created.

He was satisfied that she had followed his orders and was wearing thick leather work gloves over her bandaged hands.

They worked in silence for hours, changing jobs whenever the strain of repetition got too bad.

Covertly, Siegfried watched her while she scraped, reaching up high and worrying away at a stubborn patch of filth. The baggy front of Bill's old shirt molded tightly against her breasts, and Siegfried swallowed, hard, remembering how she had looked yesterday, wet as a mermaid. He stopped short. A wave of heat rushed through his body as he shifted uncomfortably from foot to foot to ease the sudden restriction of his jeans.

The more he saw her, the more he wanted her, and it was becoming too difficult to work side by side, and say nothing. Do nothing.

Alice finally succeeded in loosening the sticky mass from the side of the tank. She balanced it on the end of her scraper, and flicked it to her left, where it landed neatly in the wheelbarrow already piled high with other refuse. She noticed his motionlessness. "Yes?"

"Time for a break," he said, feeling as if he mumbled, the English sounds foreign on his lips. His whole body was sensitized, aware of her. Every pulse beat heightened his desire for her.

"I'm not tired. You go rest. You've been working longer than I have today."

"All right," he said, but he could not move away. He smelled her: hard-working woman with a hint of lemon cologne, and found that his feet had sent roots into the concrete floor.

Alice's scraper chewed another strip of mold away from the wood. Siegfried leaned closer to her.

"Ah-lees, I—" She turned to face him and they were within touching distance. Siegfried brushed a streak of dust off her hair, then let his fingers drift downward to touch her cheek. Her hazel eyes were questioning as she gazed up at him.

Siegfried placed his hands on her shoulders, pushing her back against the tank. He leaned close to touch his mouth to hers, hesitant and feather-light. *May I?*

She was tense and trembling slightly. "Siegfried, don't..."

"Alice?" A man's voice called from the entrance to the winery. "Are you in here?"

She shoved Siegfried away with a gasp.

Hugh Roye stood in the blaze of sunlight in the doorway. Glare and the brim of his hat obscured his face except for the determined set of his jaw, until he came right up to them. He removed his hat in courtesy to Alice, revealing sweat-crimped, thinning fair hair brushed back from a broad, lined forehead. His eyes, slightly red-rimmed from the dust of travel, were the same milky-blue, but they radiated anger and a deep-seated sense of resentment, that the world had injured him through no fault of his own.

"Is it true?" he demanded, waving a copy of this week's *Sonoma Index-Tribune* in their faces. "You *married* him?" He seemed to take no note of Siegfried's presence.

Alice nodded, her shoulders shrugging. She took another step away from Siegfried.

"You could have called to let me know, Alice, or at least sent me a note! How do you think I felt, finding out about your marriage from the *paper*?" He displayed a small, circled announcement.

"Cousin Hugh!" Siegfried put out his hand.

Hugh juggled the paper and his white straw hat until Siegfried dropped his hand.

"I'm so sorry," Alice whispered. "I didn't—- that is—- "

her eyelids fluttered nervously. "Only Tati was there."

Hugh ground his teeth together. "I thought we were friends, Alice," he accused. "But now I find you're treating me no better than the rest of my so-called family!"

"We were sorry we could not include you, Cousin," Siegfried interrupted, placing his hand possessively on Alice's shoulder. "But everything happened so quickly."

"You didn't have to know him very long, did you, Alice, dear? But then, you're just the kind of woman to make a man lose his head."

"That was uncalled-for," Siegfried said, maintaining civility despite the venom in his cousin's voice. "And you will apologize to my wife immediately."

"You— you sneaking Hun!" Hugh sputtered, his voice rising with indignation. A flush began to creep up from his collar. "I have nothing to say to you!"

"But you do have something you will say to Alice." Siegfried commanded. No man, not even his only living cousin, could insult his wife with impunity.

Alice gasped, but Siegfried merely tightened his grip on her shoulder and waited for Hugh's apology.

"I'd say you owe *me* the apology, Alice!" Hugh growled.

Contempt edged Siegfried's voice now. "You sound like a spoiled child, cousin. Apologize to my wife, *now*. I will not say it again."

Alice slipped out from under his hand. "Really, Siegfried, he doesn't have to—"

"He does, or I will thrash him."

"You couldn't!" Hugh bristled.

Siegfried wanted very badly to try. His hands curled into fists.

"Hugh, I'd like to talk to you," Alice said urgently. "Right now." She seized Hugh's elbow in a seemingly friendly grip, and started to drag him out of the winery. "Siegfried, if you come after us, you're fired."

Siegfried, surprised, stayed where he was.

"You've got every right to be unhappy about this, but you shouldn't have provoked him!" Alice said, as she hustled Hugh down the hill to where his elegant new Dodge Brothers car sat next to her shabby truck. "I thought he would kill you!"

Hugh stopped. "For all we know, he did kill Bill."

"What are you talking about?" Alice asked, stunned.

"Oh, Alice, use your head. Alsace was German territory

until we won," Hugh said bitterly. "How do you suppose Cousin Siegfried spent the War? Making wine on his estate?"

"Well, I never—"

"...considered it, did you?" Hugh sighed and shook his head pityingly. "His father was a rabid pan-Germanist. Herr Rodernwiller would never have allowed his sons to be pacifists." He paused a moment, letting her absorb the import of his words, "You married the Enemy, Alice. How could you!"

"Tati didn't say anything about Siegfried being a German," Alice swallowed heavily. She felt nauseous. "S-soldier."

"Tati. I knew she had to be at the bottom of this," Hugh spat.

"I'm sorry!" Alice cried. "You've always been my friend. If Tati had given me any choice—"

Hugh leaned against the side of his car, heedless of dust against his white suit. He squinted intently at her, settling his hat back on his fair hair. "Don't you understand, Alice? Tati duped you. She never wanted you to keep Montclair after Bill died." He looked around at the white house, the palm trees, and the hillsides rising green under their rows of vines. "She's cheated you— and me— out of it. Again."

"How can you say that about your grandmother?" Alice swallowed the bile rising in her throat.

Hugh's face twisted. "Good-bye, Alice."

Alice watched as Hugh's car bounced down the gravel drive and disappeared around the curve. She didn't know what to think. His words made dreadful sense. Why else had Tati been so insistent on the marriage? How *had* Siegfried's father lost everything?

And, thinking back, Siegfried had never mentioned where he had spent the War. Or how he had acquired his limp, his apostasy.

She *was* married to a Hun. Oh, God.

She gripped her upper arms, shivering, as a slow, dry breeze rustled the palm leaves and brought her the scents of growing grapes.

"Was that Mr. Roye?" Maria's wistful voice startled her. "Why did he go so quick? It seems like a long time since he's been here for Sunday supper."

Alice smoothed damp palms against the thighs of her overalls, bumping against the scraper she had unconsciously pocketed when Hugh arrived. "I— ah— he couldn't stay."

"Was he mad about you and Mr. R.?" Maria stood on the porch and shook crumbs out of her apron.

Alice gave an involuntary spurt of laughter. "You could say that."

"Oh. But he will come back again, won't he?" Maria's gaze followed the dust plume hanging over the drive.

"I don't know." Alice glanced up, where Siegfried stood guard at the entrance to the winery. Had he been watching them the whole time? "Maria, excuse me. I've got to—" She couldn't finish. She hated the thought of the coming confrontation, but she forced herself to march up the hill to him.

"Ah-lees, did he apologize to you?" Siegfried demanded as she drew near.

"I want an annulment. Now." Her throat hurt and her voice shook. How could she have let him touch her? He had almost kissed her, before Hugh arrived. Her lips tingled. She rubbed them to make the feeling go away.

"Why? What did Hugh say to you?" Siegfried asked, bewildered. pain in his blue eyes. And there would be more, before she was finished. She steeled herself. *He was a Hun!* Alice's memory provided lurid images, based on wartime newsreels and posters: Siegfried in a helmet crowned with a steel spike. Siegfried with a bayonet, stabbing helpless babies. Siegfried with a machine gun, mowing down rows of courageous Allied soldiers.

Don't let it be true, I don't want it to be true!

"Ah-lees! What happened?" Siegfried reached out, and Alice felt his hand on her shoulder, drawing her close.

She tried to step away from him, but his fingers tangled in her shirt, and somehow her effort to escape led her back to him, her face resting in the curve of his shoulder, her arms awkward against his bony ribs. His right arm came around her back. She couldn't bear the thought of him holding her. If he finished the embrace, she would shatter. Her fingers closed on the handle of the scraper hanging in the pocket of her denim overalls. Without thinking, she grabbed it and held it against Siegfried's throat.

"Don't touch me." Her voice quavered, but the blade held steady. When he didn't obey, she applied a little pressure. The skin at his Adam's apple indented along the edge of the flat tool.

He stood, unmoving. His eyes rolled as he tried to look at her while holding his head absolutely still. "Ah-lees, what are you doing?" he whispered.

"Is it true, Siegfried? Were you a German soldier?"

He spread his hands wide in a gesture of surrender. "Yes," he said promptly, and something in her chest turned cold and heavy. "I was."

Alice, watching him warily from close enough to kiss

him, saw past his golden-stubbled chin to his outstretched arm. The grimy bandage across his palm reminded her of his kindness to her over the past week, and the scraper wavered. She grabbed her elbow to steady it as Siegfried twitched. "How could you?" she rasped. She could barely breathe. "I *trusted* you!"

Siegfried wet his lips with his tongue and drew in a sharp breath. His skin had turned the color of milk. "May I speak?" he asked, trying to look at her again.

She nodded. Her voice would have failed. Bill's ghost stood between them, casting a chill shadow.

"Without a knife at my throat? I will not try to touch you again— or hurt you at all."

She stepped back, deliberately. She did not drop the scraper.

Siegfried closed his eyes and began to speak. "My father believed that 'All Germans belong in one Fatherland.' But Alsace has never been either wholly French or wholly German. When the War started, and the French invaded, half the country rejoiced. The other half was happy to fight back. I wanted no part of either side." He opened his eyes again and stared at her intently. "And neither did my mother, but one of the battles swept through our village, and my brother was killed by French shelling. After that, my father stood outside the army recruiter's office in Schlettstat until I did my duty. And once you are in the army there is only one honorable way out of it until peacetime."

She flinched.

"Feet first. If you still *have* feet."

"Hugh said—" Her lips failed to hold the right shape to form words. She concentrated, and after she regained control she finished. "You might have killed Bill."

Siegfried's eyes gave away nothing. His arms stayed outflung. "I might have," he answered her calmly, when she most wanted him to argue. "If not he, then others like him. It was war, Alice. One obeys orders."

"I should have sold Montclair to Hugh!" Alice cried. "At least he made me a fair offer!"

"Hugh would have torn out the vines. Tati was right. You need a vintner. You need *me*." He jabbed his thumb toward his chest in a swift chop.

Alice's mouth rounded as if she tasted something sour. "I do need a vintner, but I won't— I *can't*— be married to you."

"I will not stay here as a mere hired hand."

Alice was shaken by the anger in his voice.

His hands made fists, and they shook. "In the Kaiser's army, they made me an *Offizierstellvertreter* — a deputy officer. I had the duties, the responsibilities, but not the— the rank of a real officer." He laughed shortly and forged on. "I was never fully trusted. I was never German enough. Too many Alsatians deserted. The real officers always thought I might be next." His knuckles whitened as his nails dug into his bandaged palms. "This property belonged to my grandfather. Either I stay here as your husband, or I will seek employment elsewhere. And if I leave, Ah-lees, you will not get your altar wine."

Alice fought down her panic. He must go. But who else could she hire as vintner, with Prohibition looming so close? And if she failed to make altar wine, how could she keep Montclair?

Siegfried must have seen her hesitating, for he said, "If, after crush, after the vintage is sold to the Church, you still want me to go, I will honor your request for an annulment. I will return to my grandmother, and you need never see me again."

The scraper dropped from Alice's fingers. He was right. And there was another, darker reason she had to keep him.

He was staring intently at the toes of his work boots when she capitulated. "All right." Her face hot, she stumbled over the words in her haste to get them out. "Tati would never, ever forgive me if you... left... so suddenly."

His sudden smile was blinding with happiness and relief, and Alice had to look away, ashamed of her own cowardice.

As a soldier of the Enemy, she ought to hate Siegfried. Why, then, was it so much easier to despise herself?

They returned to work. What else was there to do?

Sunday dinner was strained. Siegfried ate mechanically while Alice sat across from him in icy silence. He felt distanced from his surroundings, as if the walls had collapsed, and what remained was only an illusion. It was like the aftermath of an artillery attack— he was alive, but had not yet begun to feel again. Peter had enjoyed himself in convivial surroundings and dominated the conversation with a slightly slurred monologue. Maria seemed sad. Afterward, Siegfried could not remember what they ate.

Alice shut herself up in her office behind a rampart of ledger books which Siegfried did not feel up to storming. He could think of nothing to say to her that would improve her opinion of him. *All is lost.*

He climbed the stairs slowly, each movement an effort. A hot bath failed to disperse the chill gray cloud that had settled on his soul. He emerged clean but in no better heart than he had started.

Too dispirited even to dress, he sat down at the little writing table in his room to compose a dutiful letter to *Oma* Tati, but the only thing he had to say was unacceptable: *I hope you are well. Today, Alice called me a Hun and tried to kill me. Why did you lie to her about me?*

He stopped chewing the pencil when he tasted black lead. Alice hated him. He had been so close to winning her regard. So close. She had almost let him kiss her before Hugh arrived. In those disastrous five minutes, Siegfried had gone from hero to villain in her eyes. It was like coming home to Alsace, and finding himself the Enemy.

He wanted to be the hero, to do right by Alice. He wanted her respect and admiration. He wanted her to sparkle with that wicked grin. He wanted *Alice*.

Before Hugh spoke, there had been the possibility that she could be wooed. Now Siegfried had no chance.

But he wanted Montclair as his home. The prospect of being merely a caretaker here left him cold, so cold. He sagged to the foot of his bed, pulled the quilt up and wrapped it around his bare shoulders.

He raked a hand through damp hair and shivered. Before she knew about his past, Alice had been close to liking him. How could he restore Alice's regard?

What if he couldn't?

He curled up in a miserable ball, pulling the quilt over his head, and retreated into sleep.

In his dreams, he lost every battle of the War.

He wrestled with corpse-shaped mold in the dark corners of the winery, hip-deep in sucking trench mud. Reddish-brown redwood melted into reservoirs of shed blood as his men died under fusillades of machine gun fire. He tried to shoot back, but his broom had no ammunition. The fighting went hand-to-hand with soldiers made of glass. A bayonet stabbed out of the mouth of a wine bottle, aimed for his heart.

He woke up crying out, and rolled off the bed, scrabbling frantically for his rifle. But only the nubbled texture of the rug met his fingers. Where was it? He had to find it, because—because—

There are no snipers here. He pulled himself upright and forced himself to go the open window, to expose himself as a target. He leaned out on the windowsill, surveying the sleeping vineyard, seeking calm in the steady moonlight pouring over the hills. His labored breathing slowed.

The night was warm. The fog must have gotten lost on its way in from the sea.

The sound of his bedroom door opening seemed louder than a rifle shot.

Siegfried jumped, turned, and saw Alice, standing in the doorway in a thin white gown.

"Are you all right?" she asked, anxiously. The moonlight silvered her face and hands, and her hair was a long dark rope falling along the side of her neck past her breast.

"I dreamt about the War."

She stepped back hastily. "Oh."

"It's nothing to concern you," he said, harshly. "We lost."

"I'm sorry," she whispered, automatically. "If you need anything—— from the kitchen, if you're hungry, or——" She bit her lip as he gaped at her.

Her nightgown moved with her breathing, outlining her body. He ached to follow the twining trail of her braid up to her ear, then her cheek, then her mouth, taking possession... He moved into the shadow of the wall, aware of his nakedness all at once, like Adam in the Garden of Eden.

Alice crossed her arms across her chest. She yanked on the end of her braid as if it were a bell-rope, and her head a bell, to be cleared by one loud ring. "Good night." She backed out of the room and closed the door.

He returned to the light flooding through the window, laid his cheek against the cool glass, and let himself imagine what it would be like to follow her into her bed and sate his hunger.

Perhaps her kisses might save him, banish the dreadful emptiness and chill that had been gathering in his soul since the day he returned home to Alsace.

The thought hit him all at once, sending a shaft of warmth into his belly, like a glass of wine on an empty stomach. *She came here. She heard me cry out, and she came.*

He smiled. *She does not hate me.* Maybe, if he tried hard enough... intoxicated with hope, he planned his new campaign in the moonlight.

Alone in the wide bed that she had once shared with Bill, Alice cursed herself, staring up at the high, pale ceiling. She should never have entered Siegfried's room! She should never have looked at his body, shadows softening the stark bones showing too plainly on his large frame. His muscles stood out as if sculpted of wire and clay. The strength that had carried him through the horrors of the War was as evident as the shocking scar puckering his thigh from knee to groin. What a hideous wound that must have been, so near his...

She threw the back of her forearm across her face as if to shut out unwanted thoughts. She shouldn't think such things, not about an enemy soldier, not about any man not her husband.

Her husband *was* an enemy soldier.

When she had heard him cry out, her first instinct had been to comfort him.

And what did that make her?

Traitor! her mind whispered. She hadn't made any protest at seeing him naked, hadn't had the decency to turn her head, hide her eyes. Should she have squeaked in alarm? She didn't know what else she might have done. *Should* have done. If only she had had a normal childhood, a decent upbringing— a decent mother! A truly respectable woman, the kind Alice pretended to be, would have retreated far sooner.

Especially when she had recognized the look in his eyes. Even through the darkness it had seared her. She knew what he felt. She had always known how Siegfried felt about her, though she had tried to deny it.

Desire.

No. He only wants Montclair. I'm not a complete fool.

The smooth cotton sheets grew warm against her skin. The back of her hand pressed against her lips as if to hold in the sound she would have made, had she been alone in the house. She must hate him. She *must* hate him. He was a Hun! Bill had made the supreme sacrifice only last year.

Married to the enemy.

She had no room in her heart for a German soldier, even one who lightened the burden of their enormous task with his contests and good humor. She needed his talents as a vintner, that's all. In daylight, he treated her with respect, bandaged her hands, called them pretty.... they both had secrets to hide. If Siegfried's past could be so easily revealed by Hugh's malice, so could hers. And she had far more to lose.

She shook her head, unwilling to feel empathy with Siegfried. Their circumstances were nothing alike! He had volunteered. She had to avoid any more personal contact with him until after crush. He was too dangerous. It would be too easy to forget why she must hate him.

She waited a long time, listening for another sound from Siegfried's room, for the hiss of bare feet across hardwood floor, or the creak of a bed frame accepting an occupant.

Little by little her heartbeat calmed and the hot tingling faded from her skin. Tiredness weighted her down, pressed her into the warm, soft pillow, and she slept, to dream of a merry smile, a solid male body wrapped close against her back, a large hand tenderly possessive on her hip.

When she woke in the cool dawn, she ached for a real husband, not just a phantom figure with Bill's face.

But she put away her mourning, and prepared for the day. They had too much to do before crush.

Montclair
Monday, May 26

Delicious scents of perking coffee and frying bacon lured Alice to the kitchen despite her apprehension at the thought of facing Siegfried in daylight.

Maria's back was to the room as she busily ladled pancake batter onto a griddle over the gas burner. Alice paused in the doorway leading from the hall, because Siegfried was already sitting at the table, fully absorbed in studying the weekly newspaper. As she watched him warily, he picked up a pencil sitting next to his plate and carefully circled a small ad.

She was on the verge of moving when she noticed the jam-jar sitting next to her coffee mug. It was crowded with pink rosebuds tied with a neat tendril of grapevine. Siegfried had obviously gathered them during his early morning walk through the vineyards— without her.

Her intake of breath must have been audible. Siegfried's face went as pink as the flowers, and he busied himself with shaking out the newspaper, folding it over, and smoothing it completely flat. When he finally did look up, his expression gave away nothing. "Good morning," he said, as if commonplaces were all that lay between them.

Alice moved forward through air thicker than Maria's syrup and as perilously sweet. How could Siegfried possibly think he could *court* her when she knew about his past? She began to sit down across from him, very gingerly, as if the flowers might leap out of their humble vase and attack her.

It got worse. Siegfried rose and helped to adjust her chair. She sat so upright and tense she was sure her shoulders would crack. He sat down as she spoke in what she hoped was a businesslike fashion. "So. How are my Grenache vines this morning?"

Siegfried gave a conspiratorial smile which made her grit her teeth. Then he donned seriousness like a uniform. "They are bearing moderately. We shall not need to thin them very much." He touched one of the pink buds tenderly. Alice noted his stroking finger with an odd shiver in her chest. "You know your roses well."

She placed her napkin on her lap and said pointedly, "Bill and I planted those bushes, just before he enlisted."

"Ah." Siegfried hastily withdrew his hand, bent his head, and began studying the newspaper again.

Maria turned around with a pot of coffee and a tall stack of golden-brown pancakes. "Mrs. R!" she greeted, glancing slyly at Siegfried. "I'll have your toast ready in a minute." She poured coffee briskly for both of them, conspicuously eyed the roses, waggling her eyebrows, and gave Alice a broad wink before turning back to the stove.

The awkward silence was broken when Peter's heavy tread sounded on the porch. Peter entered the kitchen and flung himself down with a laconic, "Morning." He pulled his chair forward with a loud scrape, and said brusquely: "Give me some of those flapjacks, too, Maria. And a couple of eggs." Peter glanced over at Alice. "Don't know how you get by, eating like a bird." his glance rested on the jam jar. "Nice flowers. Looks like you're training Sig right." He laughed loudly, and Alice winced.

Siegfried put aside the newspaper, his face shiny red now. He cleared his throat as he poured syrup over his pancakes. "Peter, what progress has your crew made in spraying the Pinot Noir section?"

"We're nearly done, but we'll need another sack or two of Bordeaux mixture to finish the Cabernet."

As Peter continued to detail his ongoing struggle against powdery mildew in the vineyard, Alice studied the roses in front of her. They *were* her favorite flowers, but it was far safer to acknowledge irritation at Siegfried's blatant attempt to butter her up than pleasure.

"Alice," Siegfried said, interrupting her contradictory thoughts. "I think you should not clean the inside of the tanks any more. It is too dirty a job, not fit for a lady." He polished his plate with the last shreds of pancake.

Peter added, "A kid could fit inside, and we'd only have to pay him half a man's wage. Herculio has a nephew who'd be more than happy to earn some extra."

"How kind of you," Alice replied, fuming in earnest. The winery was her responsibility. *Hers*. And, no matter how tempting the offer, she wasn't about to concede that responsibility to Siegfried. "But we really can't afford to hire anyone else. Besides," she produced a bright smile, "I'm already dressed for the job."

Later, inside the reeking, dimly lit isolation of the enormous vat, Alice wielded a long-handled scrub brush and reflected on the thorns that came with roses.

I shouldn't have accepted the flowers, she thought, pulling out her scraper and furiously attacking a dark ridge of deposit on the curved redwood walls of the tank. But if she had publicly rejected them, she would have seemed unreasonable to Maria and Peter.

How do respectable women discourage this sort of thing? If I make a fuss I'll seem petty, but if I accept them, he'll just get bolder.

A traitorous flutter in her midsection liked the idea of Siegfried becoming a little bolder, and of being courted, *really* courted. She pushed the feeling down, hard, trying to stomp it out of existence. He was a Hun. He had fought against Americans, killed them. And she had loved Bill, who was so charming, so gallant.

She concentrated on the memory of her first arrival at Montclair, when he helped her out of Da's touring car just as if she had been a grand lady. But that memory skipped like a bad phonograph record to the day she had to sell the Buick, just before Christmas, all alone and terrified she would not get a good price for it.

Bill was *gone*, and his legacy to her had nearly been beyond her ability to keep.

Alice turned her head to her upper arm, and wiped her eyes against a fold of Bill's shirt, then picked up the pace of her scrubbing, trying to dispel her memories along with the fossilized remnants of past vintages.

The labor brought her mind no peace. Siegfried's actions raised the specter of her own secrets. Despite his past— *soiled, like yours*, her conscience insisted— he was a good, decent, honorable man. Had he been an American, she would not have felt worthy of him, just as she had never felt quite worthy of Bill after their marriage had been so hastily arranged by her Da.

But Siegfried was not American. She couldn't ignore his past, what he had been, what he might have done. *Things would have been easier if only Hugh hadn't told me the truth!*

By the time the dinner bell rang, she hadn't decided what to do; and by that time it was too late.

Siegfried's noon offering was a bouquet of white wildflowers: yarrow and Queen Anne's' Lace wrapped by convolvolus. White, for innocence of heart and purity of motive.

What made her most disappointed with herself, in a shivery, breathless kind of way, was that she wished she could believe it.

When Alice came downstairs, Maria was waiting for her in the flower-bedecked kitchen. There wasn't an empty jam jar in the house.

"What a pretty dress!" Alice exclaimed, doubly glad Maria had gotten a new white summer frock. At least there was something to talk about besides the flowers! And Siegfried's crushingly polite, silent persistence.

"Peter bought it for me," Maria said, brushing off some invisible lint. "We had— some words, and he thought he could make it up to me. Are you in the same boat?" Before Alice could answer, Maria's face relaxed in a dreamy expression as she fondled some rose petals. "I remember when Peter used to bring me flowers, when I was sixteen. He would turn up at my parents' house just after supper, with a big bouquet of whatever he had stolen from his mama's garden here. His papa thrashed him once for cutting down her prize delphiniums, but he said he didn't care, as long as I... kissed him." Maria glanced, embarrassed, at Alice, as if unsure how her employer would take this rather risqué confidence.

Alice didn't know how to deal with it, so she pretended she hadn't heard it. She certainly couldn't condemn Maria— or anyone. Of all people, she had no right to go casting stones. "Didn't I smell some coffee?" She saw Maria accept the change of topic as a rebuke, and tried to soften it with a smile, but the other woman had already turned to produce a steaming cup from the counter.

"I'm sorry. I forgot. Mr. R left this for you."

The coffee was exactly the right shade of golden brown. It was almost frightening, that Siegfried should have paid attention to her habits to such a degree that he could make her the perfect cup of coffee. She inhaled the fragrance. It was a pity she couldn't drink it before Mass, and go to Communion.

She opened her eyes when Maria sighed. "You're such a lucky woman, Mrs. R. It's none of my business, but maybe you should be treating Mr. R. a little better. He's a good man, and he's crazy about you. Marriage isn't always easy —I should know— but—"

"It's very complicated," Alice said firmly. She didn't want to answer Maria's unspoken question, *Why is your husband sleeping in the guest room?* "Shall we go? I don't want to be the last one at church."

Alice set her untasted cup in the sink and went outside with Maria. This morning was clear, promising heat again later. The sun was bright as they came around the house toward the parking area.

Brilliant black reflections stabbed Alice's eyes.

"Oh, my!" she exclaimed as Maria gasped.

Siegfried hastily slipped a rag into his pocket and stepped back so they could better see the Model-T, spit-cleaned and polished to a fare-thee-well. He had scrubbed every inch of its battered surface until it sparkled. When he'd had the time to waste on it, Alice couldn't imagine.

He smiled at her dazed expression, then opened the driver's door with a flourish. "Thank you, Siegfried," Alice managed to say as she climbed into the truck. "But you really didn't need to."

"It's so nice to drive to church in a clean car," Maria gushed as Siegfried opened the passenger side door. "How very thoughtful of you!"

How calculating! He doesn't mean it for your good! Her rational voice shouted. *He knows what you like,* her bad angel whispered.

"It was my pleasure." Siegfried sounded as if his considerable efforts really *had* been a pleasure for him.

This is getting out of hand! Alice thought hard. She had to find something quickly to put him in his place, and keep him there. "You know it would please me more if you came to Mass with us," she said softly.

As she had hoped, Siegfried's expression turned stubborn. "No. I cannot. I am sorry."

In the glow of this minor victory, Alice ignored the fact that he had held her gloved fingers a little longer than courtesy required. "You'll be in my prayers," she responded piously. And he would be too, she promised herself, putting the truck in gear. Especially the one that went, *Dear God, make him leave me alone— before I surrender to his sweet, lying ways.*

A week later, they had finished cleaning the fermenting tanks and vats.

Alice washed her hands at the pump in the yard. In the lingering twilight, the sky shifted colors from lapis lazuli to copper to sulfurous yellow. She dipped a handful of cool water, splashed it onto her sweaty forehead, and thought longingly of how good it would feel to release her heavy hair from its tight bun, and rinse the sweat from her itchy scalp.

The work crew waited patiently for her to finish. Then they took turns soaking themselves all the way through their red union suits. It had been very hot during the afternoon, and from the look of the sky, tomorrow would be a scorcher, too.

Maria called from the kitchen porch, "Lemonade!"

There was an exodus from the pump. Gray dusty winery crew met blue-powdered vineyard crew by the kitchen, as Peter and his men welcomed their comrades with huge grins and passed along glasses of lemonade.

Alice drank. She was exhausted from her exertions of the last month, and from her effort to work with Siegfried on a daily basis without falling under his spell. His exuberance and his clever daily contests had gotten the winery cleaned faster than anybody could have expected.

As if summoned by her thoughts, Siegfried appeared on the path between the fruit trees, his hair as golden as the last line of sunlight on the hills across the valley. He climbed halfway up the porch stairs, then turned around to face the small crowd.

"You did fine work," he said, pitching his voice so that all would hear. "Mrs. Rodernwiller and I feel fortunate to have gotten such an exceptional crew. We have much left to do before crush, but I am confident that with your help, we can do it. Montclair's vines are among the finest in the world, and our goal is to make the winery worthy of the grapes. On Monday, we start on the equipment!"

After a ragged cheer from the workers, Alice stood up, her back and shoulders protesting the movement, fetched the cash box from her office, and began to pass out the five-dollar gold pieces each man had earned for his week's work.

Small groups ambled down the driveway, talking together happily, heading back toward their homes near town. Soon they were all gone, leaving only empty glasses behind. Overhead, a handful of bright stars pricked holes in the darkening sky.

Alice's pulse skittered as Siegfried approached. "That was a nice speech," she said, forcing a pleasant smile, forestalling whatever he might have said.

In the falling darkness, she was glad not to read his expression. She felt rather than heard his tired sigh.

"Did you think so?" Siegfried bent his head, and studied his pale lemonade. "I have given better. Once I persuaded twenty-five men to commit suicide all together, and they thanked me for the honor. This was nothing." He drained his glass, and set it down on the porch railing with a thump. "And I'll thank them again next week. Men like to be thanked for their work. It makes them feel as though they have done something worthwhile."

She felt the weight of his pause, his unstated accusation. "We *are* doing something worthwhile. We're saving Montclair." She thrust the last gold coin at him. "Here. This is for you."

He set his jaw mulishly. "No."

Alice's heart thumped. "But you've earned it! I just wanted to show you how much I appreciate all of *your* hard work."

He took the five-dollar piece from her fingers, very slowly. "I will accept this on one condition: that you also pay yourself. You have worked as long and as hard as the men."

"I— I can't," she said. She quashed the warm glow she felt at his praise. "That's silly. I own the place."

He held out the money to her. "Then I must return this. We have an agreement. I am your husband. Not a hired hand."

"I didn't mean—," Alice said, flustered. "I didn't want to insult you."

"No?" He looked at her, then away. "That is good."

"I only thought that you might need some money for, well, I don't know. A haircut, maybe. Or a movie. There's a new one this week, starring Marion Davies—" She knew she was babbling.

"And you do not need money for yourself?" He stood a little closer than propriety allowed, and tucked a wisp of her hair behind her ear, a gesture so startlingly intimate that she jumped and moved a half step away. "Perhaps for some ribbons?" His tone was teasing, but his eyes were thoughtful.

Alice longed for that pretty summer hat she had seen at the White House, but she shook her head. "When we make a profit. Which we will." Alice's pulse sped up again as if it knew better than she did how she *really* felt. "I don't know what I would have done without you," she said recklessly. The next moment, she reminded herself that he was a Hun, that Tati had forced him on her.

But he was already speaking. "Or I, you," he said softly. "We have much work left to do, but I am sure now we can make good wine together."

She could feel the heat of his body, barely warmer than the ambient air, and the undertow of his desire, wicked complement to all his flowery gifts— and far more honest.

"Supper's ready!" Maria called from the kitchen door.

Alice made a quick retreat, suddenly shy. But not before Siegfried tossed her back the coin. She caught it reflexively as he strode past her into the house. The metal was warm from his hand.

Tuesday, June 24

Talk at the supper table was mostly between Peter and his wife. Maria's spareribs were superb, and the first of the season's purple-green artichokes were so tender even the thorns on the tip of each leaf were harmless.

Siegfried ate with the concentration of a mystic in search of enlightenment, and Alice was too drained to make light conversation. She chased a dab of butter around her plate with an artichoke leaf, and contemplated her dilemma. She had put it off until the last possible minute but she had to ask Siegfried soon. She wished she could just forget the whole matter, but the announcements had already been printed.

The cowardly part of her wanted to stay home, and ignore the changes in her life that Siegfried had brought. The responsible part of her knew she *had* to speak now.

"The Grape-Growers Association meeting is tomorrow," she announced abruptly, doing the right thing, however late. "And it's my turn to provide the refreshments."

Siegfried stopped chewing and waited pointedly.

She added, "At one o'clock. In the Courthouse. If you're interested in coming with me."

He swallowed, then nodded. "Do you go too, Peter?"

Peter tore a biscuit and sopped up the juices on his plate. "No, no. I tend the vines, not the politics. Mrs. Roye— I mean, Mrs. R.— does fine by herself."

"I will accompany you, Alice," Siegfried said, firmly. He resumed his meal.

Later, as Maria cleaned off the table, Siegfried cleared his throat. He asked with a diffidence Alice suspected was assumed for the occasion, "This meeting— you have already chosen the wine you plan to serve?"

Alice reined in her impulse to snap at him. They hadn't been out of each other's pockets in over a month. When had she had time to go taste wine?

"No, I haven't," she said, folding the napkins. "I'll pick up the lantern from the pantry, and we can go now."

"But wine should be tasted in the morning!" he protested.

"We won't have time tomorrow before we have to be on the road."

"You waited long enough to inform me," he said, affronted.

"We've been busy," she countered. *And I've been dreading the comments we'll get from the other members of the Association when I arrive with my new* German *husband in tow.* "I'm going now. You can come with me if you like, or not, as you wish."

Why did she feel so relieved when he did follow?

❧

Siegfried carried two glasses and a long thin glass wine thief while Alice held a kerosene lantern steady.

The fragrance of the vineyard boiled up all around him, yeasty with adobe dust, spiced with cedar and eucalyptus. Stars blinked overhead and crickets sang in counterpoint to the sound of their footsteps. Across the valley a cow bawled, protesting the persistent heat.

These last few weeks, Siegfried had gained some confidence in the progress of his courtship. Alice had taken to blushing whenever his flowers appeared, and she kept them until they wilted. The look of astonishment on her face when she saw the washed and waxed Ford that Sunday had made him feel ten feet tall. He took heart from the fact that she had not spurned his offerings, but he was appalled at her lack of foresight. Waiting until the night before the meeting to pick the wines? What was she thinking?

Their crunching footsteps returned sharp echoes as they approached the stone walls of the winery. Siegfried hurried to open the door into the cool redolent darkness. The small light of the lantern rolled great barrel-shaped shadows along the walls. Alice went straight for the door in the back, waiting for him to catch up and slide it open.

Siegfried paused at the door to the tunnels cut into the heart of the hill. The tang of oak permeated the close, cool air. Gray-white walls, hand-carved by Chinese labor fifty years ago, pressed in on him with clammy hands. The wine glasses clenched between his fingers chimed as Alice and her lantern moved further into the absolute darkness.

The last time he had visited these tunnels, *Opa* Roye had held the lantern and directed yellow light down an endless row of stacked and balanced sixty-gallon barrels. The light had failed before Siegfried could see the end, leaving him with an impression of ordered infinity. His grandfather's deep, slow voice had tolled the honor-roll of grape varieties, explaining cryptic chalk signs. 'X' or 'p' or 'c' marked the liquid jewels contained within: topaz Traminer, ruby Cabernet Sauvignon, garnet or citrine Pinot Noir. A romantic young Siegfried had been certain that no pirates searching for buried gold ever came upon a trove as rich as the one beneath this Sonoma hill.

As he followed Alice's retreating light, Siegfried was jolted from his reverie. Hundreds of barrels were stacked haphazardly along the walls, dry and empty. "What happened here?" he demanded, hoarse with shock.

"What do you mean?" Alice picked her way through the crowded aisle, seeming not to notice the devastation surrounding them.

"This—" *Desecration*, Siegfried finished silently. How could Alice fail to see? But she merely proceeded, as if the ruin of masterwork was commonplace.

To her, who had let fungus grow on the fermenting tanks, perhaps it was.

"They're dry." His throat was almost as parched as the warped wood. "The barrels."

She turned to look at him. The yellow lantern light shone on the curve of her cheek like a crescent moon. "I didn't think I could make a good red wine, so I sold last year's crop out of the field. I got $15 a ton, too, enough for this year's payroll."

He remembered not wanting to see the wine caves, after facing the ruin of the winery. Now he knew why. He said harshly, "The bevels on the staves must fit tightly or the barrel will leak. When wood dries, Alice, it shrinks."

She understood now. Alice touched one of the hand-crafted barrels, as precisely made as cabinetry. "You mean these are all sieves now?" She counted wildly: "Ten, fifty, hundred, two hundred, four hundred..." The freckles stood out against her paleness like tiny golden tears.

Warring emotions held him silent: he wanted her to feel the weight of her error, but he also wanted to rescue her. "We will not know until we have tested them," he said, compromising. "But we will have to inspect and recondition each one." Another monumental task to accomplish before crush. And more money needed for labor, and materials. Why couldn't he have come here sooner? Before Bill left and let Montclair fall into ruin?

But if Siegfried had come before Bill's departure, Alice would not have been free to marry him. What had happened had happened. The casks would need work. The wine must have suitable containers in which to age. He must earn Alice's trust so she would keep him.

"I didn't know," Alice said with bitter self-recrimination. The light wavered as her hand shook.

Siegfried put the glasses in his pocket, seized the lantern, and patted Alice's quaking shoulders with a clumsy hand. Hopefully, he said, "It will be all right. They might be saved. And, if not, we can do without." How, he did not at present know. But he would manage somehow. For her.

She took a long shaky breath. "I *hate* making mistakes!"

He let his hand drop. He knew exactly how she felt. Matter-of-factly he handed her the wine thief. "And where is the wine we are tasting for your meeting?"

For a moment Alice held the wine thief as if she didn't

know what it was for, but then she brushed non-existent loose hairs away from her face, and straightened. "This way."

She picked through the tumbled welter of barrels, heading deeper into the tunnel.

Siegfried followed her to a section where the barrels were neatly stacked, labeled with chalk symbols in a round youthful hand. Alice came to a halt before a large barrel labeled "B15."

"This is Bill's last vintage." Alice surveyed the massed racks of piled-high barrels. "His Burgundy '15. Fifty acres of Montclair's best grapes; Bill promised me it would be worth $12,000 at maturity."

Siegfried felt a tremor of new alarm. "It has been aging in oak for three and a half years?"

Alice started at his tone and her eyelashes trembled. "What *else* have I done wrong?" she asked, plaintively.

At her wounded expression, Siegfried choked on his intended brusque reply, and turned away to twist the bung out of the nearest barrel.

Both of them were silent as Siegfried inserted the wine thief into the barrel. The slender glass tube took a long time to reach liquid, and Siegfried's stomach dropped as the scent of the neglected wine drifted out. He brought up the wine-thief, and dripped acrid thickness into the glass he pulled from his pocket.

He didn't even need to taste it. With a sigh, he handed Alice the glass. Viscid liquid dark as blood coated the sides of the glass as she tipped it toward her mouth. Her face spasmed. "Oh, no! It's *vinegar*!"

"Did you not top it off?" Siegfried demanded.

Her mouth pinched, she shook her head. "Bill never told me I had to."

Siegfried took a deep breath, and spoke very slowly, enunciating each syllable as if speaking to a child. It was the only way he could prevent himself from grabbing her and shaking her, hard. "The wine evaporates. You must prevent it from concentrating. And from the air come the organisms that make it into vinegar. Making wine is like raising a child. You have to keep an eye on it every minute."

"It's all worthless, then. Every bit of it?"

He had seen the same resolute despair in the young soldiers under his command when they found themselves in untenable positions, facing implacable enemies with inadequate supplies. His burst of resentment at her incompetence faded. *No one instructed her*, he reminded himself.

"I think..." he said slowly, trying to find something he could say to make this debacle an opportunity rather than a loss,

"It will not be worth anything as Burgundy, but there may be a market for good wine vinegar. And if Prohibition goes into effect— we may be lucky after all."

She made a sound halfway between a hiccup and a laugh, and stared blindly at the racks of tidy barrels. "I was c- counting on the income!"

"When did you expect it to mature?" He tried to make his question gentle.

The back of her hand moved across her face. "I— I wasn't sure," she admitted. "I can't— I c-can't believe how much I don't know!"

"Alice," he said, taking her hand, feeling the telltale dampness. "You could spend a lifetime learning about wine and still know only a little bit." He could summon no contempt for someone who hated her ignorance as much as she did. "Some of this wine may be usable for blending with this year's vintage. We will have to see. We have only opened one barrel."

He thought he was consoling her, but unexpectedly, she began to cry in earnest. Great tears welled up and spilled. Siegfried set the lantern on the floor, and wrapped his arms around her.

She shook against him, crying as if she had never wept before in her life. He had a handkerchief, thank God! He stroked her hair and wondered, even as she sobbed, what the coiled braid might feel like, unfurled, cool as silk beneath his hand.

He held her gently, all her softness pressed warm against him. The near-soundlessness of her sobbing was like the furtive tears of duty-ridden soldiers. He, too, had known such hopelessness.

He had retreated from the War into a numb and terrible refuge. Armored against the misery in his soul, he had lived through a thousand nights of terror, leaving behind as useless baggage any thought of tomorrow; leaving until tomorrow any sign of grief for comrades lost and gone, and for his youth and innocence blasted away in shards of shrapnel.

He rested his cheek against her hair. For the first time he mourned for his brother Ernst, for his boyhood friend Jürgen Bauer, for his mother and father, and even for his cousin Bill. All of them had paid the ultimate price. His own tears fell.

"*Ah-lees*, " he murmured, voice thick. He was making a damp spot in her hair, matching the one she was leaving on his shirtfront. At the thought, a half-smile lifted one corner of his mouth. "Give me back my handkerchief."

She looked up. He bent and kissed away the tracks of tears on her cheeks, tasted tears mingled together as their lips met. Her arms went around his waist, drawing him closer. His heart beat in unison with hers. The kiss lasted a timeless, blissful interval, a wordless sharing of comfort, intimate yet strangely chaste.

Alice finally stepped back from him, and taking his hand, she tucked a moistened scrap of linen into his palm. "Your handkerchief," she said, shyly.

Siegfried reluctantly let go of her shoulders to wipe his face. When he blew his nose, it sounded like a trumpet blast in the echoing tunnel.

She smiled tremulously, and somehow the dark, still air beneath the hill was full of light. There was a tear streak shining on her face. His mouth tingled from their kiss and he relished the petal softness of her skin as his thumb tenderly brushed the moisture away.

"I-I'm sorry," Alice said, studying the uneven carved stone floor. In the lantern light, her profile was a study in gold and shadow.

"I am not." Siegfried croaked. He cleared his throat and pushed the used handkerchief deep into the pocket of his jeans. "Until now, I have not been able to mourn my losses. Thank you. What you have given me is worth far more than a tunnel full of wine."

"Spoiled wine," she said, her shoulders drooping unhappily.

"Perhaps. We will not know until we have tested it all."

She looked down the rows of barrels. There were at least four hundred in this section, and the end of the tunnel not yet in sight. "I can't. Not tonight."

"But, Alice, there is your meeting to come, yes? We must find something to serve the association."

She threw up her hand as if his statement were a blow. "Don't! I said I'm sorry!"

"We must have a good wine. And we will not have time tomorrow. Therefore we must find it tonight, correct?"

"Siegfried, we can't test every barrel here tonight," Alice protested. "I can't, anyway. Maybe you can."

"I do not speak of this vintage," Siegfried said. "Of course there are too many barrels here! But what about the library wines? Or *Opa* Roye's bottle-aged vintages?"

"There's nothing else. I told you. This was Bill's last." She bent to pick up the lantern and it threw wild shadows.

Siegfried felt as if the whole mountain were tilting. Against this, the neglected '15 Burgundy was nothing.

"How *could* Bill have sold *Opa* Roye's last wine before it had finished aging? Oh, Ah-lees, I had come to despise my poor cousin. For this, I spit on his grave! "

"What are you talking about?"

Siegfried blinked. Had Bill never told her *anything*? "Come and we will see." He headed back towards the entrance of the tunnel.

"But there's nothing else back here!" she protested.

"That, we shall see!"

Montclair
Tuesday, May 26

They walked together past the empty barrels until the sliding door to the wine cave entrance came in sight.

"There's nothing here," Alice repeated. She felt light, hollow-boned and breakable, not quite sure she had cried herself out. It wasn't *real* yet, the loss of Bill's wine, the failure of his last promise to her. She would probably feel more upset once it sank in that she had no fall-back plan any more, that this year's crop was all that stood between her and losing Montclair. She *had* to get that sacramental license now. Could they even make it through harvest?

She would have to go over the books carefully to make sure they could.

She wasn't paying heed to Siegfried, but she suddenly noticed he was scrabbling at the wall behind a hulking rack of empty barrels. He pinched his fingers together, and a sheet of rock came away from the wall.

It took Alice a moment to understand what she was looking at. Against the rough limestone, a curtain of dirty white canvas hung from ceiling to floor. He was lifting up a flap of the heavy cloth, revealing a shadow where a wall ought to be.

"There's another tunnel?" Alice exclaimed, outraged.

"It was not meant to be hidden," Siegfried said apologetically. He held the corner of the canvas up as she lifted the lantern, splashing light into the wedge-shaped opening. The visible reaches of the second tunnel were empty and mysterious. "I expect you have seen this tarp half a hundred times and never noticed it."

Alice put her hand over her eyes.

For a horrible instant, Siegfried thought that she was going to cry again, but then he heard her muffled, "Stupid! Oh, how could I be so—"

"Alice," Siegfried stopped her from heaping any more abuse on her own head. "Why did Bill never show you this?"

"He didn't trust me," Alice whispered, her hazel eyes wide and stricken in the lantern's yellow light. "I don't think he hated me," she continued haltingly, "but I knew he resented—"

"Bill never hated anyone in his life." Siegfried declared. He put his hand on her back to comfort her, feeling the delicate arc of her shoulder blade under his fingertips. "He would not have kept this from you on purpose! Oma Tati was always telling him he would forget his head if it were not already fastened to his shoulders."

Alice snorted. "My Da said Bill didn't have the brains God gave bastard geese in Ireland." She clapped her hand against her mouth, eyes wide, amazed at her lapse.

"Indeed." Siegfried tried to suppress his grin. "And it was not your fault that the wine Bill made went sour." He gave her shoulder a squeeze, and wanted to do more, but she stepped out from under his hand, refusing to look at him again.

"It was, though." She shook her head as if shaking off all emotion, and asked, very businesslike, as she peered into the black tunnel: "What's in here, then? And how far does it go?"

"*Opa* Roye used this arm of the tunnel for his in-bottle aging. It is just as long as the main arm." Siegfried took her arm and drew her in. It was exactly the same as the last time he had traveled this path, during his apprenticeship. That time with his grandfather had been the last and best moments of his boyhood, the last days of an old man's life.

But perhaps something of *Opa* Roye lived on yet. "Good. Here are the library wines."

"What?"

Siegfried drew Alice up to the wooden cases, which stored the bottles at a gentle angle, their corks submerged. He found the note card tucked just where *Opa* had left it.

For Siegfried Heinrich Wilhelm Rodernwiller, upon the occasion of his marriage. Montclair Estates Burgundy. Bottled by William Winston Roye, 1912.

And the next case: *For the occasion of the baptism of "_____" Roye. Montclair Estates Port. Bottled by William Winston Roye, 1911.*

And the cases, gifts in anticipation of a future he would never see, went on: more Pinot Noir for Bill's graduation and marriage, for Ernst's, for the celebration of *Opa* and *Oma* Roye's golden wedding anniversary, for more hoped-for grandchildren. And the last stack in the series: *For Hugh Lawson Roye, on the occasion of his graduation from college. Montclair Estates Claret. Bottled by William Winston Roye, 1905.*

Alice read the cards with him. Siegfried was not surprised to see her eyes sparkling with tears once more. He himself felt perilously close to succumbing to sentiment.

She put down the final card inscribed with *Opa*'s

copperplate hope, and bowed her head. Her lips moved in prayer, and Siegfried remembered the antiphon: *And let perpetual light shine upon them.* He let the thought fly up wherever such things go. He might have walked away from the Church, but he could not give up his belief that the honored dead should receive their due. *May they rest in peace. Amen.* He thought of *Opa* Roye's confidence in the future, and his love for the family that would come after him.

Now Siegfried was responsible for that future.

He dared to look behind him. "I take back what I said about Bill. He left *Opa's* legacy to age unmolested." Siegfried reverently took a dark green, dusty bottle from the case on the opposite wall of the tunnel. *Montclair Estates Burgundy. Bottled by William Winston Roye and grandson, 1912.* There was a wall-rack full of cases, and none of them, as he well knew, were dedicated to any specific joyous event. He had a terrible curiosity to know how this wine tasted.

"How many are there?" Alice whispered.

"One hundred thirty-two cases. An acre's worth of grapes."

"Oh, my!" Alice's eyes narrowed. "Will this be any good? It's been here longer than—"

"In bottle. No air should have contaminated the wine. A good red can be aged a very long time and only improve. *Opa* Roye's wines were immediately drinkable, of course, but after seven years, they should be heavenly." Siegfried passed the bottle before the kerosene flame, checking for sediment or changes in coloration. The color had only deepened with age. Even surrounded by heavy green glass, the wine had a ruby heart. "There is only one way to find out."

He pulled out his knife, which, like that of all good vintners or soldiers, had its own corkscrew, and proceeded to open the bottle. The cork was good and firm, not brittle, not crumbly. It pulled loose from the neck with a soft pop. Siegfried held it up to his nose and sniffed— no hint of mold or vinegar.

Excited, Siegfried handed the knife with embedded cork to Alice and dug into his pocket for the clean glass. He poured carefully, swirling the glass to release the rich bouquet: blackberry and vanilla, rounded and mellow with oak.

He gave the glass to Alice, hating to let it go, and got out the used glass, wiping the last drops of the spoiled '15 away with his fingers. He poured for himself, then cupped the curve of the bowl, slightly warming the wine before raising his glass to Alice in a toast, "To Montclair's success!" He closed his eyes as he drank.

The first sip filled his mouth with memories. The heat of Sonoma's summer had brought the sugar in the fruit to its highest level, but the process of fermentation and the years in bottle had burned all the sweetness away. Only the ghosts of summer fruit remained: cherry, blackberry, plum, a hint of spice, and the vanilla promised by its bouquet.

"Siegfried, this is wonderful!"

He opened his eyes as Alice swallowed with total concentration.

Her joy was headier by far than the wine. A brilliant smile revealed hidden dimples in her cheeks, making her look suddenly younger and mischievous. He wanted to clasp her waist and spin in a dance of triumph; he wanted to drink the wine of her lips, besotted with her kisses.

"I think," he said gruffly, lowering the bottle to his side, "this will do for your meeting. Yes?"

"Yes. This should do very well," she agreed warmly. "We can pack several cases tomorrow before we drive to Santa Rosa. They'll fit nicely in the back of the truck, too." She finished the remaining wine in the glass, and then picked up the lantern. Light-footed with relief, they began the long walk back through the tunnels to the house.

She paused after a few steps, and turned slightly toward him. In the lantern light, her eyes were the translucent golden-brown of aged sherry. "Thank you, Siegfried."

If she would only look at him like that again, he would give her the world, not just some old wine in a glass.

Alice climbed into bed, her legs and back aching, her mind jumping and sparking with possibilities. Bill's vintage was useless, but she had one hundred thirty-two cases of William Roye's finest wine! She pulled her sheet up to her chin, doing mental sums as she closed her eyes. *My luck has changed at last.* With the money from the sale, they *would* be all right until harvest.

She drifted downward into sleep. Just before she reached bottom, the memory of Siegfried's kiss, imprinted on her mouth, soothed and disturbed at the same time.

In her dreams, *a chaotic jumble of tunnels led to long-halled houses with wine-red wallpaper whose doors did not fit tightly because the staves had warped and shrunk. Alice ran through the gas-lit halls, fleeing from a monstrous gray Hun. His bayonet had impaled a baby which cried, improbably, "Mama!"*

But when she finally stopped running, and faced her

pursuer, there was only Siegfried, his eyes innocently closed as he drank his grandfather's wine, the smooth muscles of his throat working, savoring a pleasure too overwhelming to share. When he came close and kissed her, she kissed him back, his mouth sweeter than wine. She drew him into one of the red-walled rooms off the corridor, where her bare skin met crisply laundered sheets —

She woke up, shaking, holding the sheet away from her as if it were a contaminating rag. Her cotton nightgown clung damply to her breasts and she felt *alive* in a hundred places she should not even think about.

Bill had been dead over a year now, and it had been even longer since she had last kissed him, been a wife to him. He had come home in April 1917 for a brief leave just before being sent to Europe. After that, there had been postcards and the occasional letter, and then nothing until the government's telegram arrived.

She had missed him, of course, but she thought she had gotten over this wretched carnal *need* for him.

Alice got out of bed and leaned at the open window, wishing the pre-dawn breeze, cool and scented with the countless perfumes of Montclair, would blow her dream away. In the east, a layer of turquoise sky preceded dawn. No fog. Birds began chirping haphazardly, and the county's roosters performed their appointed duty.

As the light increased, the day's proper colors took their place: greens and tawny gold, the black Ford truck, and splashes of red and yellow from the rosebushes bordering the vineyard.

The utter beauty of the morning was not distraction enough to prevent her from reliving the kiss she had shared with Siegfried. It had been so good to be held again, to have the comfort of a strong shoulder, to feel a man's firm mouth against her own. It had felt right, and it ought not to have. It was too soon to want anyone but Bill.

And yet, she was tempted. She wanted Siegfried to repeat that tender pressure against her mouth, the slow caress that sent a heavy pulse beating between her thighs. If they'd been near a bed, she would have dragged Siegfried to it. Then she would have woken up in his arms this morning, and seen his hair shining and tousled in the morning light, his head denting Bill's pillow.

Her heart began to beat faster, and its unfaithful pulsing filled her with remorse. She swallowed and turned away from the window. Bill's side of the bed was empty, the pillow plump and round. She had not betrayed him, but snares of the flesh and the Devil were all around her.

She had to keep her vigilance, keep her distance.

But why did it have to be so hard?

Dressed in her oldest shirtwaist, with a floppy straw hat to protect her complexion from the sun and thick gloves, Alice spent a cool morning hour in the vegetable garden, hoping the scents of soil and herbs would restore her tranquillity.

Except it wasn't working. Her thoughts kept straying into dangerous territory. How *could* she have kissed Siegfried?

There was only one reason. Alice crossed herself, praying to the Blessed Virgin for Her intercession, too ashamed of her likeness to her mother to ask God directly for forgiveness. How could she be worthy of making His altar wines if she was consumed by carnality?

She bent to her work, seeking escape from her emotions by yanking weeds and slashing dead leaves from the herb and flower borders.

The wine she had tasted last night would have honored the Mass. Perhaps she should send a few bottles to Archbishop Hanna in San Francisco? It had been nearly three months, and he had not yet replied to her petition for a sacramental wine license.

Bribery, whispered her conscience. Alice ruthlessly uprooted long tendrils of convolvulus that threatened to strangle a rosemary shrub. *It's not bribery*, she protested to her inner critic. *Just a small reminder to jog his memory.*

Yes. She would do it. And when the Archbishop saw what Montclair could produce...

Straightening up, Alice watched, enthralled, as a tiny ruby-throated hummingbird darted among the fruit trees, hovering as he inspected the promise of a generous harvest of apricots, peaches, pears, and plums. Finding no blossoms to nourish him, the bird chittered furiously and streaked away. Alice smiled in sympathy for his hunger. She wondered if Siegfried liked peach pie, and remembered warm tears soaking her hair.

I won't think about Siegfried. It's disloyal to Bill. I mustn't forget to buy Mason jars at Duhring's, she told herself, focusing on the commonplace.

She had brought a large basket with her, into which she placed various herbs for Maria's roast pork: spiky-leafed rosemary twigs, dusty green sage, and sweetly fragrant basil. Tomatoes followed the herbs into the basket, and Alice bent to dig the first carrots and a bulb of garlic from the soil.

He likes my cooking, she thought with a self-indulgent smile. *He likes to kiss me.*

Her throat closed up as she realized what she was

thinking in her weakness. If she continued on this path, she would lose her chance for an annulment. She would be stuck, married to a Hun!

She dug out half a rosemary plant before recognizing it wasn't a weed.

Mortified, Siegfried struggled out of sleep in the dark. He was kissing his pillow, having dreamt it was Alice in his arms. In spite of the fragrance of linen and feathers in his nose, he could still taste the salt of her tears, balanced against the sweetness of her lips. He had wanted to go on kissing her in the wine cave, had wanted to do much, much more than kiss her.

He flung the pillow away from him and struggled out of bed, unwilling to indulge in wishful thinking. He had promised himself he would not force Alice, that he would wait for her to welcome him, and he was a man of his word.

But he wanted her so badly now. His body had betrayed him, seeking its mindless pleasure despite his good intentions. He would not let it rule him, he vowed to himself as he washed and dressed. He would be the master.

Although he made it his inflexible habit to rise early, today he was ready to start half an hour earlier than usual. His list of tasks was nearly endless, but he thought he might achieve some peace of mind if he could study what was left of Bill's last vintage, and the last gift of *Opa* Roye.

When he was done, inventory book in only slightly shaking hand, he returned to the main buildings to join Peter for their regular dawn walk through the vineyard.

The foreman emerged from the door of his cottage, yawned widely, and greeted Siegfried. They headed towards the Pinot Noir section of the vineyard, pushing their way through long, curling vine tendrils that waved in the soft breeze and tumbled down in a fountain of tender green leaves.

They walked slowly up the hill, and Peter stopped to point out the progress of the field workers. They were already beginning their day's labors, trimming the excess leaves and shoots from the rows of vines in order to ensure maximum sunlight for the developing grape clusters.

Siegfried had no comment until they reached the row end, and he saw that the luxuriant growth had been raggedly cut short. "These plants have been over-thinned," he observed unhappily.

Peter cursed in Italian, and snatched his hat off, striking it against his thigh in anger.

"What?" Siegfried felt as if he had suddenly awaked fully from the dream of the night.

"Tell Alice she needs to buy a bag of dried chili peppers the next time she's in town." Peter examined a chewed-up grapevine tendril with disgust.

Siegfried raised his eyebrows. *Chili peppers?*

Peter let him stew a moment longer, then grinned lopsidedly. "Not my men, but deer have been at these vines. We grind the chili up and add it to the sulfur spray. The deer take one mouthful and run for the reservoir. They're pests. Papa always called 'em 'hoofed rats.' Come hunting season, we'll have some great venison, fattened on a diet of Montclair grapes and your wife's vegetables! Which reminds me— it's getting close to breakfast." He gave Siegfried a jarring slap on the shoulder. "We'd better finish up and get back to the house before Maria decides to serve us cold eggs."

"Before we go, I have something about which we must talk." Siegfried knew his grasp of English was slipping again, but he could not help it. He could not be calm. "Peter, Alice and I went into the caves yesterday. None of the wine in the '15 barrels had been topped off."

Peter stiffened. "Sig, when the influenza killed Papa—" he began.

"No." Siegfried interrupted, coldly furious at Peter's attempt to deflect his attention by a reiteration of his losses. "I measured the levels in those barrels. They had not been topped off for *two* years, at least! Your father died only last November. And you knew well enough what to do. It was simple maintenance! And not only the wine, but the cooperage— all ruined!" He drew a deep breath, his anger rising. "*Mein Gott,* Peter. More damage you could not have done if you had tried!"

Peter flinched guiltily.

Siegfried's sudden comprehension churned his stomach. "*Did* you... try?"

"I don't know what you're talking about." The foreman started to turn away, but Siegfried reached out and gripped his forearm. Peter stayed passive for a moment, then shook free.

Siegfried said, "I thought I knew what kind of man you were, Peter! How can you sleep at night?"

"Bill laid down that vintage before he went away," Peter wiped his palms nervously down the legs of his jeans. "It was no good to begin with."

"I cannot believe that your father, as a vintner, would ever allow a vintage to be ruined." Yet he had tasted mercaptan-tainted burgundy...

"If he'd had any say in it," Peter said bitterly. "Which he didn't, when Bill was in charge. Bill's wine was worthless, so Papa earned nothing for years. When we heard that Bill wasn't coming back, that he— he *liked* being a soldier-boy, oh, Papa was so mad! He told everyone that Bill had abandoned him, and left a city girl in charge."

Siegfried remembered Attilio Verdacchia, who had been a fierce old man even in Siegfried's youth, very much in command of the winery and his frail, much-younger wife. "I fail to see how this justifies the victimization of an innocent widow!"

Peter cleared his throat uncomfortably. "My father came to America with a dream." He kicked at a tuft of dry wild mustard growing between the vines. "All he ever wanted was his own land, his own house, with a vineyard and some olive trees. And Papa thought, since Hugh should have inherited Montclair in the first place, that—"

"You would let the winery crumble around Alice's ears to bring down the price," Siegfried finished, biting off each word. "I see."

"Hugh promised Papa a commission on the sale price of Montclair," Peter said, flatly. "Papa had his property all picked out. There was a place for sale in west Santa Rosa, near the Martini vineyards. He only needed a couple hundred dollars more. It was losing his down payment that killed him!" Peter's face was ugly, molded by grief and bitterness.

"What happened?" Siegfried murmured.

The foreman made a throwaway gesture. "When the influenza came, and Mario got so sick, we spent a fortune on that quack Dr. Waxler. Waxler *said* he had a cure! But he didn't. He took our money and left town. Papa— he gave us everything he had, and when Mario— when Mario—" Peter coughed and spat. "It broke Papa's heart. Within a week, he was gone, too. And then we had to pay for the goddamn funerals."

A surge of sympathy washed through Siegfried, but he resisted its effect, using the same tactic that had worked with men under his military command. "And now? Are you still working for Hugh?"

"I've done my best to keep things running around here since Bill left. Sig, look around you," Peter swept his arm wide, taking in the hundreds of trellised rows draped over the hills like a man-made quilt. "I defy you to tell me I've let a particle of harm come to these vines. We're going to have a great harvest. I know I don't have a vintner's touch— not like Papa, or your grandfather, or even you. We both know Bill never did. He would have lost this place sooner or later, anyway."

"How can I trust you, Peter?"

"You don't have much of a choice," Peter said in a hard voice, all traces of his apologetic demeanor vanished. "You could fire me, but I'd take my crew with me. The other vineyard workers have already hired out, and I know Alice doesn't have the money to lure them here with higher wages." Peter hooked a thumb in his jeans pocket. "Sig, just continue the terms of Bill's agreement with me, and I'll work for you, fair and square. After all, you know what you're doing around here."

"What terms?" Siegfried asked, anger and relief warring in him. He needed Peter and his workers through crush.

Peter must have caught something of Siegfried's reaction because he stepped back hastily. "I get ten percent of the year's profits. So, the harder I work, the more money I get. Your grandfather originally made that deal with Papa. Old Mr. Roye was no fool."

"No, a fool he was not. I will continue the agreement," Siegfried capitulated through clenched teeth. How Peter had changed from his boyhood! "But I expect you to be loyal to me."

"Look, you or Hugh— either way, a Roye is in charge of Montclair again. I just want a chance to have my own place someday, where Maria and I can grow old, and watch our kids grow up," Peter stopped at the mention of children. He took a deep breath, then continued in a different tone: "Papa died without getting his own land. You, of all people, ought to know what that's like, what it can drive a man to do." He stuck out his hand.

Siegfried took it automatically, guilt stinging him. He had married Alice for her land, hadn't he? *But I'm helping her keep it.* "What about the cooperage?" he asked, his voice sounding plaintive even to his own ears.

"Ah, Sig. It was mostly old and ruined by too much sulfur anyway. We need all new. I know a cooper down in Monterey..."

Peter continued to talk while they returned to the house, and his rough chatter was no different than any morning. It was plain that the foreman felt the matter was resolved.

Well, and if it was, Siegfried need not trouble Alice with revelations of old disasters. She had enough to worry her already— and if she became too unhappy, she might never kiss him again.

She *must* kiss him again. Nothing else in his future was certain, but this he knew, bone deep. He would *make* it happen.

Montclair
Wednesday, June 25

After breakfast, Siegfried found a hand cart in a shed behind the winery, and wheeled it into the caves. He lit the lantern, the dancing flame reminding him of Alice. Yesterday evening she had been so sweet, so trusting. This morning, she had been unapproachable, hiding out in the garden after grabbing a piece of toast.

He remembered the softness of her lips. Imagining kissing her again led to wondering how that soft white skin would feel, bare against him...

He pushed the handcart blindly through the tunnel, propelled by a wave of lust. He longed to make love to her and intoxicate them both with kisses. What bliss it would be to spend his days laboring in Montclair's winery and vineyards, and then sleep in her arms!

Siegfried reached the racks, and brought himself down to earth with a thump. He found empty cases stacked in a corner, then turned to the rows of racked bottles and made his selections, cleaning the dusty bottles before inserting them into their slots. When the wooden boxes were full, he rolled the unwieldy cart outside to Alice's truck, mindful of any unevenness in the ground that could jar the wine. As he bent and lifted the heavy cases, he rejoiced at how easy and supple his muscles had become. Even his scarred leg was less painful.

Covering the cases of wine in the Model-T with a heavy canvas tarp, Siegfried returned to the house to wash up and change clothes.

His face and neck damp from shaving, he opened the wardrobe, and suppressed a sigh. He only had Opa Roye's dark suit to wear for formal occasions. Black wool was unsuitable for summer, but he must make do with what he had.

He adjusted his stiff collar in the small mirror and put on his vest and coat. They were less loose than they had been, and likely to shrink more with Maria's delicious cooking. How wonderful not to be hungry all the time!

He combed back his hair and smoothed down a cowlick on the crown of his head with the palm of his hand. He had almost forgotten it was there. It was only noticeable now because his hair had grown out of its military cut. He was growing accustomed to being a civilian again. Safe. Sound. Working for Montclair's future.

Unbidden, Peter's words attacked like sniper fire. *Papa died without getting his own land. You, of all people, ought to know what that's like, what it can drive a man to do.*

He shook out the lapels of the coat, deliberately recalling the flavor of Alice's lips. So sweet. Her kiss had felt so right.

A last glance in the mirror to check his appearance, but he could not look himself in the eye. He would love her even if she did not own Montclair. Wouldn't he?

As she descended the porch stairs and came down the walk to the graveled driveway, Alice saw Siegfried, formally dressed and looking severely handsome, as he opened the gleaming Model T's door and stood holding it for her.

He was frowning.

Her heart gave an odd lurch, a double-thump of awareness that he had a right to be upset with her. She ought to have told him about the meeting before now; but she had been so anxious, so— she had to admit it to herself— afraid of the reaction to her unconventional wedding from the members of the Association.

She dreaded the coming hours. There would be sideways glances, and perhaps some men, less than gentlemen, might make rude comments. She didn't really believe anyone knew her background, would throw it in her face; but she feared most what was least likely.

And what if anyone asked where Siegfried had spent the War?

She had not been able to face these possibilities ahead of time.

And she was not yet ready to face Siegfried. Not when the mere sight of him could make her pulse flutter. Not when his presence, in a fine old suit, gave her a chill as she came too close, trying to get past him to climb into the truck. Not when the gaze from his dark blue eyes was so serious and direct. Bill would have laughed and passed off the tension of the moment with some pointless joke.

Alice felt breathless as she caught Siegfried's direct gaze again. She couldn't think straight, but she forced a laugh, remembering how Bill could charm his way out of any uncomfortable situation. "Penny for your thoughts?"

He smiled, a little shyly, a faint red flush staining the fair skin above his celluloid collar, and Alice knew immediately it was the worst possible question to have asked.

"I was thinking," Siegfried said softly, "that I should very much like to kiss you again, Alice."

Somehow she was trapped between the truck and the door, and Siegfried was leaning, close, and his fingertips were brushing her chin, lightly tilting her face up. She did not resist him. She was entranced, suspended in a state of waiting.

He bent to kiss her, tentatively at first, and the spell was broken in a flash like lightning. She leaned into the softness and heat of his mouth. His hunger for her was a flame that warmed her, and his slow possession of her mouth kindled a deeper need in her. Siegfried's kisses were sinful. They made her want to abandon her respectability. His large hands cupped her face, and with shocking suddenness she longed to feel those callused palms against her breasts.

Alice stepped back, pushing herself away from him with a gasp that was almost a sob, hitting the side of the truck with enough force to make it rock.

"Ah-lees?" His accent made a caress of her very ordinary name.

She felt a stab of guilt for bruising his feelings. In the next moment, she hated him, hated herself for the searing rush of desire he had ignited in her. How easily he could make her forget every scrap of propriety she had painfully learned! Her hard-won serenity in tatters, she wiped her mouth convulsively with the back of her hand.

"We'd better go," she said, in a voice she hardly recognized as her own. "We'll be late for the meeting." She slid into the driver's seat.

Alice stewed during the interminable drive up to Santa Rosa, bouncing the Ford vengefully through potholes and over ridged ruts with a grim disregard for the cases of wine sloshing around in the truck bed.

He doesn't really want *me*, she told herself, over and over again. He wouldn't care who he kissed, as long as she owned Montclair.

Siegfried's jaw muscles unclenched as they neared the white Santa Rosa courthouse with its grand cupola and huge clock. The square in front of the courthouse was crowded with parked cars and horse-drawn wagons and even a bicycle or two.

"I should have brought more wine!" Alice exclaimed, the first words she had spoken since Sonoma.

"Too late," he replied, pretending to be calm. He wasn't.

She had deliberately driven into potholes she could have missed. She might have ruined the wine they had brought.

He wished he could shake some sense into Alice! But she sat so stiffly, refusing to look at him, untouchable.

His nerves were screaming as if he were about to go into battle, and Alice's kiss had only added explosives to the incendiary mix. Even angry with her, he was ready to do more— a great deal more— than kiss her. If she ever gave him the chance again. And if he thought any more about how sweetly she had kissed him, how soft she had been against him, how she had *let* him kiss her, he might die.

He hoped he could survive this meeting with his dignity intact.

The back entrance of the courthouse was an alleyway, shaded by tall trees. She drove to where a small dapper man hovered in an open doorway.

"I'm sorry we're late, Mr. Price," Alice called as she parked the Model-T. "I know I haven't left much time for setup." She smiled apologetically.

At this mention of lateness, Siegfried jumped down and immediately started loading the wine crates onto the hand truck. Of course Alice had not allowed enough time for proper preparations. She had not wanted to come at all.

"All the arrangements are made, but we do need your wine, Mrs. Roye," said Mr. Price fussily as he helped her down from the truck.

Siegfried, setting the last crate in the stack, realized with annoyance that Alice had not made any correction of her name, nor was she going to introduce him. He maneuvered the hand truck smartly to the doorway where the two of them were now standing, and stopped it precisely. "I do not believe we have met, Mr... Price?" Siegfried bowed slightly and gave Alice a fiercely expectant look.

Flustered, Alice's head swiveled back and forth between them. She said, "I'm so sorry. Mr. Price is the secretary of the Association. Please let me present Siegfried Rodernwiller. He's, er— William Roye's grandson from Alsace. And..." She looked down at the polished hardwood floor of the corridor, blushing.

Siegfried sensed her embarrassment acutely. She was ashamed to be associated with him!

He presented his hand to Price. "Alice is now Mrs. Rodernwiller. We were married last month. It is a great pleasure to serve my grandfather's last and best vintage to this association."

Price's rather limp hand found its way into Siegfried's

grasp. He shook it warmly.

"I— well, er— that is, congratulations!" Mr. Price stuttered. "My dear Mrs. Roye— er, Rodernwiller— ah, this is amazing news!"

Siegfried winced inwardly at his pronunciation, but let the matter pass. He tilted the hand truck. "I assume the meetings are held in the same room?" Before receiving an answer, he started moving.

Alice and Mr. Price had to bustle to keep up.

"You said— your grandfather?" Mr. Price asked, puffing. "I never had the honor of meeting old Mr. Roye. I'm afraid I'm rather a newcomer to Santa Rosa." He coughed self-consciously.

"Mr. Rodernwiller trained as a vintner in Europe," Alice announced, as if it were all the explanation needed.

They paused at a set of closed, carved double doors and Mr. Price nodded to him. "It's a bad year to enter the winemaking business, Mr. Rodernwiller, as you've no doubt heard. There won't be much left of our vineyards if Prohibition goes into effect."

"There was nothing left at all for me in Alsace, Mr. Price," Siegfried said. "At least here, I have the opportunity to make for myself a place."

"Of course." Mr. Price nodded again as he pulled open the door. "In the meanwhile, I'm afraid we have a great deal of work to do."

In the meeting room, clumps of men stood talking amongst irregular rows of chairs. Nothing else had changed since the last time Siegfried was here: the same ranks of photographs and awards covered the redwood-paneled walls and the ornate brass chandeliers sparkled.

Alice and Mr. Price began setting out the bottles in a row on the long table in the back of the room. The white linen was almost hidden by trays of biscuits, cheeses, and pyramids of clean glasses.

Siegfried made himself useful by stacking the empty cases, then pulled his corkscrew from his jacket pocket and picked up the nearest bottle. Carrying it halfway down the table to make room, he saw the square announcement card, acknowledging in neat script who brought the wine: Mrs. Wm. Roye, Montclair.

Not Mr. & Mrs. S. Rodernwiller of Montclair.

Siegfried scowled, irate again. Had Alice imagined that she could keep their marriage a secret?

Of course she had!

Well, he was not going to make it easy for her. She would

find it extremely difficult to get rid of him. And if she did try anything so foolish, she would soon find herself in bigger trouble, with Montclair floundering around her ears. She needed him!

He caught Alice's eye and jerked his chin in the direction of the tell-tale card as he deftly twisted the cork out of the bottle he held.

She gravitated toward him, opening bottles as she moved.

"Mrs. William Roye?" he hissed.

Alice was suddenly intent on removing the cork from a bottle without breaking it. "The cards were made up weeks in advance," she protested unconvincingly. "And I had no idea that you would— I mean we would— I mean, I forgot to ask them to change it. I'm sorry."

She didn't sound sorry, Siegfried thought as he savagely penetrated the cork of the next bottle with his corkscrew. She sounded vexed at having been caught out. He composed and discarded a number of edifying remarks as he pulled and twisted, pulled and twisted, but Alice avoided his gaze, so he remained silent, nurturing his ill-temper as a very flimsy barrier against an emotion he did not want to acknowledge.

A prickle of goosebumps accompanied his unwelcome realization that somehow Alice's presence, her well-being, and her goodwill had become necessary to him, too. That she hadn't changed the name on the cards— hurt.

While he concentrated on his work, a steady trickle of men and a few women filled up the meeting room.

In quick glances, he recognized many of the members of the association from his summer as Opa Roye's apprentice. Louis Kunde, owner of a vineyard north of Agua Caliente, entered and waved a friendly greeting. Siegfried returned the wave.

There was a surge of conversation as a short, energetic Japanese man swaggered in, his vest-pockets bristling with Havanas, an unlit cigar clenched between his teeth. Siegfried swallowed a smile as the legendary Kanaye Nagasawa took his rightful place in the front row of seats. In his early years, he had been sent by his noble father to be educated in Scotland. He had escaped a return to his homeland by becoming a member of an eccentric religious community based at the Fountaingrove estate on the outskirts of Santa Rosa. Now in his early sixties, he was respected as the undisputed authority on Sonoma County wines. In his incongruous presence, Siegfried felt less an outsider.

Even as he had this thought, Walter Bundschu, who owned the Rhine Farm Vineyards bordering Montclair, came up to say hello. "I read in the paper that you had returned from Europe. I didn't expect you'd grow up to be the spitting image of your granddad," he said, vigorously shaking Siegfried's hand. "But I guess you're used to people saying that. Welcome back! It's a rotten time to be in the business," he added darkly. "Those damned scoundrels in Congress— begging your pardon, Mrs. Rodernwiller," he nodded across the table at Alice, then turned back to Siegfried. "It'll be a crying shame if you have to rip up Mr. Roye's vines. You've got some of the best grapes in the county."

He was interrupted by the staccato sound of the Secretary's gavel, calling the meeting to order. Mr. Price sat at a table next to the podium, a large composition book and pens placed before him. He banged the gavel again and the murmur of conversation began to die down. Like Walter, men who had been gathered in clumps near the doors found seats.

Siegfried followed Alice the very last row. She twitched her skirt aside when he sat down, ostensibly to make more room for him, but to Siegfried's lacerated sensibility it felt as if she wished to avoid polluting herself with his presence.

Alice couldn't look at Siegfried. The memory of his kiss burned, a scarlet brand of guilt and forbidden pleasure. She had let him get too far under her guard. His anger about the announcement card shouldn't matter a bit to her, but it did. She now felt like a heel for not including his name. His *German* name, she reminded herself, but she wasn't convinced.

The President of the Sonoma County Grape Grower's Association, a middle-aged man whose dark hair was liberally laced with gray, stepped up to the podium. Mr. Victor Piezzi said, "Ladies and gentlemen, I'd like to open the meeting now. Do we have any additions to the announcements or the agenda?"

Two or three people raised their hands.

"Please step up to Mr. Price and he'll write them down."

This took five minutes. In the meantime, Mr. Piezzi read out the minutes of the last meeting, and the Association voted to approve them. The announcements were mostly notices of land or equipment for sale, and Alice caught Siegfried jotting down a note about a bottle-filler being offered. Congratulations were given to Mr. and Mrs. Smith of Glen Ellen on the birth of a son.

Alice was just beginning to think that she might escape unscathed, when, to her horror, Mr. Price stood up and said: "And I'd like to offer the Association's congratulations on the marriage of the former Mrs. William Roye of Montclair, to Mr. Siegfried Rodernwiller of Alsace, France. Some of the Association members who've been here longer than I might remember Mr.

Rodernwiller as being a grandson of the elder William Roye."

Surprised hubbub broke out. As most of the Association members turned in their seats, Siegfried smiled and rose to bow. Alice's face heated. They were being stared at as if they were circus freaks on display! She studied her shoes, praying silently that the earth would swallow her up, but Siegfried just encouraged the crowd.

He slipped his arm around her shoulders, drew her up, and said "Thank you," loudly, in response to individual congratulations being shouted their way. "Thank you. I am a very lucky man."

Alice, fuming, wished he would cease this display of empty affection. When he didn't heed her subdued command, "Siegfried, stop this!" she stomped on his toe with her heel.

Without ceasing to wave, he hissed from the side of his mouth: "Alice! Do you intend to fully humiliate me today?"

His accusation pierced her. It was true. She had been unbelievably rude. She was not acting like a lady, one who owed everyone equal courtesy. Her heart sank. Her whole life was a pretense, and Siegfried had seen through her careful screens of gentility and respectability to the improper, common core beneath. She burned with shame to be discovered, to be despised by him.

She unknotted her gloved hands in her lap and raised her face to his as he smiled and waved to the group.

"I'm sorry," she whispered. She forced a smile and lightly kissed his cheek, but the effort to appear a shy newlywed for the assembled grape-growers cost her a great deal.

There was a wolf-whistle, and Mr. Price pounded his gavel. "No need to embarrass the happy couple," he chided, chuckling. When the noise died down, he said, "We'd better get on with the business part of the meeting. First item of discussion on the agenda is the report of a Phylloxera outbreak in Mr. Rossi's vineyard..."

As Mr. Rossi stood to make his report, Siegfried, his arm a solid warmth against her shoulders, crushed Alice close, giving her an odd sense of comfort as they sat down.

"I accept your apology," he said, his lips brushing her ear.

Although his warm breath sent a shiver down into the pit of her belly, his tone was completely unloverlike. He was furious with her! She wished she could crawl off and die somewhere, but the meeting continued, dragging through agenda items at a snail's pace.

She struggled to pay attention to the projected grape

prices for the coming harvest. This was important. Mr. Piezzi advised that their best estimates were between $20 and $30 per ton, if prices held steady from last year. A buzz of discussion followed this statement. Alice felt exposed again as Siegfried raised his hand and stood.

"Since my arrival in California I have heard a great deal of speculation about the effects of Prohibition. Can you tell me what might be the actual consequences?"

Mr. Piezzi rubbed his chin thoughtfully. "I wish we knew how to answer you. Wartime Prohibition is slated to go into effect July 1. Representative Lea is trying to get an amendment passed exempting wine and beer, but the vote won't be taken until early next month."

Walter Bundschu rose to his feet. "I don't believe constitutional Prohibition will ever pass," he declared. "Especially now that the War is over. The Prohibitionists are a small group of fanatics and they won't succeed in imposing their narrow-minded views on this nation!"

Alice didn't recognize the young man who objected: "But state after state has voted in favor, and those states are closing their doors to what we produce!"

The clamor swelled as the members began to debate amongst themselves. Alice saw the moment when Siegfried understood that the immediate future was just as uncertain for the entire county as it was for Montclair.

Mr. Price rapped his gavel again and called for silence. The noise level dropped by infinitesimal degrees until only a single frantically whispered debate remained, two rows ahead of Siegfried and Alice.

Even that noise stopped when Kanaye Nagasawa stood up. "Prohibition is nae better than confiscation of our property wi'out payment," he stated, in his startling Scottish burr. "Wine has held a long and honorable place in the history of mankind, and the livelihood of thousands of Americans depends on it. I canna believe that a Constitutional Amendment will be ratified." The unlit cigar clenched between his teeth bobbed vigorously as he spoke.

There was a smattering of applause, one or two more statements supporting Nagasawa's opinion, and then Mr. Piezzi called a vote to close the meeting.

Alice rose quickly and hurried to the refreshment tables. The Association members seized glasses as fast as she and Siegfried could pour.

Walter Bundschu raised his high and boomed out, "Gentlemen, I propose a toast to the new Mr. and Mrs.

Rodernwiller. Much happiness to them both!" After he drank, he winked at her. She was simultaneously shocked by his vulgar gesture, and warmed by his evident friendliness.

"Hear, hear," the others chorused.

Siegfried clinked his glass to hers, but she turned away from him. There were more empty glasses and she concentrated on filling them. But she couldn't help listening when Mr. Piezzi said, "Welcome to the Grape-Grower's Association, Mr. Rodernwiller. I once had the honor to meet your father, years ago, when he came to purchase rootstock from Mr. Roye."

She watched Siegfried closely while pretending not to. He froze for an instant, then said, very rigidly, "I regret to tell you that he passed away this spring."

"I'm very sorry to hear that. Please accept my condolences. He was a fine man."

Before Siegfried could answer, Mr. Bundschu clapped him on the shoulder. A splash of garnet stained the tablecloth, but only Alice noticed it. "Come and meet Mr. Schmidt. He came from Hamburg—a long time ago, of course." Mr. Bundschu took Siegfried by the arm and towed him to the other end of the room, leaving Alice to pour the rest of the wine by herself.

She swallowed her resentment and filled glasses.

A burst of masculine laughter came from the corner of the room. There was Siegfried, the center of attention, gesticulating with his free hand as he accepted profuse compliments for Montclair's wine.

Never her wine. Never her property. Never her dream.

Alice told herself to be reasonable. Siegfried was not a newcomer to Sonoma. Of course he would be remembered and celebrated. She smiled until her cheeks ached, and dispensed more wine, but after a short interval, she began to feel invisible. Men who had formerly been pleased to give her winemaking and winery management tips were thanking her for her hospitality, promptly dismissing her, and drifting over to talk shop with her husband.

Mrs. William Roye, who had spent the last four years negotiating with wine brokers and trading bits of farming lore with her neighbors, vanished as if she had never existed. In her place was Mrs. Siegfried Rodernwiller, keenly feeling her demotion from independent widow to a husband's appendage.

Siegfried, in an exalted state, was now immersed in conversation with Kanaye Nagasawa. The old man was tasting the wine between mouthfuls of a ship's biscuit fished from his vest pocket. "The best I've tasted in years!" he pronounced.

She couldn't look at Siegfried anymore. She seized a full

bottle and began to circulate through the crowd, refilling glasses and accepting her neighbors' compliments on old Mr. Roye's wine.

Galling though that was, she was not prepared for the chance comments she heard as she came up behind a couple of the Healdsburg-based grape growers.

"You mean he actually told you that her Traminer spoiled?" one asked. "Dammit, Hugh's a cad to do that!"

"Yeah. Poured it out at dinner, cool as you please, then made a big fuss about how his grandfather put so much work into that place. Of course, we all told him shame, her being a war widow and all, but—"

"But he's never had a good word to say about her. He's been bellyaching' about losing that property since his grandpa died, and just gotten worse since Bill died Over There."

"Now, from what I hear, Bill's widow *did* let the place go to seed. Stands to reason her wine'd spoil."

Alice stood paralyzed with shame and rage. *I thought Hugh was my friend!* He had been her ally in the dark months after Bill's death. *How could he do this?*

She hoped she could creep away before the two men saw her. The one she stood behind was tall and broad, and might hide her escape even as he obscured her presence. But before she could turn, a heavy hand fell onto her shoulder.

"I hope you do not mean to imply that my wife has been mismanaging the Montclair vineyards," Siegfried said coldly.

Where had he come from? *How much had he overheard?*

The men started guiltily and Siegfried continued. "I have walked the vineyards every morning since I arrived in Sonoma. My wife is a conscientious farmer, and Montclair's vines are both healthy and well-tended."

Why was he defending her? She did not know whether to smile gratefully or run away in humiliation. His hand anchoring her, she ended up doing neither.

"I wasn't impugning Mrs. Roy— er, Rodernwiller's farming," one of the men protested. "But that Traminer—"

"Who among us has never had a cask of spoiled wine?" Siegfried interrupted, his eyebrows raised exaggeratedly.

Both men offered sheepish grins.

"In any case," he finished, "I am Montclair's vintner now, and I have sworn to carry on my grandfather's tradition, to make only the finest of wines."

"Yeah, well, as I was saying, Hugh's had a chip on his shoulder for long time." The big man nodded at Alice. "My apologies, Mrs. Rodernwiller. Didn't mean to distress you."

"Not at all," she lied, practicing hard-learned lessons in courtesy.

"Excuse us, please. I want a word with my wife," Siegfried said, nodding to his fellow vintners. He steered her blindly toward the refreshment table. "Poor Ah-lees," he said kindly, patting her arm. His anger toward her had obviously vanished in a haze of triumph.

"What did you come to tell me?" she inquired distantly.

"I wanted to tell you— to share with you—" She could feel his pulse leaping in his fingertips. "Baron Nagasawa—" He could barely speak, who had been so eloquent on her behalf.

"I heard how much he liked the wine," she said for him, so he wouldn't have to stumble over it.

But he went on as if she hadn't spoken. "He called it 'verra excellent.'" However badly his accent mangled the Scots burr, the significance was clear, as was his deep satisfaction.

"I'm not surprised," Alice said. "After all, Mr. Roye was a great vintner, and this was his final vintage."

Siegfried came back to Earth from that far place of victory where he had strayed. "Of course. Of course he liked it." He seemed to see Alice for the first time since the meeting had adjourned. "You look quite done-in. This has not been a comfortable day for you."

She blinked, the half-full bottle of Grandfather Roye's Burgundy trembling in her hand. How dare he pity her? He had married her to gain Montclair. She did not need him, specifically. Any vintner would do.

He was smiling tenderly at her now and her response proved her a liar.

"Excuse me," she said, and stumbled away from him, her fingers cramping around the bottle. She resumed mechanically refilling glasses and responding to comments with a smile pasted on her face. She would not look back at him. She bit her lips, to stop their tingling.

The last drops of wine went into Louis Kunde's outstretched glass as he continued telling his plans to Walter Bundschu. "I'm going to raise beef cattle on my land. It's the wave of the future, mark my words."

"Yeah, Samuele Sebastiani is the lucky one. If Prohibition passes, at least he'll stay in the business, selling grapes and wine to La Fontaine," Mr. Bundschu commented, taking a sip of wine and rolling it across his tongue to release the full flavor.

"Charles La Fontaine of Fountainview?" Alice demanded. "What about him?"

"Oh, we just heard. He got the sacramental wine license for Northern California."

Her chest hurt, a stabbing pain that made it difficult to draw enough breath to speak. "H-how—?"

"He's a friend of the Archbishop in San Francisco, Mrs. Rodernwiller," Mr. Kunde said, shaking his head. "There are many of us who wish we were in his shoes!"

Mr. Martini, a vineyardist of Santa Rosa, chuckled. "I bet plenty folk'll be religious soon!"

La Fontaine got the license? Alice felt the bottle of wine slipping through her numbed fingers. The refreshment table was nearby— she had just enough strength left to put the bottle down before it fell.

She was clumsier with her dream. It slipped through her fingers and shattered. *It's over. I've lost everything.*

Santa Rosa
Wednesday, June 25

Everyone loved the wine! Siegfried thought triumphantly as the meeting finally began to break up.

He was saying good-bye to Mr. Schmidt in German, happy to be speaking with fluency again, freely connecting thought and word, when he saw Alice run from the meeting room.

After a hasty excuse, he pushed through the doors leading to the interior of the courthouse. Alice was leaning against the corridor wall, her arms wrapped tight around her as if she had been gut-shot.

Instantly, battle fury gripped him. "What happened? Who did this to you? Is this more of Hugh's mischief? By God, I will break his bones when I find him!" He started to open the door to the meeting room, but stopped when Alice shook her head. His own gut twisted. Except for ragged breathing, she was utterly silent while tears cascaded from tightly closed eyes.

All his residual anger evaporated. He closed his arms around her, stroked her hair, content that he had a strong, whole shoulder for her to hide her face against. "*Schatz,*" he murmured, wishing he knew what to do to help her. She felt so fragile under his hands, so soft.

Against his will, with blithe unconcern for the circumstances, his desire for her rekindled.

He tried to stifle the quiver that shook him, but she shoved him away and disappeared into the marble-floored sanctuary of the ladies' room.

Idiot, he cursed himself. *Next time, do not chase her away.*

Alice's first reaction when she recognized the damp, prickly wool of Siegfried's suit had been to let him comfort her; but the thought that he was witnessing her complete breakdown was intolerable. She wrenched away, ran, and threw herself onto a *chaise longue* in the ladies' room, curled up in a nest of dusty red plush, and cried until only the concrete foundation of despair remained.

I'll never be able to make wine for the Church. She admitted at last to herself. *I'll never atone that way for my mother's sins.*

She pushed herself up and tottered to the gilt-framed mirror hanging over the marble sink. Red, swollen eyes and puffy, splotched cheeks reflected back at her. A thick dusting of rice powder might have made her presentable, but respectable women didn't wear cosmetics, so she had only a comb and a handkerchief in her small purse. With a sigh, she took out her handkerchief, opened the faucet, and began to bathe her eyes with cold water.

Siegfried doesn't care what you look like anyway, as long as he has Montclair.

She tried to shake away the miserable thought, then had to unpin her hair, which had come down in messy wisps. She re-twisted it into a neat, painfully tight chignon. Then she trudged back to the meeting room, feeling ugly and empty.

Only Mr. Price remained, scribbling in his meeting ledger. "Your husband is waiting for you outside, Mrs. Rodernwiller." He paused. "Are you feeling all right?"

"Fine," she lied. His gaze was speculative, and Alice knew what he was thinking. *Newlywed... delicate condition...* "Good day, Mr. Price," she said firmly, and stalked away.

"Thank you for bringing your excellent wine," he called after her. "See you at the next meeting."

Siegfried was busily fastening down the empty wooden cases in the truck bed when she emerged from the courthouse. Alice braced herself for his flood of questions, unable to bear the thought of telling him the truth.

"They drank all but three bottles," Siegfried reported after a swift assessing glance at her. He tactfully avoided any mention of her tears. "We should be able to sell all our stock at a premium price to the sommelier at the Bohemian Grove."

Alice reached for her driving coat. Shafts of afternoon sunlight pounded dull nails into her forehead. "That's fine for the cases we have in storage," she replied listlessly. "But what happens when they're all gone? We can't raise Grandfather Roye from the dead to make more."

"I have a confession to make, dear *Ah-lees*." Siegfried opened the car door. He stood too close to her, disjointing her thoughts. She heard him say: "The wine is mine."

She slid behind the wheel and grappled with the concept while Siegfried turned the crank to start the engine, but her thoughts were so slow and scrambled that she didn't fully understand what Siegfried had said until he climbed into the passenger seat.

"*You...* made the wine?" Alice whispered, relieved that

the hot leather car seat gave her support. She swallowed jealousy like vinegar.

"Seven years ago I was *Opa* Roye's apprentice. He gave me an acre's worth of grapes on which to practice." Siegfried's brief smile was as brilliant as the sunlight. "I made the wine we drank today, Ah-lees. I can make more. I can make as much as we need. You see, I *am* a good vintner."

Without the license it doesn't matter how good you are, she thought despondently. It took three tries before she got the Model T into gear. Her hands had a tendency to shake as she drove through Santa Rosa into the open countryside.

Ironically she was trying to avoid yet another pothole on the rutted road near Glen Ellen when a tire blew. She wrestled with the steering wheel as the wheel rim hit gravel. The truck shimmied and swerved wildly and noisily over a shallow ditch into a nearby orchard. They stopped inches away from the gnarled trunk of a plum tree. The engine snarled one last time, then died. Quiet ruled.

Feeling bruised in spirit and body, Alice took a shuddering breath and thanked God there was nobody else on the road for her to run into.

"Ah-lees, are you all right?" Siegfried sounded unhurt, merely worried about her.

She pried her fingers from the steering wheel. "Get out." She remembered politeness. "Please."

Siegfried grinned like a maniac, already half down from the truck. "Do not worry. I will fix it for you!" he said, shucking off his coat with disgusting cheerfulness. Then he took off his shirt, as well, revealing the cabled muscles in his pale arms, set off by the cut of his sleeveless undershirt.

He opened her door and extended his hand. She was reminded of his strength by the ease with which he helped her down. The hot air was motionless. Soon the sun would sink behind the Sonoma Mountains, leaving this side of the valley in cooling shadow, but for now, straight beams of light penetrated the canopy of the orchard, gilding his skin in a fine layer of gold.

Her knees were weak. She resented having to depend on him and she truly did not expect him to lay his coat on the oat-brown weeds at the base of the plum tree, or to make a sweeping courtly bow and gesture her to sit down.

"Do you know how to change a tire?" she asked suspiciously.

"You can tell me if I do anything wrong," he assured her with a warm smile.

But she felt useless and stupid in comparison to his easy

competence as he turned and, without any trouble, found the wrench in the toolbox mounted on the running board.

It had taken her the better part of a year to realize that she always had to pack the right tools and a fully inflated spare tire before going on a drive. She had gotten stuck several times on this road between Santa Rosa and Sonoma, until it seemed she had discovered all the houses with telephone connections. Peter had rescued her, once, with the irritability of a man who had better things to do. She had learned how to change her own tires after that, just as she had tried to learn how to run the winery.

Another thing she wasn't very good at.

She had tried to make her own wine, and look how her Traminer turned out. She had thought Hugh her friend— but then, he had every right to criticize her management. Her memory of Siegfried's shock that day when he had first inspected the moldy vats still had the power to knot her insides. In her ignorance she had let Bill's last vintage go sour. And if she had truly been a good wife, Bill would never have run away to the army...

She was only twenty-two years old, and she was a complete failure.

Her throat threatened to close, and she coughed involuntarily.

Siegfried looked up, concerned. "Am I raising too much dust for you? Do you need a drink of water? Or," his gaze slid toward the back of the truck, "—wine?"

"N-no." She wanted nothing to do with wine just now. Montclair was one step from ruin, though she had tried her best, her very best, to save it, and herself. If she failed...

Siegfried shrugged one sculpted shoulder and returned to the tire.

She turned to look deep into the orchard. If she failed... If Wartime Prohibition went into effect before she could sell Siegfried's heavenly wine for the cash to get through harvest... if Constitutional Prohibition banned wine, and she couldn't crush, and no one ever bought wine grapes again...

She didn't have the money to switch to chickens or beef or prunes. She couldn't sell Montclair. Bill had entrusted it to her.

Everywhere she looked, there was only more failure to come.

And if she failed... if she lost Montclair, she would find herself on the road back to the City, a destitute widow, forced, for lack of anything else she knew how to do, to return to her old neighborhood, to her mother's house.

Of all her nightmares, that one was the worst. If she went back, she would lose all the shreds of respectability she had carefully cultivated, all the respect she had earned from her neighbors in Sonoma. Her poor, sainted father would roll over in his grave. He had worked so hard to rescue her from iniquity.

She would rather die than go home again. She would rather starve on the street. But if she lost Montclair...

The sun disappeared behind the hills, and the heated air in the valley seemed to exhale. A harsh caw sounded and she looked up as a couple of crows, intent on investigating the truck for food, launched themselves from branches of a tree opposite.

Siegfried suddenly bent, as if he'd dropped something. He came back up, his arm moving fast.

There was an aborted squawk, and black feathers exploded all over the road. The second crow flapped heavily away, out of range of Siegfried's next stone.

Alice leaped up. "What happened? What are you doing?"

Siegfried stood folded, one arm propped on the fender of the truck to hold himself up. His eyes were closed, his whole body shuddering.

"I hate crows," he rasped.

"What's wrong with them?" Alice was baffled. Crows weren't particularly beautiful birds, but they were harmless. Not like the starlings that came through in autumn like rapacious locusts, sometimes stripping a vineyard of its fruit before the pickers could harvest. The crow on the road was thoroughly dead, blood pooling in the dust.

"Carrion eaters." Siegfried's mouth twisted into a anguished gash. He forced a breath. "In the trenches, they never had to look far to feast. I *hate* them."

He didn't look competent now. He had been laid lower than she had been.

Oddly, Alice did not feel victorious, or superior. Her first impulse was to comfort Siegfried, to quiet his tremors. Her knees were weak, but they carried her close to him. Lines of suffering were etched into his face. She wanted to smooth them away, to return his cheerfulness. She hadn't known she would miss his smile so much.

He opened his eyes, and Alice thought for a crazy instant that he wanted to eat her up, as if she were the best, most beautiful thing he'd ever seen, as if he'd waited his whole life to stand right here and look at her. As if he might even love her.

Alice's heart pounded. Siegfried let go of the truck fender and closed the space between them with a single step. He put his arms around her and pulled her tight, leaning on her as if now hers was the strength that kept him upright.

She knew he was going to kiss her, and she wasn't ready.

But his chest was warm and solid with only the thin cotton undershirt covering it, and his arms were so strong. And now he was kissing her. Not her lips, but her eyebrows and the corners of her eyes, leaving a residue of tenderness.

She relaxed against him, tilting her face up and waiting for him to bend, as he must. His mouth captured hers at once. Her eyes drifted closed, and the only reality became what she could feel: his arms around her, his lips, his wine-flavored breath mingling with hers. His embrace circumscribed the hollow space around her heart, defining and containing it. His lips were insistent, nearly as desperate as her own.

Her hips pressed against his, and she felt him, aroused, through the layers of navy silk and black wool that separated them. Alice ached in answer, and opened her mouth to his deep kiss, to his tongue tentatively touching hers. His hands were at her waist, sliding up and down her back in a rhythm that matched the thrust of his tongue. If they continued, soon she wouldn't have the capacity to stand.

If only her life were simple, she could just sleep with Siegfried and *be* married to him—

The sound of an approaching car intruded, and she tried to step away, but Siegfried held her close, oblivious to the embarrassment of being publicly discovered in so indelicate a position with a half-naked man.

"Siegfried! Somebody's coming!" she hissed, pushing at his shoulders.

"Ja," he agreed, dreamily. He did not release her.

"What if it's somebody we know?"

His pulse beat strongly against the hollow above his collarbone. His cheek against hers was hot. "What if it is? Maybe we are on our honeymoon."

She almost agreed with him, but she forced herself back to her senses and stamped on his toe to make him let her go. She drew in a gulp of air, furious and mortified and bereft all at the same time.

Siegfried said unconvincingly, "My poor foot!" He memorized her face, brushing the back of his hand against her cheek, and stepped away from her just as another Model-T rattled around the bend.

The car pulled up and stopped. "Why, Mrs. Roy-Rodernwiller! You folks need any help? I've got a tire pump if you need one."

Alice recognized James Sullivan, who owned a vineyard near here, south of the Kundes. She served on various church committees with his wife, Betty. Had she been alone, Alice would have taken his offered help gratefully.

"No." Siegfried said. "All is under control. But we thank you."

"Sure thing. Do you want me to wait until you get moving again?"

"That's very kind of you," Alice said before Siegfried could open his mouth again. "I'd appreciate it." She wobbled, and Siegfried steadied her.

"Here, Alice. Sit, sit. I am almost finished."

She let herself be led back to the spot where he'd put his coat, and sank down onto it while Mr. Sullivan helped Siegfried pick up the flat tire to load it in the back of the Model T.

She had grown used to being Mrs. William Roye, vintner. Had found it surprisingly fulfilling. Could she accustom herself to being Mrs. Siegfried Rodernwiller? Did it matter whose wife she was, as long as she was a wife, and not—?

Alice caught herself before she crumbled the dirt clod in her hand into dust, and irretrievably stained her glove. She looked sideways at Siegfried as he wrestled with the tire, all the muscles in his arms and shoulders defined. He was strong. He was gentle.

He was German—

He wasn't. "I am Alsatian," he had declared. And a lot of the grape-growers at the Association meeting had had no trouble at all in pronouncing his name.

"Hrodanvilla," Alice practiced under her breath. She checked to be sure Siegfried and Mr. Sullivan hadn't heard, or noticed her lips moving. "Zigfhreed Hrodanvilla."

It didn't sound so ugly any more. There was a certain charm to it, now that she was used to it.

But marriage involved more than a name.

There was a definite tingle in parts of her that she knew she shouldn't recognize at the thought of lying with Siegfried. She remembered his kisses, imagined the weight of his body on hers, and the slide of skin against skin— *I could do it*, she thought wonderingly, and the more she thought about it, the more she knew she must do it.

She would give him Montclair, and in the giving, bind him to her. And no matter what happened, she would be respectable. She would say *yes* to Siegfried at Montclair, if he asked her. *When* he asked her. Tonight. Not here in the road like some two-bit dock whore.

Her head whirled, so she rested her cheek on her knees. She didn't know if she wanted tonight to come soon— or never.

❦

Siegfried unloaded the cases from the back of the truck, humming under his breath.

They loved his wine.

Alice had let him kiss her.

The other vintners accepted him.

Alice had let him *kiss* her.

He stacked the cases by the winery door, wrung out by all the emotional storms of the afternoon. Tomorrow he would put them inside. Tomorrow he would do many things. But tonight...

The faint powder scent from her skin was still in his nose as he walked back to the house.

She had gone to lie down. She was tired, too, poor thing, rocked by the news that another had gained the sacramental license she coveted, and devastated by Hugh's enmity, now common knowledge, as Siegfried knew it must be, once Hugh realized that he would not be able to buy the property *Opa* Roye had refused to bequeath him.

Standing near the porch, Siegfried watched a flock of long-necked white egrets splash elegantly into the shallow end of the reservoir. He had thought his heart abandoned somewhere in the crumbling sandstone of the Vosges Mountains, ripped apart by rusty barbed wire, obliterated by the incessant cannonade. But he was wrong. It was alive, brimming with rash hope that California earth would accept his roots, that he might thrive and be fruitful here.

"You're back from the meeting?" Maria called from the path to the foreman's cottage, carrying a basket. "Where's Mrs. R.?"

"She was not feeling well," Siegfried replied when she drew near. They both turned towards the house.

"Oh, that's too bad! And I'd just plucked a couple of chickens for supper, too." A stray feather clung to her apron, and she brushed it off. Both of them watched it float over the porch rail and drift gently down.

With sudden inspiration, Siegfried said: "Maria, *I* shall cook supper for my wife tonight. You may have the evening off."

Maria dimpled. "Is it a special occasion? Is there some good news?"

His sleeping arrangements— or lack of them— with Alice were no secret to her, he knew, but Siegfried had no intention of discussing his private life. He shook his head. "No, but I wish to be alone with her." His face grew hot at Maria's knowing look.

"Of course," she agreed, her dimples deepening. "Well, then, I'll take the other chicken with me for Peter's dinner, but I'd better show you what to do, first."

Tugged into the kitchen by the sleeve like a recalcitrant schoolboy, Siegfried patiently suffered Maria's lecture on the operation of the tall, spindly-legged gas stove. All the while, his mind was chanting joyously: *Alone with Alice! Alone with Alice!*

Lying on her bed in a ferment, under a cold damp towel that did nothing for either her headache or her heartache, Alice plotted.

For the first time in her life, she was going to do the wrong thing, on purpose, and this time she was not going to let guilt, her loyalty to Bill's memory, or the thought of what a real lady would do, rule her.

Instead, what ruled her was lustful speculation: what Siegfried's skin would taste like; how soft his hair would be under her hand, how her bed would creak with two of them in it.

I'll be his wife. I'll be safe.

A fleeting remembrance of Bill made her curl and draw her knees protectively up to her chest. If she thought too much about him, she might lose the scandalous trickle of anticipation twining around inside her.

She was going to make love to Siegfried.

No. She would let Siegfried make love to her—

No, really. She would let Siegfried think he was seducing her, when she was actually trapping him in her coils.

She would do it, too.

She would.

Really.

When she could get up.

Heavy-limbed and light-headed, she finally rose from her nap, dressed carefully, and went down stairs, following the scent of supper. She stood at the doorway to the yellow-lit kitchen, amazed to see Siegfried wrapped in one of her aprons and lightly dusted with flour, shuffling a pan out of the oven.

"I could not find any shallots," he said, as if justifying his presence in her kitchen. "So I used instead some young onions. Your tarragon is wonderful and fresh and I used some of the wine to marinate the chicken a little. You do not mind if we dine here, in the kitchen?"

Bemused, Alice shook her head.

"Let me see: there are lettuce and tomatoes from the garden, and I have made biscuits." Siegfried dusted his hands across the apron self-consciously, raising a light cloud. He sneezed and then moved around to Alice's side of the table, holding out a chair for her. "I hope you rested well. You are feeling better?"

Alice's knees gave way and she landed on the chair rather more forcefully than she intended. Her teeth clicked together. "Y-yes. I am." The scent of broiling chicken filled the room, tangy with herbs.

Alice blinked to see her usually sober kitchen table decorated with a checked cloth and candles. Siegfried had already set the salads on the table, and now busied himself with scraping the biscuits, only one shade darker than golden brown, off the baking sheet and into a bread basket.

He placed the basket in front of her. "If they are ruined, there is some bread left from lunch," he offered, apprehensively.

"No, thank you. They look lovely," she said with automatic politeness.

And they did. His biscuits were lumpy, with bottoms suspiciously shiny, but as she tore one open it steamed with hot fragrance, butter melting on it eagerly.

Siegfried wielded poultry shears and served her a portion of chicken, redolent with garlic and tarragon, then settled into his chair, opposite. He looked at her for a long moment, giving her the most unsettled feeling, and said, without crossing himself, or bowing his head, or any show of piety except his naked words: "I thank God for this food, for saving my life, and for you, Alice. Amen."

"Amen." She blessed herself, hoping God's all-seeing eye was watching somewhere else tonight.

"Oh!" said Siegfried, standing up hurriedly. He pulled the cord to turn off the overhead light. The golden glow of the candles on the table grew brighter as her eyes adjusted, until Siegfried came into perfect focus.

She could hardly take her eyes off him to eat, or eat when she took her eyes off him. The chicken was tender and she knew it must have flavor. The lettuce was crisp, and the tomatoes full of juice. But more than a bite of each left her stomach fluttering, and the rest of the wine, served thriftily with dinner, made her head swim.

Siegfried chattered about the other vintners, and the size of the crop, and the favorable weather, and how pleased he was that everybody liked the wine. His wine.

Alice nodded, and stretched her mouth in a fatuous smile and tried not to think about what she might be doing with Siegfried in just a little while.

The candle flames wore halos of gold and soft shadows slid about. Only the spicy scent of the wine and the memory of his mouth on hers were real. She took another gulp, half-hoping it would intoxicate her enough to let her forget what she was doing, knowing she wanted to feel every exquisite sensation.

At last they were done, plates clean except for bones. Alice began to collect the silverware, but Siegfried stood up. "No, Alice. Go rest on the porch. I will wash up."

In disbelief, she said, "No, really, I couldn't—" but he took her elbow and led her toward the screened door at the back of the house.

"You rest," he insisted. "I will take care of everything."

"Th-thank you for dinner."

Alice slipped through the screen door, and sat down on the slatted bench. *Oh, honey, he wants you bad*, said a cynical voice in her head, sounding perilously like her mother. The three-quarters full moon had risen over the crest of the nearest hill. Cricket music echoed under the stars, louder than the clanking and splashing of dishes being washed by her husband.

The evening air was cool, and Alice thought of Siegfried's long legs, one of them badly scarred. She imagined those limbs, pressing all along the length of her own, and between...

She grasped her elbows firmly and sat up straight.

Let's be practical, she told herself. There were mechanical aspects to a seduction that should be taken care of beforehand. She made a mental list. *Towels*. Yes. *New sheets*. Well, she and Maria had done the laundry only two days ago. *Nightgown?* No, definitely not. *Butter?* She remembered a painful session or two with Bill, and the dry burn of his entry. *Yes.*

She worried how to get these items unobtrusively. Towels were in the bathroom. Leave the sheets till tomorrow.

But the butter— her thoughts skidded around exactly why she needed butter, and slid into the difficulty of obtaining any. She couldn't just go into the pantry and pick up the cold-crock. Siegfried was in the kitchen. And she couldn't just sneak back there after Siegfried went upstairs. She knew he would come out here, and sit down with her, and put his arm around her, and kiss her, and pretty soon they would walk upstairs together, very close.

She knew it would happen just like that. And there wouldn't be any time to run downstairs and get the butter. He wouldn't want to let go of her and she wouldn't dare retreat, then, either. She had already decided what she was going to do.

She might knock him on the head so he went out cold for

a while, and she could run into the pantry and pick up the crock,
run upstairs with it, and then be back on the bench, breathing a
little hard, when he woke up.

Alice stifled a nervous giggle. *Oh, certainly.*

Or she could break out of his embrace on the way back
through the kitchen, and just calmly pick it up to bring with them
upstairs. But then he would ask her what she wanted it for, and
wonder how she knew to use it, and the thought of trying to
explain was simply too much to contemplate.

She sighed, the urge to laugh gone now.

Siegfried pushed open the screen door. "Are you feeling
better?"

"Mmm-hmmm," she croaked.

"I am sorry about the meeting," Siegfried said, as he sat
down next to her on the bench. "Hugh is a cad."

She shook her head.

There must have been enough light for Siegfried to see
her expression, for he said, "You are brave, and kind, and so you
think Hugh is, too. But he is not."

She put out her hand, and felt Siegfried's fingers close
around hers, warm and intimate in the darkness. "I'm sorry I was
so rude to you today."

"*Macht nichts,*" he said, dismissively, then lifted her
hand to his mouth and kissed it, tickling her skin.

So far, so good.

"I wanted to protect you, Alice."

Alice's heart began a slow, heavy beat. *Now.*

"I'm not used to having anyone worry about me." She
closed her eyes, waiting for his lips to conquer hers again. Long
seconds passed, and to her keen disappointment, nothing
happened.

Her heart began to pound with a new terror. What if he
didn't want her after all? Then Siegfried's words came out
quietly, next to her ear. "Look."

Alice, dazed, opened her eyes. "What?"

"Shhh." Siegfried put his forefinger over her lips, and she
parted them in an automatic kiss. "Look... there." He pointed.

Two dark forms emerged from the shelter of the fruit
trees, stepping delicately into the moonlit open of her vegetable
garden, huge ears swiveling, large liquid eyes searching
cautiously for dangers.

Alice leapt up and ran to the porch railing. "Shoo!" she
called, waving her arms wildly. "Go away!"

The mule deer were startled into immobility, then
bounded off into the darkness.

Siegfried chuckled and came up behind her, brushing the nape of her neck with a light kiss that sent a pleasurable jolt through her. "Peter told me about them."

"Pests," Alice muttered darkly, eliciting another chuckle from Siegfried. "I used to think they were lovely animals."

"Those encroaching deer will not dare return tonight." He pulled her back against him into the silver-dappled shadows. Thigh to thigh, his arm heavy and possessive around her shoulders, every inch of her body tingled where he touched her.

Siegfried's breath on her cheek raised goosebumps, as if she could feel not only her own flesh, but his, too, and the desire that was present and rising in both of them. She took hold of his right hand and intertwined her fingers with his. She felt Siegfried's breath catch. His lips were soft and warm and it was so very easy to return his kiss. His hesitation— and her own— melted away in the pressure of mouth on mouth.

His free hand cupped the back of her head, keeping her close. Her arms crept around his neck.

The deliciously wicked melting sensation she had experienced in his arms earlier that day returned, and Alice realized that all of her worries about the butter had been unnecessary.

Siegfried raised his lips from hers long enough to murmur something in German, then he kissed her forehead, her eyes, her cheeks. Electricity skittered through her as he traced the curve of her ear and gently nipped it. His mouth continued downward along her throat, raising more delightful shivers as his kisses followed the perimeter of her high-necked blouse.

He put an arm around her waist, and led her back to the seat. Alice allowed him to guide her, unresisting, then deliberately sat down on his lap.

He perched stiffly on the edge of the bench until she put her hands on his shoulders. "Relax," she said, tracing her own line of kisses along his jawbone. "I won't bite you."

"No? " He grinned. "Too bad." He leaned back, drawing her with him. The bulge in his lap pressed against her leg, wildly satisfying. His hands rose to cover her shoulder blades. Alice kissed him slowly, tasting the now-familiar pleasure of his mouth.

Then Siegfried's hand slipped down under her arms, to her breasts, and rested there lightly. He brushed the sensitive tips. At her twitch, he jerked his hands away. "Did I— hurt you, Ah-lees?"

She made a small sound of deprivation, and broke the kiss, startled by how *right* his hands had felt. "No."

Wearing a hesitant expression, Siegfried did not move. "I do not want—"

"I'll tell you if it hurts."

His gaze never leaving hers, Siegfried touched her cheeks and lips, then his fingers molded her breasts. Slowly he reached up to open the top button of her shirtwaist, then, when she did not protest, the next, and the next, until the blouse lay open to her waist. He pushed it off her shoulders, trapping her lower arms in a tangle of fabric. Leaning forward, he kissed the bare skin above her thin silk slip. His breath was warm, and her heart beat heavily again. *This* was why she had left off her corset when she dressed for dinner.

Siegfried said something in German again, of which she only caught *Liebchen*... beloved... and then his fingers were drawing wandering circles, cupping and lifting her breasts, testing the weight and texture. She leaned shamelessly into his touch, gasping a little, begging him wordlessly for more. She kissed him, hard, as his hands continued their wicked magic.

Alice had never felt anything like this strange, hot longing with Bill. Then again, she had never sat on his lap half naked in the moonlight, letting him fondle her. The thought of Bill, lying in an unmarked grave while she embraced his cousin, instantly sobered her.

"Ah-lees?" Siegfried asked unsteadily as she wriggled hastily off his lap.

What *had* she been thinking?

"I— I want to go now," she stammered, backing away from him and holding her blouse together. She turned away from his distress, but he rose and followed her inside. He didn't try to touch her, but his jaw muscles bunched as he escorted her upstairs.

She berated herself for a coward by her bedroom door. She did not want to slam it in his face without an explanation, but what could she say to him? *Thank you for a very enjoyable evening*?

Alice was horribly aware of his presence behind her. She had wanted this; she had encouraged him. And now she was running away. She put her hand on her doorknob.

"Ah-lees, please— I burn for you," Siegfried whispered. "Do not leave me!"

She turned slowly and, knowing she should not, knowing she could do nothing else, took a single step into his arms.

CHAPTER
12

Montclair
Wednesday, June 25

He kissed her again, his mouth hard and possessive, then carried her down the hall into his bedroom. She clung to him, the pulse between her thighs beating wildly in flagrant anticipation.

He pushed her blouse open and down over her shoulders past her wrists. She freed her hands from the clinging material and reached for his shirt, but her hands were trembling so badly that she couldn't work the buttons through the holes.

"Ah-lees— *lass mich.*"

She didn't need a translation. His hands flew down his buttons, and then it was easy to push off his shirt.

She rested her cheek half against his sleeveless undershirt and half on bare shoulder, tasting his skin, clean and smooth, with a faint remnant of soap. He must have washed while she was resting.

Oh, God. He wanted her so much. Enough to bathe, and to cook, and to beg.

He pulled at the waist of her long skirt, undoing the fastenings. She let go of him just long enough for it to fall at her feet. She stepped out of her shoes, shivering even though it was warm in the upstairs room.

"Ah-lees," Siegfried whispered, as his fingers traveled the length of her slip straps over her shoulders, down to her breasts. "You are so beautiful..."

She rubbed against him for the lascivious pleasure she obtained from the slide of silk against skin. There were trousers in her way. She removed them with Siegfried's willing help. Somewhere along the line he had shed his shoes, too.

His hands undid her chignon, tugging the pins out and letting them fall. As he fanned the mass of her hair across her back, strands came down, curtain-like, framing her face and his in a suddenly private world. Outside that barrier their bodies touched in increasingly intimate communion, but within that compass, they were alone together, soul to soul.

Alice closed her eyes as he urged her gently towards the bed. She did not want to see the secrets behind Siegfried's dark blue eyes. She did not want him to see hers. It was enough that she was here, with him, giving him what he wanted for her own ends.

⁓⁕⁓

Siegfried had spent his youth in the country, and he was familiar with bulls and stallions and the mechanics of sex. He had heard improbable-sounding stories from his fellow soldiers, and he had applied his imagination freely, but these were theories he had never put into practice. Until now.

He combed Alice's unbound hair with gentle fingers, his heart singing. She was almost his, and she did not know the enormity of the gift she was giving him. *Lieber Gott*, let him not fumble too badly. He had waited all his life for this moment.

He had never wanted to hurry more, but he knew, deep in his bones, that patience was his only hope. When he was sixteen, plagued with a breaking voice and the first sprouting of whiskers, *Opa* Roye had taught him the vintner's secret: to make love the way that he made wine, slowly, and with careful attention to detail.

He smoothed his hand lightly over Alice's right breast, rounded under the silk of her slip, and felt an answering response in his loins as his thumb brushed the firm berry of her nipple. He let his hand linger, cupped under the swell. She arched slightly.

Opa had been right. If he was patient, Alice would show him the way to best please her. He need not be ashamed of his inexperience. He had done well enough on the porch, although her squirming weight on his lap had been torture.

All those weeks of watching her, remote and lovely even in her grubby men's clothing amidst the filth of the winery, wondering what it would be like to kiss her and hold her... now she was in the bed with him, nestled in the curve of his chest, hip to hip through the thin barrier of their underclothes. The silky strands of her hair tangled on the pillow and brushed against his wrist as he traced a slow spiral around her breast with a dexterous finger. He heard the pattern of her breathing change as he neared the crest, and break in a gasp as he flicked it lightly. Once again, he felt an answering shock, now urgent. *I'll die if I cannot join her soon.*

Her skin was hot as he brushed it with kisses, and her scent surrounded him, unmistakably her own, like a Riesling, spicy and sweet, apple and vanilla with a backbone of flint. Her mouth against his was delicate, and her kiss was like freshly pressed grape juice, sweet and full and hinting of the flavors in the wine to come. He let his kiss trail downward, and closed his lips around the tip of her left breast. A sound like a deep sob escaped her, and to his delight, she opened her thighs and pressed upward against the burning length of his erection. He wanted to see her naked in the moonlight. He wanted to cool his fires in her moist depths.

Siegfried raised himself up slightly, and tugged at the hem of her slip. Alice's eyes opened, wide and shining in the faint silvery light. He froze. Had he done something wrong? But no. Her fingers came against his, aiding him as she lifted her hips. She sat up to pull the ivory silk over her head.

The garment disappeared as he rose to his knees and worshipped her, fantasy made flesh. Her breasts were perfectly round and white, just as he had imagined them. But he had not dared to imagine the tender dimple punctuating the smooth curve of her belly, nor the dark triangle of curls at the joining of her thighs. They were open for him, but shrouded in shadow, so that his ultimate destination was a mystery.

Alice smiled self-consciously as he continued to look at her, at a loss on how to proceed. He wanted to throw himself upon her, and mount her like a stallion his mare, but he dared not... Then she leaned forward and freed his undershirt from his shorts with a sharp jerk upwards.

Siegfried raised his arms to aid her task as her hands skimmed upwards over his torso and chest. He flung away the garment as Alice continued to touch him with feather-light strokes. He was on fire all over and trembling as she kissed him. Her hands began to wander lower, stopping momentarily at the buttoned waistband of his shorts. He groaned as she placed her cool palm against the thin cotton, afraid she would scorch her hand on his heat. The muscles in his thighs bunched with the effort not to disgrace himself by spilling his seed explosively.

Then she pulled down his shorts and her hands were at his waist as her mouth devoured his. Siegfried shook as he pressed against her, and felt the folds of her secret flesh against the tip of his penis. Alice whimpered as he butted against her. He tried to pull back, sure he had hurt her, but she reached down and guided him smoothly inside.

Ach, Gott. Why had he waited so long?

They were one flesh now, arms wrapped around one another, as he rocked in her embrace. Blind instinct overcame him, and he thrust repeatedly. She lifted her hips to receive his strokes, her heels curled around the back of his knees.

The heat and the pressure mingled. He was made all of molten metal, red-hot, glowing yellow, intent on reaching his goal before the fire consumed him. One more stroke, the low sound of Alice's murmurs, the pressure of her fingertips digging into his back, and a white-hot fountain begin to spout from the base of his spine. He poured himself into her, blind, confounded, shouting with the ecstasy of it, so near pain. A pattern of platinum and gold burned behind his eyelids. Then the last of it was gone in a glorious blast of sparks, and only dark alloy was left behind, their intermingled metal cooling in the slight draft from the open window.

He collapsed limply on top of her, and kissed the molded curve of her cheek. Alice, dearer to him now than his life...

"*Ich liebe Dich*," he mumbled.

His eyelids drooped. Dimly, he felt her touch on his hair, and then he fell asleep in cozy intimacy with that beautiful, scented flesh.

Siegfried woke when Alice shifted beneath him. He could not have been asleep very long. He was lying on top of her— he must be crushing her.

He rolled to one side, and propped himself up on his elbow to study her in the diffuse moonlight. She sighed deeply, her eyelids fluttering, and he wondered if he had been too selfish with her. *Opa* Roye's untested instructions had been clear: always make sure the lady had her pleasure first. He had been too keyed up for that, but now...

She had seemed to like his touch on her breasts, so Siegfried reached out and felt her nipple change from yielding resiliency to stiff pushing against his palm. He stroked teasingly, trailing his fingers across slopes of smooth, warm skin. Alice's heartbeat fluttered against his fingertip caresses, but her eyes stayed closed.

He touched the tip of her breast, pebble-hard now, and was rewarded with the gasp he sought. He leaned closer, and kissed her sweet mouth. Passive at first, the next brush of his hand over her nipple woke her mouth to hungry life.

Siegfried kissed her thoroughly, enjoying this game of leisurely arousal, then moved his mouth lower, kissing her shoulders, the hollow of her throat, the shallow valley between her breasts. He rested his head there for a moment, listening to the precious sound of her heartbeat, then kissed the tender underside of one breast.

His own desire sated, he enjoyed touching her in this unhurried fashion, each caress a new and subtle revelation as he studied her reactions. It *was* similar to the vintner's art of courting and coaxing the grape to develop all its potential.

He needed to taste this vintage again. He drew her nipple into his mouth, suckling it, and smiled as Alice arched under him. He repeated his caresses on her other breast, then he inched down the bed, daring to kiss the soft expanse of her stomach, his hands shaping the indentation of her waist and coming to rest on her hips. A muted giggle told him that she was ticklish. Siegfried raised his head and grinned at her, wordlessly announcing that he had filed away the spot for future reference. He was charmed to hear her giggle emerge full-force.

He kissed the slight swell of her belly, amazed at smoothness. When he reached the patch of curls, the fine hair and musky scent reminded him of a tale of pleasure he had thought improbable at the time. His comrade Jürgen had freely shared all the details of his recent conquests during the silent watches of many a starlit night, but Siegfried had never quite believed his bragging. Now, he thought this particular attack was perhaps worth a try. Alice would surely let him know if she was repulsed. She was so honest, so good...

Siegfried felt her surprise as he gently nudged her legs apart. His lips slid across the velvet-soft skin of her inner thighs. Gently he kissed the warm, mysterious place that had delighted him earlier, letting his lips and his tongue learn the secrets concealed from his eyes.

Alice let out a low sound as he discovered a small hidden berry. He stopped, unsure whether he had mortally offended her. He was reassured when her fingers tangled themselves in his hair and she whispered, "Please."

He bent his head once more to his work, like tasting a young, firm grape. Alice's fingers flexed as if she might pull a hank of his hair out by the roots. Her tender folds swelled and became slickly moist. She squirmed, and he remembered how it felt to be inside her. The renewed force of his desire made him thrust his tongue into her sweet depths, to taste her fiercely in response to the cries she made. He was drowning in the scents of musk, Riesling and vanilla, the complex flavors of Alice.

He could not drink deeply enough.

I didn't expect this— oh! Alice thought, on fire and ashamed of the noises escaping her throat. But Bill had never done this to her when he claimed his marital rights. If she had only known how different it would be with Siegfried, she would have—

—dragged him to bed the night he got here, her mother's voice whispered to her, cynical and amused. But, for once, Alice agreed.

Dear God, she did not want him to stop. She wanted Siegfried to continue forever with his slow, gentle devotion of her carnal self, to strip the pretense from her and let her wallow in lust. She wanted... she wanted...

This. The pressure, clenched tight within her like a fist, building, building as Siegfried lay between her thighs and tormented her sweetly with his scandalous kisses. She gave a muffled scream at the pulsing waves of joy.

Her heart pounded as the last ripple died away. She became aware that Siegfried's head shared her pillow again, his arm held her shoulder, his arousal, renewed, pressed against her hip in an unspoken question.

She answered unreservedly, welcoming him inside again.

Afterwards, Alice lay nestled in the curve of Siegfried's elbow, her arm draped over his waist. She felt safe, protected, and, for the first time in this horrible day, relaxed and calm. She drowsed, her cheek against his skin, his breath soft against her hair. He would not leave her now. Montclair was safe, and she was, too. Even if Wartime Prohibition came, they would have the land—

Oh, God.

The land! Alice withdrew her arm from Siegfried's skin, and tried to cover her nakedness. *Oh God, I didn't need to sleep with him!* She could have sold a portion of the land, and used the proceeds to plant a cash crop. Instead she had just sold herself for material security. And enjoyed it.

All her education, all her efforts to escape the influence of her background, all her prayers for strength of character had been useless. When put to the test, she acted not like a lady, but a whore.

She had always been afraid she would discover this truth. Now she knew.

She was no better than her mother.

In the middle of the night, Siegfried half-woke. Something was not right. He reached out, expecting warmth, only to find a cool spot beside him in the bed. Alice was gone.

He came fully awake as he heard the faint sound of weeping. He was well acquainted with its irregular rhythms from the long nights of the war, when too-young draftees stopped pretending they were men, and called for their mothers.

Siegfried rose, groping with his toes for his undershorts. He pulled them on, clumsy with haste, and followed the sound of sobbing to the bathroom.

The light was on, and the door stood partially open. He peeked around the corner. Alice, clad in her crumpled slip, holding the long tail of her hair in one hand, wept over the commode. The sour smell of vomit hung in the air.

"Alice?" Siegfried took a cautious step inside. "What is wrong?"

She didn't answer him, nor did she look up. A cold chill crawled down Siegfried's spine, and the last of the golden haze lingering from his sexual initiation dissipated. He awkwardly put a hand against her back. "Alice? Please, tell me! Are you ill— or, or— hurt?"

"Go away." Her shoulders shook, displacing his hand.

Her eyes met his in the mirror, and her gaze was filled with despair, her cheeks red and blotched with tears. She was still beautiful to him. But he remembered her adamant statement, "There *will* be an annulment!" Had he taken unfair advantage of her precarious emotional state last night? Had he pressured her into consummating their relationship when she did not actually wish it?

"Do you regret what we... did tonight?" he asked, not wanting to hear her answer.

Alice nodded, and wiped at her lips with trembling fingers.

"I— I only want your happiness," he blurted, his tongue tripping over suddenly unfamiliar English sounds. "If this has made you so unhappy, then I— we— can pretend it never happened."

"You mean you won't—" She swallowed a hiccup. "We can still get an annulment?"

Pain ripped through his chest. He was right. She did not really want him. His throat turned dry with the effort to force out the word, "Yes, of course." He raised his chin. "You see, I would never force you to— to—" He could not say the rest.

"Thank you," she whispered, twisting her hair into a coil, revealing the naked relief on her face. "I'm sorry that I— I didn't mean..."

"Come," Siegfried said, putting his arm around her shoulders.

She flinched, and he leapt back as if burned. *Lieber Gott, what does she think of me?*

He escorted her down the hall to her own bedroom, moving with numb decorum. The metallic scrape and click of the key, locking the door behind her, sent his spirits plummeting even lower.

He returned to his own bed and spent the remaining hours

of the night staring at the dim ceiling, berating himself for his foolish nobility in renouncing the consummation of their marriage.

He burned for her now, more than ever.

Alice crawled into bed and pulled the sheets over her head, trying not to listen to the sound of Siegfried's slow, uneven steps retreating from her door.

Expecting to toss all night on the shoals of self-recrimination, she was surprised when she opened her eyes to curtains glowing with gray dawn light. She plumped her soft pillow, feeling wonderfully buoyant and languid, complete in some indefinable way... and then she remembered.

Alice shivered, and drew the sheets tightly around her shoulders. She did not want to recall sprawling on Siegfried's bed, wantonly urging him on, making *those* noises. Having those feelings.

The thought of having to meet his eyes across the breakfast table made her cringe. So, for the first time since Bill's death, she did not rise with the sun to begin the endless round of chores. Instead she rolled over and went back to sleep.

Siegfried struggled awake, a foul mood hanging over him like the gray blanket of fog outside. He dressed in his work clothes, then stomped down the hallway to the stairs, pausing to glare at the closed door of her bedroom. Why had his wonderful first time been so terrible for her? Alice's musky scent still filled his senses. Her flavors lingered on his tongue like the delayed finish of a truly great wine.

He had waited so long. At first, he had been abstinent from the knowledge that he would have to marry any girl he got in the family way. As heir to the Rodernwiller vineyards, his father had cautioned him to marry wisely. During the War, the prostitutes repelled him; he could not stomach the idea of sharing a woman with every soldier in a German uniform.

Outside, he began his walk alone through the Cabernet section of the vineyard, pacing down the trellised rows, staring absently at the leaves and tendrils.

Alice had been so responsive, so passionate. Afterwards, she had reacted as if he had raped her. But he had not! He had given her numerous chances to pull away, to tell him "no." She had been willing... more than willing. He would swear to it.

A cloud of starlings soared over the vineyard, and landed

a few yards away. Siegfried picked up a clod of dirt, and desultorily threw it at them. Some of the birds were startled into flight, but soon settled down again among their unruffled companions. He gave a despairing snort, and continued walking without really seeing the vines until the clanging of the kitchen bell summoned him to breakfast.

In the kitchen, across from Peter, Siegfried munched steadily through a plateful of scrambled eggs and potatoes fried with bacon and onions. The food was flavorless and dry. He replied to Maria's cheerful prattle with monosyllabic grunts as she refilled his coffee cup. He glanced up at the doorway several times, but Alice didn't appear.

Maria, coffeepot in hand, followed his glance. "Is Mrs. R. still sick? It's not like her to be late for breakfast."

"Yes. Let her sleep," Siegfried mumbled uncomfortably around a mouthful of potatoes.

"The poor dear. I wonder if I should bring her some chamomile tea and toast?"

"Let her be, Maria. You're not a doctor," Peter growled. "Er, sorry to hear that Mrs. R. is sick," he apologized to Siegfried.

"M-mnh," Siegfried said, returning his attention to his plate. It was empty, like his hopes.

Siegfried spent the next hour stalking around the winery, grumbling at his busy workers and listlessly picking up tools to start a task then putting them down again with not the faintest idea what to do with them.

Last night he had made love to his wife, had given and received in measure far beyond what he could have imagined, and this morning he felt like hell. He wanted to make love to Alice again and again, every night, every morning for the rest of his life. He wanted to feel her supple skin, to make her giggle again, to hear her soft cries, to taste her rich bouquet. He wanted her kisses, her warm breath in his ear, the softness of her breast in his hand, the *rightness* of their joining.

He wanted to be her husband. Not just in name, but in fact.

And he wanted Alice to want all these things, too.

He *was* her husband, by God. He had only offered her the chance of annulment to give her the time to realize it herself, so she would not feel like he had stolen Montclair from her. *If she needs more time*, he gritted his teeth, *then she shall have it.*

But he hoped she would not leave him burning long.

There must be some way to prove his good intentions, to

demonstrate how much she really needed him. At Montclair. In her bed.

He turned ideas over in his mind as his feet led him unaware into the vineyard, through the riot of vines. The one scheme he came back to, again and again, was the license.

She had wanted a license from the Archbishop of San Francisco to produce sacramental wine, but La Fontaine got it instead.

In a flash of platinum and gold, inspiration struck Siegfried. He would show her how useful he could be.

Opa Roye had shared Charles La Fontaine's quest to make a California Burgundy that would compare with the finest French reds. Siegfried would presume on that acquaintance, and assure the fortunes of Montclair. He would bring some of his wine to Mr. La Fontaine, and convince him to contract with Montclair as a secondary supplier. He would return, triumphant, and lay his victory like a laurel wreath at Alice's feet.

And she would take his hand, and kiss him, and draw him down to her soft bed...

Fired with enthusiasm, Siegfried strode back to the door of the winery, where a crate from the meeting still held three bottles of the 1911 vintage.

Peter, walking by with an armful of empty sacks as Siegfried loaded the case in the back of the truck, cocked his head inquiringly. "You going somewhere?"

"I am going to run an errand. Please tell Maria that I will miss dinner, although I should be back in time for supper."

"You— miss dinner? That must be some errand," Peter joked, dropping the blue-stained sacks and hooking his thumbs in his jeans pockets. He pointed at the Ford with his chin. "You know how to drive?"

"Of course!" Siegfried replied, stung. "My father owned a Daimler."

"Oh, yeah? Well, this ain't no Daimler. You know why the man named his Ford after Theodore Roosevelt?"

Siegfried shook his head, but Peter was already laughing. "Because it's a rough-riding son of a gun! Know why another fella named his after his wife? Because he couldn't control it!" Peter snorted, and came to the end of his short burst of mirth. "Better get the seat off while I go get some gasoline for it. You'll want to fill 'er up before you go."

The bedside clock read 10:00 AM. The wonderful languor of her earlier awakening had disappeared. As she rose to dress, she felt sluggish and out of sorts. She finished buttoning her blouse, opened her curtains, and saw that a leaden sky perfectly accompanied her mood.

The kitchen was warm, and smelled of coffee and bacon. She entered reluctantly, afraid of finding Siegfried there.

"Oh, Mrs. R., you're up at last. Mr. R. said you weren't feeling well and that I shouldn't wake you. Are you better? Would you like breakfast?" Maria asked, wrist-deep in bread dough. She stopped kneading and wiped her hands with a dishtowel.

Alice sighed. "I don't know, Maria. Don't worry about me. I just want some coffee and toast. I can make it myself."

"Coffee's on the stove," Maria said, sprinkling a fresh layer of flour on the wooden kneading board and beginning to work the dough again. "You know, Mr. R. didn't look so well, either. Did you two have an argument?"

Alice twitched as she picked up the enamel coffeepot from the stovetop and poured herself a mug. "Not 'zactly." She opened the icebox and added a too-generous amount of cream to her coffee. She couldn't control her hand, and she hadn't meant to confide in Maria, but her next words tumbled out before she could help herself: "It's only— he's so *different*... from Bill."

"He loves you, though," Maria commented with a worldly-wise smile. "I can tell."

"No. He loves Montclair." Alice said bitterly. And why did that suddenly matter so much to her? Yesterday, she had selfishly seduced him in order to keep Montclair and her position in the community. By doing so, she had not only betrayed Bill's memory, but confirmed her worst fears about her own nature. Siegfried had done such things to her! She winced in embarrassment.

Maria, wide-eyed, had stopped kneading.

"Oh, never mind." Alice grabbed a slightly stale loaf of bread from the breadbox and sawed off two slices for her toast. "Yesterday was a bad day."

Maria raised a skeptical eyebrow at this, but said in her most neutral tone, "Well, then, I hope today's better, Mrs. R."

"Thank you," said Alice, fervently. "Where is my— where is Siegfried?"

Maria shrugged. "Peter said he went off on an errand."

He was gone! She wouldn't have to face him, yet.

Alice enjoyed a solitary breakfast in the dining room, but thoughts of Siegfried kept distracting her: his boyish grin as he discovered her ticklish spots; his look of intent concentration as he devoted himself to pleasuring her; the soft demand of his mouth on her breasts.

At the memory of their lovemaking, arousal woke between her thighs again and the warmth of the house became stifling. She rose hastily from the table, longing for the coolness of the foggy morning outside.

"I'm going to fetch the mail," she told Maria, as she rinsed out her coffee mug.

Once on the driveway, Alice drew a deep breath of the moist, eucalyptus-scented air and hoped that the quarter-mile walk down the hill to the road would calm her fevered recollections. Otherwise, how could she face Siegfried on a daily basis? Assuming that he still wished to serve as her vintner.

Of course he does, Alice reassured herself, fighting down a stab of panic at the thought of losing him. *He won't give up Montclair that easily.*

The mailbox contained several bills, an advertising circular for Princess Hair Tonics, and a white envelope bearing the return address of the Archdiocese of San Francisco. She weighed the letter in her hand for a moment, knowing what it must say, then shoved it in her skirt pocket.

There was one more item in the mailbox: a package addressed to "Mrs. Siegfried Rodernwiller."

The return address on the package gave her an unpleasant surprise: Florence Campbell O'Reilly, San Francisco.

Alice tore open the brown paper covering the package and soon balanced an enormous, gaudy brooch in the shape of a dragonfly on her palm. The fluttering wings, covered with a thin layer of blue-green enamel and outlined by a row of diamonds, were cleverly attached to the gold body by tiny springs. Two large diamonds set into the enamel head formed the insect's faceted eyes, and the legs were heavy gold.

As she studied the wild glitter in her hand, Alice gave a despairing laugh. At five inches across, it was the most vulgar piece of jewelry she had ever seen, the sort of thing that a demimondaine might wear to the Opera, pinned to a gaudy sash over a *décolleté* evening gown.

What in heaven's name had prompted her mother to send this?

At least she didn't deliver it in person. Alice choked back another laugh, this one edged with hysteria. She imagined her mother invading her Montclair refuge. How would she introduce Florence to Siegfried? To Peter and Maria? To the ladies at church?

A note, written with appalling penmanship, had been wrapped around the brooch.

Dear baby girl,

The paper said you got married again, and I was thinking about you. I think about you a lot. I know you dont want nothing to do with me, but I hope you are happy and that you got yourself a good man. I hope the grape farm is doing well. If you need anything, let me know. I love you, honey.

Your loving mother, Florrie.

Alice stood next to the mailbox for a long time, re-reading the note, sick at heart. Last night, driven by desperation, she had betrayed everything that mattered to her— her honor, her respectability, her chastity.

Like mother, like daughter. I can't escape her taint.

Back at the house, she tossed the bills and the Archbishop's letter on the desk in her office. Then she trudged upstairs to her bedroom and dumped the gaudy dragonfly brooch in the jewelry box on her dresser. It was utterly out of place among the scanty items already there: a pair of cultured pearl earrings, a simple pendant on a silver chain. She touched one of the earrings regretfully, reminded of her pawned pearl necklace.

Then it hit her. Eagerly, she picked up her mother's gift and held it appraisingly to the light. With all those diamonds, it might be worth enough to buy plum trees to replace the vines. She put the dragonfly brooch in her box and closed the lid, already planning her next trip to San Francisco.

Sonoma
Thursday, June 26

Siegfried stalled the truck a few times before he crossed the railroad tracks by the gray stone Sebastiani winery on the edge of town.

He finally puzzled out, through trial and error, the unfamiliar gearshift: clutch, reverse and brake pedals on the floor, throttle and spark levers on the steering column, and one floor lever to the left of the driver. Failing to correctly set the steering wheel levers stalled out the engine. The leftmost pedal put the Ford in first gear if the floor lever was upright. To shift into second gear, the lever had to be pushed forward while the pedal was depressed. Stepping on all three pedals at once locked the transmission.

It was, as Peter had warned, quite different from Father's Daimler, but by the time Siegfried turned left onto the dirt road that led east to Napa, he had the hang of it.

The truck, properly handled, eagerly traveled mile after bumpy mile. Summer sunlight and blue sky leaked through cracks in the gray cloud cover, altering irregular dun hills to heaps of gold tarnished by gnarled old oaks. As he passed isolated homesteads protected by lines of cypress or eucalyptus trees, he was stung by homesickness for sights he would never see again: the perfect mountain cone of Haut Königsbourg, its slopes blanketed by rich green pines and glossy-leafed beeches, its castle-crowned peak guarding the verdant plain of Alsace; roads shaded by cherry trees and poplars; a mosaic of vineyards and fields dotted with villages where ornate church spires guarded red, sharp-roofed houses.

Instead, around the next bend, he was treated to an immense vista of silver-green San Pablo Bay stretching south to the Golden Gate. A red-tailed hawk flew in serene circles overhead. San Francisco was a slash of white along the far distant shore.

He drove on.

Rattling down the rutted Main Street in the so-called City of Napa, memory superimposed the pastel stuccoed houses and *Winstuben* of home over this rough little railroad town of plain wooden stair-step storefronts and telegraph wires.

All the way to Calistoga, driving past vineyards and

orchards of plums and olives, while the the stony irregular peak of Mount St. Helena crowned the sky, he tried to shake off the mood of nostalgia. *The past is dead. Montclair's future depends on me.*

Siegfried slowed the Ford to a crawl and turned left just past a large tile-roofed winery covered with ivy. He had arrived at Fountainview. Flat vineyards stretched away on both sides of a narrow unmarked lane, while the Sonoma-Napa mountains loomed high ahead. After a half-mile drive, he parked next to an outbuilding and fetched one of the wine bottles from the case in the truck bed.

Opa Roye had once described La Fontaine's house as a country cottage, unpretentious yet luxurious. There was a large, rambling, English-style garden, vibrant in pinks and purples. Wicker furniture on the verandah looked comfortable and well-used. As Siegfried climbed the steps to the front porch he noticed lace curtains in the windows. He remembered *Opa* telling him that Madame La Fontaine was Alsatian, and tried to quell his anticipation. He couldn't wait to hear a familiar accent again.

He lifted the heavy brass knocker, let it fall, and waited.

No one came to answer the door. Siegfried tried the knocker again. There was still no response.

His heart sank. Had the family left Fountainview for the day to picnic? Had they gone into town for some shopping?

Siegfried kicked himself for not telephoning first. But then, Alice would have known where he was going, and his surprise would have been ruined. Well, it was ruined anyway. He trudged back toward the truck, all his hopes dashed.

Footsteps sounded from behind the outbuilding, a painted wooden shed. A man appeared, wearing the denim overalls of a vineyard worker and carrying a large pair of pruning shears. "What are you doing here?" he asked in a gravelly whisper.

There was something wrong with his voice, his face. Siegfried realized that the man's mouth hadn't moved when he spoke, and the words were strangely distorted, even allowing for a French accent.

"Ah, hallo," Siegfried said, uneasy under the man's baleful dark-eyed glare. "I was seeking Mr. La Fontaine."

The man's eyes narrowed in sullen dislike. "I am Jean Aramon, Monsieur La Fontaine's foreman. What do you want with him?"

Siegfried hefted his bottle. The wine inside caught the light, garnet filtered through dark green glass. "I am Siegfried Rodernwiller, an acquaintance of Monsieur La Fontaine. When will he be back?" Siegfried spoke in French, and instantly knew he had made a mistake.

"'Back?' He won't be 'back' for several weeks, *boche*," Aramon rasped. "And if you were indeed acquainted with *M'sieu* and *Madame* La Fontaine, you would know they live in San Francisco, and only come here to take summer holiday and for crush. Now, get off this property."

"Could you at least give Monsieur La Fontaine my regards when he returns?" Siegfried asked desperately. He could not believe his poor luck. It had taken him nearly two hours to drive to Fountainview. He held out the bottle of wine.

"I said, *out*, you filthy German pig!" the other snarled, the upper part of his face contorting as he swung his long-handled pruning shears like a sword.

Siegfried stepped back and parried the blow with an unthinking motion born of long hours of bayonet practice. There was a numbing impact and the bottle exploded in a shower of liquid and long, jagged shards of glass. Only the neck remained in his hand. Red wine spilled like blood onto the dust of the road.

The foreman brandished his weapon again and the lifelike mask concealing his face fell off. A hole gaped where a nose belonged, and where his lips had been was a mass of pink scar tissue puckered into a permanent sneer. Siegfried recoiled: he had seen similar scars on men whose faces had literally been torn off by shrapnel.

Hanging onto the shreds of his dignity, Siegfried spread his hands in surrender and dropped the bottle remnant. It landed close to the false nose, the faintly smiling sculptured lips. Although they had been on opposite sides of the late conflict, Siegfried felt an uneasy kinship for Aramon, a fellow casualty. "I will leave now," he said, then slowly backed towards the Model-T.

"Good riddance!" Aramon spat. Hatred emanated from him like a bad smell, but he did not attack while Siegfried cranked the truck to a reluctant start.

He was a mile south of Calistoga before he noticed that there was blood mingled with the wine staining his right hand and shirtsleeve. He had not felt the cut before; now, perversely, it began to sting mightily. He cursed and bound his purple-stained handkerchief around his palm, tightening the knot with his teeth and a grimace.

He drove without seeing the road. *I am a coward.* He had backed down from a fight, hoping to avoid trouble. What kind of a man was he? He couldn't even face down an insolent farm hand. A wounded man.

And he hadn't gotten the contract. Shame rose sour in his

throat. He was penniless, worthless. It was no wonder Alice did not want him.

On a desolate stretch of sere countryside he heard a sharp *swop*! from the front end of the car. The Model-T lurched and abruptly listed to one side. Siegfried stamped on all three pedals, bringing the car to a slithering white-knuckled halt. He emerged to inspect the damage.

The tire was in tatters. It had burst and could not be patched. And the spare was also flat, unrepaired from yesterday's misfortune.

"*Verdammter Reifen!*" Siegfried kicked the offending wheel. He spent a few moments more venting his wrath on the silent black hulk. "*Verdammtes Fahrzeug!*"

He was shaking. His hand hurt, his stomach burned, and a headache throbbed behind his eyes. He had missed dinner; now it looked as though he would miss supper, too. He wished he had gotten Maria to make some sandwiches for him, but he had only the remaining bottle of wine. And that was not, as he well knew from hungry nights in the trenches, a sustaining meal by itself.

He rummaged in the toolbox mounted on the running board for the tire-repair kit and pump. He applied a vulcanized rubber patch to the flat spare, then waited impatiently until the cement dried. He slammed air back into the tire with vicious bursts of the pump handle. The task, so easy under Alice's admiring gaze yesterday, took him nearly an hour and half and left him weak with impotent rage.

When he re-started the motor, the kick-back of the crank almost broke his thumb. The steering wheel fought him and it seemed hours later when he finally reached Montclair's long drive. Dusk and fatigue blurred the vines and the white house above. In a daze he started driving up the hill. As the engine sputtered and died halfway up, he remembered, belatedly, what Alice had told him about backing the truck up the slope.

The porch light came on. She was waiting for him.

His humiliation was complete.

Alice ran down the hill. Her initial relief on hearing that Siegfried had gone had turned eventually into annoyance that he hadn't said where he was going, but exasperation had long since deteriorated into worry. "Are you all right?" she called.

As she drew nearer, Siegfried climbed slowly out of the truck, moving stiffly. He steadied himself on the doorframe, and stood staring at the Ford as if he couldn't quite comprehend what it was doing there, a charcoal gray shadow in the mauve twilight.

Her steps slowed as she saw dark stains on his shirtsleeves and caught the reek of stale wine. *He's drunk!?* "Don't worry about the truck," she assured him soothingly. "We can move it tomorrow morning."

"I'm not—" he said haltingly. "I'm sorry about..." he waved vaguely, and staggered.

Alice suppressed the urge to catch him. She had never seen him under the influence before; she didn't know if he'd fall over, be sloppily grateful, or start swinging at her. "Why don't you come inside?" she coaxed. "I'll fix you some supper and some hot coffee."

"Supper," Siegfried echoed. "Yes. That would be good." He pushed himself upright, and tottered up the hill.

Alice was unsure of her diagnosis by the time they entered the house. Even though the scent of wine was stronger than ever, Siegfried was white as a sheet instead of being flushed with drink. Then she saw the bloody handkerchief bandaging his hand. Had he been fighting again? "What happened?"

"Nothing. I broke one of the bottles. I should wash up." He wandered toward the stairs.

She caught at his sleeve. If he fell in this condition, she couldn't carry him. "Why don't you use the kitchen sink while I make sandwiches?"

Siegfried washed his hands in numb silence, grateful for Alice's solicitude. When he collapsed into a chair at the kitchen table, she placed a plate of thick-sliced roast beef sandwiches before him. He fell upon them as Alice ground coffee and set water to boil.

After the first few bites, his headache began to recede. He was appalled at how soft he had become. After all the privations he had suffered during the War, missing only two meals had put him into this weak and quivering state.

Alice, her color high, poured coffee for him. She did not sit down.

Siegfried finished one sandwich and then started in on the second one, letting the pleasant sound of Alice's bustling about the kitchen flow past him. The next time he lifted the coffee cup to his lips, his hands had stopped shaking. He finished the last bite and pushed his plate away with a contented sigh, astonishingly revived. He cleared his throat and steeled himself to tell her the unhappy news of his day. "I am sorry to have taken your truck without asking you."

"No, no, that's all right," Alice said, fidgeting with a fork in the sink. She refused to meet his eyes. "You don't have to account for every minute to me."

"I went because—

"You should know—" Alice bit her lip. She reached into the pocket of her apron, drew out a crumpled envelope. "This arrived in the mail today."

Siegfried took the proffered envelope and pulled out the letter.

My dear Mrs. Roye,

I regret to inform you that I am unable to testify to the quality of the wines produced by the Montclair vineyards as I am unfamiliar with your products.

When we do grant a license to produce wines used in the Holy Sacrifice, we require that they be produced under the direction of practical Catholics who have the proper reverence and appreciation for the holy purpose for which they are to be used.

Thank you for your inquiry, and God bless you.

Very sincerely yours,

† John Hanna

Archbishop of San Francisco

"...I suppose he felt that wine made by a woman wasn't appropriate for Mass. I'm sorry you won't have the chance to offer him your wine," she was saying in a low voice, very fast. "It looks like Wartime Prohibition will go into effect, so this harvest we can sell table grapes, grape juice, grape syrup, even raisins. But Hugh was right. We should pull out the vines after this harvest and plant plums."

Plums? Plums for prunes?

The last of the dishes landed in the sink with a muted clatter.

"Alice."

She kept her back to him. "You're a wonderful vintner. I would hate to see you waste your skills here on just plain farming. You should practice your art where it will be appreciated." A long pause. "But, of course, you're welcome to stay here until you find a new position."

A new what?

She was giving up? His mouth went dry. She had no use for him? After last night perhaps she did not, but he refused to believe this! If she annulled their marriage, he would lose Montclair. Where else could he go?

His intention to tell her about what had actually happened at Fountainview died. He couldn't allow her to give up on his dream! He stood abruptly, and the chair skittered away behind him. "I drove to Fountainview and made a deal with Mr. La Fontaine," he blurted, lying through his teeth. "He will buy wine from us, if we can meet his standards."

She had to believe him. Stretching the truth a little would save him. It wasn't *really* a lie. Mr. La Fontaine would love Montclair's wine when he tasted it.

"Of course, we cannot tell anyone until after crush, when we will know if the wine is good enough," Siegfried amended, hastily. He wasn't good at this kind of deception. She would know...

"This is wonderful news. How did you arrange it?"

He tried to swallow. "I-- I presumed upon *Opa* Roye's acquaintance with Mr. La Fontaine, and brought him some of our wine today. That is where I went." Frantically he tried to think of something else to say. He stepped close to her, saw that she was staring at the dirty dishes, her bottom lip white between her teeth. "I did this for you, Alice. Is this not what you wanted?" *Since you don't want me as a husband?* "This should make you happy."

She forced a smile. It faded. "Yes. Yes-- of course it does. I always wanted my wine to serve a higher purpose than the liquor trade. I'm... grateful that you took the trouble. It was kind of you."

"Trouble? Kind? Ah-lees," he said, confused, desperate. "I did this for Montclair." *I did this for us.* Her perfume tantalized him. Struck dumb, he leaned forward and kissed her. He was afraid she would flinch away, as she had done last night, but she kissed him back. She *did* like him, after all!

He drew her closer, burning for her, and put a possessive hand on her breast. *My wife!* When she stiffened in response, he brushed his thumb across her nipple, expecting her to sigh.

A moment later his leg exploded and he doubled over in agony, clutching his thigh. Her knee had narrowly missed his groin. Her ferocity had reawakened the pain beneath his scar, and the damage to his pride was worse.

"Oh, Siegfried, I'm so sorry! Are you okay?" Alice hovered anxiously. "Did I hurt you? I didn't mean to! I'm sorry! But you shouldn't have—"

"I...shall... be... fine," Siegfried gritted, every word a boulder rolled uphill.

"Can I help you?"

"*Bitte. Geh weg!*"

"I'm sorry?"

"Go. Away."

Alice, still apologizing, disappeared upstairs. Siegfried allowed himself one whimper as he found the chair and saved himself from falling down, holding his leg out straight before him. He should get up and assure Alice he was perfectly all right. Maybe he would do so, when he was able to walk again.

In about fifty years.

How could I do that? Alice asked herself, appalled at her extremely unladylike behavior. *How could I hurt him like that?*

Her mother's voice, matter-of-fact, answered her. *Because he was offering that sub-contract to pay you for—*

She clasped her hands over her ears, as if she could shut out the sound of her thoughts that way. "A bath. I need a bath," she muttered to herself, and went to her room to take off her clothes. She felt soiled and jittery and utterly unlike her normal restrained and careful self.

The hot water threw up clouds of steam and she breathed deeply, trying to quash her recriminations. *You shouldn't have hurt him.*

She most definitely should not be thinking about it— about Siegfried's— about the way he had touched her last night—

She dropped her robe and splashed into the water, hoping the heat would cure her shivering. She tried to concentrate on the little thunder of the water rushing from the faucet, and the hollow echoes in the big, deep tub, but the water was velvet, and lapped her in sensitive places.

Sitting up, she rubbed at her sore knee, which bore a red tender splotch, proof of her violent and essentially base nature. Her father would be so ashamed of her. She was her mother's daughter, though she tried to wash it away, tried to pretend otherwise. She *knew* Siegfried wanted her. She knew how he wanted her to repay him for getting the subcontract with La Fontaine.

At least, she sniffed, she had made a clear response. Hugging her shins, resting her cheek on her knee, letting the warmth of the water seep into her muscles, she wished she were not so smart.

That first moment of Siegfried's kiss had been so nice. She'd felt so safe, so cherished, so desired... She'd wanted him, too, before she realized what he was doing.

And now it was all so sordid.

She turned off the water and steeped.

After the worst of the spasms in his leg faded, Siegfried

limped down the hall from the dining room to the study. He poured himself a medicinal glass of port and settled down behind the large mahogany desk to contemplate his wreck of a life.

The port was soothing, lubricating his thoughts. He had bungled very badly with Alice, when it was most necessary to succeed. He did not want to leave Montclair! He caressed the old, polished wood of the desk possessively. A spark of heat in his groin reminded him he did not want to leave Alice, either.

He groaned and hung his head in his hands, calling himself all kinds of names for fool. He loved her, and he had done everything wrong. Let him only have another chance to win her!

He swallowed the last drops of the port, deciding what he would do.

In a moment he took paper and pen and began composing a letter to Charles La Fontaine. He got as far as the salutation, then rolled the fountain pen restlessly between his fingers. How to make a dignified request? If only he could have spoken to La Fontaine in person! His good news to Alice might be premature, but he was determined that it would not prove to be a falsehood.

Liar. And coward.

Siegfried could not even complain about Aramon's rudeness. He concentrated and forced out the first resistant sentence: *My late grandfather, William Roye of Montclair, often spoke of you. On numerous occasions he mentioned your respect for fine red wines. I have recently returned...*

It took him another half-hour of heroic wrestling with his rusty English grammar to complete the brief letter. He copied the text of his rough draft, with its many corrections and crossed-out lines, onto a clean sheet of paper, and then addressed and stamped an envelope.

He pushed back from the desk and poured another glass of port. This had to work. He had to make Alice understand that they could keep the winery going, that his skills as a vintner would not be wasted, that she really did want to keep him.

First, he would apologize to Alice for his ungentlemanly behavior. He had heard the water running in the pipes for her bath, and he wondered if she was finished yet.

Siegfried pictured her in the tub, her soft white skin beaded with water, her face flushed and moist, her copper hair curling wildly. At the now-familiar spark of arousal, he tried to stand. His thigh gave a complaining twinge.

He drank off the port in one swallow, and made his slow way up the stairs.

Her bedroom door was ajar. When his tap produced no answer, he pushed it open and stepped inside.

Alice's room was furnished with the same cherrywood furniture from his grandfather's day. Closest to Siegfried was the large bed with its massive scalloped headboard and plump goosedown pillows peeking out from under a crocheted lace bedspread. He longed to sleep here, next to Alice. The master of Montclair, with his lovely wife curled up next to him...

A wedding portrait in a simple silver frame stood on a lace doily on the night-table. Siegfried bent closer, recognizing Bill. The Alice in the photo was extremely young. Siegfried recognized her terrified expression.

How little he actually knew about his wife. A large carved armoire against the far wall, its door half-open, revealed a modest collection of dresses, skirts, and blouses. A dresser, mounted with a beveled mirror, stood next to the lace-curtained window, scattered items on its top: long, bead-tipped hatpins bristling from a pincushion; hairpins tumbled in a blue-and-white porcelain bowl; a silver-backed brush and comb framing a near-empty bottle of eau-de-cologne. There were postcards of Paris and London stuck in the oval frame of the mirror. With a stab of jealousy, Siegfried realized that Bill must have sent them to her from Europe.

Something glittered at the edge of his vision. Siegfried saw an open jewelry box and a huge dragonfly brooch sitting inside. He blinked— the gaudy pin seemed wildly at odds with Alice's style. Where had it come from?

"What are you doing here?" Alice asked sharply.

Siegfried spun around.

She wore a long robe and her hair was wrapped in a towel. The delicate scent of lemon soap drifted to him.

Siegfried drew himself up straight, clicked his heels together, and gave her a stiff, formal bow. "I took an inexcusable liberty earlier this evening, Alice, and I beg your forgiveness."

Her bare feet, small and white, peeked out from beneath the hem of her robe, unbearably erotic. Siegfried swallowed heavily and straightened.

Alice's expression was wary again. She held the neck of her robe protectively closed. "Thank you for your apology, Mr. Rodernwiller." She indicated her bedroom door with an austere nod. "Good night."

She was very angry with him. 'Mr. Rodernwiller,' indeed. "Good night." He dared not look at her again, standing so deliciously damp next to her bed. He hobbled into the hallway and heard her door shut firmly behind him.

Back in his own room, he undressed and crawled, frustrated, into bed. He fell asleep planning how he would make good on his rash promise, how he would redeem himself in her eyes. La Fontaine would love Siegfried's wine. How could he not?

Alice lay awake for a long time, pondering the abrupt reversals in her life in the last two days. She had failed to obtain a sacramental wine license, but Siegfried had gotten a subcontract to supply wine to La Fontaine, the licensee. She had seduced Siegfried for her own selfish ends, but he had nobly renounced the consummation of their marriage. She had rejected his sexual overtures tonight, but she still wanted him, his mouth on hers, his weight over her. She wanted to show him the things she knew, to bring him as much pleasure as he had given her. But then he would know just how unworthy she truly was...

She was acutely aware of Siegfried sleeping in the next room, no differently than any night since he'd arrived, except for one. And that night had apparently made no difference in their life together.

But it had.

She rested her forearm against her eyes. One night together. One night apart.

All her plans had come to nothing. She wondered if God was laughing at her.

Sleep brought a welcome end to her thoughts.

Alice pushed her cup forward as Maria refilled Peter's mug, then Siegfried's. She needed more coffee this morning. The kitchen was too bright, and too full of Siegfried. Maria winked at her as she poured, and Alice busied herself with buttering a piece of toast. The simple task seemed to take forever and she was clumsy, dropping the dull knife.

Siegfried snatched it from the floor and handed it to Alice without losing a beat in his debate with Peter. "Once the red wine comes out of the fermenting vats it *must* age in oak. And the old barrels— if they are not ruined already— will need reconditioning before I will let any wine touch them."

"There's thousands of them!" Peter protested, "Even with Herculio's crew, you're going to be outnumbered, and I can't spare any more men."

"If we do not have enough barrels, your workers' efforts will be wasted. We will have to sell grapes, not wine," Siegfried warned, lifting his coffee cup to his lips.

"With Wartime Prohibition starting next Tuesday, you

may have to, anyway," Maria said, picking up the remains of a platter of meatless Friday eggs from the table.

"No, we won't," Alice said with satisfaction. "We have a subcontract!"

Maria's congratulatory murmur was drowned by Siegfried's question: "And if we need more workers, we will have to hire them, is that not so, Alice?" He looked hopeful, overlapping his fingers as he warmed them on the fresh cup.

She said doubtfully, "If we can sell Mr. Roye's library wines to the Bohemian Club for at least four dollars a bottle—"

Maria clucked as she picked up empty plates. "*If* all the rest of the wineries weren't dumping their stocks, you might."

"And what do *you* know about it?" Peter jeered.

"I can read the paper." Maria nimbly sidestepped the hand he reached to pat her hip, and deposited the dishes in the sink.

"Little woman, you're a great cook, but don't—"

"She is correct," Siegfried interrupted him. He took a gulp of coffee. "In these conditions, if we negotiate well," he continued gloomily, "and if the Bohemian Club sommelier is the same man I remember, we might get two dollars a bottle."

Only two dollars for a premium vintage! Alice put her toast back on her plate, her appetite gone. She addressed Siegfried for the first time this morning, and it was just as difficult as she had expected. "Siegfried, may I speak to you, privately?"

He walked with her out of the dining room, slightly puzzled but polite enough to wait for an explanation. She ushered him into the office, closed the door, and faced him, trying to shut out all the memories of his hands, his mouth against her skin... She took refuge behind her desk. "We can't afford to spend any more money."

Siegfried scowled, unlover-like. "Why not?"

"I was going to use the profits from your wine for everything we needed, but if we can't get a high price for them—

Siegfried folded his arms. "This habit of economy is very tiring, Alice. One must spend money to make money, after all. You agreed to abide by my decisions. Are we now to battle over each penny?"

"I can't spend what I don't have."

Siegfried sat down cautiously on one arm of the wooden chair. "What about all the money Bill inherited from *Opa* Roye? *Opa* was a wealthy man."

"I didn't spend it, if that's what you're thinking!" Alice took a moment to master her voice. "I don't know what Bill did with the money he inherited. All I know is my dowry was embezzled from the First National Bank in Santa Rosa. Frank Brush and Will Grant got away with over three quarters of a million dollars before they were caught! When we found out, Bill tried to get the owners of the bank to pay us back, but they'd made as much restitution as they could. That's how Hugh got his start as a chicken rancher: old Mr. Brush deeded over some land he owned in Healdsburg. And when he couldn't get our money back, Bill went into the army."

Not trusting her voice to continue, Alice unlocked the book cabinet and pulled out the ledger detailing Montclair's finances. Opening it, she put it on the desk for him to read. Then she busied herself raising the window to let some cool morning air into the stuffy office. She stood there as Siegfried sat fully down and began to study the figures, muttering to himself in German.

Through the window she saw Peter and his men walking the rows, trimming every third cluster by Siegfried's command. At a sudden silence, she turned.

Siegfried's face was propped in his hands. "*Oma* Tati warned me that you had ruined Montclair." His voice was flat, dry.

Alice gave a faint huff. "We're not bankrupt yet. I've been doing this for years. We just have to keep on being careful, until harvest."

"Careful?" Siegfried slammed shut the ledger, and Alice jumped. "I cannot make good wine without decent equipment *and* barrels!"

"Might Mr. La Fontaine give us an advance on our vintage?" Alice spread her hands, then dropped them as Siegfried shook his head vehemently. "Well, but you—"

"No."

"All right, then," Alice fought to keep the irritation out of her tone. "Since you can't have everything you want, you must decide what's most important: new barrels or new machinery."

"We will try to save most of the existing barrels with our current crew," Siegfried said, without much enthusiasm. "But we need a new crusher, and bottler, and piping."

"We'll have to see how much we get for your wine."

"Is there no other source of funds?" Siegfried asked, closing the ledger with a snap.

Guiltily, Alice thought of the dragon-fly brooch. "I'll... see what I can do."

He was nodding to himself. "I will make a telephone call to the Grove, and arrange an appointment today. There is not much time left."

She placed the ledger back on its shelf. "Before you go out, let me know."

He looked up sharply. "I would not have taken your truck without your knowledge if you had been awake yesterday, Alice."

Waving her hand, she dismissed his unstated apology— and criticism. "I just want a ride to the train station." Siegfried frowned, and took a breath as if to start a question, but she forestalled him. "It's such a relief to have told you the truth about our finances. And I'm grateful— you've saved Montclair by getting us this contract with La Fontaine."

It was a successful distraction. Looking unexpectedly stricken, he swallowed, and lowered his gaze. "We must survive crush first." He shook himself. "There is a great deal to be done. We must be at it." He stood, bowed, and left the room. A moment later she heard him cranking the telephone in the hall.

She sat, planning what to wear for the journey to the pawnbroker. Her navy wool, with the high, plain collar, her leather gloves, and her coat— because no matter how hot it was in Sonoma, you could count on the chill in San Francisco.

Siegfried ran all the way down the hill to the mailbox to post his letter so Alice wouldn't see it.

CHAPTER
14

An army of barrels marched in ragged rows across every level square foot outside the winery, all the way up to the house. Siegfried and his crew had spent yesterday afternoon hauling hundreds of oak barrels from the tunnels, discarding those too badly warped to save, and setting aside the rest for testing. The ones that passed would receive a thorough scrubbing-out with soda ash.

This morning, Siegfried had converted Alice's truck into a makeshift water pump and was using an old canvas hose to fill the barrels with water from the reservoir. The soaking made the wood swell, and showed whether the staves were tight enough to store wine.

Alice hesitated before stepping off the porch. She was supposed to call them in for lunch, since the kitchen bell had been drowned out by the noise of the Model-T's engine. Reluctantly, she walked to the low fence. She waved at Herculio, who manned the hose where it attached to the pump. He mouthed, "Dinner?" and she nodded.

Siegfried, filling yet another barrel, caught sight of her, and the nozzle of the hose slipped from his hands. The hose writhed wildly, spraying water in all directions. Siegfried jumped away, but was instantly soaked head to foot. He pounced on the thrashing hose, yelling, "Snake! Snake!" and laughing so hard he almost dropped it again. The other men in the crew goggled at his antics, then began to share his mirth.

Herculio frantically killed the engine and the powerful flow of the water slackened to a trickle.

Siegfried grinned, water dripping from his hair. He ran his hand over his head and a spray of droplets flew out behind him. His thin shirt molded to his body. In this heat, he wasn't wearing an undershirt. Alice saw his nipples through the translucent cotton, and a bolt of desire sizzled along her nerves.

She wanted him in her bed, doing those dreadfully wicked, indulgent things to her... He made her want things that no respectable woman would tolerate.

"Dinner is served," she called weakly, then turned and escaped into the house.

Thursday, July 3

Alice came to supper after a long afternoon spent doing sums. She had been trying to figure if they might have enough extra to pay a mechanic to perform much-needed maintenance on the destemmer and pumps. She had scarcely spoken Siegfried this week, except at meals, and he was so exhausted by supper time that she sometimes caught him nodding off before dessert was served.

At least she didn't have preparations for the Fourth of July to contend with, too. In 1917, when Bill was first sent to Europe, she had worked with the wives of other Sonoma servicemen for weeks to create a float for the parade. She had been so proud and excited to drive them all around the Plaza, Bill's beautiful Buick draped in red, white and blue bunting, waving to everybody they knew. It was the first time she had truly felt accepted by her neighbors.

Because of Bill's death, she had not attended last year's parade and picnic. This year, both Siegfried and his past would make the public holiday too uncomfortable. She wondered if she could use the excuse of too much work not to attend.

"What do you mean, not attend the Fourth of July picnic?" Maria demanded when she mentioned this idea over supper.

"*Quatsch!* What foolishness!" Siegfried added.

"We're so busy, and—"

"Mrs. R., that's unpatriotic!" Maria protested, setting down a bowl of creamy whipped potatoes.

"And the crew wouldn't stand for it," Peter added. "Not after we won!" He looked at Siegfried, and then away.

"We all understood why it was so hard for you last year," Maria said sympathetically, "but things are different now."

"I know," said Alice miserably. Thanks to Gertie Breitenbach's not-so-subtle interrogation, Alice was sure her hasty marriage had been the subject of speculation in town. It was just a good thing nobody knew how Siegfried had spent the war. "I didn't mean that *you* all couldn't go."

"I'll pack a nice picnic basket," Maria encouraged. "And you need a bit of a rest. Just an afternoon. You don't want to miss the fireworks!" She returned to the kitchen.

Alice bit her lip.

"That is settled, then," Siegfried said. "Peter, remember when we were boys, and *Opa* Roye used to give us pennies to buy firecrackers?"

Peter nodded. Maria said from the kitchen doorway, "All little boys like them." A soft expression came over her face.

"Mario always clapped at the fireworks——"

Peter, busy pouring gravy over his mashed potatoes, knocked the ladle against his plate and slopped a large pool over the tablecloth.

"Oh, no!" Maria rushed over and began dabbing at the spill.

"Just stop it!" Peter snarled, batting aside her arm.

She leaped back and, on the verge of tears, met Alice's horrified gaze. In the next instant, she vanished into the kitchen, yanking the swinging door closed behind her.

"Sorry," Peter mumbled into the dead silence in the dining room.

Siegfried's stern look was spoiled by a smothered yawn.

"Excuse me," said Alice, sliding her chair back from the table. She found Maria gripping the edge of the sink, staring fixedly out the window. She wasn't crying, but as she stood there motionless, she let out the lungful of air she was holding and gasped for another breath.

Alice stood nervously next to her, wanting desperately to help, but unsure how. She didn't know if putting her arm around Maria's shoulders would be taken wrongly, so she kept her hands at her sides. "Maria, I'm sure Siegfried didn't mean to bring up bad memories..."

Maria ran water from the faucet, and splashed it across her forehead and cheeks. "I know Mr. R. didn't mean anything. That's not what——" Her voice wobbled on the edge of a sob, and she cleared her throat. She smoothed her hand down her apron. "I just *hate* it when Peter yells at me. He says I'm not supposed to speak about Mario anymore. But I forget. I keep wanting to talk about him." A single tear fell. "He was such a good boy, wasn't he, Mrs. R.?"

"He's with the angels now," Alice murmured. She ignored her doubtful scruples and gave her friend a hug.

"Peter says we'll have more children," Maria whispered after a while, "And I want to, I do, but... It's so hard."

"Maria! Where's the rest of dinner?" Peter bellowed.

Maria started and Alice hastily let her go. "I better—— they're hungry."

"Let me help," Alice commanded.

Maria handed her a bowl full of green beans. "Go on. I'll be all right," she said. "I'll just be another minute."

But she never came back into the dining room.

☙❧

The day was pure California summer: sunny and hot and dry. Alice, Siegfried, Peter, and Maria stood on the sidewalk in front of Duhring's closed Hardware and Grocery, watching the stately Fourth of July parade wend slowly around the streets that formed the perimeter of the Plaza.

Most of the parade entrants consisted of flag-decorated cars or horse-drawn wagons carrying local politicians and merchants, interspersed with groups of schoolchildren in various pasteboard costumes.

The Bundschus, who annually hosted Shakespeare plays in their own hillside theater, had put together the most elaborate float of the parade. A huge, papier-mâché Bacchus with a brass spittoon for an empty cup lolled under a vine-covered trellis built on the back of a flatbed truck. A large placard read: "Here Lies Another Victim of Prohibition."

The Bacchus was attended by four young women wearing wilted vine garlands in their flowing hair, draped in Greek robes made of black-dyed bed sheets. The Rhine Farm winery and vineyard crews, also draped in bed sheets and garlanded with grape and ivy tendrils, carrying long pine cone-tipped staves, marched in solemn formation around the truck as it crept slowly forward.

They were singing in ragged, mostly inaudible disharmony. Most of the stanzas seemed to end with a loud and mournful "Hey!" punctuated by the sound of dozens of stave ends hitting the street. Whenever this occurred— every ten or twelve paces— the maidens attending Bacchus would reach into ivy-draped baskets and scatter handfuls of paper confetti towards the bystanders. But most of the confetti did not make it quite that far, ending up on the street and in the hair of the sheet-clad bacchantes surrounding the float.

Alice forgot her troubles and smiled as the float passed. Some of the men were wearing brick-red union suits in misplaced modesty under their pseudo-Greek attire. At her right shoulder, Siegfried chuckled as he noticed the same thing. It surprised her, how good it made her feel to hear him laugh. Alice glanced up and saw that Siegfried was staring at her. His face held the same intense expression that she had seen several times since their night together. Hurriedly, she looked away.

When the parade ended, all the residents of the town and surrounding countryside converged on the grassy Plaza around the dollhouse-like City Hall. They settled down to eat their picnic luncheons in the dappled shade of dozens of young trees.

Children in pinafores and sailor suits ran wildly around the bunting-draped speaker's platform, shrieking and laughing as they pursued runaway balls and smaller children, completely ignoring their mothers' repeated admonitions to behave like Christians, not heathens.

After everyone ate, the sexes segregated themselves by some mysterious alchemy. The men, customary glasses of now-outlawed beer and wine in their hands, organized an impromptu game of horseshoes, and their women gathered to watch and cheer them on.

Alice and Maria shared a large, plaid wool blanket with several card-playing ladies from church. The main topic of conversation was not horseshoes, but the Freschi family, who had lost everything in a house fire the night before. Gertrude Breitenbach was organizing donations of household goods to tide over the family until their insurance money arrived. Pots and pans had already been pledged in abundance, so Alice volunteered towels and sheets.

While Betty Sullivan was offering some clothing, Alice's gaze drifted to Siegfried, taking his turn at the horseshoe toss. Mrs. Breitenbach, who was simultaneously winning at cards and declaiming the tribulations of Mrs. Freschi, nevertheless noticed Alice's straying attention. She interrupted her own story to comment: "He *does* look like poor Billy, doesn't he? It's quite remarkable."

Maria's cheese-and-tomato sandwiches turned into an indigestible lump in her stomach. Alice swallowed dryly, put aside her cards, and busied herself with a lemonade refill. "Um. I suppose so."

"I've noticed we haven't yet seen him at church. Is your husband still Catholic, dear?" Mrs. Breitenbach asked, her bright blue eyes intent.

"Yes, he is," Alice said, devoutly wishing herself elsewhere. She picked up her linen napkin and assiduously wiped imaginary crumbs from her already-clean fingers.

Mrs. Breitenbach continued, "And you've been married now, what— six weeks, dear? When are you two going to make it right in the eyes of God?"

Alice gritted her teeth and took a deep sip of her lemonade. Gertie was still waiting for her answer when she finished swallowing. "I— I don't know. Maybe after crush..." She twisted the napkin into a tight coil around her fingers.

"And how are you *feeling*, Mrs. Rodernwiller?" Betty Sullivan interjected. Her hand rested protectively on the slight curve of her belly under a pretty pink voile maternity dress, making her meaning clear.

"Perfectly well, thank you," Alice snapped. She continued in a more conciliatory tone: "We've been very busy preparing for harvest."

"If there's even going to *be* a harvest," Betty sighed dramatically. Her husband, who had helped change the Model-T's tire on the day of the disastrous Grape Grower's Association meeting, owned a small vineyard north of the Kunde estate. They did not make wine themselves, but sold Alicante Bouschet and Charbono grapes to those who did.

Alice had to bite her tongue to keep from sharing Siegfried's good news— but he had said they mustn't tell anyone.

"I'm all for keeping men out of saloons and away from whiskey. Keeps them from drinking up their wages while their wives and children go hungry at home," Maria said abruptly. "But it's not fair that the government's restricting wine as well as hard liquor. Which reminds me—" She stood up, but she must have done so too fast, for she turned deathly greenish-white, and swayed uncertainly.

Alice sprang up, concerned. "Are you all right?" She slipped her arm through Maria's to steady her. Gertie Breitenbach was on her other side.

"Oh— oh yes, I'm perfectly fine," Maria said, although she belied her words by clutching Alice tightly until blood came back into her cheeks. She loosened her grip with embarrassment.

"Do you need to lie down for a little while? Shall I drive you back to Montclair?"

"No! Don't trouble yourself," Maria protested. "I was just a little dizzy. I really want to register to vote." She pointed at a flag-draped booth on the other side of the horseshoe pit. A large, hand-lettered sign identified it as belonging to the National Women's Party. "You should come too, Mrs. R."

"I— ah—" Alice stammered.

Maria was standing more solidly now. Gertie let her go as well.

"Oh, didn't you register last year?" Mrs. Breitenbach seemed assured that Maria was all right now.

"I was too busy." Perhaps it was a feeble excuse, but she hadn't considered it with Bill's death coming so close on the heels of her twenty-first birthday last April. And this year, the weeks had passed in a hazy blur.

"Why don't we both register?" Maria tugged at Alice's arm. "It's so important. Maybe someday we can vote in federal elections, too," she said wistfully. Eight years ago, women had won suffrage in California, but for state elections only.

"I— I don't know if I should," Alice hesitated. In her experience, ladies left politics, like cigars, to the menfolk. As a girl, Alice's Da had spoken disparagingly about suffragettes making the newspapers when they marched and protested and even went on hunger strikes. And Tati had never even mentioned...

"And why not?" Mrs. Breitenbach's loud, imperious voice asked. "Aren't you patriotic, Mrs. Rodernwiller?"

"Of course I am," Alice said indignantly. "I—I just don't know if it's respectable!"

A chorus of replies overwhelmed her.

"Yes, of course it is!"

"I'm registered to vote!"

"I always go with my husband." Betty Sullivan coughed, then smiled slyly at Alice. "But I don't always vote the way he tells me to." Every woman laughed at that.

"Well, all right, then," Alice said, self-conscious. She turned back to Maria. "I didn't mean to imply that you weren't respectable."

Maria grinned, her first smile since Peter's sharp words the night before.

At the booth, Alice concentrated on keeping her handwriting neat as she filled out her registration form against the bumpy plank. Despite her best efforts, the letters looked crooked, her pencil no match for the grain of the wood under the paper. She was frowning down at the form when she heard a familiar voice.

"Hello, Mrs. Verdacchia, Alice!"

Startled, she looked up, to see Hugh Roye approaching, impeccably clad in a khaki suit and a tan pencil-curl fedora. His smile, as he drew nearer, was not like Bill's smile, confident of its charm, but more like Siegfried's: unexpectedly sweet and genuine. Alice caught herself making the dangerous comparison and firmly quashed her thoughts. "Hugh," she said, coolly, offering him her hand. *Why are you in Sonoma?*

"You're looking very lovely today," Hugh said, as he gave Alice a hearty peck on the cheek. He seemed to have completely forgotten his earlier rancor as he looked past Alice at Maria.

"Thank you," Alice said. She would have believed him if he hadn't also winked at Maria. "Too bad you didn't 'phone to tell us you were coming. I'm afraid we've eaten all Maria's luncheon."

"I would have packed some extra sandwiches for you," Maria said shyly.

Hugh's face lit up. "And how are *you*, Mrs. Verdacchia?"

"I'm very well, Mr. Roye," she said, offering her hand. "It's very nice to see you again."

"The pleasure is all mine. Too bad the Fourth falls on a Friday this year. Picnics just aren't the same without your wonderful fried chicken. I miss your excellent cooking."

"Oh, no," protested Maria, laughing.

"Did you come down all the way down from Santa Rosa for the celebration?" Alice asked, working hard at being polite. She was uncomfortable, especially as Hugh kept holding Maria's hand.

"Yes. I'm afraid I missed the parade, though," Hugh replied. He asked Maria, "Did you see it?"

Maria began to describe the Bundschu float, blushing rosily and laughing breathlessly. Her gaze never left Hugh's eyes.

Alice frowned. Hugh was acting like an infatuated schoolboy, with Maria, of all people! And Maria, instead of rebuking him with a stern glance and a firm step backwards, was smiling up at him, standing closer than was strictly proper, as if she couldn't help herself. Alice coughed discreetly, and Maria seemed to recall her manners. She retrieved her hand from Hugh's grasp, but Alice thought she did so involuntarily.

A quick glance behind showed Alice that Peter was just stepping up to the horseshoe pitch, oblivious to the scene taking place. Siegfried was in a clump of men sharing a newspaper article. She could hear their unhappy comments about the Prohibition situation from here.

Low-voiced efforts to move Maria away were disregarded. Oh, God, what should she do? Indecision kept her rooted, but all her senses were heightened in anticipation of disaster.

Rodern looked like this before the war. Busy. Lively. Undamaged. Siegfried gulped beer while Peter took his turn to play. The clang of tossed horseshoes striking metal stakes underscored the laughing shrieks of children.

On a day which celebrated independence, Siegfried rejoiced in being tied to this small community. After four years spent adrift on the bleak tides of war and loss, he stood once again in the familiar company of farmers, men such as he had known in Alsace, sharing their jokes and their concerns.

He took another sip of the pleasantly bitter beer, and wished fervently that Alice would consent to bind him closer. Even after wearing himself out day after day in the necessary work of refurbishing the winery, the slightest brush of her sleeve against his arm was enough to kindle the embers of his desire into flame.

But she kept him at arms' length, and no doubt would, until harvest and the fruition of his scheme to save Montclair. He hoped Mr. La Fontaine would respond to his letter soon.

His musings were interrupted by his companions. They were passing around a copy of Tuesday's *San Francisco Chronicle*, and Siegfried caught a glimpse of the headline: *SF Saloon Licenses Voided; Strong Liquor Doomed Today.*

"Damn' nonsense," growled Samuele Sebastiani, one of the richest men in town. He shook out the folds from the paper with a vicious flick before passing it on to Siegfried. "It will never work. Take away their beer and wine— people won't stand for it!"

"Well, then why did they all vote for it?" asked Frederick Duhring, sarcastically. He pushed back his hat, and wiped his brow with his red handkerchief.

"Wartime Prohibition? Haven't those blasted fools in the government heard? The war's been over for nearly eight months," drawled Mr. Sullivan. His comment was greeted by harsh laughter.

"Yeah, and not a moment too soon. Too damned many gold stars," commented Duhring, who caught Siegfried's puzzlement, and explained: "On our service flags. There's a silver star for every boy who volunteered for service Over There. Sonoma County's got one hundred seventeen in all. The fifty-seven gold stars commemorate the ones who made the Supreme Sacrifice." He doffed his hat, and held it for a moment over his heart.

"I see," Siegfried nodded. "It is good for a soldier to know that someone thinks of him."

"Your cousin Bill's gold star is on the flag hanging in St. Francis. You should look for it the next time you're there." Duhring turned to watch Sebastiani toss a horseshoe. His question, when it came, was elaborately casual. "So, you never did say: what did you do in the War, Mr. Rodernwiller?"

It was the question Siegfried had been dreading, and he could avoid it no longer. Well, out with it: "I served in the artillery, at the Front in Alsace-Lorraine."

"At the core of the conflict!" Mr. Sullivan enthused.

Peter's last horseshoe landed, and a puff of dirt hung in the air.

"For which side?" asked George Breitenbach, a round-faced, deeply tanned man in his forties . His usually genial expression was closed, waiting for Siegfried's answer.

Siegfried raised his head proudly, though his heart was thudding. He thought fleetingly of how much he had enjoyed the company of these men. But he would not lie to them. "If you ever met my father on his visits here to buy rootstock, you know what were his politics. He was pleased when the trench lines formed with his land in German hands, until the French invaders, calling themselves liberators, shelled our village, hit our house. They killed my young brother in his bed. I enlisted to fight, as my father wished, to avenge my brother, to protect our homeland." Siegfried's voice threatened to shake, so he took a breath to steady it. "I failed. My father and his Kaiser's cause are dead—and, as you might guess, I found no welcome home in Alsace."

Siegfried waited for an eternity, then there was a soft sound of feet shuffling, and someone's tongue clicked in sympathy or shame.

Peter, at the fringe of the crowd, said loudly, "Sig's a good fellow. It wasn't his fault that he was living Over There when everything happened."

Something in Siegfried's chest unknotted at this public display of loyalty. He had not expected the foreman to defend him. Peter had kept close to the kegs of beer this afternoon, downing mug after mug, avoiding the hordes of children.

Mr. Breitenbach's expression relaxed. He clapped Siegfried on the shoulder. "Too right, son. We all did what we had to do. At least you didn't shirk your duty."

"Better a Hun than a coward," someone said, and the tense moment broke in uneasy laughter.

Siegfried shook his head mutely, grateful beyond words for his unexpected reprieve.

"Thank God the War is over," said another. All around him, men were nodding in slow approval.

"And what are *your* politics, Mr. Rodernwiller?" Breitenbach asked.

Siegfried said firmly, "I will be an American, as was my mother, God rest her soul. I hope to follow in my grandfather Roye's footsteps, and fight only Phylloxera from now on."

More nods, and someone refilled Siegfried's mug of beer. He was left to stand, dazed, as the men moved on to the next topic of conversation: "Anyone see Marc Freschi? I thought for sure he'd be out here today, beating us all at horseshoes."

"Didn't you hear?" asked Mr. Breitenbach, who always got the news first from Gertie. "They had a house fire last night—lost everything. My wife is taking up donations of clothing and household goods from the ladies."

"Collect some money, too," Samuele Sebastiani suggested. "We all know the insurance never cover everything. I will give twenty dollars."

"Good idea. I'll pledge ten," Mr. Duhring volunteered.

As the pledges swelled into a chorus, Mr. Breitenbach pulled a fountain pen and a small notebook from his coat pocket and began recording names and amounts.

Siegfried made his way forward, eager to include his name in Mr. Breitenbach's notebook. Never mind that he had no money. He would find a way. It was the least he could do.

He had just opened his mouth to give Breitenbach his pledge when he heard Maria cry out: "Peter— no! Stop it!"

Siegfried whirled in the direction of her voice, and saw Peter in front of a red-white-and-blue booth nearby, swinging wildly at Hugh. Alice held tight to Maria, who covered her mouth as if to keep from crying out again.

As he ran, dodging picnic baskets and seated women, his leg aching with the sudden effort, he wondered at Hugh's presence. Reaching the booth, he caught hold of his cousin, dragging him away from the fight. Herculio, following close on Siegfried's heels, did the same to Peter.

"What are you doing here, Hugh? And why in God's name are you fighting in the street?" Siegfried demanded, pinioning his cousin's arms at his side.

Hugh's left eye was reddened and there was a thin trickle of blood drying on his upper lip. He tried to shrug Siegfried off. "I didn't start anything! I was just saying a friendly hello to Alice and Maria, er— Mrs. Verdacchia."

"Is that so?" Siegfried asked, skeptically. He judged that Hugh was not about to go charging back into the fray and loosened his grip.

"Yes, that's so," Hugh shot back, trying vainly to straighten his creased jacket. "That drunken fool attacked me."

"Liar! You bastard! You were accosting my wife!" Peter shouted from ten feet away, struggling to free himself from Herculio's grasp.

"That's not true," Maria protested.

Peter ignored her. "It was bad enough when Bill Roye was alive. Every Sunday— *every* Sunday— he came for dinner." He spat into the dirt toward Hugh. "I saw how he looked at her then! Now he's practic'lly kissing her in public! I'm going to kill 'im."

Herculio shook him. "Peter, stop. You're going regret this when you sober up."

Peter paid no more heed to Herculio than he had to

Maria. "I'll bet you thought I never noticed, but I did!" he glared at Hugh. "I noticed! She's my wife!" His voice rose to a shout again. "I won't let her disgrace me!"

"I would never do anything to dishonor Mrs. Verdacchia," Hugh said, his face flushing darkly.

"Then come away from here," Siegfried commanded.

Hugh shrugged off Siegfried's hand and started walking. He wiped vainly at the smears of blood on his face and accepted his crumpled fedora from a boy— evidently a boxing fan— who wished him better success in his next match.

"I think you may take it as given that Peter is no longer working for you," Siegfried said directly after Hugh had completed his adjustments. His words made an impact on Hugh, but his cousin merely smiled grimly.

They reached Hugh's elegant little car.

"And you should know better than to chase after married women," Siegfried warned him.

Hugh opened his car door.

"Have you nothing to say for yourself?"

"Not yet. And you won't like what I do have to say to you, when I get around to it. Just— enjoy Montclair while you can." The look Hugh gave Siegfried took him aback.

It was full of— not anger, or shame, or justified resentment, but pity.

Hugh got in his car and drove away, leaving Siegfried puzzled, and though he did not like to admit it to himself, worried. What would Hugh do next?

Alice, watching Hugh depart with Siegfried, was released from her horrified inertia when Maria began to cry in stifled, racking sobs. "I didn't— do anything— wrong!"

The helpless sound of it tore at Alice. She put her arms around Maria and drew her out of sight of the curious bystanders. In back of the voter registration booth, Maria wept against Alice's shoulder, her tears soaking warmly into the thin silk of Alice's dress. "What— am I going— to do?"

"What do you mean?"

Maria pushed herself away from Alice, and sniffled wetly, wiping angrily at her reddened eyes and cheeks. Alice reached into her purse and handed over a handkerchief.

"I feel like I'm suffocating!" Maria said in a tiny voice, as she accepted the handkerchief. "Peter is— he's being—" She blew and the handkerchief fluttered. She dabbed at her eyes. "I mean, I still love him. If he'd only let me— He used to be so different, before Mario—" Maria sighed resignedly and seemed to crumple into place. "Before Mario died he was a different person. Now, everyone is his enemy. He doesn't even trust *me* any more! I can see him watching me, wondering about me... And Mr. Roye— he's so kind. And so—, so—"

"Oh, Maria. I'm sorry," Alice said in shocked realization. "I knew you liked Hugh, but— there's nothing you *can* do. You're already married. I know you'd never do anything so improper!"

Maria straightened, and looked Alice in the eye. "It doesn't mean I haven't thought about it." She looked down again. "You're so lucky. Mr. R. loves you so much, and he's a good man." She pocketed the handkerchief. "I'll wash this with your regular things this week. I guess we should get back to the picnic now."

As they walked back around the booth, Alice reflected on how lucky she was. She hadn't had to make a choice between Bill and Siegfried. And she finally had the leisure to reflect on what she'd overheard by the horseshoe pit.

Alice shook her head, blinking in astonishment at the unpredictability of people. Not only was Maria showing a hidden side, but Siegfried had told the most influential men in the community about his wartime service— and they still accepted him!

She was happy for him, she really was.

But men had it so much easier in life all around. The community would never do any such thing for her, if they knew about her Barbary Coast background.

She bit her lip, and focused on helping Maria. Many hours remained until sunset, and the fireworks.

But she wished they could go home *now*.

It was Independence Day, after all. Maybe she just would.

Once Hugh was safely on the road back to Santa Rosa, and Peter had disappeared into the care of a cool wet cloth wielded by Herculio, Siegfried sought out Mr. Breitenbach.

He had been accepted today. It was only right that he should help an unfortunate neighbor. Siegfried found Breitenbach shaking out crumbs from a picnic blanket.

"Twenty dollars— you sure about that, son?" Breitenbach asked as he scribbled Siegfried's pledge in his notebook. It was, after all, a month's wages for a field worker.

"I am sure," Siegfried said quietly. "I will have the

money for you next week."

Then Siegfried saw Alice seated behind the wheel of her truck, waving at him to climb in. She was going already? Maria, wilted as her white frock, sat next to her. Clearly, Peter's whereabouts were his own concern.

Siegfried nodded his understanding and said his good-byes to Breitenbach. He loped over to the Model-T, clambered in, and braced his back against the cab. His thigh twinged at the position.

The truck lurched forward, gears grinding. Neat rows of houses went by, and he considered how to fulfill his pledge to Mr. Breitenbach. He knew that Alice would never sanction any such expenditure. Then he remembered the small metal biscuit tin shoved far back in the drawer of his night table. Stored in it were letters from his family and his father's signet ring, inside a bloodstained scrap of folded paper.

He had not re-read that note since the terrible day of his homecoming. He had not needed to. The words were burned into his memory.

The ring was the last remnant of his birthright. He would sell it on Monday morning and leave Alsace behind forever.

CHAPTER
15

"You did *what?*" Alice exclaimed furiously when Siegfried finished speaking. After going to check the morning's mail, he had found her in her garden, where she had retreated after lunch to wage a relentless battle against weeds, shovel in hand.

He looked abashed for a brief second, then gave her a grin— half proud and half sheepish— as he repeated his news. "When I sold my father's gold signet ring to help the Freschis, I had some money remaining. So I have bought nickel-plated fittings for the bottling system."

"After all the discussions we had? Siegfried, we could have used that money to pay the picking crews their bonuses during crush!" She had been slaving over her books for days, trying to find a way to squeeze a little more money out of the household budget. They had actually sold the wine for two dollars and fifty cents per bottle last week, the last day before the deadline, but it hadn't been enough. And the dragonfly had not brought as much as she expected, either.

Siegfried narrowed his dark blue eyes, and set his jaw mulishly. "I am your husband. If I use my money to—"

"You're not *really* my husband," Alice shot back, incensed. "And if you were, it wouldn't be *your* money any more, it would be *our* money. And it could have been spent better elsewhere!"

"I did what I thought best—"

"You stubborn, bullheaded German!" Alice snapped. All her frustrations came boiling out in a geyser of resentment. "You've ignored everything I've told you about Montclair's finances! All for a new toy!" She slammed the shovel into the dirt.

Siegfried, infuriatingly, ignored her outburst, too. He said mildly, "Mr. La Fontaine wants only the finest from us. That old equipment would have ruined our vintage." He waited in the strained silence for her agreement.

Alice gave a short, impatient huff. She couldn't argue against his expertise. But to buy such a system without even consulting her meant that he felt more confident about his position here. *I am your husband.* Well! "You know what the winery needs, but I've been running Montclair for the last three years. Tell me before you make a major purchase like this again!"

"I'll be in the winery. I hope you feel better later," he said, turning away.

She hacked into the ground with her shovel, imagining the hard dirt to be Siegfried's back. *How dare he patronize me! 'Hope you feel better later!' Hah!* She jabbed again at the base of a dandelion, which fell over and bled white droplets.

She had told him! He wasn't going to push her around! She had sounded...

Like a complete shrew. Alice stopped her assault on the weeds, and sagged over the shovel handle. *What was I thinking?* He had every right to spend his own money. He hadn't needed to buy anything for the winery at all. And she'd shouted at him like a fishwife! What must he think of her?

She scooped the decimated weeds into a pile, left the shovel leaning against the fence, and left the garden to wash up. She would talk to Siegfried when she saw him at dinner. She would apologize, and admit that they did need the bottling system.

She would eat crow, and be nice, because she needed him— at least until harvest.

Thursday, July 17

"Are you nearly ready with the next batch, Mrs. R.?" Maria called.

Alice came back to reality with a start. The air inside the kitchen was steamy with the tangy smell of cooking fruit, and it was oppressively hot. She had drifted into a pleasant memory of her weekend honeymoon at the Sutro Baths in San Francisco with Bill. All those pools of cool, refreshing water... The movements of her paring knife, steadily halving and pitting the near-endless supply of reddish-purple plums, slowed and stopped.

Late last week, the apricots had ripened. Now it was the plums, and the peaches would be next. Alice felt like she had been imprisoned in this unbearably hot kitchen for months, trapped in a purgatory of sticky fruit juice and endless regiments of Mason jars, their empty mouths opened wide in silent demand.

"Almost," Alice replied, asking herself, as she always did this time of the year, *How can eight trees produce so much?* When she finished with this basket of fruit, two more were waiting for her on the floor next to the kitchen table.

Maria stood at the stove, stirring the bubbling mixture. Jars, lids, and melted paraffin were at hand for the canning and sealing.

Alice reached for the next plum and let her small knife bite deep into the smooth skin. A swift flick of her wrist, and the fruit fell in two halves, revealing translucent yellow flesh. Alice removed the pit with the point of her knife and tossed it into the waste basket.

Last summer, every pit had been saved for the war effort, to be used in gas masks for the boys going to the Front.

Alice dabbed angrily at her eyes, thinking of Bill again, and wondering why she was shedding tears over him now, more than a year after his death.

"Are you feeling all right?" Maria asked. She finished filling and sealing another jar.

Alice blinked, annoyed that she had drifted off into reverie again. "I'm just tired, Maria. There's been *so* much to do this month." She sighed. The fruit needing to be canned. The vegetable garden. The barrels to recondition. The ledgers to balance and bills to pay.

"Well, I'm sure I can finish here if you want to go lie down," Maria offered, but she looked fatigued herself, with plum-colored circles under her eyes.

"No, I'll help you," Alice said stubbornly, despite the intense wave of longing at the thought of a nap.

"Well, if you're sure. But I don't want to see your name in the paper like Mrs. Johnson if you cut yourself!"

Alice laughed. "I won't." She found it endlessly amusing that the *Sonoma Index-Tribune* reported minor injuries, out-of-town visitors, vacation plans, and detailed accounts of weddings and even engagement parties, like Dorothy Breitenbach's.

She reached for the next plum with grim determination, and managed to finish the contents of the basket in front of her. But it was a struggle. The air had become a thick blurred syrup, and she could hardly keep moving. She yawned.

Maria shook a wooden cooking spoon at her. "Now, Mrs. R, you take a nap. That's an order!"

"I can't—" Alice interrupted herself with another yawn, and Maria gave her a wry look.

"All right," Alice said. "But just for an hour. I don't know what's wrong with me—"

Maria's mouth twitched.

Moving very slowly, Alice put down her knife, untied her apron and hung it from one of the pegs on the wall near the door.

As she walked out, Maria said in a strained voice, massaging the small of her back with her knuckles: "You take care of yourself, Mrs. R."

Alice forced her reluctant body to move slowly forward with the promise of cool sheets and soft mattress awaiting her upstairs. "There's just... so much... to do."

Almost three weeks later, Alice was still exhausted. She woke up tired before she could crawl out of bed. Even this morning's clear beauty couldn't inspire her as it usually did.

She dragged herself down to breakfast, late, and picked over the remnants. Siegfried and Peter were already hard at work, Maria's cheerfulness jarred, and nothing looked appetizing.

The single welcome prospect for the day was shopping. On the first Monday of each month, Alice opened her purse to buy necessities for Montclair. She never bought fripperies, but she let herself enjoy purchasing the things she needed to buy. And when they got paid for this year's harvest, she might be able to indulge in a new hat, and more of her favorite cologne.

Today the thought of driving into town seemed too much work. She felt leaden and wandered listlessly through the kitchen and pantry with her notebook, making a list of most-needed items.

"Boraxo soap," Maria said. "Shoelaces and bootblack. Sugar and flour. Butter!"

Alice felt herself flush, and was grateful that Maria hadn't noticed. She went on with her list.

Molasses, lard, pectin, and another bag of coffee. Siegfried drank so much of it! Alice wondered briefly if she should mention how expensive it was, but then she remembered how his face softened when he drank it. He finished each sip with such smacking enjoyment that it would be cruel to deprive him of it.

She plodded through the house, searching out other items. Toothpowder. Bluing for the laundry. Shaving soap for Siegfried— *not* the same brand as Bill's, thank goodness.

When she was finished with the household list, she forced herself outdoors to find Peter and ask him what he needed.

Today was blessedly cooler than it had been, the sky bright blue and cloudless. A freshening breeze blew in from the ocean, riffling the rows of vividly green vines.

It was too beautiful to have such trouble putting one foot in front of another. The dry dirt seemed to suck at her feet like sticky mud.

When she reached the border of the Pinot Noir section, she paused, panting, holding on to one of the rooting stakes. "You're not sick, Alice Mary! You can't afford to be sick!" But she felt so weary that, if there had been a place to lie down, she would have done it.

But there wasn't, so she trudged on after Peter and his crew. She stopped at the peak of the ridge, and surveyed her domain while she caught her breath and wiped sweat from her brow. To the southeast she could barely see the red and plaid shirts of Peter and his crew, dusting the vines blue with Bordeaux mixture.

The rising range of hills running northwest shifted as her vision blurred; each ridge now stood out sharp as etched glass. Her connection with her feet was as tenuous as dawn mist. A meadowlark gave voice to the glory of the morning, but she could barely hear it over the thunder in her ears.

"I can't be sick," she repeated to herself. "There's too much work to do."

She bent over, hoping that blood would rush to her head, and her heart would stop pounding.

It took another half hour to walk to Peter's dusting acre, and for nothing. He had all the supplies he needed.

She faced the long, wearisome walk back to the house with as much fortitude as she could muster.

It wasn't much.

Mrs. Duhring filled her order with supplies and gossip in equal measure.

Within ten minutes, Alice had learned that the Freschis were starting to rebuild their house and that Betty Sullivan's mother had come to visit. Walter Bundschu had just signed a contract to sell his entire crop of grapes to Inglenook over in the Napa Valley, and at a good price, too. His brother Carl, the winemaker and general manager at Inglenook, was telling everyone that he was going to write a letter of protest to President Wilson regarding Wartime Prohibition.

Alice nodded politely throughout the monologue, signed the account book when Mrs. Duhring had totaled up her purchases, and thanked Mr. Duhring as he loaded the truck for her.

"Don't mention it, Mrs. Rodernwiller," he said. "My wife says you're looking a mite peaked. Have to take good care of yourself, you know, being a newlywed and all. Thank you for your business!" He waved her on, and turned to his next customer.

She drove back to Montclair, seething at his implication. The nerve of some people!

But it wasn't until she was putting away the most embarrassing of necessities, the cheesecloth and cotton for her sanitary supplies, that she saw that last month's supply had not been touched. *Oh, no.*

She slammed the cabinet door shut.

"You're just sick," she told herself. "You've been working too hard."

It was past time to leave for Mass, and Maria still hadn't shown up. Alice walked over to the foreman's cottage to fetch her. Perhaps she, too, had overslept. They'd been canning something from the garden every single week for the past month and a half, along with all their regular chores. It was no wonder they were both exhausted.

But Peter, unshaven and haggard, answered the door with a curt explanation: "She's not feeling well."

Alice commiserated with him, and drove to Mass alone. Her friends there no longer asked when Siegfried would join them. They were too busy offering help to her and Maria, should there be a need. Alice was grateful for their generosity. She was feeling pretty low herself, and the Mass's lesson, "A man will surely reap whatever he sows. If he sows in the field of flesh, he will reap from it a harvest of corruption," lowered her spirits even more.

She'd missed another monthly, and she had the sensation of doors in her future closing against her. *So what if you can't claim an annulment?* She tried to jolly herself. *You might get Siegfried to do* that *to you again.*

She tried to quell a sinful anticipation, but her flesh was very weak.

When Alice returned, Siegfried was just finishing his breakfast. The smell of scorched bacon hung heavily in the air, and he felt a twinge of protective pity and embarrassment when she grimaced at it. She was so drawn and pale.

"Please, sit down." He rose to pull out a chair for her, fighting the impulse to take her in his arms.

She looked surprised, as she always did at his little courtesies. The faint scent of her eau-de-cologne tormented him, as did the memory of her soft hair and softer skin. His fingers curled around the back of her chair with helpless longing.

He swallowed heavily, and said, "I will pour you some coffee. I have cooked: would you care for bacon and eggs?"

Alice shuddered. "No thank you. Just coffee, please. And a little toast."

As he had hoped, the kitchen provided a refuge while he made toast and waited for his lust to subside. He filled a mug from the enamel coffeepot warming on the stove, then added a generous dash of cream as he knew she liked.

In the two months since their lovemaking, Alice had been unfailingly pleasant, but distant. She performed many small kindnesses for him without ever meeting his eyes, made polite conversation that touched on nothing personal, and let him know him in a hundred subtle ways how much he had gambled and lost that June night.

And yet, certain intimacies had been established. Alice always read aloud from the weekly paper when she returned from Mass. Siegfried suspected that she did this to fill the silence over breakfast without actually having to converse with him, but he had grown to treasure these quiet Sunday mornings alone with her.

Alice smiled and thanked him as he placed the mug and plate of toast in front of her. As he seated himself and handed her the pot of strawberry preserves, she asked, "Did you hear that Carl Bundschu wrote the President a letter?"

Siegfried raised an eyebrow in surprise. "No. Did he?"

"Everyone at church was talking about it this morning. Apparently it was printed in this week's paper." Alice took a sip of coffee and buttered her toast. "I'll read it to you, if you like."

"Please." Siegfried inclined his head gravely as she took a bite of her breakfast. A single crumb of toast clung to her upper lip, and he longed to lean forward and brush it away with his forefinger.

As if unnerved by his thought, Alice fumbled her toast, dropping it on the table. After scooping it quickly back onto her plate, she began to ruffle though the paper energetically. "Oh, here it is:

To the Honorable Woodrow Wilson, President of the United States

My dear Mr. President:

You must pardon me if I request a little of your valuable time, but this matter is of such great importance to thousands of people in this State that I must appeal to you personally for relief.

When the people of this State read your message to Congress, they approved of your recommendation to refuse Wine and beer from the War Prohibition measure and the vineyardists had good reason to believe that Congress would take action, so that this year's crop, which is now hanging on the vines would be saved and harvested.

Congress refused to act, and why? Politics is evidently more impirtant—

Alice broke off her reading to comment: "The linotypist must have been upset. This is the third error I've seen so far."

Siegfried motioned her to continue.

—important than the welfare of an industry which in this State represents an investment of over $150,000,000. 'Political Congress' has refused to accept your recommendation. Thousands of people who have their all invested in wine grapes—

"Like ourselves," Siegfried said. "Left to the mercy of this ludicrous legislation."

"Not quite, since you made that deal with Mr. La Fontaine." Alice smiled warmly, sending an acid shaft of guilt through Siegfried's stomach. He had not received an answer to his second and third letters to Mr. La Fontaine, either.

—which they planted under the encouragement and direct supervision of the United States Department of Agriculture, and are now facing ruin. Should any legitimate industry of the United States, no matter how small or large, suffer on account of political differences? Is that justice?

You, Mr. President, now that Congress has refused to accept your recommendation, are the only one that can help us and we appeal to you at this time when we see a total loss to our crops.

Would it not be possible for you to give the vineyardists, the winemaker, and the merchants who have invested their money in a legitimate business some idea as to when the 'ban' will be lifted? The bill plainly states the 'date of which is to be determined and proclaimed by the President of the United States.' We therefore feel we are entitled to know so that we can adjust affairs and not continue from day to day with an uncertainty which is breeding a dissatisfaction and discontent among the people that at one time were the most loyal and patriotic citizens of the United States.

I know I am voicing the sentiments of many of my fellowmen and trust that we might receive some information from you as to what we may expect.

I remain, Yours very sincerely,

C. E. Bundschu.

"That's quite a letter. I hope it does some good," Alice finished.

"I don't know if I would have been as polite," Siegfried said. "Politicians are worse than bankers."

"At least we have nothing to worry about," Alice gave

him an unexpected smile. "Thanks to your efforts."

"It is nothing," Siegfried mumbled, grabbing for his mug of coffee. He had lost the habit of prayer in the trenches, or he would have been on his knees, begging for a reply from La Fontaine.

After Alice finished washing dishes, she went behind the big house to the cottage that Peter and Maria shared.

Maria didn't answer when Alice knocked, so she hesitantly pushed open the front door, and went inside. The front room was much as Alice remembered it from infrequent visits. Family photographs stood on a small, round table covered with a fringed shawl and there were crocheted antimacassars over the backs of the sturdy armchairs. But there was a poignant absence: no toys lay scattered about the floor.

"Hello? Maria?" She heard a sound like a sob coming from the back of the house, but no one replied. Feeling like an intruder, Alice walked slowly down the short hall.

Through an open door she saw the bed was torn apart in the main bedroom, blankets heaped to one side. The horsehair mattress was badly stained with blood. Alice felt sick at the sight and hurried down the hallway toward the little kitchen.

Maria was bent over the deep sink, shaking with silent, wracking tears as she scrubbed weakly at a huge brownish blot on a sheet. She did not seem to notice Alice's arrival.

Alice dizzily realized what must have occurred. She had not known Maria was pregnant.

"Maria, should you be doing that?" she asked, pity softening her voice. "Here, let me—"

"It's all my fault," Maria whispered, pouring more powdered soap onto the ruined bedclothes. "Peter says I lost the baby because I work too hard. What am I supposed to do? We can't afford for me not to work."

"You could have said something— asked me—" Alice said, breathlessly.

"You work too hard, too. And where would Peter and I go if you lost Montclair?" Maria's face went chalky and she swayed.

"Come sit down," Alice ordered. She pulled up one of the wooden chairs and guided Maria's half-fall. "You should have left the washing-up till later. Do you need a doctor?"

"We can't afford one." Maria shook her head. "The last doctor cost Peter all our savings. No. I'll be fine. In a while." She wiped tears from the corners of her eyes.

Alice busied herself making tea.

"Mrs. R., you shouldn't be doing that," Maria protested feebly.

"Why not?"

"It's my job—"

Alice presented her with a cup of chamomile tea, and didn't move until Maria had taken it from her.

"You are officially on a paid vacation until you're feeling better," Alice pronounced.

"That's kind of you."

Alice wasn't sure whether she was really being kind, or just a bully. "You take as long as you need."

"I'll be fine. It usually only takes a day or two, and then I'm as good as new."

"Usually?" Alice gasped. "You mean this has happened before?"

Maria closed her eyes. "This is my third miscarriage since Mario was born. I don't know what's wrong. I pray and pray to the Blessed Virgin, but she doesn't listen."

"Oh, Maria," Alice said, sympathy brimming over. "Does Peter know about the other times?"

"One of them," Maria admitted. "I haven't wanted to get his hopes up." She pushed damp wisps of hair off her forehead.

Alice couldn't think of anything to say, so she only gripped Maria's hand in friendship.

"Peter wants a baby so badly." Maria's face crimsoned. "He exercises his marital rights all the time." She sighed. "But it's like he doesn't see *me* anymore. He just wants another son. When I was in high school, even right up until his father died, he had eyes for no one but me. Now I— I can hardly wait until he leaves me alone. Oh, Mrs. R. What's wrong with me?"

"I'll 'phone Dr. Stillman for a house call, and I'll pay for it."

"Mrs. R. You're so good. And— and when the doctor comes, you'll let him look at you, too, all right?"

"What do you mean?" Alice's heart thumped erratically.

"You've got to take care of yourself," Maria insisted, her voice scratchy. "You might lose your baby from overwork, too."

"But I'm not—" Alice began the automatic denial, but her strength to speak drained away. *I can't be pregnant!* But the evidence of her body witnessed a different truth. Even Maria knew.

She would have to tell Siegfried. If the doctor confirmed it.

"Mr. R. loves you," Maria said softly. "I've seen the way

he looks at you. He'll make you very happy."

"I hope so." *Because he's gotten everything he wanted.* It was just odd that the thought, which should have made her squirm and beat her fists with anger at the unfairness of the world, was a warm spot of contentment riding low in her belly.

She didn't need the doctor's word. She knew: she carried Siegfried's child.

Friday, August 22

Fillet of sole almondine. *New potatoes with parsley, green peas fresh from the garden, and a bottle of Sylvaner. Tati's formal china. The best silver trays...* Alice gathered her courage by planning her dinner, because it kept her from fretting about the outcome of her announcement at the end of the meal.

She and Maria cleaned silver companionably in Maria's kitchen. Bored after five days of enforced bed rest, Maria had insisted on helping as long as Alice carried the heavy tableware cases back and forth from the house. Maria chattered about inconsequentials, never mentioning the cause of her illness. The sound of her voice was a soothing background noise for the turmoil in Alice's mind.

Apple pie. Will I have time to bake one?

"There's one in my pantry," Maria said, responding to Alice's muttered note to herself. "I just couldn't stay in bed a moment longer yesterday, and Peter had brought home a sack of apples, so I baked two."

"I couldn't—"

"Don't be silly. You think you need to sweeten up Mr. R.?" She smiled sadly. "I think he won't even taste the pie, if you tell him your news before you serve it."

Alice blushed as her stomach twisted with nerves. "I hope you're right."

Siegfried sighed, sitting back in his chair and wiping his lips with his napkin. Although it had been a delicious meal and his stomach was happily full, he wondered what was wrong with Alice. She had been so skittish, scarcely eating more than a bite of anything, leaping up from her chair every two minutes to fetch something else from the kitchen.

The clink of cup against saucer roused him from his postprandial bliss. "Coffee in a minute!" she called from the kitchen. She appeared, placed the tray, and lit candles against the drawing dusk. The light gilded her skin and brought out flame highlights in her hair. She watched him warily as he took his first sip of her brew.

The coffee was hot, black, and strong— just the way he liked it.

A growing realization blossomed that he was being prepared for *something*. Puzzled, he put his elbows on the table. "Yes?"

Alice fidgeted with her napkin. "Siegfried, you know I always wanted an annulment. I didn't want... well, but we..." She trailed into silence, chewing her lower lip, and Siegfried began to worry in earnest. She still wanted an annulment? What had he done wrong lately?

"Ah-lees, please, what is it?"

She took a deep breath, obviously steadying herself. "We— we can't claim nothing ever happened between us. You're going to be a father."

"Das kann ja doch nicht sein!" Siegfried exclaimed, incredulously. *After only one time with her? What a miracle!* "You are certain?"

"You know Dr. Stillman came to see Maria." She bit her lip again, and he wanted to kiss her, to wipe that little pain away. "He examined me, too. It's definite."

He reached for Alice's hand, and found it cold. "You have made me the happiest of men, *Liebchen.*"

"I know," she said, dully. Her eyes shone with unshed tears.

A warning klaxon sounded at the back of his mind. *She never wanted you. Now you have to convince her that she has not made the biggest mistake of her life.* "Ah-lees," he said, deliberately keeping his voice low, so as not to frighten her. "Although *Oma* Tati may have pushed us together, my esteem for you has only grown deeper upon our further acquaintance. I know I am not worthy of your regard, but I will do everything in my power to make you as happy as you have made me."

He stood up, and drew her up with him. He put his arms around her and pulled her into a tender embrace.

She was going to be the mother of his child! Let him be a better father than his own had been. He would protect Alice and serve her all his days.

Tati would be ecstatic.

"Ah-lees," he murmured, kissing her forehead. *"Ich liebe Dich."*

He felt her tremulous smile, her lips pressed against his cheek. "What did you say?"

For a moment he almost withdrew the words, afraid that

she would disbelieve him. But it was too late for that. "I said 'I love you.'"

She melted into his arms with a shaky sigh and raised her face to his. "You're truly happy about the baby?"

He answered her with a deep kiss, and she responded—then grew heavier, a dead weight. He staggered, then carefully picked her up, peering anxiously into her face, which had gone bone white, and unconsciously tranquil.

She had fainted at his declaration.

As quietly as possible, he carried her upstairs and to her bed. He placed her on top of the coverlet, and held her hand, listening to her breathe. "*Mein Schatz, mein Liebchen, Du bist mein Herz, mein Leben.*" He knew she did not hear him, but it did not matter. *You are my treasure, my love, my heart, my life.* They were going to have a child together, and be a family. Siegfried thought his heart might break from the joy of the gifts he had been given.

They were truly married. There would be no annulment.

Montclair was his, forever.

CHAPTER
16

Montclair
Friday, August 22

Alice opened her eyes. Siegfried, wrapped in Bill's old, richly colored dressing gown, was hanging up his suit inside the vacant half of the closet.

Unconsciousness seeped away like wine out of a leaky bottle, leaving her cold. *Idiot! Why can't you think anything through ahead of time?* "What are you doing?" she asked stupidly, although she knew. Siegfried was moving into her room.

"I am your husband." He straightened the coat upon its hangar, and bent to align the too-polished dress shoes with military accuracy.

"We never discussed...sleeping arrangements," she countered, striving for at least as much politeness as Siegfried displayed. *But I've been thinking about it,* her mother's voice purred. *Mmmmm.* Abruptly, Alice sat up straight.

"I did not expect that we would need to." Siegfried nodded, but he did *not* nod, and smile, and say, *Of course, since you are so against it, I will go away, right now.* He merely set his battered hairbrush and comb next to her own silver set upon the dresser.

Alice shivered and clutched her elbows. She was on top of the spread, fully dressed. He must have carried her to her room. How could she have slept through that? "You can't—"

"I *can!*" he blazed, his eyes fixing hers. "You have told me that you bear my child. Very well. We are husband and wife. We shall sleep together."

She marveled at this flare of Teutonic stubbornness and his instantaneous repudiation of what he *expected* her to say. What a real lady would say. Knowing herself a complete fraud she spoke the line: "But *sleeping* is all—"

"No!"

Now she was shocked. Siegfried had never raised his voice to her in anger before.

Carefully he collected himself. "Saint Paul himself— an authority, you will agree?— said, 'It is better to marry than to burn.' For you, Ah-lees— I *burn.*"

She believed him. She felt the heat from his body across the room and she recognized the matching flame within herself.

Her heartbeat stuttered and a tremor, deep inside, shook her. She had to say something, anything to deflect his intention, or she would be lost forever, living her mother's life in Siegfried's bed.

"That's a sin!" she declared desperately. "We haven't been married by a priest!"

He took a step closer. "I do not care what some pious old men— who are not married, and have sworn they never will be— call a sin!"

"Siegfried! That's—" she faltered. That was an ineffective argument, then. "But I'm— I'm in a delicate condition—"

Another step, and she could tell that he had bathed. His skin had an allure like the ripest of peaches, downy softness wrapped tightly around firm flesh, promising a sweetness that would cure all her hunger and thirst.

Siegfried tempted her. "Ah-lees," he breathed. "I have seen you working. If you have the strength to weed the garden, can the fruits, beat the rugs, you cannot call yourself 'delicate.'" Slowly, slowly, his hand came close to her face, and gently his fingers traced the line of her jaw. "Please do not deny me."

She trembled again. She knew what she ought to do: say yes, endure, and remain unmoved. All the years outside her mother's house had taught her that.

But she knew she couldn't do it. She was on fire where Siegfried touched her, as he brought his mouth down along the line of her neck, across her collarbone, trailing kisses along the top of her breast, breathing hot upon her nipple.... She wanted him, too, despite the fact that he had won everything: respect as a vintner, Montclair, and even herself. If he touched her again, she would beg for more.

She had tried so hard to become a lady. Tried, and failed.

She only had strength for one last effort to keep him from shattering her defenses. She would pretend, just as she had always done.

"Of course," she said coldly, her voice dripping with simulated disdain. "It would be most improper of me to deny you your marital rights."

Siegfried recoiled, standing with his back to Alice, his passion drenched by her icy response.

Once was more than enough, to touch her, and cause a flinching gasp, as if his flesh burned her. He had not meant to hurt her!

He clenched his teeth against uttering an apology. He was

her husband, for the love of God! He had a right to enjoy her body. He wanted to hold his wife, to love her and hear her cry out in her ultimate pleasure.

"...most improper..." Her words rang in his ears. "...deny you your marital rights..." Where had this cold unfeeling woman come from? Where was his adorable, ardent Alice? *We haven't been married by a priest!*

He felt like slapping his thick-skulled forehead. Of course she was unhappy. She had married him before a judge. They had not been sanctified in their union. She was devout, as he had once been, before the War had devoured his piety.

She would feel better once they were truly married under heaven. He would ask her in the morning. A brief fantasy of Alice, sweetly smiling, raising her face for his kisses, was interrupted by a very real, anxious question.

"S-Siegfried?"

He turned back to her. She looked so woebegone, frightened and defiant and *lonely,* that his heart went out to her. "No, Ah-lees, you are right. I have no wish to impose myself on you if you are not willing."

Something flared in her eyes before she veiled them, lowering her lashes in a parody of submission.

"But I am sleeping in this room!"

She sniffed, as if she did not care, stood up, and brushed past him to gather her nightclothes and disappear into the bathroom.

While she was gone he finished settling his few things in amongst hers, filled with a delight that threatened to curl up the corners of his mouth. He felt like shouting in triumph, laughing out loud, dancing all night long. It was almost as good as making love to her would have been.

He replayed the memory, and another grin was born. That flash in her eyes had been *disappointment.*

He climbed into bed, happily anticipating his next move.

He would *beg* her, in the morning.

And she would say yes.

Siegfried rose early to bathe, shave, and dress himself in Opa Roye's old suit. As he came down to the kitchen, Maria's eyes widened. "Morning, Mr. R."

Peter was hunched over the table, gulping down a forkful of hashed brown potatoes. He chewed furiously, and swallowed. "What are you all dressed up for?"

Alice, in the act of pouring herself a glass of water,

turned and saw him. One eyebrow quirked before she smoothed away her expression. "Church?"

But he had seen that spark of her true nature, before she hid it. "Indeed. It is past time that I came with you, Alice," he said, bowing slightly.

"Well past," she agreed dryly.

Siegfried looked longingly at the big breakfast Maria had made for Peter. Fasting in penance before Mass was harder now, since he had known real hunger. But he would do it for Alice. "Shall we go?"

Maria nodded as she hastily untied her apron, and settled a wide-brimmed straw hat on her head.

"Are you sure you feel well enough to go with us?" Alice asked her with concern.

"I'm fine now," Maria assured her, putting a hatpin through the back of her hat to secure it. "Really, I am."

As they went out on the porch, Peter's voice rang from the kitchen. "Pray for a son, Maria *mia*. Remember— tell God that He doesn't see me again until we have another son."

St. Francis de Solano church hadn't changed since his grandfather's funeral. It had overflowed then with *Opa* Roye's friends and colleagues. Tati had been so very brave, tiny and frail in black silk, refusing to lean on Bill's arm.

Siegfried held Alice's hand as he followed her to her accustomed pew, and only relinquished her when she genuflected before seating herself. He bent his own knee to the Presence on the altar, then joined his wife, pointedly oblivious to the stares directed at him. His neighbors deserved to enjoy their astonishment at seeing him.

Alice knelt, moving her lips in prayer. Maria, sliding in on the other side, knelt too, her hat brim brushing Siegfried's sleeve as she bowed her head.

Siegfried sat stiffly. The wooden seat was hard, and his old injury ached more than it had in weeks. He scowled, remembering his denial when the shrapnel tore through flesh and bone. There had been no pain at first, only horror. *I am dead.* He had not called on God then, either for mercy or for help. He had known too many comrades whose prayers had gone unanswered. Only Siegfried's own vigilance and determination had preserved his limb from the saws of the army doctors.

The congregation rustled, then stood, as the young priest appeared, flanked by altar boys.

Siegfried went through the old familiar motions,

standing, sitting, kneeling, responding to the Latin prayers, conscious that he was not alone. Alice was with him. And their child.

He did not pray. He only hoped his plan would work.

Alice was annoyed when Siegfried towed her out of the pew the moment Mass was over. Unable to discreetly disengage herself from his grip, she stood on the porch outside the church. The sun reflected blindingly off the whitewashed stucco, and sparrows chittered in the arbor lining the eastern side of the building.

He had been sleeping when she finally went to bed last night, a small, secret smile softening his face. She didn't trust him at all. What mischief was he up to?

Young Father Byrne, who had replaced the mortally ill Father Moran, took up his position at the foot of the steps, awaiting the exodus of the congregation. He caught sight of them, and nodded, smiling.

Siegfried went directly to him and shook his hand. "Reverend Father, I am Siegfried Rodernwiller. You may know that Alice and I were married in a civil ceremony—"

The first few people trickled out through the double doors, blinking against the bright daylight.

"...my grandparents were active in this county for many years, and my mother's fondest memories were of Montclair. I came here, seeking a new home..."

Oh goodness, more people were outside the church now, and all of them were listening, fascinated, as Siegfried spun out his story. Alice had an inkling now of what Siegfried planned to do, and knew he was waiting for the maximum audience. She could not free her arm from his grip. He looked at her, briefly, his eyes pleading.

"I hope you will be my witness here..."

Alice felt a tide of heat wash upward from her heart as Siegfried went down on one knee before her with the whole congregation watching.

"My dearest Alice, please do me the very great honor of solemnizing our marriage in this church, as soon as may be possible."

"You know I can't refuse." Her voice was a little louder than she had intended, but she was strangely pleased. He didn't *have* to do this. He'd already won Montclair.

The young priest beamed and patted their joined hands. "What a wonderful plan. We can post the banns next Saturday! I *love* weddings."

Alice was startled as a ragged cheer rose from the crowd on the steps.

"Well, I'm glad they're doing the right thing," Gertrude Breitenbach commented.

"She'll be such a beautiful bride!" Adele Livernash sighed.

"They're getting married during *crush*?" a masculine voice asked in disbelief.

Alice met Siegfried's eyes and saw joy there, mixed with a healthy dose of awareness of how foolish he must appear, kneeling at her feet.

He had done it again: made his decision and left her no option but agreement. She wanted to hate him for his high-handedness, but she couldn't, not when he grinned at her like that, boyish and so pleased to have given her an unexpected gift.

As Siegfried brought her hand to his lips and brushed her knuckles lightly with a kiss, she smiled back tremulously.

Maybe he did love her at least as much as Montclair.

It took all Alice's courage to prepare for bed that night. She spent an hour in the bathroom, brushing out her hair, trying not to remember Siegfried's glances during supper. The pleasant shock each one had caused her. The way he had looked at her.

She recognized lust when she saw it, but Siegfried's attitude had been more like... worship. It left her feeling vulnerable, and very unworthy. He plainly wanted her, and yet seemed to feel as if she were something he dared not aspire to. As if she were too good, too pure for him. What a joke that was!

And it terrified Alice, how much she wanted him too. Wanted to feel his weight over her, his mouth everywhere. She wanted to show him all the things she knew about, to bring him as much pleasure as he had given her. Even if he discovered how unworthy she truly was.

She was leaning sleepily on the door, too tired to move, not yet ready to face going to bed, when the wood under her ear gave out a series of explosions. No. It was Siegfried, knocking firmly.

"Ah-lees! Are you all right?"

"Yes. 'M fine."

"Come to bed, then." He sounded patiently amused, as if he understood very well exactly what she was doing. "I will not eat you."

She answered him with frosty silence.

"Unless you wish it," Siegfried coaxed.

She threw open the door. "How dare—!"

He grinned at her, then put on his serious face. "Ah-lees, you are exhausted. You must come to bed. You know I will do nothing to you that you do not like."

She was just tired enough to let slip the truth. "That's what I'm afraid of."

His grin reappeared, and he took her hand, gently leading her to the bedroom. Their room. She wobbled and he put one arm around her waist to steady her, bringing hip and thigh into close contact. Every place he touched her tingled and she wanted him to kiss her. No. She wanted to kiss him, but she couldn't risk it because... because...

He had pulled back the covers for her, and he helped her sit down on the bed. Tenderly, he lifted her feet, then drew up the sheet. It was pleasantly cool tonight, but that wasn't why she shivered.

He turned off the lamp. Soft moonlight washed through the curtains. He took off Bill's robe, laid it carefully over a chair, and got into the other side of the bed. The springs groaned and then adjusted.

She knew he had worn nothing under the robe. She knew what he looked like, moonlit in silver. The image tormented her.

"Good night, Ah-lees," he whispered.

She tried to hold herself very still, but her hand moved of its own volition. She reached over and found his arm, softly furred, muscles at rest, his skin cool. She ran her fingers lightly down his arm, electricity leaping up from his skin to hers everywhere she touched. She wanted to touch him everywhere. Across the breadth of his collarbone, down his chest to the small, smooth nipple, back along the midline of his body to his flat belly, finally encountering what she sought.

Siegfried groaned. "Ah-lees, I am not made of stone!"

"No, but you're certainly hard," she whispered, glad that the darkness hid her smile. "I want you." She squeezed lightly, luxuriating in his exquisite resilience.

"I had hoped you would say that!" he gasped.

"I know," she said, just before she closed the gap between them and kissed him, forestalling any other speech.

And in the bliss that followed, she forgot all her reservations.

In the foggy morning, Alice awoke worn out and disgusted with herself for feeling so... satisfied. She only had three weeks to prepare for her church wedding.

After breakfast, while Maria cleaned up, she sat down at her desk with paper and pencil, and listed all the tasks she had to do. She filled two sheets of paper, then stopped, defeated. It was more than humanly possible.

She would not cry. She would *not*. This pregnancy of hers had already brought too many easy tears. She had to keep a clear head now, and *think*. What were the most important things to complete? Alice pulled out a fresh sheet of paper.

If they had to marry again, she would have preferred a private wedding, but Siegfried had already invited the whole church. Where would she find the money for invitations, the reception, the fees for the priest and the organist?

By the time she finished calculating the cost of the reception, she was in despair again. There went her hope of solvency at the end of this year.

Setting her teeth, she bent to her task again. *Flowers for the ceremony: Montclair's garden.* After a pause, she noted: *'phone Tati— and Hugh.*

Alice sighed. She missed Hugh's friendship. He had been such a support to her after Bill's death.

More notes: *Food. Cooking. Transport the food. Bridesmaid and best man: check with S. if Maria and Peter can serve. Wedding dress?*

Alice put her well-chewed pencil down, feeling slightly heartened. She still had her first wedding dress. Relieved to escape her depressing list of uncompleted tasks for a little while, she left the office and went upstairs.

The dress came out of the linen closet with the rustle of silk and the pungent scent of camphor and cedar. The heavy messaline skirt slid through her fingers and pooled like cream on the carpet until she spread it across the bed. The bodice was relatively simple, a fichu-like wrapping of one swathe of fabric over another, finished with a five-fold silken girdle. But there were layers upon layers of lining, interlining, silk, lace, beaded braid and trim applied to the skirt and sleeves until the whole thing was as beautifully decorated as a wedding cake.

She pulled her middy over her head and unfastened the waist of her skirt so she could try on the dress. It had been over four years since her marriage to Bill, but she remembered how excited she had been to wear it.

The skirt stuck a bit, going over her hips, but it wasn't until she tried to fasten the tiny button at the waist that Alice realized how impossible everything had become.

A two-inch gap remained no matter how tightly she

sucked in her stomach. And no corset could correct that, even if she had been willing to wear one in her condition.

She tugged the skirt back off and slumped onto the bed. She was numbly counting the number of seams which would have to be picked out and re-sewn to successfully alter the dress when Maria knocked apologetically on the door frame.

"It's dinner time, Mrs. R. When you didn't come down—" Maria stopped, and her kind face filled with concern. "What's the matter?"

Alice thrust the offending garment at Maria. "Oh Maria, it doesn't *fit*!"

Maria took the dress and examined it. "It seems all right to me, Mrs. R. Oh, no. Don't cry!" Maria sat down next to Alice and patted her shoulder.

Alice folded in half, burying her face in her hands. "I don't have time to alter it! I already have too much to do! And I c-can't afford to buy a new one!"

Maria stroked Alice's back. "It'll be all right, Mrs. R. You'll see."

"Bu—but who will help me?"

"I will," Maria vowed. "And I bet, if we let Gertie Breitenbach know, she'll come up with something. You don't need to do everything by yourself. You have friends. You're not alone."

Friday, September 19

On the afternoon of the day before her third wedding, Alice stood by the lace-curtained window in her bedroom, watching Siegfried and Peter load disassembled trestle tables and benches into her Model-T so that they could transport them to the reception hall.

Preparations for harvest and crush and the wedding had continued at a frantic pace. True to Maria's prediction, the congregation of St. Francis pitched in. Betty Sullivan volunteered to decorate the church. Several parishioners who played accordion and fiddle offered to provide music for dancing. The Kundes and Bundschus each pledged a keg of beer and a case of wine.

She found herself watching the movement of Siegfried's broad shoulders, and wondered if she would ever be able to follow the rules of respectable conduct between man and wife.

She turned away from the window and opened the bottom drawer of her dresser, retrieving a stack of dog-eared advice columns clipped from women's magazines and pamphlets.

She had been collecting them for years, trying to make up for the lack in her own upbringing. Glancing over them now, she realized how far short she fell of the mark.

She sat down on her bed, placed the packet of papers on her lap and untied the ribbon that bound them. Then she leafed through the sheets, seeking an answer for her present dilemma. There was a battered copy of the *Ladies' Home Journal* near the bottom of the stack. Alice opened it, and the magazine fell open to an article entitled "A Girl's Preparation for Marriage."

In it, Mrs. Preston offered advice to a young girl who had dared let a man hold her hand before they were properly engaged:

...this sort of familiarity... acts directly and subtly on the nerves of the body, renders them morbidly sensitive, rouses the emotions and passions which it is physically harmful to have roused and played upon... it wakens and stimulates feelings and instincts and desires that should not be wakened...

How true! Alice chewed on her lower lip. She had already allowed Siegfried to waken those inappropriate passions within her. Now they smoldered, like embers under cool gray ash, needing only his touch to flare.

She put aside the *Ladies' Home Journal*, and selected a yellowed pamphlet written by a minister's wife about the danger that lust posed to proper marital relations.

Alice shivered as she read. Rather than finding Siegfried's attentions revolting, they engendered in her the basest sort of excitement and arousal. Oh, yes, she was definitely treading dangerous waters with him.

Through the window, she heard the Model-T's engine cough to life, and slowly drive away. She did not hear Siegfried enter the bedroom.

"Alice?"

She jumped involuntarily, dropped the pamphlet, half-rose, then clutched frantically at the papers cascading from her lap.

Siegfried chuckled and knelt to gather up the papers that had eluded her grasp. "I did not mean to startle you." He settled himself down next to her, and put an arm around her. "What are you reading, *schätzchen*?"

He brushed a wisp of hair tenderly off her forehead, tracing the outline of her ear with his finger. Alice shivered pleasurably as he leaned closer and she felt his warm breath on her neck.

"Just some instructions," she replied, fighting to keep her voice calm as he began kissing her cheek, his lips traveling down to the side of her throat, sending delicious tingles to the place between her legs. "On being a good wife." She gasped as his teeth closed gently around her earlobe. "Siegfried, please! It's the middle of the afternoon!"

He sighed, and pulled away. "I find you a perfectly good wife," he protested, snatching up the pamphlet from her lap. He read a few lines, a frown deepening between his fair eyebrows. "*Nichts als Quatsch!*"

"I beg your pardon?"

His lips moved as he read. At her question, he glanced up. "What utter nonsense!" He tossed the pamphlet to the floor with a contemptuous flick of his wrist.

"It's *not* nonsense, it's how respectable women behave! And I wish you wouldn't make fun of it!"

"Perhaps I don't want a respectable wife," Siegfried suggested. "I like you very much just the way you are." His arm tightened around her and then he was kissing her. Alice's world narrowed down to the warm pressure of his lips against hers. Siegfried's other hand briefly cupped her cheek, then stroked lightly downward to her breast, where her nipple contracted almost painfully, seeking the heat of his palm through thin layers of cotton and silk.

Siegfried's kiss deepened at her gasp, and he began rubbing his hand over her breast in light, sensual circles. Alice's breathing became ragged, and she arched against his hand, allowing the thrust of his tongue into her mouth, wanting more, *more....*

Dazed, she let him push her back onto the bed, welcoming the abandoned thrill she felt as he continued to caress her. Then he captured her hand and placed it against the front of his trousers. "Perhaps I want my wife to be a little wicked with me in our marriage bed," Siegfried said, lifting his mouth from hers momentarily, his voice uneven.

She loved the feel of his arousal, knowing she had the power to satisfy him. She touched him gently, searching out his buttons, and remembered suddenly a conversation she'd had, shortly before her father had whisked her away from her mother's house.

The girl had called herself Katie and hadn't been much older than Alice in age. But in worldly terms, she'd been far Alice's senior. New to her chosen profession, Katie was cheerful about it, and very grateful to have found a place in Florence's upscale business, catering to gentlemen. She had befriended Alice on the sly, and had been a fount of extremely interesting information. In particular, Alice recalled an amazingly instructive session with a Coke bottle which had simultaneously appalled and fascinated her. All these years, and she still wondered if Katie had been pulling her leg. Maybe she'd find out.

Siegfried's grin widened as she slid off the bed and onto her knees in front of him. "I can be *very* wicked, Siegfried. Just for you..."

As she finished unbuttoning his trousers, she felt his fingers fumbling at the pins in her chignon. Her hair tumbled down and spilled across his thighs like a copper curtain, giving her the privacy to be bold in the bright light of day.

"*Das fängt ja gut an!*" Siegfried exclaimed, quivering as her mouth touched him. He pulled her head closer.

Alice kissed him intimately, making him groan, and his fingers threaded through her hair.

"Don't stop," he begged, the last English phrase he was capable of for quite some time.

She discovered what she had known all along: she was very good at being wicked.

It was time to leave.

Alice tried futilely to tuck the last wisp of hair into her chignon, but it wouldn't go. The spray of flowers was too tightly pinned, and there wasn't room to maneuver her fingers.

Outside, Peter hit the Model T's horn again.

Maria, wearing her best beaded blue dress, bustled through the hallway. "Mrs. R.! You look just beautiful. Now come on!" She dragged Alice bodily out the front door. "It's one thing to be late for your own wedding as the bride, but we've got to get the whole wedding party to the church in your truck! Hurry!"

Maria handed her up into the passenger side of the Ford. Peter scowled impartially at them both. "About time! Hurry up, Maria!"

Maria scrambled into the back of the truck, where Siegfried sat, very correctly upright, in a new suit, courtesy of Tati. He had covered the truck bed with a clean blanket, so their clothes would be protected. Placed carefully next to him was the bouquet of white roses he had cut early this morning.

As Peter bounced them down the hill toward town, Alice nervously smoothed the loosely cut, high-waisted wedding gown loaned to her by Gertrude's daughter Dorothy, now Dorothy Murdoch.

She felt like such an impostor, because she wasn't the virtuous woman her neighbors thought her. She remembered the sinfully delightful things she had done with Siegfried, and how good it had made her feel when he shouted her name. Even now, on her way to church, she ached for him.

Peter pulled up in front of St. Francis and Siegfried hopped out, wincing a little as he landed on his bad leg. He helped Maria down, then opened the door for Alice. She was so lovely today, all chiffon and lace and white roses. Her face was nearly as pale as her flowers.

He brought her cold hand to his lips. "Courage, *mein Schatz.*"

She smiled wanly as she accepted the bouquet from him, then Maria led her to the entrance. The two women would stay there until he and Peter were in position at the altar.

"Daydream *during* the ceremony," Peter advised gruffly as they walked up the aisle of the crowded church. He had grudgingly agreed to attend as best man for Siegfried's sake.

Siegfried nodded. "You have the ring?" he asked, probably for the fiftieth time.

"Nah," Peter elbowed him in the ribs. "I left it back at the house. Come on."

The church was packed. People who had no business being here during the busiest time of the whole farming year had come. Alice saw a blur of all their faces as she walked slowly up the aisle. The organ music was deafening. The multitude of candles around the altar burned with a noonday glare, obscuring the black-coated figures of her groom and his best man.

Tati beamed at her from the front row. Hugh, in the pew behind her, glowered.

She clasped the roses in her arms. A stray thorn pricked her, and she focused on that single spot of reality as she joined Siegfried in front of the altar.

She remembered her first wedding, the reluctant releasing of her arm by her father. She missed him, his funny jokes, his fast-talking blarney, his dedication to bettering her life. *If only he could have been here today.*

Father Byrne faced the congregation, spread wide his arms, and began the Nuptial Mass.

Most of it washed over Alice with no more meaning than wind amongst the trees. But as she stood, then knelt, then stood again for the various parts of the rite, some sections stood out too clearly:

"Wives should be submissive to their husbands as though

to the Lord..."

Siegfried smiled at her after that command, and she felt him take her hand, helping her support the weight of the flowers.

Father Byrne continued: "Henceforth you belong entirely to each other; you will be one in mind, one in heart, and one in affections. And whatever sacrifices you may hereafter be required to make to preserve this common life, always make them generously. Sacrifice is usually difficult and irksome. Only love can make it easy; and perfect love can make it a joy. We are willing to give in proportion as we love. And when love is perfect, the sacrifice is complete... *Greater love than this no one has, that one lay down his life for his friends.*"

Alice felt the eyes of the whole congregation fasten on the service flag, standing a little forlorn now in the·corner of the chancel. Bill's gold star shone there, the last gleaming remnant of his life. Someday, when the flag was put away for good, his memory, too, would be tucked out of sight.

A single tear escaped from her eye as she knelt for the blessing. *Good-bye, Bill. I did love you.*

She stood up, with Siegfried's help, for the recitation of the vows. He stood close enough that the warmed-wool scent of his new suit was nearly as strong as the fragrance of the roses that she carried. He gazed at her tenderly as the priest coached him through his promises. Siegfried's hand, clasping hers as he spoke, was warm, truer than any promises he might make.

Then it was her turn.

"I, Alice Mary O'Reilly Roye, take you, Siegfried Heinrich Wilhelm Rodernwiller, for my lawful husband, to have and to hold, from this day forward, for better, for worse, for richer, for poorer, in sickness and in health, until death do us part."

Father Byrne mumbled something about authority and the bond of matrimony; then he was blessing them, and speaking to the congregation: "I call upon all of you here present to be witnesses of this holy union which I have now blessed. 'Man must not separate what God has joined together.'"

There was a collective sigh, and not a few fluttering handkerchiefs. Alice heard at least one full-fledged honk, then it was time for the next part of the ceremony.

Siegfried imperiously held out his hand to Peter, who pantomimed dropping the ring before grinning lopsidedly and handing it over. Siegfried gave the ring to Father Byrne, who made the sign of the cross over it several times, praying, "Bless, O Lord, this ring, which we are blessing in your name, so that she who wears it, keeping faith with her husband in unbroken loyalty, may ever remain at peace with you according to your will, and may they live together always in mutual love."

Father Byrne gave the ring— Bill's ring -- back to Siegfried, saying, "Now that you have sealed a truly Christian marriage, give this wedding ring to your bride, saying after me, 'In the name of the Father, and of the Son, and of the Holy Spirit. Take and wear this ring as a sign of our marriage vows.'"

Siegfried followed the directions, taking Alice's hand and slipping on the ring that she had not taken off in the last five years except to have him put it back on again.

She was married to him. Again.

Sonoma
Saturday, September 20

Siegfried laughed and joked as the people filed past their short receiving line on their way into the hall. Standing beside him, her hand clasped firmly in his, Alice felt the somberness that had clouded her in the church dissipate and vanish. She felt giddy with happiness despite her new shoes, which pinched her feet dreadfully and made her long for the moment when she could sit down and surreptitiously slip them off.

Overwhelmed by the open-handed charity of her friends and neighbors, Alice sneaked a glance at the buffet table. Everyone had brought dishes and platters of food. There were deviled eggs, sliced ham, potato salad, bowls of ripe summer fruit, plates of bratwurst, platters of sliced cheeses, apple strudel, pear tarts, and a magnificent, tiered cake from Romeo Cantoni's bakery.

There was even champagne, unlabeled, shipped from somewhere in the City.

Siegfried ate, and drank, and laughed, his hand frequently seeking hers for a quick squeeze. There were so many people to talk to, so many acquaintances to acknowledge, so much joy to share.

It seemed only a moment, then it was time to cut the cake. Maria appeared with an engraved silver knife, her face glowing, and Alice received a quick kiss on her cheek. "I'm so happy for you," Maria whispered. "You're so lucky."

I am lucky, Alice thought, surprised, as she lowered the knife to her wedding cake. Siegfried's hand settled over hers, and they pressed down together. Being here with Siegfried seemed so right. Nothing else mattered any more— not the opinion of her neighbors, not his wartime service. Only Siegfried mattered. Dear, sweet, passionate Siegfried. Her husband.

I love him. The thought sent an intoxicating shock rippling up from the soles of her feet. *I do! I love him!*

Absorbed in her transcendent discovery, she missed the wedding toast, but came back to herself in time to share a glass of wine with Siegfried. To the din of good-natured whistles and applause, they fed each other pieces of cake. Alice's new awareness filled her to overflowing, but she did not know how to tell Siegfried.

Not now. Not in public. Maybe later, when they were alone... Siegfried placed a sweet, crumbly morsel between her lips, giving her a slow smile that made her heart speed up and a slow flutter begin between her thighs.

She smiled back, silently promising him a private feast of something sweeter than cake.

Another round of hand-shaking and backslapping, and it was time to throw the bouquet. Alice raised the mass of flowers, hooking a thorn in her thumb, and the bouquet soared askew.

Maria was standing on the sidelines, chatting with Hugh. Alice saw her catch the bouquet reflexively as it sailed toward her. A disappointed shout rose up from the eager maidens who had been awaiting the lucky flowers. "Oh, no, Mrs. R!" Maria said, laughing, and lifting the bouquet to toss back to Alice. Even Hugh was smiling.

Over the racket rose Peter's thunderous voice. "Maria!"

Maria turned pale as she saw him bulldozing his way through the mass of people toward her. She flung the bunch of roses blindly at the knot of young women, and moved hastily away. Hugh did not try to follow her, but stood watching the scramble to catch the bouquet before it hit the ground.

"Siegfried, maybe you should—" Alice began, but he was already gone.

"But that bastard Hugh—" Peter protested as Siegfried grabbed his arm and steered him towards the champagne table.

"You must try this vintage," Siegfried interrupted, hastily pouring. He thrust the glass at Peter. "Doesn't it taste like Opa Roye's?"

Peter grunted and drank blindly, his eyes scanning the hall for his wife. Siegfried did not release him until Peter had finished a second glass. The dull brick color left the foreman's cheeks and he started responding to Siegfried's banal chatter. Another glass, and Siegfried felt he could safely leave Peter and trust that he would not initiate any violence.

The church hall was beginning to clear. It was the harvest, after all, and most of the guests would have to rise early to work the next day, even though it was Sunday.

He found Alice again, forced into a corner by Mrs. Breitenbach, who was gushing, "My dear, you should have asked for a photographer, too! I have a cousin in Petaluma— Oh, Mr. Rodernwiller, I have been telling your bride that you really should commemorate this lovely occasion with a photograph. My husband has a Kodak—"

"Yes, thank you!" Siegfried responded, mostly to get the woman away from Alice, who appeared ready to fall down. "Alice, *liebchen*, you should sit."

He fetched a chair in an instant, and helped Alice into it. She settled with a tiny sigh, and Siegfried knew he should get her home, soon.

He put his hand protectively on her shoulder, then heard the command, "Turn around! Smile!"

He obeyed, and a flash of light overwhelmed his vision. Instantly, he was ready for the gun's retort.

But there was only a cloud of acrid white smoke, drifting away from George Breitenbach's large, complicated-looking camera.

"Thank you," Siegfried managed to say civilly, despite the pounding of his heart and the sudden cold sweat prickling his temples, "I look forward to seeing the photograph."

"We'll bring it by," Mr. Breitenbach promised. "Many happy returns of the day."

"Thank you," Alice murmured, placing her hand over Siegfried's.

"Do you need something to eat?" he asked anxiously, after the Breitenbachs drifted away like their smoke.

"No. I'm fine," she insisted. "Oh, look. There's Hugh." She pointed to a pillar towards the entrance of the hall. "He seems so unhappy. We really should—"

"Your wish is my command," Siegfried said gallantly. "I will go talk with him." He left her, and wove through the remaining guests toward his cousin.

He had not thought much about Hugh since the Fourth of July. It rankled that he had been so enigmatic then, and that he had never apologized for his ungentlemanly conduct towards Alice.

"Thank you for coming to our wedding, cousin," Siegfried said, at his most polite.

"How could I miss it?" Hugh sneered. "You invited half the county."

Siegfried was taken off guard. "Hugh—"

"Come outside with me," Hugh said. "I've wanted to say a few things to you, and now is the time."

Siegfried looked back. Maria had come to stand next to Alice, and they were chattering gaily about something. The remaining wedding guests had smiles on their faces and plates and glasses in their hands full of tasty food, good beer, and fine champagne. He followed Hugh out of the hall, and they stopped under the rose-covered trellis that shaded the back patio.

"You think Alice is so wonderful," Hugh began, harshly, shaking his head. "You have no idea."

"I will not tolerate further insult to my wife," Siegfried warned.

Hugh ignored him. "I told you that you wouldn't like what I had to say. But you'll listen to me. Her father the wine-broker bought Grandpa's champagne for the whorehouse her mother managed. The only reason Bill married her was because O'Reilly paid him for wine that spoiled— and charming Billy couldn't pay him back. Your sweet demure little Alice is a complete fraud. She's a whor—"

Siegfried's fist found Hugh's filthy mouth, connecting with a satisfying *crack* and knocking him back against a square redwood trellis support. The climbing rose overhead shivered and white petals dropped softly onto their shoulders.

Hugh struggled to his feet, his hand cradling his injured jaw. Blood dripped freely from his lip. "You don't believe me? Just ask Tati." Hugh spat redly onto the shade-dappled ground. "Montclair should have been *mine*." His voice sliced through Siegfried with the force of shrapnel. "I was the oldest son! I always knew Bill would never be able to keep it. But then he died, and *you* came. Well, you may have married your way into the property, but, by God, you've married a whore's daughter." Hugh laughed hoarsely. "Congratulations on your marriage, *cousin*. Drink your wine to the dregs."

Siegfried was paralyzed. He knew the flavors of falsehood. He had commanded enough men in the army to tell when one spoke the truth.

Hugh was not lying.

What he said was so improbable, so terrible, so... consistent. Alice had not invited her mother to the wedding. *She lives too far away*, she had insisted, almost panicked, and then she had quickly changed the subject. None of Alice's other relatives came, either, and Siegfried wondered if his new wife had even invited them. If there were any.

Siegfried settled for shoving Hugh roughly. "Get out of here. Go home. I never want to see you again."

"It's mutual," Hugh agreed, rubbing his jaw in a satisfied way that only aggravated Siegfried more. "I wish you joy of your wedding day."

Hugh walked slowly away, not turning around as Jim Sullivan emerged from the reception hall. "What happened?"

Ah, God, he hurt, and Hugh hadn't even touched him. And his eyes— something had gotten into his eyes. He couldn't see. The world swam in a dazzling blur.

"Hey," Sullivan asked. "Are you all right, Mr. Rodernwiller?"

"Yes," Siegfried whispered. "It was nothing."

He walked unsteadily back toward the wide doors of the hall.

Maria stood there, eyes wide with apprehension, gazing in the direction of Hugh's departure. "What happened?" she asked in a low voice, as soon as Siegfried drew near.

"*Nichts,*" he mumbled.

"Something happened!" she persisted. "What?"

"It does not concern you, Maria," he said heavily. "Where is my grandmother?"

Maria blinked rapidly. "Was it about Peter?"

Siegfried gathered his fragmented attention. "No, Maria. What happened was not about Peter."

She nodded in relief. "Mrs. Roye's over by the punchbowl."

Tati was talking with Mrs. Duhring, and both of them were chuckling about something. Siegfried stopped in front of them and bowed, punctiliously. "May I have a few words with you, Grandmother?"

Tati frowned suspiciously, but disengaged from Mrs. Duhring and followed him out the back door of the hall to a deserted porch.

"What can I do for you, Siegfried?" Tati asked.

"Give me some answers, *Oma.*"

"My dear, you know I'm always happy to oblige you."

Siegfried considered her, his mother's mother. She had such a sweet, lined face, and it did not seem possible that she was a master of manipulation. But he had known her all his life. "*Oma,* Hugh has just told me the most despicable *things* about Alice. Why would he do that?"

Tati's expression hardened. "I have *never* been able to fathom that man's mind."

Siegfried took a step closer, well aware that his height was intimidating. "Why did Alice marry me?"

"Darling, I knew that if I could just get the two of you together, everything would work out. I have a great deal of affection for Alice, and she needed someone to help her run Montclair." Tati stopped, her gaze trapped in his. "I merely encouraged—"

Suddenly, the remaining pieces fell into place. "You blackmailed her to ensure that she married me. What exactly does she fear?" Siegfried asked implacably. He did not want to hear Tati's answer, but he had to know the truth about his wife.

Tati blinked at him, then recovered herself. "Siegfried, I am *astonished* at your tone of voice. Oh, I can tell that you are annoyed—"

"*Ich bin wütend.*" He was indeed furious, his rage a flat, steely taste in the back of his throat.

Involuntarily, Tati stepped back. She forced a laugh. "My dear, you wanted Montclair. I got it for you. Don't quibble about the methods now. You have exactly what you wanted." She tugged at her gloves again. "Alice will be a wonderful wife. She is a perfectly decent girl." But her eyes slid away from his searching gaze.

Siegfried's heart broke.

Tati was lying to him.

"Then you must have a great deal in common," he snarled. He turned on his heel and walked away.

The reception ended at last. Alice received the last beer-scented good wishes from the departing guests, then let out a sigh. The ordeal was over. She sank down in a nearby chair as Siegfried approached. "I'm so sorry that Tati didn't want to stay overnight. I see her so seldom, but she seemed determined to return to the City."

Siegfried's expression darkened momentarily, then became carefully blank. "Perhaps the idea of staying with newlyweds made her uncomfortable," he suggested, without conviction.

"Perhaps. What happened to Hugh? He didn't even say good-bye." Alice remembered his ill-humored face in church. Maybe it was a good thing that he hadn't stayed very long.

Siegfried didn't reply, but leapt to his feet and helped steady a tottering tower of floral decorations in Mrs. Breitenbach's arms as she passed by on her way out the door.

"What— you two still here?" Gertrude Breitenbach made a shooing motion with her chin. "It's your wedding night," she said, clucking. "You should be home, taking off your shoes and having another glass of champagne."

She put down the burden in her arms, reached into a wooden case partially concealed by a tablecloth, and retrieved one last bottle of the unmarked vintage. Siegfried had earlier pronounced it very good, but Alice had been too keyed up to do more than take a sip or two. She had clutched her one glass for the remainder of the reception, the champagne growing tepid and flat as the hours passed.

Siegfried accepted the bottle. "We thank you," he said

with grave formality. "For everything." He gave Mrs. Breitenbach one of his sweet smiles, lifted her hand, and kissed it.

Mrs. Breitenbach turned pink. "Go, go! Mr. Breitenbach and I will take care of the rest here."

She picked up her burden again, and continued out the door. Maria, just entering the building, stepped aside and let Mrs. Breitenbach pass through the door first. Then she hurried over to Siegfried and Alice.

"We are about to leave. Where is Peter?" Siegfried asked curtly.

"Mr. R., he's out back. He had too much to drink. Again," Maria reported. "He doesn't usually—" she began to add, defensively, at Siegfried's disapproving scowl. Then she stopped, her shoulders slumping.

Siegfried gave Alice a sideways glance, not quite meeting her eyes. "Please excuse me." Then he turned to Maria, and said in a resigned tone of voice. "You had better show me where he is."

It was nearly dark by the time Siegfried managed to partially revive Peter, who had passed out near the necessary facilities. Maria insisted on riding in the bed of the Model-T with her inebriated husband, leaving Alice to gather up her silk skirts and climb into the passenger seat.

Siegfried drove the bumping, rattling truck back to Montclair without speaking.

The silhouette of his profile was stern in the faint twilight, as he gazed out at the road and the dark shapes of the passing bushes and trees. "What's wrong?' she asked, when the silence grew too heavy.

"Nothing." His voice was low, and a little husky.

Back at Montclair, Alice staggered wearily upstairs to her bedroom and slipped out of her high-heeled pumps with a moan. Siegfried had not said a word to her since their brief exchange on the drive home.

But then again, it had been a long and exhausting day for both of them, Alice reassured herself.

"Will you unbutton me?" she asked, presenting her back with its long row of tiny buttons to him.

He drew close, and she felt a series of slight tugs, followed by a sudden give in the fabric around her bosom and waist. She arched her neck ever-so-slightly in anticipation of the kiss she knew he would place there, as he always did when helping her with her buttons.

But he didn't kiss her. Nor did he place an affectionate hand on the curve of her hip when he reached the last button at the base of her spine.

"There." She felt him move away, and a second later, heard him open the wardrobe door.

"Thank you," she said timidly, glancing over her shoulder as he hung up his suit jacket.

"*Macht nichts*," he replied dismissively, without looking at her, occupied with hanging up his clothes.

Alice slipped the borrowed wedding gown off her shoulders, carefully stepped out of it, then hung it in the wardrobe. Siegfried moved away from her as she did so, and occupied himself with laying out his pajamas. Alice suppressed her hurt feelings as she continued undressing. *He's tired,* she told herself, trying to make herself believe it. Since his public proposal, even when he had been exhausted, Siegfried had always managed at least a quick cuddle before falling asleep.

He was moving very stiffly, his usual easy movements gone slow and mechanical. As she watched, he stepped out of his trousers, the long muscles in his legs flexing. He folded the dark wool along the knife-crease before hanging the pants up next to his jacket. He did not lift his head to look at her when she rolled down her silk stockings and stood there, clad only in her slip.

Alice felt the air in the bedroom darken with unspoken tension, and she wondered what was wrong. Snatching her nightgown off the bed, she went down the hall to wash her face.

She emerged from the bathroom some time later, hoping that Siegfried was waiting to pounce on her as soon she slid between the sheets. It was their wedding night, after all. Alice hesitated a moment outside her bedroom door, feeling a certain guilty excitement at the prospect.

But when she entered the bedroom, the lights were already turned off. Siegfried was lying on his side of the bed, his body turned away from her.

He's as tired as I am, she told herself, yet again. But he had not even met her eyes since the wedding reception. The sick certainty that something awful had happened began to constrict her chest.

"Good night, Siegfried," she murmured as she climbed into the bed. She was surprised further when he ignored her. She knew he was not asleep yet. She had shared a bed with him long enough now to recognize the relaxed sprawl of his limbs and the deep, gentle breathing that marked his genuine slumber. Tension radiated from his too-straight back, encased like a mummy in sheet and blanket despite the stifling summer heat.

Alice stared miserably up at the dark ceiling. Why was he acting this way?

She had grown accustomed to his open affection. She liked the way that Siegfried treated her, as if she were irresistible. Alice threw back her sheet in a vain attempt to circulate some cooler air to her sticky skin, and thought back over the last three weeks: Siegfried sneaking up on her in the hallway for a quick but fervent embrace before mealtimes; a morning kiss on the cheek that ended with him nuzzling the sensitive nape of her neck; his slow, sensual worship of her breasts before he made love to her at night.

Had she done something to offend him? Alice cast her mind through the day's events. He had been his usual easygoing, calm self at the wedding, a pillar of strength. It wasn't until after the reception that she felt shut out... after she had seen him in a serious discussion with Tati.

Oh, no. A cold vise closed around her lower belly, and she cupped a protective hand over the slight swell there, shielding her baby from the sudden surge of dread.

What did Tati tell him? And why? She had done everything Tati had asked of her, even made her marriage to Siegfried a permanent one. *Why would she betray me?*

When Alice awoke, Siegfried was already gone, but he had left evidence of his passing: Bill's dressing gown thrown over the chair, spatters of shaving soap on the mirror in the bathroom, and red-dotted swabs of cotton in the wastebasket.

This untidiness was so unlike him! She finally caught up with him in the kitchen. He was dressed for Mass, and the shaving cuts stood out vividly against his fatigue-pale face.

Maria and Peter were nowhere to be seen. Siegfried said without meeting her eyes, "Maria will not be joining us this morning. Peter is feeling unwell. I will get the truck. We will go soon." He left the kitchen.

Alice watched him through the window as he bent stiffly and turned the crank to start the Ford. He looked as sad as she felt. She suddenly couldn't bear the constriction in her throat. Yesterday they had pledged sacred vows. Now they were not even talking.

She hurried to join him, but standing next to him was like standing next to a pillar of salt. She felt bereft, and anxious. *What did he know?*

Siegfried heard God speaking to him through His instrument, the Mass.

Today's lesson was from the Gospel: "Now while he was at table in his home, even many tax collectors and sinners came to join Jesus and his disciples at dinner. But the Pharisees saw this and complained to his disciples, 'What reason can your master have for eating with tax collectors and sinners?' Overhearing the remark, he said, 'People who are healthy do not need a doctor; sick people do. Go off and learn the meaning of the words, *It is mercy I desire, not sacrifice!*"

Siegfried did not want to be counseled towards mercy and forgiveness. He wanted to burn with righteous rage. He had been deceived in all that he had believed about Alice. He had thought her modest, chaste, and of good family. But none of it was true. His yet-unmet mother-in-law was a whore; his father-in-law had been a supplier to brothels. As for Alice herself... Siegfried's stomach churned at the thought. Thank God his father could not know his shame!

He stalked out of the church as soon as the Mass was ended, only to encounter a knot of gesticulating men, standing on the sidewalk in front of the church steps, passing a newspaper from hand to hand.

"Not only does he not answer my brother Carl's letter," Walter Bundschu was saying heatedly, "But he lets Judge Van Fleet in San Francisco go ahead and declare that Wartime Prohibition is legal. It's going to be enforced! Right before harvest!"

Irate mutters accompanied this declaration, and somebody passed Siegfried a copy of Saturday's *Santa Rosa Press Democrat*, which detailed the Federal judge's decision.

"We can't even make our two hundred gallons of wine for personal use!" protested another man, reading over Siegfried's shoulder. "That's infamous!"

"That's what Mr. Price said. There's going to be a special meeting of the Grape Grower's Association on Wednesday," Walter announced. "Everybody needs to be there."

The man behind Siegfried commented, "That lawyer Bell sure knows how to call it. Listen to this: 'Wartime prohibition so far as winemaking is concerned, has been a lie, a subterfuge and a fraud from the beginning. Thank God the right to a jury survives in this country!' Good thing he's appealing the decision!"

Siegfried finished scanning the article, and passed along the paper, stunned.

Except for medicinal, religious, and non-beverage uses, the refrain ran through his head. *Please God, let La Fontaine answer me soon. It has been over two months.*

"How can they do this to us?" Sullivan wailed. "I'll lose

everything!"

"Come to the meeting Wednesday!" Walter repeated. "We'll decide what to do, together."

Siegfried added his assurances to the mass response. He would be there.

On the steps, the wives and sisters of the wine-men shared their own anxieties about the future.

Mrs. Breitenbach said kindly, "It's a blessing that none of this marred your wedding yesterday, Mrs. Rodernwiller. It's such a shame."

"Yes," Alice agreed.

Betty Sullivan, her pregnancy now visibly advanced, said, "But it was too bad that your husband and his cousin had that fight. Hugh Roye, he's a troublemaker."

Alice controlled her first reaction to this news, and waited for Mrs. Breitenbach's question: "What did Hugh do?"

Only her question was directed at Alice, not at Betty. "I don't know," Alice had to admit.

"You mean your husband didn't tell you all about it?" Betty asked innocently.

"I— no, we didn't discuss it." Alice felt the knot of anxiety in her stomach grow. What would they have to fight about, except her? *So Siegfried's sudden coldness wasn't Tati's fault after all, but Hugh's. Oh, God, help me.*

"Well, I'm sure you had other things on your mind," Mrs. Breitenbach said, smiling broadly.

"We all have something else on our minds," Betty said, watching the men.

Back at Montclair, Siegfried grunted an acknowledgment when Alice placed a plate of bacon and eggs before him, but when she brought out the paper and prepared to read from it as usual, he said curtly, "I have already heard the news."

She read to herself the account of their wedding, with its sanitized account of her origins. The article ended with, "All had a good time," which was patently false, if Betty Sullivan was to be believed.

She wondered if Siegfried knew the truth about her. If Hugh had told him whole ugly story. She was afraid to ask, so she hid behind the paper, glad of Siegfried's silence.

※

That night, despite the exhaustion of an afternoon spent laboring in the heat, Siegfried lay awake, miserably aware of Alice sleeping a few inches away.

She stirred, dreaming, and rolled towards him with an unintelligible murmur, reaching out to slide her hand across his bare chest.

Siegfried clenched his teeth until his jaw muscles hurt, then deliberately picked up her hand and moved it away.

He could not bear her touch until he had proven to himself that Hugh was lying. Until he knew in his own heart that Alice was not a whore.

Siegfried, embraced by shadows, remembered all that Hugh had said and all that Tati had so unconvincingly denied. He had never heard a person other than Hugh speak ill of Alice, in this small town where everyone knew everyone else's business. The Bundschus, the Duhrings, the Breitenbachs, the Sullivans, they all accepted Alice for what she claimed to be.

And yet... and yet... all of the other evidence against Alice damned her: her refusal to invite her relatives to the wedding, her reliance on those bloodless pamphlets, her shocking inventiveness after he had begged her to be wicked for him. Siegfried remembered the occasions when Alice had claimed to go shopping in San Francisco all day, only to return empty-handed. There had always been a miraculous infusion of money the day after: money to hire cleaning crews for the winery, money to replace ruined cooperage...

What had she actually been doing in the City to obtain so much money?

And then, Alice had become pregnant after *one night* with him. Was such a thing possible?

Siegfried felt his heart harden into a frozen lump as he remembered how she had vomited the night they first made love. Didn't women do that in the early stages of pregnancy? Had she already been expecting before they consummated their marriage?

No! part of him protested, remembering how kind, good, hard-working, and dedicated to Montclair she was. But Hugh's words were undeniably true.

It could not be true. Alice, a whore? It must not be true!

Siegfried fell asleep still trying to resolve the terrible muddle in his own mind.

...he was walking the vineyard when the long row of vines transformed into coils of barbed wire stretching out along the barren, artillery-pitted earth of the Front.

Panic clawed at Siegfried's chest as he realized he was standing out in the open space of No-Man's Land. He whirled around and saw Peter methodically working down the row of barbed-wire tendrils, using clippers to thin out clusters of ripe bullets hanging on the rusty wires. The new brass casings shone like polished gold in the dim, smoky light.

The distant whump of artillery shells grew louder.

Siegfried looked around frantically. Where was he? Where was his trench? Where were his men? Franz, Jürgen, Karsten, Helmut— surely they would not abandon him in the middle of No-Man's Land? But the battlefield was eerily deserted. There was only Peter's stolid presence, performing his bizarre harvest.

"Peter! Peter! For God's sake— we have to get under cover!" Siegfried tugged at Peter's blue work shirt, but Peter ignored him, continuing his task— snip, snip— his clippers opening and closing with slow efficiency, sending bunches of ripe and half-ripe bullets falling to the blood-black earth.

The booming of the big guns drew nearer. The bones of Siegfried's feet hummed with each impact. Tiny ripples began to appear in the pools of scummed water filling the bomb craters. Cover— they needed to seek cover. When the shells began to fall, it would not matter if the bombardment was from German or enemy guns.

A low whimper caught his attention. It was Alice, imprisoned in a coil of barbed wire, her face white and terrified in the dim light. Behind her, Peter screamed, "Whose baby is it?"

Siegfried began to run towards her, but the air had become thick as mud. The explosion of a shell deafened him and he braced himself for the numbing rip of shrapnel in his leg—

"Shhhh, shhhh."

Siegfried awoke with a start, every muscle tensed in the anticipation of imminent injury. He was cradled against something soft and warm, smelling faintly of lemon. *Alice.*

He lay half atop her, his face nestled in the cotton nightgown between her breasts. She held him tightly, murmuring to him. Her comforting touch moved through his hair, down the back of his neck, and over his bare shoulders.

It had only been a dream. He was safe in his own bed with his wife, her thighs pressing pleasantly against his groin, her yielding breasts soft against his mouth under the barrier of fabric.

"Siegfried? Are you all right?" Alice's voice was low and warm, inviting his confidence.

She stopped stroking him, and he felt her palm flatten against the middle of his back, drawing him closer. He shifted slightly, unwilling to talk, and drew up her nightgown, needing to bury himself in her and expel his poisonous dream in the act of love.

Alice's breathing quickened at the touch of his hand on her leg. Against his cheek, her nipple grew hard.

Like a bombshell tearing into his heart, the image of his wife in the beds of other men came to him. In particular, he imagined Hugh, his high, sun-freckled forehead flushed and sweaty as he thrust between Alice's soft white thighs.

Siegfried shuddered and rolled away from her, seeking refuge from her betrayal behind a barrier of blankets and a turned back.

Sleepless, racked with the ache of unsatisfied desire, he was aware of every shift and breath that told him that Alice, too, lay awake until dawn blanched the darkness.

Montclair
Wednesday, September 24

The alarm clock's shrill jangle woke Alice from her doze. She fumbled for it, staring blearily at the black numbers circling its white face. She was tempted to fling it across the room. She had spent another sleepless night, enduring Siegfried's pretense that he was alone in their bed.

Beside her, he stirred and grumbled, rolling away from the sun's rays lighting the lace curtains. Now facing her, he opened his eyes. Just for an instant, she saw a sleepy smile curl his mouth. Then his expression became remote.

But he said nothing.

Awake now, Siegfried saw Alice bite her lip, revealing her suffering. She was haggard, the warm tones of her skin faded to yellowed ivory, with bluish shadows under her eyes.

The warm coziness of their marriage bed had become a field of barbed wire. Siegfried's nerve-endings felt raw, exposed. Was there any greater torture than the night he had just spent, unable to bring himself to touch his wife, unable to stop wanting her? How could he despise Alice and desire her at the same time?

He turned away, studying the cruelly bright streaks of sun on the faded rug, and cursed himself for imagining fanciful stories about a family of noble wine brokers. Instead, he, a Rodernwiller, had been tricked into marrying into a clan of whores and pimps.

Damn Tati and her meddling!

Alice made a small, hopeless sound that tore at Siegfried's heart as she threw back the bedclothes. She padded out of the room silently, leaving Siegfried to wrestle his demons in the knife-edged morning light.

Maria made an early lunch of sausages and fried potatoes to feed them well before the tedious journey to the emergency meeting in Santa Rosa, but it was too hot and smoky to eat. Fires far to the north and east were consuming thousands of acres of brush, filling the air for miles with drifting ash.

Alice picked at her food. She wasn't hungry. She peered

at Siegfried, and saw that he was shoveling in Maria's good food as if he had been starving for years.

"Mrs. R, if you don't eat, you'll be sorry before you get to the meeting," Maria predicted.

"She is not going," Siegfried pronounced around a mouthful of sausage.

Alice looked up at him in shock. "What do you mean, *not going*?"

Siegfried swallowed, wiped his lips, and set his napkin down deliberately. "You do not need to attend this meeting." He spoke at an angle across the table, as if he could not even look straight at her. "Peter and I will go."

"I always go to the meetings!"

"You always went when you were a widow alone," Siegfried corrected. "Now I will attend the meeting, and you will stay here."

Alice glared at him. How dare he forbid her to do anything! "I'm coming with you. You can't stop me."

"You must take care of the baby, Alice," Siegfried said, gently. As if he cared for her.

Maria dropped her fork, and it clattered loudly against her plate. "Please, listen to him." She was studying her plate with passionate intensity, two spots of red burning in her cheeks. "In this heat, over the potholes— it wouldn't be good for you. I couldn't stand it if something happened."

"Er, well," Peter cleared his throat, hastily. "I'll be happy to stand in for you, Mrs. R. Just until the baby is born, of course. Congratulations, by the way," he added, in falsely hearty tone. He opened and closed his fist convulsively, crumpling his napkin into a tightly compacted ball. He glared at Maria, clearly speaking to her although his words were addressed to Siegfried. "You're a lucky man, Sig. At least *your* wife isn't barren. A man needs a family— *sons* —to look after him in his old age."

Alice gasped, but Maria continued to push a slice of fried potato listlessly around her plate, shrinking under the weight of Peter's baleful scrutiny.

"I am sure you will have another child someday, Peter," Siegfried said quietly.

"Yeah, I hope so, too." Peter said, savagely mincing a sausage.

"Now, then," Siegfried leaned back and folded his arms. "Maria has given you some excellent advice, Alice. I hope you will not argue further."

Alice itched to slap the smug expression off his face, but she was suddenly too tired, especially with Peter and Maria against her. She threw down her napkin and pushed herself up from the table. "Fine! I'll just go take a nap, then."

She had been hoping to shock them with her slothfulness, but to her dismay, everyone nodded approvingly, as if naps were a normal and accepted practice during the busiest season of the year. Maria gave her a weak smile.

Alice pulled herself slowly up the stairs by the banister and plodded to her bedroom. She was a coward. She ought to have defended her right to attend, but even her friends had become Siegfried's allies. She didn't have the strength to stand against all of them.

As she sank down onto her bed, she tried to tell herself that she hadn't really wanted to go to the horrid old meeting, anyway. Siegfried had saved her from hours of sitting in a room filled with men who hadn't yet prepared themselves for the inevitable.

Siegfried may hate me, but thank God Montclair has been spared the fate of the other vineyards, she thought, as sleep washed over her. *Thank God.*

Siegfried stopped the truck at the Montclair gates and walked over to the mailbox, where the mailman, a ruddy-faced fellow with grizzled hair and whiskers, had just pedaled up on his bicycle.

"Mornin'— terrible day, ain't it?" Mr. Tester complained at Siegfried's greeting, wiping his forehead with a large red handkerchief. He pointed northwest toward an ugly tower of khaki smoke rising high into the sky. It was unthinkably huge to be visible from so far away. "I heard the fire's nearly out of control, way north of Healdsburg. I wish it'd start rainin'."

"Not until after harvest!" Siegfried exclaimed. He was sorry for anybody in danger from fire, but his grapes needed at least another day of sun to develop the right amount of sugar.

"Didn't they pass a law against the harvest? Damn politicians," Tester said, rummaging in his satchel. "Ah, here you are." He handed Siegfried a small bundle of mail. "There's a real nice envelope for you from Mr. La Fontaine. Hope it's good news for you!" He waved, and remounting his bicycle, continued on his way down the road.

Siegfried held the envelope, struck dumb with anticipation. Here was his fate, wrapped in creamy linen with an imprinted name and address.

"So— what is it?" Peter demanded. "Did you ask La Fontaine for a contract?" His eager gaze was riveted on the envelope. "That was damned clever of you, Sig."

His fingers trembling, Siegfried tore an edge down one short side of the envelope, and extracted the thick note paper from within.

My Dear Mr. Rodernwiller:

While I am sensible of the debt of gratitude which I owed to your grandfather, I am most heartily sorry to inform you that I have already contracted for as much additional wine, over the products of my own vineyards, as I may sell within the license granted Fountainview.

I may, however, in future, have the need and the sanction to sell a greater volume of wine than, at present, I am allowed. If such occurs, I will gladly consider your offer to provide me with the highest-quality Burgundy from Montclair. I do recall with great fondness the superb vintages that your grandfather used to make. If you can match them, you will be his worthy inheritor.

I remain yours most sincerely,

Charles La Fontaine

"*Ach Gott*," Siegfried grunted.

"Don't tell me— he turned you down? God damn." Peter slumped in the passenger seat of the Model-T. "What do we do now?"

Siegfried set his teeth and put the truck in gear. "Now we go to the meeting."

Santa Rosa

Wednesday, September 24

The sun was an evil penny in the tawny pall of smoke covering the sky. Flakes of ash fell like dead snow as Siegfried and Peter climbed the steps to the Sonoma County Courthouse.

Siegfried wrenched open the door to the Supervisors' chambers and a babel of voices escaped the crowded room. Every winemaker and grape-grower in the county from Agua Caliente to Windsor— representatives from over two hundred and fifty businesses — had come to this meeting.

Peter followed Siegfried toward a pair of seats remaining open, amidst a gaggle of Dry Creek vineyardists from west of Healdsburg. The Sonoma contingent had already filled up the rows closest to the speaker's podium, and all were shouting at one another.

Mr. Victor Piezzi, President of the Association, appeared at the speaker's podium, but no one noticed for a while. Eventually pockets of silence grew, then there was a concerted scraping of chairs and almost everyone sat down. There were more attendees than chairs, though, so the walls were lined with standing men.

Piezzi got right down to business. "As you all know, Judge Van Fleet ruled Wartime Prohibition constitutional. He stated that wine grapes are a food or fruit to be conserved for the army, which means we will not legally be able to make wine from this year's grape crop."

Although this was no surprise, a discordant groan answered the bald statement of fact.

A small man stood, holding his hat against his chest. "I'm the manager at the Asti vineyard. We've converted to grape juice. I can recommend this as a measure to avoid a total loss on this year's crop."

"You're a big operation!" an anonymous voice called out. "Most of us little guys don't have the facilities to switch over to refrigeration— or the money!"

"Those Prohibition biddies give me a pain! 'Just make grape juice!'" Peter muttered to Siegfried. "You can't *stop* fermentation once the grapes have been pressed!"

Angry shushing from their neighbors silenced Peter. Siegfried had barely heard him; his head was still whirling from La Fontaine's letter. He had ruined Montclair. They would lose everything. *How can I tell Oma Tati what I have done? Or Alice?*

"So what are we going to do?" Mr. Piezzi asked, rhetorically. "Mr. Price, our Secretary, has some suggestions."

Walter Price took the podium. "The California State Department of Agriculture advised us in August that we have three options. One: get a permit from the government for the crushing of grapes for sacramental purposes—"

There was a rumble of protest: "Which La Fontaine got!"

"And he's sewn up contracts with only a couple of suppliers!"

Out of the corner of his eye, Siegfried saw Peter fold his arms angrily.

"If I may continue?" Silence obtained, Mr. Price went on. "Two, produce non-alcoholic grape juice, and three, ship the grapes to market in refrigerator cars. Now we've already covered numbers one and two, but I have further bad news. There aren't enough railroad cars to service all of the vineyards. We've asked the Department of Transportation to schedule more since all railroad traffic is still under their jurisdiction for the 'war effort,' but we're aware that the smaller growers don't have rail spurs." Another uproar greeted this announcement.

"We'd have to truck our grapes, and there are nowhere near enough trucks, either!"

"And we don't have the weather to make raisins. It's mighty hot now, but that won't last into November. Let the Central Valley make raisins. We're wine-men!"

"So we really— we really only have two choices." Mr. Price shouted over the din. "Wait until the President declares demobilization and lifts Wartime Prohibition; or, defy the government and crush our grapes."

The roar that rose from the assembly was deafening.

Mr. Piezzi stepped up, raised his hand to gather the crowd's attention. "Justus Wardell cautions that penalties will be heavy if we crush."

Peter whispered to Siegfried: "They're just trying to scare us."

"Here's an excerpt— please, let me speak!"

Mr. Piezzi pounded his gavel, attempting to reestablish control of the meeting.

Mr. Price waved a piece of paper. The din lessened, and he continued. "This is from Mr. Wardell's letter: 'The fact that the manufacture and sale of alcoholic liquors is prohibited under the law, the production of such is not relieved from tax liability, and it must be understood that the payment of the tax in no way conveys a right to act contrary to this law. Any person, incurring liability to the tax is also liable to prosecution under the prohibition law.'"

"That does it," Peter shouted, standing up and flinging his Stetson to the floor. "You're saying if we make wine they'll tax it, take it, *and* put us in jail!"

Mr. Price also raised his voice. "What I'm trying to say is, we must all stand together in this!"

"Or we'll all hang separately?" someone shouted. "But we aren't at war with the government!"

"Ain't we? They just stole our livelihoods! Talk about taxation without representation!"

"Gentlemen! Gentlemen, I beg you! We must keep our heads! I propose that we proceed to harvest and crush our crops in expectation that the wartime ban will be lifted either by appeal or by demobilization. In the meantime, I will personally present a guarantee to the Internal Revenue Service on behalf of all the members of this Association, that none of the wine so made will be sold nor exported until it can be done legally."

Siegfried took no part in the tense debate which followed. He was too busy fighting down an attack of panic worse than any battle terror he had ever experienced. He had no difficulty imagining Alice's reaction to being told that La Fontaine was not going to buy their wine after all.

Yet dare he break the law without telling her?

In the acrimonious debate the followed, Siegfried was brought to realize that he had no choice. When Mr. Price called for a vote in favor of the motion to crush despite the ban, Siegfried stood with the majority.

Toward the end of the long, weary afternoon, an impromptu committee was organized to draw up an agreement for the members to sign. It provided that court costs would be paid by the Association should any one of the members be prosecuted for harvesting and crushing his crop, excluding any member who might try to sell his wine before Wartime Prohibition was lifted.

Siegfried signed. He was numb by then, and might have signed anything, even his own death warrant, just to be free of this assembly and its doom-crying.

"Gentlemen!" Mr. Price addressed them for the last time. "National Prohibition will not go into effect until mid-January. We hope there will be a window of time in which to sell our wine before then. However, if you violate the law, you do it at your own peril. Thank you for coming today."

"Aw, Sig. This is it, isn't it?" Peter was twisting his battered hat. "We're finished. All that work— for nothing."

"It was not for nothing!" Siegfried insisted. "There must be *something* we can do."

They exited with the stunned and mostly silent crowd. Outside, the heat and the burnt-spice smoke hit them again, worse than before they had gone inside.

"What a day!" Peter exclaimed, coughing.

Siegfried found the truck and cranked it to life. He drove, abstracted. Once they were on Fourth Street, on the route back to Sonoma, he ventured, "Please do not tell Alice anything about La Fontaine. I need a little time to— to make things good."

"Man, you're a dreamer worse than your granddad," Peter shook his head ruefully.

"I *will* think of a way to save Montclair," Siegfried said. He was clenching his teeth so tightly that his jaw ached.

Peter shrugged. "Okay, then. I won't tell her if you don't. But you're only making it worse for yourself."

Alice awoke with a start when she heard the familiar rattle of the Model-T's engine. She squinted groggily at her bedside clock. Then she sat up, suddenly fully awake. It was nearly six— she had slept all afternoon, leaving poor Maria to do all the work of preparing supper!

She leaped out of bed, hastily washed her sleep-flushed face, put on a clean shirtwaist, and rushed downstairs. She found Siegfried standing on the porch steps, hands on his hips, telling Peter: "—and we will start with the Traminer section tomorrow morning."

Peter frowned as he caught sight of Alice. "But what about
the—"

Siegfried spared Alice a single cold glance, and said, very firmly: "Tomorrow. Have the picking crews start at dawn. It will be too hot to harvest after midday."

"Whatever you say. You're the boss." The foreman shrugged.

Alice was asking herself if she had just imagined the slight sneer on Peter's face at those last words, when he tugged on his hat brim and strode off. She cleared her throat. "Ah, Siegfried. How did the meeting go?"

"It was chaotic," he said shortly. He stared out toward the vineyard, refusing to look her way. "Everyone was angry, desperate. We all voted to defy the government, and crush our grapes despite Judge Van Fleet's ruling. I am sure you will read all about it in the newspaper on Sunday."

"Thank God *we* don't have to worry about breaking the law," Alice said fervently. ""I need to speak to you about the harvest arrangements."

"I am very busy right now," Siegfried began. His hand slipped inside his trouser pocket, making a fist, and Alice heard the sound of crumpling paper. In his stillness he seemed to be the focus of two opposing forces, one urging him away, one insisting he stay.

"It's only going to get busier. If you could just answer my questions now... Will you come inside and have a cup of coffee?"

Awkwardly, he ran his hand through his hair, breaking the tension. "Very well. We should speak."

Alice felt a chill prickle the back of her neck at his tone. They went into the cool, darkened parlor. "I'll be back in just a moment," Alice promised, as Siegfried settled into one of the stiff plush-upholstered chairs.

He looks so weary, she thought as she made her way to the kitchen and filled two mugs of coffee from the enamel pot warming on the stove. His eyes were haunted and his cheekbones pushed sharply through drawn skin. He had not been sleeping, either.

Siegfried was grinding his teeth as she re-entered the

parlor, his gaze focused vaguely on a watercolor of the vineyard hanging on the wall. His fingers tapped nervously on the carved wooden armrest.

He thanked her without meeting her eyes as she handed him his mug of coffee.

Alice took a tiny sip and started with her primary concern. "How does Mr. La Fontaine want us to deliver his wine to Napa? The Sebastianis have always let us use their depot, but I need to know how many railroad cars to order. Or do you think it would be better to hire flatbed trucks?"

A flush crept up from Siegfried's shirt collar. "Do not worry about those details, Ah-lees. Everything I will take care of."

Alice narrowed her eyes. His accent had grown stronger, as it always did when he was emotionally moved. He was hiding something. Did he intend to shut her out of the management of Montclair entirely? "And when did Mr. La Fontaine say he would make his first payment?" Alice asked, more sharply than she had intended. "You know how difficult our finances have been this summer. Bill once told me that the usual payment schedule is—"

Siegfried finally met her eyes, his dark blue gaze burning with repressed animosity. "I don't care what *Bill* said. I am your husband now."

"You're not as much of a husband as he was," she retorted, overcome by the instinct to return blow for blow.

"I am *exactly* as much of a husband as Bill was!" Siegfried shouted, losing control. "I am told your father purchased *him* for thirty pieces of silver."

"Makes *you* a bargain, doesn't it?"

"If commerce is all you care for," Siegfried replied with icy contempt.

"*I'm* not the one who let his grandmother marry him off for a piece of land." Alice gripped the arm of the plush love seat. She had never, ever argued with Bill. She had never wanted to hurt him the way she wanted to hurt Siegfried now, to make him feel the torment of her bruised heart, her bruised pride. "Or is selling yourself for acreage more honorable than selling yourself for money?"

"Haven't you done both?" he shot back.

"And what do you mean by that?" She struggled to keep her tone restrained while nails were being driven through her heart.

"At the wedding—" He stopped. The blood rose in his fair skin and Alice knew that they had finally touched upon the unspoken thing that lay between them. "Hugh told me. About you. About your... family."

"I knew it," Alice murmured. Her wounded heart was pounding so loudly that she thought he must be able to hear it.

"Was your father really a pimp? Is your mother a— a—" Siegfried's voice cracked, "whore?"

Alice struggled to breathe. A nursery rhyme ran maniacally through her mind: *Sticks and stones may break my bones, but names will never hurt me!*

"Is it true, Ah-lees?" Siegfried pressed, his expression silently begging her to deny it. "Were you a—"

Her chest felt as if she had been hit with fists, not words. She wanted to hurt him back, as much as he had just hurt her. "Yes! Everything Hugh told you about me is true. Where do you think I learned those— those *things* you liked so much? My mother is a madam. I lived in her Barbary Coast parlor-house until I was thirteen. My father arranged my marriage to Bill." Alice had meant to shock Siegfried, but she startled herself. She had not known the extent of her own regret. "Bill owed him money, and Da offered to cancel Bill's debt as a wedding present. He threw in a big dowry to sweeten the pot, but Bill loved me!"

She stopped. *What was the use?*

Siegfried sat frozen in devastated disappointment.

Alice could not bear it an instant longer. Her carefully constructed life was shattering, her soul bleeding from the shards.

"Don't think I don't know what's going on." She pushed herself up out of the love seat, and lurched toward the parlor door. She gripped the doorframe, holding herself upright. "Now that we're beyond an annulment, you c-can stop pretending that you actually had s-some regard for me. I'm just sorry I— I believed you, before."

Siegfried glared after her as she stalked out of the room, her head held high, her shoulders squared. How dare she compare their circumstances! *He* had never prostituted himself—

Really? asked his conscience.

Siegfried slumped back in his chair, his anger draining away, leaving him chilled with remorse.

Alice had woven a complicated tangle of truth and deception in her passionate confession. Her story had matched Hugh's and Peter's, detail for detail— except the most telling point.

She had said 'Yes' to his question 'Were *you* a—'

And she had lied.

He knew it. He could always tell when someone was

lying.

Oh, God. How could he have had said those unforgivable things to her, to his sweet wife? He had seen how much he hurt her with his terrible questions. But the thought of what she might have done with other men had just about killed him... How could he have allowed Hugh to poison his mind?

Siegfried rubbed his temples vigorously, trying to straighten out his tangled and contradictory thoughts.

And after all that had just passed between them, how could he now face Alice with his part in Montclair's ruin? How could she ever forgive *his* lie?

He had to find a way to make things right.

The gilt-and-enamel French clock on the office bookcase chimed ten o'clock. Alice took a slender brass key from the top desk drawer, and reached up on tip-toes to wind the clock, putting off the inevitable moment when she would have to go upstairs and face another night of her husband's stony presence. She had dreaded what might happen if Siegfried ever found out about her mother and her past. Why had she told him that she had worked there as well as lived there?

But he believed me. And that made her feel worse than she ever could have imagined.

She finished straightening up her office, and then went outside on the porch, searching the veiled glitter of the summer stars vainly for any hint of cool air.

When she was unable to delay going to bed any longer, she went back inside.

It was dark as she cautiously pushed open her bedroom door. Alice fumbled along the wall until she reached the switch to turn on the electric chandelier. When the light came on, the first thing she noticed was the open wardrobe.

All of Siegfried's belongings were gone.

She felt nothing, and the lack of sensation frightened her a little. She went out into the darkened hallway. There was a line of light coming from under the guest room door.

She undressed and climbed into her solitary bed. Perhaps the pain would start tomorrow. For now, she just wanted to sleep, and forget everything.

I used to love this so much. I lived all year for this moment. And now it doesn't mean anything.

Alice stood on the porch, watching the pickers work their

way rapidly up the slope of the vineyard, sunlight flickering from the sharp, curved blades of their swift knives.

She surveyed Montclair, and found it barren even as the bountiful harvest began. Why did Montclair's success no longer matter to her? It was all she had lived for, since Bill left. Before Siegfried came.

Peter drove the Model-T slowly between the rows of vines, letting the men empty their full thirty-five pound lugs of grapes into the big bin mounted on the truck bed. She knew most of the pickers by sight if not by name. They came back to Montclair year after year, arriving at her gates when the apple harvest ended. *And they'll be back again next year, and the year after. But where will I be?*

She watched Siegfried as he tried doggedly to be everywhere at once. He had filled out on Maria's good food, and his shoulders were quite breathtakingly broad and well-muscled now. His skin glowed amber in the sun, and his blond hair shone bright in the dimness of the winery.

And she knew, without wanting to, whenever he was near. Her nerves had become morbidly sensitive, acted upon directly and subtly by his presence. She didn't have to see him to know he was there. Her skin would begin to tingle and the constant ache in her center would erupt into a blaze of need.

She suffered for the lack of him in her breasts, in her palms, and all up and down the insides of her thighs. She wanted Siegfried with every part of her, despite his rejection of her, whether he wanted her or not. And how had she gotten so involved, that his withdrawal from her hurt this much?

The solid railing under her hand was suddenly insubstantial. All of Montclair seemed no more solid than a cartoon drawing in the newspaper, which might crumple and blow away in a stiff breeze.

Friday, October 3

A cloud of bees and wasps buzzed inside the winery, attracted by the sweet, sticky grape juice flowing from between the slats of the press. Siegfried rubbed at a welt where he had been stung, and breathed the fragrance of the golden-green juice as Herculio tightened down the screw another half-turn.

Essence of honey and pears. If he were a bee, he would be after it too.

"Enough!" he called, and Herculio stopped. The flow of juice began to lessen. "The rest is to go in the press tank."

"Bill used to get twice that from a ton of grapes," Alice

observed worriedly from behind him.

"As you may recall," Siegfried snapped as a bee lighted on his wrist and stung him. "Bill's wine tasted like piss." He scratched away the stinger and collected his temper. "He never cared that the last gallons of the pressing are the harshest, because the skins and seeds are bitter, when bruised. The best wine is made from the free-run juice of a gentle pressing." As is the best loving, Opa Roye had taught Siegfried, ages ago. Too bad he had been such a poor student.

Alice sucked in air, and visibly calculated the volume of this pressing. He knew she was figuring how much they needed to charge for each gallon; he could practically hear chalk squeak as she did sums in her head. And every dime of future payment a fantasy, as he knew too well. *If Alice does not already hate me, she will when she discovers the truth.*

"Peter, switch the hose to tank number four!" he ordered.

As the foreman complied, he gave Siegfried a hostile look that communicated clearly: *Why are you bothering?*

Siegfried cursed himself for a coward, and rushed to inspect the next load of fruit for the press.

"Well, I'm sorry to have interrupted you," Alice said to the empty air, and left.

It was difficult for Siegfried to concentrate on the grapes when he was blinded by the memory of afternoon sunlight striking copper sparks from her tightly coiled hair.

Montclair
Thursday, October 9

"Why are you all dressed up?" Suspiciously, Siegfried eyed Alice's black frock and the dark coat she was wearing despite the evening's warmth.

"Father Moran's funeral Rosary, of course. Don't you remember? We discussed this over dinner." Alice's voice was cold.

He had spent the day finishing up the white grape crush. He had twenty thousand gallons which might possibly metamorphose into drinkable wine if he was lucky, and vigilant. Had he eaten dinner? "I— ah— my mind was elsewhere," Siegfried admitted as Maria knocked on the back door.

"Are you ready? Hello, Mr. R!" Maria entered, also dressed for church. "Oh. You're not going? I know Peter isn't, but—"

"Please, go without me. I should not leave the wines."

Alice skewered her straw hat to her head. "Certainly. After all, it's not as if you ever met Father Moran." Her gaze, meeting his in the hallway mirror, pierced him.

Maria clucked her tongue at the sight of a gap between Alice's buttons. "Mrs. R., if you didn't have time to alter that old dress, you could have asked me to."

Alice pulled the coat tight. "I didn't want to trouble you."

Holding the screen door open, Maria grumbled, "I keep telling you it's no trouble—"

Then they were gone. He was fiercely glad when the noise of the Model-T's engine receded in the distance. Siegfried went to the phone in the alcove under the stairs. His hands shaking with nerves, he cranked the phone, and asked Florine Lynch, the night operator, to connect him to Samuele Sebastiani. It was his first chance to use the 'phone alone since crush had started, because Alice was always near it.

On the third ring, Mr. Sebastiani answered in his Italian accent. "Yes? I am late to the Rosary. What can I do for you, Mr. Rodernwiller?"

"You know what fine grapes we grow here at Montclair," Siegfried began, breathlessness robbing his voice of any power. "Might you need some white wine in the near future? I have five thousand gallons each of very promising White Riesling and

Sylvaner, with ten thousand gallons of Traminer—"

"I wish you had called me earlier this summer!" Sebastiani interrupted, regretfully. "I just bought all the crop of white wine from your neighbor, Carl Dresel. And Montclair always had such fine Sylvaner, too. What a shame! I'm so sorry I can't help you. Have you tried Wente Brothers or Concannon in Livermore?"

"I shall 'phone them tomorrow. Thank you for the suggestion." Siegfried's stomach turned over. Something cold and heavy had settled in it.

"Good bye! I must go— See you at the Rosary!" He rang off.

Siegfried stumbled outside to the porch. The cool breeze blowing in from the Pacific was fresh. He inhaled deeply, trying partly to calm his driving pulse, and partly to exhale his despair. *God, why did you let me live through the War?*

His wine would not be ready for its first tasting until the middle of November, but Siegfried felt an imperative need to go to the winery to check on its progress.

Inside the building, he was momentarily taken out of himself, overpowered by the fruit and yeast scent of fermenting wine. He stepped carefully over a large puddle on the concrete floor, which was damp from being hosed down before dinner, and climbed a ladder to one of the vats.

He hung his head, gripping the legs of the ladder, suspended ten feet above the hard floor, mesmerized by the slow rolling boil of the fermenting must, so agitated it sounded as if a hive of bees was caught in the vat. The miracle in motion, work of his hands. Sweet water transforming itself into wine.

He watched it for a long time, fatigue settling over him like a warm, heavy blanket. Sebastiani had been his last hope. He would have to tell Alice the truth about their situation when she returned from the Rosary.

When the rattle of the Model-T echoed up the hill, he climbed down the ladder. But he didn't return to the house. He sat down on the wet floor, his back against the slightly vibrating bulk of the giant redwood tank, and closed his eyes. He'd get up in a minute. He just wanted to feel his child kicking...

The sharp scent of something burning woke him. Siegfried opened his eyes in alarm. Was one of the brandy stills being used?

He ran up the stairs to his grandfather's room and unlocked the door. At first, it seemed as if nothing but the ladder was missing. There was the heavy desk, the green leather chair, the small still on the corner of the table. Then he saw: the spot under the missing ladder was also empty. The large still was gone.

He cursed. Only two other people at Montclair had keys to this room.

He picked up the scent of smoke again as he came downstairs. He tracked its source slowly around the inside perimeter of the building, and found it strongest by the door leading into the wine cave. He followed the smell of burning wood, spirits, and pungent fermenting fruit down the dark tunnel, until the faint yellow glow of a kerosene lamp appeared up ahead.

He paused behind a pyramid of stacked barrels and peeked around the edge.

Peter sat on a low wooden stool in the alcove at the end of the tunnel, nursing a fire under the pot of the still. Crates filled high with oozing mounds of pomace— the discarded crushed grape skins— competed for space with dozens of oak barrels bearing a red chalk "X." Siegfried's jaw tightened. Now he knew why Peter had volunteered last month to dispose of all the discarded cooperage.

The stink of fermenting pomace was augmented by the steel-sharp reek of pure grape spirits leaking from several of the old barrels. A case of green wine bottles, four of them filled with liquid and corked, sat by Peter's feet. Whistling tunelessly, he began to fill a fifth bottle with clear liquor.

Siegfried's face heated, and his temples throbbed. The fool— had he really thought his activities would escape unnoticed? "What are you doing?" he barked, stepping into the light.

"What the hell—?" Peter sprang up, startled, kicking back his stool and knocking over the green bottle. As liquid gushed, a metal funnel rolled free, clattering on the limestone floor. "Jesus Christ, Sig, you scared the daylights out of me!" He twisted a small spigot, turning off the flow.

"What are you doing?" Siegfried repeated.

"Making *grappa*," Peter replied, trying unsuccessfully to match Siegfried's cool tone. "Like I always do. Your grandpa gave my father permission to use the pomace any way he wanted, and Alice never said contrary."

"And did you tell her what you were doing?" Siegfried gritted. "I think not."

"Tell her?" Peter gave a short, derisive laugh. "Now there's the pot calling the kettle black!"

"So, you were going to sell it, and pocket the money," Siegfried growled, suppressing the urge to overset the still and throttle his boyhood friend.

Peter put one hand on his hip and gave a derisive sigh. "You're going to lose Montclair, Sig. I'm just trying to salvage what I can, before Maria and I have to look for a new place."

Siegfried reached out and grabbed the front of Peter's shirt. "It is illegal, what you are doing! With your greed, you are endangering us all!"

Peter shoved violently at Siegfried. "Let go of me, you Kraut bastard. Everything around here was fine until *you* showed up."

Siegfried regained his footing and clenched his fists.

"So, what now? Are you going to try and beat the tar out of me?" Peter taunted.

"No." Siegfried pointed towards the exit, damping down his anger. "I am dismissing you. You have until tomorrow morning to vacate the foreman's cottage. Go."

When she returned from the Rosary with Maria, Alice went to her office, although she didn't want to look at her ledgers tonight. Instead, she scribbled speculative sums on sheets of paper. If La Fontaine paid them only ten cents a gallon for their 52,000 gallons of white and red wine, that would be enough to keep Montclair running until next year's harvest. If he paid twenty cents a gallon...

She straightened up as a little cramp— more of a flutter, really— in her abdomen reminded her that she would need a nursery soon. Would there be enough money for a cradle?

She rubbed her tummy, barely rounded yet. She didn't want her child to grow up having a mother and father bitterly at odds with one another. That pain was too familiar.

For the first time since her father took her away from her mother's house when she was thirteen, Alice let herself remember warm white arms, a beautiful voice singing along with a ragtime piano, lullaby lyrics she was ashamed to recall. Air redolent of perfume and cigar smoke. Playing dress-up in her mother's diamonds and silks. Being very good and quiet in her room late at night, when the jangling, syncopated music sounded loudest. Feeding Mama coffee and orange juice when she woke up in the early afternoon and began to put herself together for another evening's work.

"Love you, baby girl," Mama always said, before she said good night, wafting away in a cloud of perfume so strong Alice had to sneeze. And then on the day her father came to take her away: "You be good. Do everything your Da tells you,"

Da had put her into school with nuns and little girls who

didn't know anything about the life that women had to lead when they didn't have a man of their own. Da had instructed her not to talk about her past, not to ever *ever* mention her mother, not to say 'boo' to a goose.

He had tried his very best to secure a respectable future for her. And Bill, to give him credit, had also tried his best, burdened with a too-young wife and the loss of her dowry from a supposedly secure bank.

She had done her best, too, but Siegfried hadn't found her good enough. She gave a strangled laugh. She had never forgiven herself for her mothers' sins. How could she expect Siegfried to?

The kitchen door squealed and slammed, startling her. Angry footsteps clumped down the hallway.

"Do you know what he's done?" Peter shouted, before he even entered the office. "That goddamned Hun! I don't know why you married him, Alice. He's ruined Montclair! You can't let him do this to me! Thinks he's God in a wine barrel, but I'll show him!"

"W-what's going on?" Alice rocked back, buffeted by his raving.

"He *won't* get away with this! A man's gotta make a living! I only want a place of my own, and he's trying to take that away. You can't let him do this to me!"

He paused with an audible sob, and Alice realized with disgust that he was drunk, some powerful spirit on his breath, staining his work clothes. "Peter, you'd better sit down and tell me what happened."

The sound of the front door opening roused Peter to new belligerence.

"It's all his fault, the son of a bitch. Do you know what he *did*?" Peter leaned over the desk, wrinkling her papers, leering owl-eyed at her. "You don't know, 'cause he didn't want me to tell you." A malicious chuckle escaped as he stood up and flung his arm out, pointing melodramatically toward Siegfried, who was now standing in the doorway. "Now you'll see."

"Peter. You will remove yourself from this office immediately!" Siegfried ordered.

"Or what?" Peter scoffed. "You'll fire me? You can't do that. I work for your wife." He turned to her again. "Did I tell you what he jus' did? He *fired* me, the bastard. Tell him he can't do that! I've worked here all my life! My father worked here, and my sons— my sons—" He snatched off the hat perching precariously on the back of his head and kneaded it like dough.

Alice glanced questioningly at Siegfried, who offered as evidence a dark green bottle. "I caught him making *marc schnaps* — he calls it *grappa*— from the pomace. That is illegal, and he knows it. There is no legal market for such alcohol, even if they lift the Wartime Prohibition—"

"No legal market," Peter sneered, back in tenuous control. "Why don't you tell your wife about *your* market? You can't look down on me! You're lower than dirt!" Peter rested one haunch on the desk and addressed Alice. "He told you he had a deal with La Fontaine, didn't he? That he could *sell* all that wine he's making now?" He laughed scornfully. "And you *believed* him!" His laughter degenerated into snorts. "Tell her yourself, Sig. You got *nothin'*!"

One glance at Siegfried's face told Alice that Peter's tirade held at least a grain of truth. Possibly a whole wheat field, but she would deal with that next.

First, Peter. She recoiled from the passionate spectacle he was making of himself. In all the years she had lived at Montclair, he had always been decent, hardworking, conscientious. What had happened to him to break him down like this?

She knew the answer to that question before she finished asking herself. She had seen him cracking piece by piece this disastrous year, until he was nothing but a fractured shell held together by weekend binges.

Siegfried said quietly, "Peter never told you that the aging wine must be topped off, or that mold would contaminate the vats and dryness ruin the barrels. He conspired to bankrupt you, so that Hugh could buy Montclair cheaply."

"You're a liar!" Peter roared. "You think you know so much about wine? My father knew twice what you know!" He stepped forward heavily and threw a wild punch at Siegfried.

Siegfried sidestepped and grabbed Peter's wrist, spinning him around. The foreman flailed with his free arm, shouting incomprehensibly. His body arched and he gave a choking gurgle of surrender as Siegfried forced his forearm high against his spine.

Alice herself felt choked on too much truth. Suddenly the whole pattern of her life at Montclair since Bill's departure took on a different color. All the incidents that made no sense, all the failures that she had claimed for her own had been—

Sabotage.

Cold rage erupted from the pit of her stomach. She hated to side with Siegfried, but the scope of Peter's treachery, however imperfectly revealed, left her no choice.

"Peter, I must agree with Mr. Rodernwiller. You *are* fired." She stopped to take a breath. Her heart was hammering hard enough to shake her voice.

"You can't!" Peter, held perfectly immobile, could only roll his eyes. "You can't fire *me*! I run this place! I grow the best damn grapes in the county! You *can't*—!"

"We can," Siegfried contradicted him. "We have. Go."

Peter tried to struggle, but Siegfried's biceps tightened and swelled, preventing his escape until he conceded defeat. "Okay, okay! I'll— go."

Siegfried loosened his grip, but did not relax his vigilance.

Peter, unsteady on his feet, glaring balefully, shook his arm vigorously at them, not quite making a fist, before stomping down the corridor.

In a swift motion, like a ruffled dog settling his fur, Siegfried shook himself. The spell between them, composed from unity of purpose, broke.

"I can't believe what Peter said about La Fontaine, about your contract!" Alice did believe, but she needed to deny the awful possibility. She was just beginning to come to grips with the potential consequences. No deal. No money. Useless harvest. Montclair lost...

"Unfortunately, it is true," Siegfried said, his face an expressionless soldier's mask.

Her voice caught. "A—all of it?"

He gave a tiny nod, regret, guilt, and heartbreak plain. Then he mastered his face to impassivity again.

"You *lied* to me!" Rage ignited, ice burning in the wasteland of her hopes, and she began to laugh.

Hysteria a voice whispered, but it was drowned by the wildness that consumed her, transforming her from respectable matron to elemental fury. She pushed back from the desk, leaned back in her chair, and lifted both arms, knowing that she raised her breasts as well. She brought her hands to the knot of her hair, yanking the pins from the tight bun, loosening the penitential pressure on her scalp. She ran her fingers through the wavy strands, and fanned the hair out before letting it drop where it willed, along her arms, down her shirtwaist, a few locks coiling in her lap. For good measure, she unbuttoned her collar, and took a deep breath.

I worked so hard to be a lady, and for what?

"Ah-lees, I am sorry—"

"You are," she agreed. "You're the sorriest man on God's green earth."

Siegfried was startled out of his incipient justifications.

"Or, since we're in California, I guess it's God's *brown* earth." She clenched her teeth lest she give in to the urge to bite him. "You accused me of— of—" Even in this wild remorseless state, she couldn't say it out loud. "And all the time you *knew* we couldn't sell our crop, you miserable, traitorous, lying *bastard*."

He stood, stiffly at attention, but he flinched the merest fraction, as if her words were bullets.

She leaned forward, picked up a scrap of paper from the desk and tossed it into the air. It swooped and swirled, and settled at an angle against his shoes, half on the braided rug. "You lied about our future. About your baby's future." She leaned back once more, raising her arms again, clutching the sides of the high-backed chair by her head, relishing the sight of his eyes, helplessly tracking the motion of her bosom.

Siegfried recoiled, and half turned away. "I— I did not mean it as a lie, Ah-lees. I swear to you. I meant it to be true!"

"Bullshit," she said, deliberately using the most vulgar word she knew. It was amazing how easily it passed her formerly pristine lips. "You just wanted to look good, so I'd take you to bed." She smiled at him, showing off her teeth. "Well, guess what?"

He shook his head. Shock had turned his face the color of paper.

"Your days of feather-bed soldiering are over." She stood up, and leaned over the desk, mirroring Peter's stance of only a few minutes ago. "You have been found unfit for this woman's army."

She laughed again, at Siegfried's uncomprehending expression. "You're usually faster off the mark. You. Are. Fired. You are hereby required to vacate the premises. Remove all your belongings—" she paused, and drew her hand caressingly along her abdomen, "except for this little one. You've forfeited that right." She looked directly at him, and saw reflected in his face the terrible creature she had become: no longer good, or kind, or sweet. She was no lady now. She was far, far stronger, possessed of her mother's spirit. "I never want to see your face again."

"But, Ah-lees. We are married!"

"I don't give a bright blue damn. *Get the hell off my land!*" she shrieked, surprising them both. Her hands seized the papers littering her desk, and she threw them at him, for lack of anything heavier. They swooped in the air like white crows, the tangible expression of her rage. She took one stamping step around the desk. "*Get out! Go away! You LIAR! GO AWAY!*"

He broke and fled.

She stood at the doorway, panting, feeling the strain in her throat, the restless energy coursing through her. Soul-deep satisfaction filled her. She had routed him. She had sent him packing.

She held on to her triumph as she listened to the muffled sounds of his valise opening and closing. She watched him as he stumbled down the stairs, out the door into the cool evening air, until his dark form was a wavering spot against the night. She locked the front door against his improbable return, and sagged against the door frame. He was gone!

Then the blaze burned out.

Her back slipped against painted wood. Her feet skidded out from under her, wrinkling the hall runner, and she was sitting in the entryway. The flooring was cool. An edge of the door jamb poked into her back. Her body was heavy, so heavy that the air held her down.

After a while she coughed, because her throat was sore. She swallowed dryly. Thirsty. She was thirsty.

She clambered up, and wavered in search of the *grappa* bottle left behind by... left in her office. She was thirsty. She would drink.

The aroma from the open bottle seemed to her the essence of Montclair: potent, fascinating. She thought of drinking straight from the bottle, and found her training wasn't overthrown so easily. She drifted to the kitchen and found a coffee cup, and poured. She took a sip.

It burned on the way down.

It did not taste like wine, thank God.

She took another, bigger sip, then another, and managed to finish the cup. Then, wearily cradling the bottle, she took herself up to her bedroom.

Gulping down burning mouthfuls of the *grappa*, Alice took off all her clothes, and left them strewn about the floor. Naked in front of her mirror, she plied her brush, until her auburn hair crackled and sparkled, and the fine strands drifted onto her face. She smiled lopsidedly, feeling her mouth twice its normal size.

She didn't want to feel anything. She finished off another mug of *grappa*, and refilled it. This time, she spilled more than went into her cup. She shrugged, testing if her shoulders were numb yet.

They were.

"Goo' riddnnce," she mumbled, and poured two more shots of *grappa* in rapid succession. The room began to spin slowly. She felt as if she were riding a merry-go-round *around and round and round...* She giggled, spilling more liquor before it reached her mouth, and the cooling effect as it splashed against her skin made her resolve to put on a nightgown. She lurched to her dresser, bracing herself against the momentum of the room, and jerked open a drawer. Pulling the clean white cotton over her head, she flailed a while before she found the arms and settled the garment. Then she grabbed cup and bottle, staggering toward the bed, and oblivion.

His battered suitcase grew heavier by the step as Siegfried trudged slowly down the dark road. The ruts and stones were treacherous under the soles of his shoes. He paid little heed, aware only that every step carried him farther from Montclair, and Alice.

He did not care where he was headed; he was homeless, and hopeless, once more. The silhouettes of the rounded hills were the hips and shoulders of giant sleeping women against the faint wash of starlight. Crickets creaked with harsh repetition: *geh-veck, geh-veck, geh-veck.*

Go away, go away, go away.

Should he go to San Francisco, and throw himself on *Oma* Tati's mercy? The thought repelled him but he had no choice. Her well-meaning interference had brought him nothing but grief— worse than the fear he had endured in that hospital on the Front, his leg rotten and stinking like the wounds of the men dying around him.

He had healed, he had survived only to endure *this.*

Alice. He luxuriated in a dream of returning to Montclair, begging her forgiveness on his knees. She would place her hand on his head, her hazel eyes glowing with tender emotion, and say softly that she forgave him.   And then he would carry her upstairs, let down her beautiful hair, and...

Siegfried stifled a groan. No such thing would happen. He had lost another war, defeated by his own stupidity.

His feet crunched on gravel. He had arrived at the long driveway leading to the Rhine Farm house, south of Montclair. Should he go up? Lighted windows upstairs beckoned him, so he walked to the door, put down his suitcase, his fingers tingling, and knocked.

"Coming!" came the faint call.

When Walter Bundschu opened the door, it appeared that he had already retired for the evening; his graying hair was mussed, and he was tying the sash of a paisley dressing robe. "Mr. Rodernwiller! What are you doing here?" Bundschu exclaimed. He saw Siegfried's suitcase. "What— you're going on a trip? At this hour of the night?"

"I am a fool, Mr. Bundschu. A damned fool who has just

lost everything he loved. May I beg a bed for the night? There is no train leaving for San Francisco until morning."

Mr. Bundschu ushered him in, tut-tutting with understanding sympathy. "Oh, come now! All newlyweds have their trials, but surely it can't be so bad!"

"Walter, who's that at the door?" Mrs. Bundschu appeared at the top of the stairs, securely wrapped in a flower-print kimono, her faded fair hair hanging in a two long plaits over her shoulders. "Oh, hello, Mr. Rodernwiller! My goodness— what happened?"

"Nothing you need concern yourself with," Bundschu said, winking broadly at her. "I was just about to offer our neighbor a glass of wine and the advice of an old married man. Could you make up the spare bedroom?"

"Oh. I *see*, " said Mrs. Bundschu, with sudden grave comprehension. "Let me take your suitcase, young man. Walter, I think you should open a bottle of the reserve port."

"I was just thinking that, my dear." Bundschu took Siegfried by the elbow and steered him gently into the parlor. "You look awful, Siegfried— you don't mind if I address you so familiarly?"

Siegfried shook his head. He felt like hell.

"No? Good. Please, call me Walter. Now, what exactly has happened?"

"...and then she ordered me out. *Ach Gott*, I've been the worst sort of cad." Siegfried leaned back in his armchair some time later. He blinked away moisture from his eyes. "I have ruined everything by my deceit. I am a fool," he said glumly, for the tenth time. "A stupid, arrogant, lying fool."

"You certainly have got a lot to answer for," Bundschu said sternly, peering at Siegfried over the tops of his steel-rimmed spectacles. "And I can't say I blame your wife one bit. I would have done the same, and thrashed you into the bargain." He leaned forward. "But are you *really* going to abandon a pregnant woman to run Montclair by herself, without a foreman, and the black grapes still left to harvest?"

Siegfried swallowed hard, thinking of Alice, growing thinner and paler every day. What if something happened to her baby? *His* baby.

He set down his empty port glass. "You're right. I have to go back. Tomorrow morning, I'll beg her to let me make amends. I will continue working for her. I'll sleep in the cottage, I'll even eat with the pickers—"

A giant *boom* shivered through the windowpanes, making the reflections on the smooth black glass quiver and dance. The air rang like a monstrous bell.

"What was *that*?" asked Bundschu, leaping to his feet.

"An explosion," said Siegfried, with horrible certainty. The echoes reverberated through the valley as the two men lifted up the window in joint effort, and stuck their heads out to look around.

An orange glow rose up over the trees. Siegfried's heartbeat quick-marched. "My winery! My winery is burning!"

Footsteps sounded outside the library door, then Mrs. Bundschu flung it open. "Walter, what's going on? What was that noise?"

"There's a fire. The Montclair tanks just exploded! Telephone the fire department. I'll take the car and see what we can do!"

As Bundschu stopped at his door and bent to slip galoshes over his bare feet, Siegfried sprinted outside and began cranking the Bundschu's parked Ford. *Lieber Gott, ich bitte Dich,* Siegfried prayed as he turned the handle with desperate strength. *Let Alice and our baby be safe. Please, God.*

The engine caught on the upstroke, springing to life with a vicious growl. Clad in his pajamas and robe, Bundschu came trotting out of the house and jumped into the car as Siegfried put it in gear.

"I *know* I put out the fire under the still," Siegfried fretted. He took the ruts in the ridgetop road leading to the back of the winery at a far higher speed than he would have dared in daylight. Fortunately, the side-lights on the old car shone brightly enough. "I sent Peter away, and then I put the fire out. I know I did!"

"Won't know what happened till we get there," Bundschu tried to soothe Siegfried. "Keep driving, son."

They jounced and skidded as he took a turn too fast. Bundschu hung on for dear life, and craned forward beyond the range of the side lamps. He clucked his tongue.

"What?" Siegfried demanded.

"The winery's a solid wall of flames." They both flinched as another boom rent the night. "I'm so sorry."

The car's tires slid across dirt as Siegfried smashed all three pedals to the floor. He was out before the car came to a full stop at the loading platform, running down to the winery entrance.

He tried to outrun the thought that now he would never know what flavors this child of his hands would have shown at maturity.

He stopped short of the building. It was no use trying to save it. Even if the fire department arrived now, there wasn't enough water in the pond to begin to put out a blaze like this. The roof was ablaze, as was the interior of the stone building. The stones cracked and popped from the heat, and oozed wine from cracks. The fire laughed as it devoured his precious cooperage.

A gush of liquid two feet deep sloshed out as the front door gave way. The broken, burning tanks were bleeding wine. Splashing runnels cascaded down the path. The wine put out the fire at the door's foot, but the old wood lintel burned blue.

Siegfried stood staring at the inferno, turned to stone by the Medusa face of fire at the winery's entrance, her snaky locks writhing skyward.

The heat blistered his skin. He retreated, and heard Bundschu shout, "The house— the house is burning, too!"

Siegfried ran downhill, racing the river of wine, heedless of slippery gravel and slick mud, sliding and leaping as his heart stood still. The back wall of the house stuck out a tongue of fire. He lengthened his stride.

As he rounded the corner by the vegetable garden, he saw Maria, dressed in her nightgown. She sat on the ground against the picket fence, seemingly insensible of the flood of wine that foamed around her. She held something in her arms— something large, and dark, and limp.

Firelit tears streaked her cheeks. She rocked back and forth. Her eyes gazed in Siegfried's direction, but she did not register his presence.

Siegfried crossed himself.

Peter's body lay in Maria's arms, his sightless eyes open. Something had smashed in one side of his head. The shoulder of Maria's gown was stained with his blood.

"Maria!" Siegfried gasped. "Maria! Where is Alice?"

Her face turned blindly in his direction. "Hugh Roye killed my husband." She started shaking, and her next question was pitifully plaintive. "What am I going to do?" She bent her head, resting her cheek against Peter's untouched hair. "What am I going to do?" She resumed rocking back and forth over her husband's corpse.

Terror seized Siegfried. *Hugh.* He had come, and set the fire. Peter must have surprised him at it and paid the ultimate price trying to defend Montclair.

In another moment he spotted Hugh, a shovel dangling loosely from one hand, standing near the smoking porch steps. As Siegfried approached, Hugh did not turn around. He seemed mesmerized by the burning house, lit in lurid reds by the flames leaping from the winery.

"*Du Scheißkerl*!" Siegfried grabbed his cousin from behind, and shook him like a rat. Hugh's head snapped back and forth and he almost fell. Siegfried grabbed his shirt collar and hauled him around. "How could you do this!" His hands slid up a centimeter or two, and closed around Hugh's throat.

"Stop! Stop it! I didn't—!" Hugh clawed at Siegfried's hands but was unable to loosen their strangling grip. His lips moved: *Alice is still inside!*

The unvoiced words left Siegfried feeling gutted. He flung Hugh roughly out of the way and ran up the porch steps. The kitchen door was burning, thick wisps of smoke coiling up to the night sky, so he followed the porch around to the front door. The door knob refused to turn. He rattled it with wild incomprehension, trying to force it open. It had *never* been locked as long as he had been living at Montclair.

He pushed himself away from the unyielding door with a frustrated growl. He scanned the exterior of the house, then dashed several steps to his right. Pulling back his arm, he punched a hole in the parlor window.

The impact numbed his hand, but there was no time to stop and examine it. He reached through the hole, forcing his forearm through the barrier of jagged shards, and fumbled open the small metal latch. Then he was able to slide the window up with a mighty heave and scramble over the sill, awkwardly tumbling inside.

The house was black with choking smoke. Siegfried rolled to his feet and shouted Alice's name, doubling over in a fit of coughing.

He groped for the parlor door, then blundered down the front hall. Acrid clouds of smoke billowed from the kitchen, and flames hissed and crackled in the dining room. Red streamers of light reflected off the hallway walls.

Siegfried slammed shut the dining room doors, trying to keep the fire from the stairs for another minute. Then, dangerously lightheaded and gasping for breath, he ran upstairs. He pushed open Alice's bedroom door. "Alice!"

She lay curled on the bed, limp and unmoving. Siegfried's heart contracted painfully. *Was she hurt?* He shook her shoulder. "Alice— wake up! The house is on fire!"

Alice muttered something incoherent and tried to roll away from him. A wave of pure alcoholic fumes rose up as the empty green *grappa* bottle fell from her fingers.

Of all the times to abandon her habit of moderation!

He bent, scooped her up from the bed, flung her over his shoulder in a fireman's hold, and stumbled back out into the hallway. His throat and lungs raw, Siegfried coughed steadily as he descended stair by stair, gripping the sturdy banister, his precious burden balanced carefully. A hot draft blew upwards, and he tried to hurry his painfully slow descent, but the blinding smoke grew turgid in a living nightmare. He wanted to run, but he could not.

At every step down, his knees felt increasingly rubbery. He could not see for smoke, and tears, and darkness. He was aware only of the solid wood under his feet, and the warm bulk of Alice's body.

After an eternity of reaching down cautiously with his foot for the next step, he realized that he was at the bottom of the staircase. Dizzy now, he wavered as he clung to the rounded newel post. He marshaled the last dregs of his strength to let go of the newel and sprint to the end of the hall. He knew the tall square of the front door stood guard there. He just couldn't *see* it. It was an unattainable distance away down the dark hallway.

He took one step forward, but a cold, tenacious, winter-in-the-trenches chill seized him deep in his bones. He couldn't feel his arms any more. He glanced sideways to make sure Alice's legs and derriere were firmly encircled by his grip. He froze in horror.

A huge, dark stain spread over her white nightgown, starting where his right arm crossed the back of her thighs. *The baby! Please, God, don't let her lose our baby!*

He locked his knees together. The roaring of the fire was drowned out by a shrill whine of blood in his ears. He had sworn to save Montclair— or die trying.

He had failed. Utterly failed. He had worked so hard, and yet brought nothing but ruin. *Ah-lees, I am so sorry.* He pressed his cheek into the soft curve of her hip. She squirmed, feebly, then fell still. *Ah-lees.* Was she dead, too?

The smoky darkness filled with blue and yellow sparkles. He tried to take another step forward, but someone had amputated his legs. He did not feel his body hit the floor.

Alice was having the strangest dream. She was hot, and someone was jumping on her stomach. Her head hurt, and everything was swinging wildly about. She coughed, trying to keep nausea at bay, and tasted smoke. But she did not quite wake up from her *grappa*-induced stupor because Siegfried had his arms around her, and that meant she was safe. But why did it feel like she was hanging onto him... *upside-down?*

She moved, trying to relieve the pressure against her stomach and ribcage. "Si'gfr'd, get off me," she mumbled, trying to push him away. She couldn't breathe, and besides, wasn't she angry at him because—?

She was falling.

Alice woke up with a scream when she hit the floor.

Her hips and backside hurt, and she couldn't breathe. Siegfried lay sprawled on her, and the hall runner was rough and prickly through her nightgown. She blinked, and recognized the regular pattern of bannisters towering above them.

What are we doing at the foot of the stairs? she thought, in the same instant that she coughed again. She had not been dreaming the smoke.

Wriggling backwards from beneath Siegfried's limp form, she braced her arms against the carpet and raised herself to a partially sitting position.

Her heart, already pounding from the shock of her awakening, accelerated further when she saw the lurid red light shining under the kitchen and dining room doors.

Fire!

She grabbed Siegfried's head by the hair, and lifted it up from where it lay. His eyelids fluttered briefly, but he did not respond. His arm— blood welled up from deep cuts in his arm and dark blotches stained her nightgown. Oh, dear God, she was soaked with his blood.

"Wake up!" She shook him as hard as she could. "Siegfried, get up!" The light increased fractionally. "Siegfried!" she screamed, "Oh God, please help me. *Siegfried!*"

He did not rouse.

She had to get them out. Soon everything would be ablaze. But what was she going to do about Siegfried? Alice's thoughts ran in a panicked circle.

She inhaled a lungful of smoke and, coughing, scrambled up on her knees. She hooked her hand under Siegfried's armpit, trying to drag him toward the front door. She managed to straighten out his limp form, but he moved barely an inch.

She tried again. All the weight Siegfried had gained this summer made him too heavy to move. He was a dead weight—Frantically, she tore open his shirt, pressing her hand against his chest. But her own heart was beating too hard to feel anything except her own hammering pulse in her fingertips.

A red flame licked through the dining room door with a wave of heat. She fell off her knees onto her bottom, jarring frozen thoughts loose.

This was no place to quit! The fire didn't care whether she was ladylike or not, where she came from, who her mother was. She would burn— more importantly, Siegfried and his child would burn if she could not get them away.

The hallway swam unpleasantly. She would have to pull Siegfried to the door. But she didn't have the strength.

No. She would find the strength. God would just have to give her the strength to do it.

"I won't leave you here!" she yelled, angrier than she had ever been, angrier even than when Siegfried had confessed his lie. "I don't know why you came back, but damn it, I'm not going to leave you!"

She pushed herself to her feet and grabbed Siegfried's unresisting arms. He was so heavy, and the hall carpet grabbed at his legs and held him back. She clung to her anger to keep panic at bay, dug in her toes, and *pulled*.

This time, they moved six inches. Alice's breath hissed between her teeth as she shifted her grip under Siegfried's armpit, tightened her stomach muscles, and raised Siegfried's back and hips off the floor. She inched forward, and he moved with her, only his heels dragging. *Thank You, oh thank You*, she prayed in silent gratitude as she fought not to cough.

Another foot, then another, each seeming easier than the last. *We're going to make it out,* she thought, almost disbelieving, until she hit a mountain.

Not a mountain, not really, only the ridges in the hall runner she had kicked up earlier that night. But they might as well have been a range of hills. She couldn't lift Siegfried any higher. Her knees trembled. In another moment they would give out, and she would fall... The fire would leap upon them, and devour them... and she would never have the chance to see Siegfried hold his child...

She looked over her shoulder at her goal, gathering her strength. It flew open in a shower of wood splinters and a crash that was barely audible over the hungry roar of the fire pursuing her. A man with a shovel stood sihouetted momentarily in the doorway.

"Alice!" Then Hugh was there, scooping up Siegfried, gasping and coughing. He was saying something, but she couldn't hear. She bent as Hugh pulled Siegfried past her, and caught Siegfried's feet, lifting them, helping Hugh the last few feet towards the door. Then they were outside on the porch, and the night air was cold and fresh after the heat and choking atmosphere in the house.

Hugh's words finally became comprehensible: "Alice, I didn't do this. I didn't set the fire," he said, over and over again. Sweat and tears rolled down his face, leaving tracks in the soot.

"Of course you didn't— *set* the fire?" Another spasm of coughing interrupted anything else she might have said, anything else she might have thought.

They wavered and lurched across the porch. Walter Bundschu appeared. "Let me," he urged. He slipped his hands under Siegfried's calvess. Smoothly, he lifted her husband from her numbed grip.

Alice clung dizzily to the porch railing as she watched the two men bear Siegfried's unmoving form toward an unfamiliar Ford. *Is he dead?* A great yawning emptiness opened at the thought.

Behind her, fire raced down the hall runner, leaping up to the doorway, sending hungry sparks across the porch after her.

She stumbled down the stairs and across the narrow strip of yard, the ground rising and falling like the deck of the Transbay ferry. She collapsed onto her hands and knees in the drive under the palm trees, the gravel yielding and slippery beneath her fingers, fragrant with— wine?

Siegfried's wine? She looked around and saw, blurrily, that he was being bundled into the back of Walter Bundschu's car, and that Walter was tying a rough bandage around Siegfried's bleeding arm.

He was going to be all right. He was being taken care of.

Her face felt funny— stiff, and tight. *I'm going to be sick.* But she felt no repugnance, only blessed relief. She let her head hang. No braid fell down. She smelled burned hair and her stomach revolted.

When she finally finished bringing up the evil-tasting remnants of the *grappa*, she did not think she would ever be able to move again. And she didn't want to move, even if the volunteer firefighters, just now arriving, did see her like this.

A loud shriek made her head snap up. Toward the back of the house, lit by the fire's leaping light, Maria broke free from the fireman who was attempting to restrain her. There was a blanket-shrouded body at her feet, and as Alice watched, Maria screamed. "No! No! NO! Don't arrest him!"

Behind Maria, Hugh Roye, his head bowed, did not resist as Sheriff Albertson put handcuffs on him. He never glanced up as Maria's screaming reduced to sobs. He only shook his head briefly in response to something Albertson asked him and ducked awkwardly into the sheriff's car.

Oh, no, Alice thought. *Not Peter. Not Hugh. Oh, please.*

"Mrs. Rodenwiller," a male voice said. She felt a jacket being draped around her shoulders and hands lifting her up. "Are you all right?"

She saw someone blurrily. It was Mr. Duhring. "Siegfried?" she gasped, and bent double, coughing. Mr. Duhring held her until she could breathe again, then gently turned her.

"Oh, my God!" he said, appalled. "Quick! Get that car over here!" he yelled. In a more soothing tone, one she found infinitely more frightening, he said to her, "Mr. Bundschu's going to drive you to Doctor Stillman's office, Mrs. Rodernwiller. Hang on, okay?"

As Mr. Duhring lifted her into the car, she saw firemen turn a hose onto the burning house, their little pumper truck valiantly sucking water from Montclair's reservoir. A thin arc of water touched the flames and the back half of the house collapsed in on itself in a violent cloud of red and yellow sparks. Alice's breath escaped her in a long sigh.

"I'm so sorry about your house, Mrs. Rodernwiller," Mr. Bundschu said, aiming his car down the drive to the gate. "And about Mr. Verdacchia."

She didn't say anything, or look back. It was over. They might extinguish the fire, but the house was gone.

Siegfried was slumped in the other corner of the back seat, his head propped at an angle against the canvas of the raised top. She wondered dully if she could force herself to move far enough to arrange him into a better position.

In another moment she was sliding toward him, easing his position by leaning his body against hers. He was still breathing, and she touched the base of his throat, feeling his pulse beating.

Thank you, God!

❧

Drifting through the darkness that had overtaken him in the house, Siegfried drew a breath, and coughed harshly, his lungs burning. It was dark. He was sitting upright, and the jostling of the train's movement was uncomfortable.

Why am I on a train? He tried to open his eyes, to advise the conductor that there must be some mistake. *The last place I wish to be is on a train.* He wanted to see Alice, he wanted to be with her.

Grief fountained in the darkness. *I am on a train because Alice is sending me away. Has already sent me away.*

He wondered briefly where he was going, then decided he did not care. He had failed. He had sworn to succeed or die trying, and now he must pay the price. It would be far easier just to sleep and pretend that he was not being exiled from his home— again.

He let the rocking motion of the train draw him deeper into peace and forgetfulness, imagining the golden-brown hills of Sonoma County slipping away from him in the darkness.

Walter Bundschu raced along Lovell Valley Road, bouncing Alice and Siegfried together.

"Do you have to go so fast?" Alice asked after another pothole set her head nearly into the canvas top of the touring car.

"Oh— Oh, Mrs. Rodernwiller. You're awake?" Bundschu slowed down immediately. "The way Mr. Duhring was talking, I thought you were—"

"I'm not dead yet," Alice said. She coughed again. Siegfried coughed too. "But don't slow down too much."

Bundschu's pace increased until he was going moderately fast. At least the car wasn't jouncing so much. He glanced at Alice in the rear view mirror, his gaze full of concern for more than her safety. "You know, your husband, he came to us tonight. He was real sorry about what he'd done."

Selfish curiosity bit Alice. She had thought she could feel no higher terror than this night had already brought. *He talked about us. He talked about* me. "What did he tell you?"

"That he lied to you, when you wanted to switch to prunes earlier this summer," Bundschu said, and shook his head sadly. "Because he was scared of where he would go. Not much call for winemakers, these days. That he was sorry you didn't want to stay married to him."

Alice felt guilty relief. Siegfried hadn't revealed her circumstances. "He only wanted the land I inherited from Bill. It was supposed to stay in the family. The *Roye* family, whose coattails I am not worthy to touch," Alice added resentfully, before deciding she had already said too much.

"But when he saw that you were in trouble—" Bundschu clicked his tongue expressively. "The way I see it, if the land's all he cared about, then he could have just wrung his hands on the sidelines. He would have been a rich widower. He didn't need to run into that burning house."

She remembered her panic when she thought Siegfried might die, and her desolation at the thought of living without him.

"Sounds like you two need to talk. If you'll accept some advice from an old married man," Bundschu kept his eyes straight ahead on the road, "when the two of you are stronger together than you are alone, then you should fight hard to save what you have. From what Siegfried told me earlier, he was willing to fight. Are you?"

She loved Siegfried, but could she ever forgive him for his betrayal of her trust? "Maybe," she said, realizing that she wanted the chance to find out. Her hand curled around Siegfried's shoulder, as if she could anchor him to this world, as if she were afraid that she needed to hold him lest he escape.

Sonoma
Friday, October 10, just after midnight

The doctor's home office was a pretty gingerbread house near the Sebastiani winery. Alice was swiftly examined, pronounced sound except for a minor case of smoke inhalation, given hot peppermint tea to soothe her raw throat, and ordered to go to bed.

Though she was stumbling with fatigue, she insisted weakly that she wanted to stay and keep vigil while Dr. Stillman stitched up the long, jagged gash in Siegfried's arm. The young doctor frowned at her sternly and asked his wife to take Alice to their guest room. Mrs. Stillman lent Alice one of her own sensible nightgowns and her husband's robe, and made her free of their bathroom, filling the deep tub with hot water and the mirror with steam so Alice couldn't see herself.

When she emerged from the bath, her own bloodstained nightgown was gone, and Mrs. Stillman was there, ready to put her to bed.

But before she could allow herself the luxury of sleep, Alice had to make two phone calls. Mrs. Stillman let her use the doctor's telephone in the parlor. The first call was to Giuseppa Ambrogi, Maria's widowed mother, who lived on the outskirts of Sonoma. Once she had recovered from the shock of the news,

Giuseppa promised to go immediately to Maria.

Then it was time to make the second, more difficult 'phone call, to Grandmother Tati in San Francisco. Alice hesitated before picking up the receiver, the taste of smoke suddenly flooding her mouth. Should she inflict this news on the old lady now? Perhaps it would be better if she waited until the morning... *Don't be a coward*, said her conscience. Alice sighed, and asked the night operator to connect her.

The phone rang many times before Tati's voice, quavery and frightened, answered. "Hello?"

Alice thought the old woman had some experience with bad news coming in the middle of the night. She took a deep breath. "Grandmother Tati, it's Alice. I— have to tell you. There's been a fire at Montclair."

"Siegfried?" Tati's voice broke, and Alice hastened to reassure her.

"He was injured. The doctor is with him now. But the house and the winery— they're gone, Tati."

"Montclair is gone?" Tati asked, disbelief clear. "The house William built for me when we married? Where my children were born?" Alice heard the unspoken accusation against her. "And what about the winery, William's pride and joy?"

"I'm sorry, Tati," croaked Alice. Guilt strangled her.

"I spent the happiest years of my life at Montclair. I gave it to young Bill," Tati continued, in a soft, detached voice, speaking to herself, not Alice. "Even thought I knew he couldn't hold onto it. What a sunny, good-natured boy he was! But weak— so weak! And then you came—"

"Tati," Alice forced her statement past the rawness in her throat. "Peter's dead and they've arrested Hugh."

The detachment in Tati's voice was replaced by ice. "So, he's murdered someone else! I always expected it. Now he's brought shame to us all— again."

Alice's knees threatened to give way. "I don't think he did it, Grandmother Tati. He helped me rescue Siegfried." Tati thought her grandson was a *murderer*?

"Does it matter? Siegfried was supposed to save Montclair. Now it's gone. Gone!" Alice heard Tati's sigh. "Someone competent should be watching over my grandson. I'll take the first ferry out in the morning, dear." She disconnected abruptly.

Mrs. Stillman allowed Alice to hang up the receiver, then took her arm firmly when she tried to return to Siegfried. "Your husband's still unconscious, Mrs. Rodernwiller," she said, kindly. "You can sit with him in the morning, when you've had some sleep."

"But—" Alice protested.

"I know," Mrs. Stillman gave her a small smile, and added: "You must think of your baby."

Too weary for more words, Alice allowed herself to be steered. Once they reached the spartan guestroom she didn't notice Mrs. Stillman leave the room, and barely managed to pull the covers over herself before collapsing into utter exhaustion.

When she woke up in the gray hour before dawn, Alice's throat felt scoured from the inside with steel wool. She opened her eyes and lay staring up at dim, unfamiliar walls while she sorted out last night's events from the troubled dreams that had followed.

Montclair is gone. Siegfried lied to me— and almost died for me. Tati's on her way from San Francisco.

Alice groaned and tried to sit up. She fell back against the pillows on her first attempt: her back, shoulders, and bottom were stiff and painful, and her head was two or three times larger than it should be. But she knew she had to get moving. Siegfried was downstairs, somewhere. He might be awake.

Slowly, she levered herself out of bed and shuffled to the bathroom. In the stark electric light she could see her reddened, blistered face in the mirror above the washstand. She leaned closer. She had no eyebrows, and the short ends of her hair were ragged and blobby-looking. *My hair is gone!*

Yesterday's happenings were suddenly, horribly real. She wanted to cry, but she couldn't spare the time.

A chamomile infusion left for her by Mrs. Stillman, scented with the honeyed fragrance of dried flowers, felt heavenly against her outraged skin. She brushed out the sorry remains of her hair and dressed herself in the blouse, skirt, and underthings Mrs. Stillman had also left. The stiffness decreased fractionally as she moved through her toilette.

She found her way downstairs, where Mrs. Stillman refused her abject thanks for her hospitality and forced her to eat breakfast "for the baby's sake" before she would allow Alice to go to Siegfried's room. Alice obediently chewed ashy toast and swallowed tasteless coffee. *Had the doctor stopped the bleeding? Was Siegfried going to be all right?*

When Mrs. Stillman decreed she had eaten enough, she led Alice to the infirmary.

Her heart lurched when she saw Siegfried's poor, scorched face against the white pillows. He struggled for every breath, and his right arm was mummified in bandages.

Dr. Stillman didn't offer much hope. "There's no more I can do. I'm sorry. His injuries don't appear grievous, but he hasn't regained consciousness. Sometimes such a trauma..." The doctor checked Siegfried's pulse, then set his wrist down gently. "He's in God's hands, now." He closed the door softly behind him.

Alice sat down next to the bed. She took Siegfried's limp hand and pressed it to her cheek. It tore her apart to hear his raspy breathing. He had come for her, had tried to save her from the fire. What did that mean? Alice wondered if she would ever have a chance to learn Siegfried's true heart.

She wanted her baby to know its father. "Please wake up. Please, Siegfried. Get better. Please, God, let him get well." Her tears trickled across her fingers, his fingers, as if they were one flesh.

It was a weeping dawn, the first rain of autumn. Shooed away from Siegfried's bedside so that Mrs. Stillman could bathe him and change his sheets, Alice sat on a brocaded sofa in the palm-crowded parlor, fretting about the grapes remaining on the vine. Would their flavors be hopelessly diluted? She remembered Siegfried's boast that his palate was more accurate than the Brix scale used to measure the sweetness of the fruit and its readiness for harvesting. Would he ever taste a grape again?

When she realized what she was thinking, she leaned her forehead against her arm and watched the pale mist bead on the windows, trying to damp her thoughts into nothingness, trying to be patient until she could *do* something.

Tati found her there, some time later, when the world outside had lightened a few more shades of gray. "Grandmother Tati," Alice said, rising and offering her hand.

Tati seated herself in an armchair opposite and began to take off her gloves with trembling fingers, none of her usual briskness evident. Tiny droplets of water dewed the wool of Tati's long, button-trimmed black coat, and the feather on her hat drooped. Wisps of her silver hair floated free. "That quack can't tell me how Siegfried's going to be."

"No, he's still... sleeping." Would he ever wake?

"We'll have to move him to a hospital in San Francisco. Country doctors are useless."

"Doctor Stillman's a fine doctor. He and his wife have been very kind to me."

Tati sniffed. "He did tell me you're pregnant. You could

have shared this bit of important news sooner, Alice."

Alice bit back an automatic apology. She would have told Tati the minute it was happy news, and not a bone of contention between Siegfried and herself. Now, her baby was another burden of responsibility that she shouldered alone, unless Tati might be willing to help. "We've been so busy. Crush..."

Tati looked away, her lips pressed in a thin line. "Indeed," she said after mastering her emotions. "I have been busy, as well. I spoke with the sheriff this morning. Hugh's preliminary hearing is tomorrow at nine in Santa Rosa I hope he gets everything that's coming to him." Her eyes blazed with grim satisfaction.

"Grandmother Tati, you can't really believe he murdered Peter? Hugh told me he didn't set the fire."

"Then he's a liar as well as an arsonist and a murderer."

Alice was aghast at the naked hatred the old woman revealed. "How can you say that?"

"If you only knew—" Tati leaned forward, gripping the arms of her chair. "Well! I suppose you should know, so you can stop wasting your sympathy on him. I learned Hugh's real character during the '06 earthquake and fire. The most terrible day of my life..."

Tati's eyes slid from Alice, focused on empty air. "We lived on the western slope of Nob Hill in a beautiful house William built for me. It had every convenience. Running water, an elevator, gas...." Tati patted her eyes with her handkerchief. "Betty had married Heinrich Rodernwiller and moved to Rodern. Our son Teddy had no head for business, and he liked to play cards. William insisted that they live with us, so that Julia and the boys would always have a roof over their heads."

"April sixteenth was Hugh's birthday. Although William was away on business, we had a lovely party. I remember how thrilled I was that Hugh would start at Berkeley in the fall. The only consolation I have—" A fault of long-suppressed grief threatened to crack Tati's serenity, but she contained it, and went on, "—was that Julia never discovered where Teddy took Hugh that night. When the earthquake hit— you remember how it was, Alice?"

Alice nodded. She had hidden under her bed, shivering, until the earth's endless shuddering finally stopped.

"Just before dawn, I woke up to a rumble, like waves beating against a cliff. A huge jolt shook the house, and it... just... dropped. I heard the chimney fall through the roof. The shaking didn't stop. It got stronger and stronger. Churchbells were ringing, and Julia was screaming. Then everything went quiet, and I ran down the hallway. I opened the door to their room—"

Tati swallowed convulsively. "It wasn't dawn yet. There was so much dust, I could hardly see. But the bed— the chimney lay across the bed. There was only the headboard— and Julia's face— and that hideous sound she was making. I tried to lift the bricks, but they were too heavy. There were too many! I pulled and I pulled and... the house started to shake again. Billy was crying in his room. So I told Julia I would come back for her, and went to get my grandson.

"Somehow, we made it out to the street. We were standing there in our nightclothes, with the rest of our neighbors, when the shaking finally stopped. It was so quiet. No one spoke; it was as if the entire city held its breath. Then Teddy and Hugh came running up. They were fully dressed, and I will never forget until the day I die how they stank of stale champagne and cheap perfume."

Tati's eyes met Alice's now. "Of course I knew exactly where they'd been. Teddy asked me where Julia was. He told Hugh to take care of his little brother, and rushed into the house. I heard him trip over something downstairs, curse the lack of a light, and then— he must have lit a match, the fool! The house— coughed, and fire burst through the living room windows. The gas lines—"

Alice drew breath in a sharp hiss of sympathy, but Tati wasn't finished.

"I tried to go up the stairs, but Hugh held me back. He held onto Billy, too. I screamed at him, but he wouldn't let me go. He just stood there in the street, and let his father and mother burn. He let my son burn..." Now Tati wept, old tired tears. She stared off into the rain and a single tremor shook her. "If he had only tried, he could have saved Teddy."

"And *that's* why you hate him? He saved your life!" Alice froze as Tati's contemptuous gaze swept and dismissed her.

"I could never look at Hugh again without seeing Julia, in that bed." Tati held the much-abused handkerchief to her lips. She took a steadying breath. "The firemen came, but of course they couldn't do anything: the water pipes had broken. I took Billy home to Montclair. Betty was an angel. She came all the way from Europe to help me. I don't think I would have survived that summer without her. It was months before I could sleep."

"Where did Hugh go?"

"I didn't know. I didn't care. William must have sent him some money, but I didn't want to hear about it. As far as I was concerned, he could go hang—"

"He might yet," Alice said, shocked to her core at the

unfairness of it all. Poor Hugh! Reviled all his life for an act of courage. "Don't you care that, if— if Siegfried dies, Hugh will be the last Roye?"

Tatiana Roye aimed an artificial smile in Alice's direction. "But he won't be the last. Dearest Alice, you're carrying the Montclair heir. And I intend to take very good care of the both of you if anything— happens to Siegfried."

Loathing formed a scratchy ball in Alice's throat. When she could speak again, she said, "Hugh may not have been a perfect gentleman toward me, but I won't let my personal feelings stand in the way of justice. If you won't help Hugh, then I will, even if I have to sell Montclair to do it."

"I won't allow you to sell." Tati's voice rose, but she brought it under control. "I wouldn't expect someone with a background like *yours* to understand."

"I understand well enough. You value a piece of property over your own flesh and blood."

"Alice, you never deserved my land. You were never good enough for either of my grandsons. If you try to sell, I will fight you with every weapon I have." Tati pursed her lips. "I have connections, my dear, and they will agree with me that my great-grandson should not be raised in a gutter by a whore's daughter. I'll take Siegfried's child— it *is* Siegfried's child? —and raise him to be a true Roye."

Alice snarled, "Over my dead body!" How had she ever thought she wanted to be a lady like Tati?

Mrs. Stillman knocked politely on the open parlor door, then peeked around the doorframe. "You can see your grandson now, Mrs. Roye."

Sonoma
Friday, October 10

Quivering with the aftereffects of her confrontation with Tati, Alice ran blindly out of the house, through the neighborhood. *Could she really take my baby?* Her face burned in the cool, humid air. She considered Tati's feud with Hugh, and the ruthless way the old lady had blackmailed Alice into marrying Siegfried. *Oh yes. She's capable of anything.*

Alice kicked aside piles of wet leaves with her borrowed shoes, kindling her anger to the same strength-giving rage that had sustained her through her confrontation with Siegfried last night. She placed a protective hand over her belly. *No. I won't let her.*

But who would help her now? Siegfried might, if he woke up. *When* he woke, she amended.

The sky began to lighten and blue sky appeared through thinning clouds as she strode along, propelled by her turmoil. The sparkle of a stray sunbeam on a water-beaded spider web caught her eye, reminding her of the dragonfly brooch.

Alice had tried so hard to remake herself, to become someone Tati would approve of. And what good had it done her? She laughed, giddy with anger and defiance. Well, she wasn't going to knuckle under this time. Betrayal, arson, murder: she had survived them all. She was strong. Strong enough to send Siegfried packing when her heart was in shreds.

Strong enough to say no to Tati and her blackmail this time.

A sign on a plain frame building caught her eye: *Meals with Wine, 25 cents.* The 'with Wine' had been crossed out. She realized she had walked blindly through town as far as the Toscano Hotel on East Spain Street.

Alice pushed open the door and went inside. She smiled at the clerk behind the lobby desk. He was painfully young and neat with wire-rimmed spectacles and his pomaded hair in a ruler-straight part. He smiled back brilliantly.

She would show them all. No more hiding. No more lies.

"Good afternoon, Ma'am," the clerk said in Italian-accented English. "How may I assist you?"

Alice heard herself make some polite noises. Her blood was singing with excitement and fear, warming her gloveless fingers. It was such a small town: the news would spread fast. "I'd like to rent a room, please," she said. "And I need to make a 'phone call to San Francisco."

Of course, Gertie Breitenbach was the telephone operator on duty.

Gertie greeted her, then said, "I was so sorry to hear about your fire, Mrs. Rodernwiller. Poor Mrs. Verdacchia! I hope your husband recovers from his injuries soon. Where are you staying? With Dorothy married now, we have a spare bedroom..."

"That's very kind of you." Alice wondered if Gertie would regret her offer once she learned whom Alice was 'phoning. "But I've got a room at the Toscano Hotel for now."

"If you change your mind, you know you're welcome to stay with us for as long as you like. Now, how may I help you?"

Alice took a deep breath. "I'm trying to 'phone my mother. I have her address— it's a business." She gave Gertie her mother's full name and Commercial Street address.

"It'll be just a minute while I flip through the San Francisco directory," Gertie said, then said conversationally, "We've never met your mother, dear. What sort of business does she own?"

"She owns a parlor house," Alice said, defiantly. *No more lies*. "We haven't seen each other in years, but the wedding present she sent me had the same address."

Dead silence on the line.

Alice's anger cooled instantly to a cold lump. She closed her eyes. *What was I thinking?* While it lasted, it had been so nice to belong here, among respectable people.

"Oh, my." Gertie finally said. "Is this it? The directory lists a Mrs. Campbell and Restaurant Florence at that location. Shall I connect you?"

Alice was beyond mortified by now. *Was* it the right place? "Yes, please," she replied, finding herself a little short of breath at the prospect that it was. "Thank you for your help, Mrs. Breitenbach."

"You're welcome."

There was a click, a conversation between Gertie and the San Francisco operator, another long pause, then a woman's French-accented voice. "Restaurant Florence. We are not open until six o'clock."

"I'd like to speak to Mrs. Campbell, please."

"Who, may I ask, is calling?" the woman asked, haughtily enough to make Alice smile.

"Her daughter."

"Oh," The haughtiness disappeared along with the spurious accent. Her voice became soft, hesitant, and entirely American. "Alice, honey, is that you?"

"Mama." Alice voice emerged as a croak. She cleared her throat and started again. "Mama?"

"Oh, baby girl, I'm so happy to hear from you! Are you all right? When I read about the fire at your grape farm in the *Chronicle* this morning I almost broke my promise not to ever see you again. I was so worried about you!"

"You promised *what*? Da never said anything about that!"

"Oh, well. Your Da and me decided it was best— But what do you need?" she asked shrewdly.

"Mama, I need your help. You know the house burned down. Before the fire, I told Siegfried to leave. Then he— the doctor says he should be okay but he won't wake up. I'm going to have a baby—" Alice couldn't continue. *And Siegfried's grandmother wants to steal it.*

"Imagine! Me a grandma!" Her mother gave a delighted laugh. "I'll be there on the next ferry, baby girl, and I'll bring my car with me. I can run whatever errands you need: call your insurance man, whatever. You just tell me what you want done."

"Mama, this is terrible of me, but I need clothes— I have nothing but what the doctor's wife gave me to wear—and money for my lawyer. Tatiana Roye wants to take the property back— and she's threatened—" Alice swallowed. She would *not* cry. "She's threatened to take my baby because I'm your daughter. And I'm not going to let her do it!"

"That's my girl," Florence said, a proud smile audible in her voice. "I'm coming right away. Now here's what you do first. You go to your bank and get them to give you some checks. You go next to your lawyer there in town, and you make sure your name is on the title to the property, and you see if that lawyer's good and sharp enough for you. And if he's not, don't worry. I know plenty of lawyers, and judges, and nobody's going to take nothing from you. I'll be there this afternoon."

"Thank you, Mama. Good-bye, Mama." Alice heard the connection end. She tried several times to hang the ear horn on its hook, but she couldn't quite see it, and her hand trembled too much. Eventually she made it. She rubbed her hands across her eyes and straightened.

First— the bank.

She arrived at Lee Crabbe's law office on West Napa Street, new checks in her pocket. Alice forced herself to unknot her hands and enter.

Lee, a tall, lean man with curly light-brown hair and a friendly smile, had been one of Hugh's friends. He always looked as though he would be more at home in a workingman's jeans than his dark professional suits.

"Mrs. Roye— er, Rodernwiller," he greeted her, in his soft-spoken way. "I was so sorry to hear about the fire, and about Mr. Verdacchia. I want to let you know that I'm ready to do everything I can to help you." He directed her to sit down in a comfortable leather armchair.

Alice plucked self-consciously at her ragged hair. "Mr. Crabbe, it's possible that I will have to sell Montclair, and my husband's family doesn't want me to. I need to know if they can stop me. Plus, I have a question about the insurance."

"I see. Well, I hope I can clarify some of the issues for you. Let's first discuss the property ownership, then I'll go over your insurance policy with you. I have a copy in my files. May I get you a cup of coffee before we begin?" When Alice shook her head, he seated himself behind his large oak desk, and uncapped his fountain pen. "Now then, where shall I direct your correspondence?"

"I don't know where I'm going to be, but Maria will be living in the foreman's cottage at Montclair. She can forward any mail."

"Well, we know you've owned the property since Bill died," Mr. Crabbe continued, calculating the elapsed time. "About a year and a half? And it was a probated inheritance. I remember the settlement of his estate quite well."

Alice nodded.

"So that means it's a separate property.

"Does that mean what I think it means?" Alice asked, leaning forward in her chair.

"Since you are the sole inheritor, Montclair is your separate property even though you have remarried," Mr. Crabbe clarified. "Unless— did you put your new husband on the deed?"

She shook her head. "I haven't changed anything."

"All right. Did you use any of your husband's money to pay the mortgage or make substantial improvements on the land?"

"No mortgage, thank God," Alice said. "Siegfried did buy a bottling system, though. Does that count as an improvement?"

"Only to your business. He can claim a small share of

your profits, if any, after harvest, but he doesn't have an interest in the property itself." Mr. Crabbe put down the pen and steepled his fingers under his chin. "Based on what you've told me, Mrs. Rodernwiller, the property is yours alone. Neither your husband nor his family can stop you from disposing of Montclair as you wish."

Alice let out a sigh of relief. "That's good. Now about the insurance... Will there be a problem?"

"Possibly, because it was arson." Mr. Crabbe got up, and rifled through the drawer in a tall wooden filing cabinet, muttering, "Roberts... Rogers... Roye— ah, here it is!" He pulled a folder from the drawer and spread it open on his desk. He picked up his pen again as a reading aid down the closely-packed lines. "Yes," Mr. Crabbe said at last, "you are the primary beneficiary on this policy."

"I remember we put Peter Verdacchia on the policy, too. Will Peter's widow get his portion? If we get anything, that is?"

"Well, I'm afraid this policy has a restriction in it that you can't will away your interest, or even a portion of it. Since your foreman was listed as contingent beneficiary, you'll receive the total, if there is a payout. The money would only have been paid out to him if you were dead."

Alice looked squarely at the lawyer. "Hugh Roye was arrested for Peter's murder, but I can't believe he did it. If he goes to trial, can you defend him?"

Mr. Crabbe tried unsuccessfully to keep his face expressionless. "I've known Hugh Roye a long time. I remember how disappointed he was when his Grandfather's will passed over him, but I never considered him capable of arson— or murder." Crabbe put down his pen and started wiping ink splatters off his fingers with his handkerchief. Visibly composing himself, he looked up at Alice and said, "It may be a considerable expense, and the insurance money may not be forthcoming."

"Then it's a good thing that Montclair is mine," Alice said. "I wouldn't sell it *to* Hugh, but if I have to, I'll sell Montclair *for* him."

"He should be very grateful you're on his side."

"He doesn't know it yet. But he will."

She shook hands again, and was already in the office doorway when she remembered to ask, "And what do I owe you, Mr. Crabbe? You've been so helpful."

He smiled, and Alice was reminded that, however friendly, he was still a lawyer. "There's no charge for a *first* consultation, Mrs. Rodernwiller."

Back around the Plaza, the borrowed shoes a bit loose and chafing, Alice returned to the doctor's house to inform them that she would be staying at the Toscano Hotel and to see how Siegfried was doing.

Mrs. Stillman had laundered Alice's nightgown and provided another change of clothes, a carpet bag, and a toothbrush for Alice to take with her. Alice, touched, thanked her profusely, thinking, *Your attitude will change when you find out about me.* She tried to regret that soon her years as a respectable woman in Sonoma would be just a wonderful memory, but the thought, *No more lies*, was wonderfully emancipating.

Carpetbag in hand, she peeked into Siegfried's room and saw Tati sitting at his bedside.

Alice took a deep breath, and entered the room, seating herself down on the other chair, keeping Siegfried's bed between them like a barrier. Alice kept her head bowed as she settled herself, but watched Tati from beneath her lashes.

Without acknowledging Alice's presence, Tati tenderly touched Siegfried's scorched face. Two streams of tears dripped down her cheeks, but she was dignified, even in her grief. She did not sob, or even dab futilely at her eyes with a handkerchief. She simply sat there, ramrod straight, her rosary beads knotted around her hands, weeping for her losses.

Despite herself, Alice's heart began to soften towards the old woman. This was such a difficult time for all of them. Surely Tati had meant no harm to Alice.

When Dr. Stillman came in some time later, Tati had dried her tears, and was whispering her Rosary. She lifted her head, and fixed her gaze upon the doctor. "Can you tell me anything yet about my grandson's condition?" she asked stiffly, not acknowledging Alice's presence.

Dr. Stillman's eyes went to Alice. "I'm afraid not," he began uncertainly.

"Then I must insist that he be removed to a hospital where he can receive proper care!"

Alice lifted her chin, and took Siegfried's hand in hers. "Dr. Stillman, I'm quite happy with your care of my husband. I have no intention of making any changes."

Tati glowered coldly at Alice. "How dare you!"

"I am his wife, Mrs. Roye. You may stay with him if you like, but he won't be moving."

After a long moment, Tati looked away first.

"Very well," Tati said icily, struggling to her feet. She addressed Dr. Stillman. "I will be at the Swiss Hotel. You must 'phone me the moment my grandson wakes up." She swept past

Dr. Stillman, the very portrait of outraged dignity.

Dr. Stillman relaxed when she was gone. "Well, she's quite a battle-ax, isn't she?"

Alice struggled not to smile. She had won— this round.

The train idled at a station, waiting for more passengers. Siegfried sat tucked into a narrow seat, his throbbing right arm crowded painfully into the side of the car. He searched into the misty gray rain outside the window for a familiar face, but there was no one he knew.

A little girl in a schlumpfkapf waved at him, but her grandmother angrily jerked her away. Rank after rank of gray-uniformed soldiers waited at attention for their proper transports, with neighbors and townspeople waving flags and throwing streamers at them.

Nobody waited for him. Nobody came for him.

Where is Alice? Siegfried wondered. *And if I saw her, would she wave to me, or turn away?*

He rested his forehead against cold, damp glass and coughed, each breath a claw ripping apart his lungs.

Alice...

Alice held Siegfried's unmoving hand for an hour, until she couldn't sit quietly any longer. There was no change in him. He coughed, he struggled to breathe, he didn't wake. She did her share of bargaining with God in that hour, but none of the offerings she was prepared to make seemed to catch the divine fancy. Siegfried didn't wake.

She thanked the doctor and his wife again for caring for Siegfried, and returned to the hotel to await her mother's arrival. She made some more telephone calls: to the telephone company, ordering an emergency line installed in the foreman's cottage at Montclair, and to the Sheriff's office, to try to get some news about what was happening at Montclair.

Sheriff Albertson assured her that the fire was put out, that the damage was being assessed by her insurance agent, that Maria was being taken care of by her mother, and that Hugh was safely behind bars, even if he was refusing to say a word about what had happened. He seemed surprised to learn that Hugh had been the one to rescue Siegfried and herself. He was even more surprised when she mentioned that she was offering her own lawyer to defend him.

"Mrs. Verdacchia saw the whole thing, ma'am. We got a

short statement from her last night. Mr. Roye definitely killed her husband."

Alice thanked him politely, and rang off. But she still didn't believe him. She didn't know *what* Maria had seen, but she had no doubt that whatever had happened, it hadn't been Hugh Roye cold-bloodedly ending Peter's life. Peter had been so drunk. Maybe they fought— maybe it was an accident—

But what was Hugh doing at Montclair, at that time of night?

She didn't know, yet. But she would find out. And tell Siegfried, when he woke up. *Please God, let him wake up.*

She was standing in the hotel doorway, peering anxiously down the street when Gertie and George Breitenbach parked their Ford in front of the hotel.

"Mrs. Rodernwiller!"

She turned, astonished, and saw that Gertie was waving at her. "Alice!"

Bewildered, Alice waited. She couldn't imagine what Gertie and George wanted, or why they were willing to speak to her in public, in light of Alice's earlier revelation.

"We've taken up a collection for you and your husband, dear," Gertie said, as she got out of the car. George lifted a small box from the back seat. "But we didn't know where to bring it, until I realized you were making all your calls from here." As she approached Alice, she held out an envelope.

They had collected for *her*? Tears pricked Alice's eyes as she opened the flap and saw the bills and coins inside. "Oh— oh, thank you, Mrs. Breitenbach!" Then she burst into tears.

Gertie handed her a handkerchief, and patted her back comfortingly until Alice regained control of herself, then she asked, "And how is Mr. Rodernwiller doing? We're all praying for him."

"There's been no change in his condition," Alice reported. "Ta— I mean, Mrs. Roye, came up from the City." She tried to sound casual about it, but her true feelings must have shown.

"Don't let Siegfried's grandma scare you off," George advised as he changed the grip on his box. "I think her bark is a lot worse than her bite."

"She used to live at Montclair years ago," Gertie confided as George took the box into the hotel for the bellman to carry to Alice's room. "But we never got to know her very well." She shrugged. "She was pleasant enough, but I always had the feeling that she thought we were all hicks. Even though you're from San Francisco, too, Alice, we never got that feeling from you."

To Alice's surprise, Gertie gave her a quick hug. "If you need anything, you let us know."

The warm feeling in Alice's chest evaporated and she felt like sinking into the sidewalk when she saw, over Gertie's shoulder, the long, sleek, Buick touring car pull up in front of them. She watched her mother get out of the car at the same time as George came out of the hotel. She couldn't miss his reaction to her, either.

Florence Campbell O'Reilly was a fine-looking woman in her early forties, discreetly rouged, her lustrous blonde hair daringly bobbed under a narrow-brimmed brown velvet hat. Her clothes were expensively fashionable but restrained——a long, narrow skirt with matching belted jacket cut ·from heavy chocolate silk taffeta and trimmed with dark green ribbon, worn over an ivory silk blouse. A tasseled drawstring purse, silk stockings and low-heeled pumps completed the ensemble. She looked like any respectable City matron. Any *rich* matron.

"Alice?" Florence looked toward Alice, then came to an uncertain stop. "Baby girl? Oh, your poor hair!"

Gertie let her go, and Alice was certain she was just going to collect George and leave quietly, but instead, she turned around, took a step forward, and offered her hand. "You must be our dear Alice's mother," she said with real welcome in her voice. "I'm Gertrude Breitenbach, and this is my husband, George. We go to church with Alice, and we're very fond of her."

Alice felt like sniffling again at this unexpected tribute. Her mother, slightly baffled but very charming, shook hands graciously and responded, "How do you do? I'm Florence... O'Reilly."

"Oh, but we mustn't keep you from your reunion. We just brought by the first of a few things the parish is donating to help Alice and Siegfried get back on their feet. Such a tragic fire! So nice to meet you. We hope to see you in church with Alice on Sunday."

"Pleasure to meet you, ma'am," George said, tipping his hat.

"Remember, you call me if you need *anything*, Alice," Gertie said, and smiled. "All you need to do is pick up the 'phone."

Grateful beyond words, Alice smiled back at her, then found herself in her mother's arms, her head on her mother's shoulder, the familiar spicy scent of jasmine evoking a hundred childhood memories. Mama was shorter than Alice remembered, but she was still as soft and warm.

Alice had often wondered what she would feel if she ever saw Mama again. Shame? Loathing? Now she knew. It was overwhelming relief, the child's confidence that everything would be all right now that her mother was here.

Florence held her tightly, cheek laid against Alice's hair, stroking her shoulders, her back. "Baby girl, my little Alice blue, you're all right— you're safe," Florence murmured, over and over again, as they rocked gently back and forth, in the street, visible to anybody.

And Alice didn't care.

After Florence checked into the hotel, she dragged Alice into the deserted dining room, and sat her down to a late— and very needed— dinner.

There, over warm bread rolls, milky Italian coffee, and cheese-stuffed ravioli in tomato sauce, Alice confessed, "I never knew about your promise. I thought you didn't want me any more, because, well— it might interfere. With your business."

"Oh, no!" Florence exclaimed. "It wasn't like that at all! Your father and me, we wanted you to grow up in better circumstances. He said it would be for the best, and I knew it was. But I thought about you all the time." Florence gave a forced-sounding chuckle. "I must be the only woman in San Francisco with a subscription to that two-cent Sonoma paper of yours. I wanted to know about where you lived, and what you were doing. I read all about your wedding—"

"Mama," the words stuck in her throat. "All those years I never contacted you— I'm so sorry!"

"Oh, that's all right. I understand."

"But you're my mother. It was wrong of me! I've spent so much time worrying what people would think."

"It's what you have to do, baby girl, to get along in this world."

"Well, the world can get along with *us*, for now on!" Alice said, wiping up the last of the delicious sauce with a piece of bread. She'd been as hungry as Siegfried used to get...

"Alice?"

"I was just thinking about—"

"You love him a lot, don't you?"

"Yes, and I shouldn't! He lied to me— over and over again. He lied about his wartime service, and he lied about a contract he said he got and he didn't, and he—" but she couldn't think of another lie that Siegfried had told. He hadn't even actually lied about his service, just not spoken of it until she had asked about it. And the contract: Mr. Bundschu had said, *he lied to you, when you wanted to switch to prunes earlier this summer, because he was scared of where he would go. Not much call for winemakers, these days.*

He had been afraid, because she wanted to send him away. She had brought it all on herself.

She covered her eyes with one hand.

Her other hand was taken in a warm, maternal grip. "We'll go see how he's doing right now, honey. Waiter!" Florence paid the tab and drove Alice the short distance to Dr. Stillman's.

They were both surprised to see Tati at Siegfried's bedside.

Tati was even more shocked at the sight of Florence. "Alice, what is *that woman* doing here?"

"This is my mother, Mrs. Patrick O'Reilly," Alice said, at her most dignified.

"So pleased to meet you, in person, at last," Florence said with a small smile and perfect diction. "I've heard so much about you, over the years."

Tati's mouth opened and closed, but no sound came out. Finally she looked at Alice. "I refuse to stay in the same room with her. I'm warning you!"

"That's your choice, Mrs. Roye. But I should warn you as well: you may have to vacate a fair number of rooms from now on."

Tati stood up, pale and trembling. "Well, Alice, if this is the thanks I get for all the things I've done for you—"

"Alice, honey. You two don't need to quarrel over me. I have a number of errands I have to run. I can come back later to pick you up." Florence nodded politely to Tati, who continued to ignore her completely. "I'll be back by supper time. 'Bye!" And she was out the door.

"— of all the unmitigated gall!" Tati was muttering. "How dare you bring that creature here!"

"She's the grandmother of the Montclair heir." Alice smiled grimly at Tati. "Do try to accustom yourself."

"I won't have it!"

Siegfried's raspy breathing stopped, and he erupted in a paroxysm of coughing. Alice and Tati, on either side of him, held him up as best they could, and kept him from falling out of the narrow bed. When his fit had subsided, Tati wiped his face and Alice his mouth, and they settled him as comfortably as possible.

Alice tried to wake him up. "Siegfried! Siegfried!" But he remained unconscious.

Tati found her chair again, and sat, pale and very ill-at-ease.

Alice looked over the senseless body of her husband and saw a frail, frightened old woman staring at the only family she had left. "Are we going to argue over Siegfried, Mrs. Roye— Tati— or will you pray for him with me?"

"I—" Tati dashed tears from the corner of her eye, and bowed her head. "Let us pray."

They had time for half a Novena before Alice's mother returned, the smooth noise of her big car alerting them. She was waiting in the parlor when Alice found her.

"No change," Alice reported.

Florence looked up from her novel, and smiled sympathetically. "Is Mrs. Roye still here?"

Alice nodded. "We came to an understanding, I think. She won't insult you anymore."

Florence's smile was a bit lopsided. "It must be hard for her. I've been doing business with the Royes for twenty-odd years— paid for plenty of her hats, I imagine— but she's never had to acknowledge me before. Isn't it interesting the way the world turns?"

The doctor appeared in the doorway. "Mrs. Rodernwiller, we'll be sure to call you if there's any change at all. You should get a good night's rest, yourself."

"Thank you, I will," Alice promised. "May I introduce my mother, Mrs. Patrick O'Reilly?"

Dr. Stillman nodded politely. "We met earlier, actually. Mrs. O'Reilly, I trust you will take good care of your daughter. I certainly don't want her as a patient here— at least not for another five months!" They all smiled dutifully, and Alice and Florence took their leave.

"Mrs. Siegfried Rodernwiller," Florence rolled the syllables around in her mouth as they walked to her car. "That's quite a mouthful."

Alice laughed despite herself.

When they came to the hotel room after a light supper (*with* wine, despite the Prohibition) Alice was astonished to see the number of parcels and clothing bags strewn about the modest furnishings. "What have you done, Mama?" she said, half-laughing, half inclined to cry again.

"I just bought you a few things I thought you'd need, baby girl." Florence smiled broadly, seating herself on the bed. "You said you needed clothes. I hope you like these."

Alice couldn't help herself. She opened package after package: soft silk blouses with intricate lace; dresses with hobble-skirts in crepe-de-chine and messaline; sturdy corduroy skirts and hard-working middies; nightgowns, stockings, shoes and the frilliest underthings she'd seen outside her mother's house. "Mama!" she protested, laughing.

"Can't fault a girl for hoping, can you?" Florence grinned back. "I heard you two praying," she said, seriously, touching the lacy hem of a camisole. "This is my prayer, for you."

"Oh, Mama." Alice set the lingerie down. "I don't even know if he's going to—"

"You never know," Florence said.

Alice swept a heap of clothes from a chair and lowered herself into it. "Was it like this for you when Da was sick?"

Florence shook her head. "No. Well, he was pretty bad off. He didn't want you to know—" she said, interrupting Alice's attempt to speak. "He wanted you to enjoy your honeymoon, and be successful in your marriage. He spoke about you, every day. He was very happy for you, honey."

"You were... with him— at the end?"

Florence drew a gold-plated cigarette case and lighter from her purse and started to smoke, taking nervous puffs, and making a show of searching the bedside table for something that could serve as an ashtray.

"I guess I never thought of you getting back together."

"We weren't 'together.' But we never divorced, either, even though Patrick could never forgive me for what I had to do for us to survive."

"Survive? What happened to you?" Alice had always assumed that her mother was morally weak.

Florence tilted back her head, closed her eyes, breathed out a stream of smoke. The scent recalled all the days of her childhood to Alice.

"Your father was a very proud young man with big dreams when he came to work for my Pa's carting business in Wichita. Lord, Patrick could turn heads, with his hair afire and his eyes laughin'. Well, my Pa caught us, er, together, and stood over Patrick with a shotgun till he said 'I do.' We went to live in San Francisco, but there wasn't any work for him then, him bein' Irish, with no family to call on. We just got hungrier and hungrier, and by then you were on the way..."

Alice listened, fascinated.

"I...had to do some hard things, then," Florence continued, her voice growing husky. "There wasn't any work for decent women at decent wages. But for indecent women— oh, honey. I made enough as a 'seamstress' to feed us and to set Patrick up in his own business as a wine-broker. He wasn't too proud to take my money, but he couldn't stand to think how I had earned it."

"But you continued working," Alice observed, reproachfully.

Florence sighed. "Do you know how much a *real* seamstress makes? Or an office girl? When Patrick left me, I didn't want you living in a rat-infested tenement somewhere. You always had new clothes, and you never went hungry. But listen to me go on!"

"I'm listening, Mama," Alice said, openly showing her happiness to be doing so. "But your house is a restaurant now?"

"It's hard times for Sin these days." Florence chuckled. "And it's all the Government's fault, too— like this silly Prohibition, taking away *your* livelihood. First they made it illegal for foreign girls to work, then in '13 the Coast— the Barbary Coast! went dry. It was either give up girls or liquor, and guess which went? Then the state passed the Red Light Abatement Act, trying to close all the parlor houses, and in '17 Reverend Paul Smith went on a Crusade to clean up the City. He was a pious fool, but he had 'Right' on his side."

Florence took another long puff. "I heard Reggie Gamble—a very good businesswoman— give a speech back to him in his own Central Methodist church. I remember what she said, too, 'You can't trust in God when shoes are $10.00 a pair and wages are $6.00 a week.'" She stubbed out the cigarette. "Most of us in the life shut our doors. I couldn't just do that. I owned that property, and Shih Wing didn't want to stop cooking, so..."

"So now you run a restaurant."

"My band plays a little jazz, and a lot of boys home from the war come to eat, dance, and have a good time. It pays a little less—" Alice saw the contentment that pervaded her mother's face. "But I have as much money as I need, I suppose. Or I did, until I went shopping for you!" Florence laughed at the expression on Alice's face. "It's a joke, honey."

Alice went over to her, knelt on the floor, and laid her head in her mother's lap. Comforting hands stroked her hair. "Oh, Mama, what am I going to do if he doesn't get better?"

"Hush, baby. I know. You'll do whatever you have to."

Sonoma

Saturday, October 11

Alice wanted to see Siegfried first thing in the morning, but Florence wouldn't let her leave the hotel room while her hair looked like a dust-mop.

"It's not important, Mama," Alice insisted.

"It is if you're to be seen with me, Alice-blue. I have my standards!"

Alice impatiently submitted to her mother's expert touch with the scissors, but as she put on one of the fashionable cloche hats Florence had purchased yesterday, she quirked her eyebrow. "So why did it matter? Nobody can see my hair, now anyway."

"It never hurts to look your best. *And* you will have some breakfast, young lady!"

"Yes, Mama." It felt *so* good to be taken care of.

Doctor Stillman wasn't very hopeful when they arrived at eight-thirty. "There's been no change for the better. His breathing has eased somewhat, but we haven't been able to get him to eat or drink anything. I must tell you, Mrs. Rodernwiller, this is not a good sign. Perhaps Mrs. Roye is right, and he should be moved to a fully-equipped hospital."

Alice glanced swiftly at her mother, but she had no advice. "I— he's all right for now? I have to check on my property this morning, but I'll be back after lunch. We can make that decision then, can't we?"

The doctor agreed.

Alice spent a difficult half hour with Siegfried, holding his unresponsive hand, praying to an uncommunicative God. She had so many things to say to her husband. She wanted to quarrel, to yell and rip up at him for leaving her, for endangering himself, for lying, for believing her own stupid lie: that she wanted him to go away.

Before she left, she kissed his cool forehead and said, "Get better, Siegfried. I'll be back in a little while."

He never moved, except to take another racking breath.

Siegfried wrestled with a demon in the aisle of the

motionless train. It was winning, barring him from searching the rest of the cars for Alice. He was convinced she was here, somewhere. She had to be nearby. He felt her presence, smelled her lemon cologne.

"You're a puny shadow of a man, a lying coward," whispered the demon. "You don't deserve to be loved. Your father knew that. Give up!" The demon leered. "You'll have to surrender— eventually."

Siegfried had no strength to fight. He was being smothered. He couldn't breathe.

He didn't want to fight. It was too much effort.

Alice didn't want him.

Florence interrogated Alice during the entire muddy drive out to Montclair, discovering the exact details of the estate's financial condition, and offering practical advice to which Alice was too anxious to pay much attention.

She didn't have the heart to appreciate the beauties of the morning, either. The rain yesterday had dampened the dust so the air sparkled now. The hills and the vast stretches of uncultivated land bore the remnants of gray-brown grass, but the first promise of winter's burst of green life had been given.

When they arrived at the gates, Alice opened and closed them, and Florence drove straight up the driveway with nary a cough nor sputter from the Buick's engine. Alice craned her neck— there were picking crews busy at work in the Cabernet section of the vineyard! And the level grounds around the blackened stone shell of the winery looked like a fairground, with tarpaulins of all sizes shading stacks of grape-filled crates. "What...?" she whispered.

"Looks like a harvest to me, honey," Florence said, winking. "This a self-running grape farm?"

Alice shook her head, dazed. "It must be. Or—"

Herculio caught sight of them as Florence negotiated through the stacks, parking next to the remains of the house. He waved and came trotting over.

"Mrs. R.!" Herculio called. "You'll never believe how much we've been offered for the grapes. Sixty-five dollars a ton! Mrs. Verdacchia has contracts for you to sign!"

"How much?!" Alice shrieked. Florence patted her knee.

Herculio leaned against the side of the car, laughing and nodding gleefully. "It's true! I swear to God on my father's grave!"

At that price, she could pay her debts and doctor's bills,

make the payroll, defend Hugh, and rebuild— even refurbish— the house, all without having to care whether the insurance settlement arrived or not.

Herculio gave her a gallant bow and opened the door when he judged she wouldn't fall out of it. "You should thank Mrs. Verdacchia. She talked to Mr. Crewe, the agent for Rosenberg Brothers, when he came around this morning. She sold them your entire crop. Ah—" he hesitated. "I hope that was all right with you."

"Yes!" Alice could hardly believe that she was finally hearing some good news. "Thank you! Oh, thank you!" She wasn't sure if she were thanking Herculio, or God.

"Is that a good price?" Florence asked, as Herculio excused himself and went to direct the next unloading of the Model T.

"It's *wonderful*," Alice said, heartfelt. "They were only offering twenty-five dollars per ton at the beginning of summer."

Her joy at the news drained away a little as Alice slowly walked to stand next to a fragment of porch railing. The site of the house was little more than ash and a few unidentifiable melted lumps. A single beam stood, leaning precariously against the blackened chimney, but otherwise, everything was gone.

"Going to be quite a job," Florence said quietly. "Are you planning to rebuild?"

"I don't know," Alice said. She had loved Montclair, but would she be able to stay here if Siegfried didn't recover?

Maria came running out of the foreman's cottage. "Mrs. R.! I'm so glad you're all right!"

"Maria!" She ran to her friend, and swept her into a hug. "I'm okay. But how are you? I was so sorry to hear about Peter."

Maria raised her hands as if to push Alice away. "No. Don't say that to me. I have to tell you something terrible." Her face was strained, and traces of many tears had left invisible, indelible marks.

Alice, confused, separated from Maria. They all went into the cottage, where Maria's mother Giuseppa insisted on serving them coffee and cakes. Alice introduced her mother— to Maria's brief amazement— and they found seats in the sturdy chairs.

Maria refused to eat the little cakes her mother brought. "I don't know what to do. The insurance man came yesterday, but he didn't ask me— nobody asked me *why* Hugh killed Peter. How the fire started..." Disregarded tears fell from her red-rimmed eyes.

Queasiness threatened Alice. "I know Hugh told me he

didn't set the fire. And I believed him. But if he didn't— who did?" *Not Siegfried. Please, God, not S—*

Maria said baldly, "It was Peter."

Alice gasped.

"Tell us what happened, Mrs. Verdacchia," Florence urged.

Maria wiped at her eyes. "Peter was so angry that night. He was drunk, and yelling that Mr. R. had no right to fire him, to steal his *grappa*. I was scared— I had never seen him like that before. And then he— he made me 'phone Mr. Roye..." Maria sniffled, her olive complexion deeply suffused. "I'm sorry—"

"Go on when you can," said Alice.

"Peter said that he would kill me if I didn't make the call." She tugged at the neck of her blouse revealing purplish-blue fingerprint bruises.

"Oh, Maria!"

"Peter made me tell Mr. Roye that I was running away. And— and— that if Hugh— wanted me," Maria's voice dropped to a humiliated thread, "he should come get me."

Alice's eyes widened in sudden comprehension. *So that's what Hugh was doing.* "The sheriff told me that Hugh refused to say anything at all about that night. He must love you very much to try so hard to preserve your good name."

"At the expense of his life!" Maria wailed. "I don't care about my *good name*! I just want him to be safe! And if they convict him—" She blew her nose defiantly in the handkerchief her mother handed her.

"What happened next?" asked Alice.

"Peter drank some more, then forced me to go over to the house with him. He— he gagged me, and tied me to the porch." She shuddered, but continued after a moment. "While he was setting the fire in the kitchen, Hugh arrived. Peter rushed out, and Hugh grabbed the shovel, and— and— *hit* him. It was self defense!"

My God! Alice felt pale with shock, comprehending the enormity of what Siegfried had saved her from. "Peter meant to kill us all."

"But why?" Maria begged.

"He was a beneficiary on the insurance." If she had not sent Siegfried away, they would *all* have perished in the fire. "Maria, we have to see the sheriff, right away."

Alice's mother stayed outside in the car while Maria went in to give her statement to the sheriff. "I... don't care for jails," Florence said with a self-conscious smile.

A deputy led Alice to the cell where Hugh was being kept. As he unlocked the door he said, "Let me know when you're finished in here, Mrs. Rodernwiller."

Hugh was sitting on a simple cot, his head in his hands, his elbows digging into his knees. He didn't acknowledge her, and perversely, his despair gave her courage.

"Hugh? I came to thank you."

"For what?" he responded, in a monotone.

"For rescuing me— us— the other night. It was very brave of you."

He shrugged.

"Maria is making a statement to the sheriff right now."

Now he looked up. "Is she all right?" he demanded, hands clenched on the edge of the cot. He was a wreck, gray-blond stubble thick on his cheeks and puffy eyes, one of them magnificently blackened.

"She's fine." Alice smiled to see his concern. "She told us what happened. All of it. Don't you think that you were being foolishly noble to keep silent?"

"Noble? I?" Hugh gave a short, hard laugh. "Don't you know about all the things I've done?"

"I know about some of them. The sabotage—" She was still angry about that, despite her best intentions.

Hugh shook his head. "You had something that should have been mine, and you just wouldn't sell it to me. I never understood that. *Why* wouldn't you sell Montclair, Alice? It wasn't like you knew what to do with the winery."

Alice thought of all the lies she'd told Hugh— outright, and by implication. "You've always known where I came from, Hugh. But, like Tati, you never brought it up— out in the open, at any rate." She sat down next to him. "I was afraid. I thought, if I gave up Montclair, I'd have to go back, to live my mother's life."

Hugh looked at her as if she was stupid, or out of her wits. "You would have been a very wealthy young woman! You could have gone anywhere, done anything!"

"I wouldn't have been part of the Roye family anymore." Alice did feel stupid at this point, and close to tears. "That was worth more to me than—"

"Hey— hey, Alice," Hugh said, patting her arm with clumsy sympathy. "I'm sorry. Please don't cry."

Alice took a deep breath and held it. She saw Hugh's anxious face and started laughing. She took some more breaths, and finally was able to say, "I also wanted to tell you that I hired Lee Crabbe as your lawyer— but I don't think you're going to need him, once Maria finishes with the sheriff."

Hugh's mouth twisted. "How can she ever look at me again? I have her husband's blood on my hands."

Alice heard the door at the end of the hallway open. "Ask her yourself. Here she comes."

As Maria walked hesitantly forward, just ahead of the deputy, Hugh leapt up. His fingers gripped the bars whitely. "Maria?"

Maria's steps quickened, then she was there, her hands covering his, curving around the bars. "I told Sheriff Albertson the truth!" she exclaimed. "He says they'll probably drop the charges. They have to let you go!!"

"Oh, Maria," Hugh whispered. She pressed her face through the narrow opening, and his lips sought hers. Neither of them noticed the deputy opening the cell door, or Alice leaving, unwilling to intrude on their private happiness a moment longer.

She meant to keep her mother company until Maria had finished her visit, but before she got out the door a deputy advised her that Dr. Stillman's call had been forwarded from Montclair.

She picked up the 'phone with a sick feeling.

The doctor spoke gravely. "I'm very sorry, but your husband has taken a turn for the worse. I called for Father Byrne. I hope—"

"No. That's fine. I'll be right there," Alice said, calmly, just as if her heart wasn't crumbling.

Siegfried dying? *It can't be true!*

The denial beat through her brain as her mother drove to the doctor's house.

She rushed into the infirmary, not sure whether she believed the report. But Siegfried lay so still on the bed, and the young priest, white surplice and purple stole over his black cassock, looked up, unsurprised, at her breathless entrance.

"Mrs. Rodernwiller. God bless you. I haven't started yet."

Alice followed his slight gesture, noticing the white cloth covering the top of the bedside table, the crucifix between two lighted candles, the towel, a flat dish of water, and a flat dish containing cotton balls.

"F-father Byrne," Alice said shakily. "You're giving him Last Rites? But he's not— he can't be—" Her knees gave way, and she half-fell into the hard chair near the door. This was worse than any of her nightmares, any of the day terrors that had ruled her for so long.

The priest came close and comfortingly seized Alice's hand in both his own. "I know. I know. You must be strong. God willing, he may be healed. Or we will have done our best to prepare him for his meeting with our Maker."

"There's no *reason* for him to die! The doctor said his wound wasn't grievous!" Alice wanted to shout her denial, but the mighty hand squeezing her chest left her air only to whisper. "He can't die! We... we haven't t-talked since..." Oh, God, if she started crying now, she would never stop.

And maybe she would never want to. What good was knowing she owned Montclair? What good was sixty-five dollars a ton for some worthless grapes? She didn't want any of it without Siegfried.

Father Byrne's handkerchief was huge, and his hand on her shoulder was warm. At some point, Alice heard her mother come into the room, give a sharp intake of breath, and ask the Doctor's wife to be sure to call Mrs. Roye.

She felt her mother's hand replace Father Byrne's. "Honey, you gotta let the priest do his job."

Alice tried to compose herself. She blinked fiercely to bring the room into focus, dried her eyes, staggered to her feet, and found herself by Siegfried's side.

His breathing was still ragged. She stroked his cheek, then held his hand, clasping it tightly until her wedding ring bit into her finger. He didn't respond at all.

"Father Byrne," she managed to say. "I know you like weddings better, but..." She tried to smile her readiness, but her lips couldn't hold a shape. She drew up Siegfried's hand, to stop the trembling of her mouth with the pressure of his flesh.

He didn't feel her kiss.

She laid his hand down gently, but didn't let it go. "We're ready."

Father Byrne made the sign of the cross, and she echoed him. "Peace to this house," he began.

"And to all who dwell herein," Alice responded.

The priest blessed the room with holy water, intoning, "Sprinkle me, O Lord, with hyssop, and I shall be purified; wash me, and I shall be whiter than snow. Our help is in the name of the Lord."

"Who made heaven and earth." Alice said, praying, *You made me too. Make me whiter than snow, or blacker than soot. I don't care. Just let Siegfried live.*

The rich, trained voice of the priest filled the room. "As I enter here with a sense of my own unworthiness, O Lord Jesus Christ, let abiding happiness enter with me; may the blessings of God and unmixed joy accompany my visit... Let no evil spirit gain entrance here. May the angels of peace be present, and may all harmful discord leave this house."

Alice felt the peace descending on her. She felt her mother's strength behind her, and turned her head slightly. Her mother stood solemnly, hands clasped together, eyes tightly closed.

The priest said, "As Mr. Rodernwiller is not conscious, we will recite the Confession together for him: *Confiteor Deo omnipotenti, beatae Mariae semper Virgini, beato Michaeli archangelo...*"

Alice caught up with him, the words from the Mass reverberating through her as she said them for Siegfried, and for herself. "*I have sinned exceedingly in thought, word, and deed; Through my fault, through my fault, through my most grievous fault...*"

Father Byrne's handkerchief was well used again before he spoke alone once more: "May almighty God have mercy on you, forgive you your sins, and bring you to everlasting life."

"Amen!" agreed Alice with a whole heart, feeling herself forgiven for the first time in her life.

Extending his right hand over Siegfried and making the sign of the cross, Father Byrne continued, "...May any power that the devil has over you be utterly destroyed..." With holy oil on his thumb, the priest made the sign of the cross on Siegfried's eyelids. "May the Lord forgive you by this holy anointing and his most loving mercy whatever sins you have committed by the use of your sight. Amen." He repeated the anointing on Siegfried's ears, nose, lips, hands, and feet, continuing to recite prayers for forgiveness of each sense and faculty.

"...We implore you, our Redeemer, that by the grace of the Holy Spirit you cure the illness of this sick man and heal his wounds; forgive his sins, and drive away from him all pains of mind and body. In your mercy give him health, inward and outward, so that he may once more be able to take up his work, restored by the gift of your mercy.... look with kindness on your servant Siegfried, who is growing weak as his body fails. Cherish the soul which you created, so that, purified and made whole by his sufferings, he may find himself restored by your healing....Be present in Your kindness as we call upon your holy name...."

In *darkness the demon slipped away, defeated by his victory.*

Siegfried, pliant with surrender, found no opposition to hold him back. At last, he arrived at his destination.

He descended through the long dark tunnel of the train,

exiting suddenly into the station. He blinked at the brilliant light and recognized the clean-swept platform, the tubs of flowers, the steeply peaked red roofs of the town's houses against the pale midsummer sky: Schlettstat. He was home again.

Standing on the platform, he looked around. No one else was disembarking here. He was alone. But somehow, this did not disturb him. He could not feel any sadness while standing in light as warm and as caressing as this. Siegfried slung his duffel across his back, feeling strong and curiously free, and strode forward.

There, in the wide cobbled square of the Bahnhofplatz, *he saw* Mutti, Vater, *Ernst and* Opa *Roye waiting for him. They were smiling and waving eagerly. Mutti— how beautiful she was!— was wearing her favorite hat, wide-brimmed and decorated with silk roses. The men were in their Sunday best, their hair blazing gold against stiff white collars and dark jackets. Ernst was holding his favorite toy— the sailboat Siegfried made when he was twelve. Behind them, Father's Daimler gleamed, ready to bear them all home to Sunday dinner.*

He ran to them.

They surrounded him with their love, even Father, awkward and embarrassed for something that to Siegfried was a distant memory. Serene and finally at peace, Siegfried had no wish to remember his sorrows and his failures.

Father Byrne gave the final blessing, and Alice bent to press a kiss to Siegfried's lips. To her horror, she heard the labored rasp of his breathing catch, stop, then start again.

"Oh no, please God, no," she murmured, clutching Siegfried's hand with all her strength.

Siegfried's breath gave that odd little catch again, then he exhaled in a long, grateful sigh.

And did not inhale. His chest remained inert, and his face seemed to relax.

"No!" Alice took Siegfried by the shoulders and shook him, "Damn you!" Furious, she slapped his face, hard, ignoring Father Byrne's shocked protests. "You son of a bitch! How can you die and leave me alone? You bastard! You— you—" She turned half toward her mother. "Mama! Help me! I don't know anything worse to call him! Mama—" The sob rose in her throat and stole her breath.

Her mother's arms enfolded her. She accepted their soft consolation for a moment, shielded from the tremors rearranging the landscape of her soul.

But she had so much left to say to him! She fell to her knees beside the bed, rested her temple against Siegfried's pillow. Her hand crept up to touch his eyebrows, his closed eyes. Her fingers felt the faintly smiling, quiet mouth.

"Don't you know how much work there is left to do? Don't you know how empty my arms will be, without you? Who will make the champagne for our child's wedding? Who will I read the paper to? Please, God— I forgive you. Everything you've done. Everything I've done. May God forgive us both.... Oh, Siegfried, don't you know how much I—" Anguish burned hotter than a burning house. "—love you?"

In the midst of his family, happy at last, Siegfried heard a sound that slashed him like shrapnel.

A woman wept.

He felt the sweet kisses of his mother on his forehead. His little brother held his hand. Opa Roye beamed. His father, shame forgotten, put his arm around Siegfried's shoulders. The moment was perfect— then it shattered.

Like Orpheus, he glanced back.

Glanced— down?

The bright light was painful, but he saw. Alice was weeping at the bedside of a burned and blistered corpse. A woman, very like Alice but older, blonde, stood behind her, crying too.

Alice spoke. "Oh, Siegfried, don't you know how much I love you? Don't leave me alone!"

Confusion shredded the last of his serenity. He had found Alice at last, and she wanted him, too— but why should he return to a place where all his efforts ended in failure?

Not all, whispered his father. *Not like me!*

Not all, Opa Roye said, grinning widely. *Your wine was pretty good.*

Not all, his mother laughed. *You loved your wife and made her happy. Don't hold still, here, Friddy, though we love you. This home is always waiting for you.*

She pointed, and he saw: Alice wept for him now. Her tears flowed like a fountain where he might wash his soul and be clean at last.

He loved her more than his life. He was willing to sacrifice his life for her— dare he live with her, chancing the possibility of failure again and again?

She loves me! Siegfried's heart jolted with happiness. If she wanted him back, he would go to her. He would follow her anywhere, do anything for her. She was the home he longed to return to.

He reached for her hand, and the brightness increased, until his family—Vater, Mutti, Ernst, Opa Roye, and Another he did not notice before— were lost to sight. But their happiness remained with him, in him, an honor and a glory he would keep, and return, forever.

I will bring Alice to meet them someday, he thought. *Mutti will like her.*

Siegfried opened his eyes to a room almost as bright as where he had just been. "Ah-lees," he croaked, tasting the salty-sweet moisture of her tears on his lips, a sacrament of love.

He willed his vision to clear, and saw the priest reverently kissing his narrow purple stole.

"God be thanked! He has granted us a miracle!" Father Byrne said, jubilant. "Welcome back to the world of the living, my son,"

With an effort, Siegfried turned his head, seeking Alice.

There was a well-dressed woman, blonde hair bobbed under a close-fitting hat. Her face was familiar. She was the woman in his...dream. Like—Alice. Her mother? She supported a sobbing Oma Tati.

But Alice was kneeling at his left side, smiling tremulously at him, her whole heart shining in her eyes. "Ah-lees," he said, smiling too. He closed his eyes and slept again, a sleep of healing rather than escape.

Siegfried awoke at twilight to find Alice still sitting at his bedside. He struggled to push himself upright. He needed to tell her something very important, but when he tried to speak, only a coughing spell emerged.

Alice stooped to brace her arm behind his back, and held a glass of water to his lips. He drank eagerly, feeling the brush of her mouth against his temple. When he finished, he rested for a while, readying himself to try to talk again.

"Ah-lees, *mein Herz*," he squeezed out before he had to cough some more. "Are you all right? Our baby?"

"The baby's well. It kicked me! And I'm just fine— now," Alice said, joyfully. "You saved our lives, you know. How are *you* feeling?"

"Like I have been through the crusher-destemmer."

She gave a watery chuckle. "Siegfried, you were dying,

We thought you were dead!"

"I thought so, too." The memory filled him, so that he felt curiously light and at peace. He could not speak of it, only hold Alice's hand until he could master himself. "I heard you say that you— love me."

She blushed, the color rising under her fair skin like the most beautiful of sunrises. She did not admit it— out loud, and he knew too well what prevented her. Releasing his hand, she began to pleat the bedsheet with nervous fingers. "Your grandmother threatened to take the baby away from me if you— didn't recover."

"Why would she do such a thing?" *How dared she?*

"Because of my past. Even you asked me— if I'd been a...you know," Alice whispered. "And, afterwards, you moved out of our bedroom." Now anger smoldered in the back of her eyes.

It took all his strength to recapture her hand and hold onto it for dear life. "*Schatz*, I was wrong to let you think I believed you when you said—" His fragile voice dissolved in a torrent of coughing, and he fought for breath. "I have been a terrible coward. I could not tell you about my own lie because I knew you would want me to go away."

"That's what Mr. Bundschu said—"

"I am so sorry. I promise, I will never lie to you, or leave you, again. Can you forgive me?"

"I already have," she said, softly, her eyes shining with that familiar, glorious light. "But—"

He raised his eyebrows in question. His heart sank at the determined set of her lips. "But?"

She looked away from him, over her shoulder as her mother came into the room. Siegfried wished that Alice's brilliant welcoming smile could be directed at him, too.

"How's our Lazarus doing?" Alice's mother examined him closely, her gaze assessing but not unfriendly.

"I am well, thank you." He stretched his burned mouth into a painful smile, and gave Alice a significant look.

"Oh— um," she said, blushing again. She raised her chin. "Siegfried, this is my mother, Florence O'Reilly. And Mama, this is my husband, Siegfried Rodernwiller."

"Is that how you pronounce it? It sure looks different when you read it in the newspaper." Alice's mother nodded to Siegfried, and winked.

"I am very pleased to meet you," he said, sincerely. "I am very fortunate to have married your daughter."

"You do know it's all gone? The house, the winery, the

wine, everything. You love Alice even if Montclair don't come with it?"

"Mama!" hissed Alice, turning red, at the same time Siegfried answered, "Of course!"

Florence's eyes narrowed as she studied Siegfried.

He felt himself weighed and found wanting, so he sat up a little straighter, though the abused muscles in his back and shoulders protested. "I am sorry to hear Montclair is gone," he spoke from the heart. "But I was an utter fool to think that anything was more important than my wife."

"Alice's lawyer says she owns Montclair free and clear. You got no claim on it, even if you did marry her."

Siegfried remembered that, when he first arrived in California, owning a vineyard had been the most important thing to him. Now he knew better. He turned to Alice. "*Mein Leben.* You are my life. My home is where you are. We may not have a house, but I will gladly live in a tent if you will give me another chance to be your husband. Ah-lees, will you take me back?" As she hesitated, he added, "Please?"

Alice took a deep breath, and looked straight at him. "I'm tired of pretending that I don't have a family." She gave her mother a swift, apologetic smile. "Of hiding the truth about my past, of worrying what people will think."

"Of course, Ah-lees." She was going to give him another chance! He was intoxicated with joy, floating on champagne bubbles. "I love you just the way you are. And as for your mother— Mrs. O'Reilly—" he addressed her. "That seems very formal. May I call you 'Mother'?"

"Honey, you can call me anything you like. *If* you treat my baby girl right." Florence grinned.

Alice brought his hand to her cheek and kissed his fingers. He felt her tears on the back of his hand as she said, "I do love you. And I have good news about the crop—"

"Not now. Now you kiss me." He touched her cheek as her lips sought his. The taste of her tears was replaced by the warm flavor of her kisses, hesitant at first, then fierce, as she flung her arms around him.

He was truly home, at last, and forever.

Montclair
Saturday, April 17, 1920

Spring sunshine lay soft over Sonoma's rolling green hills, and wild mustard bloomed in yellow profusion between the rows of newly-leafed vines in Montclair's vineyards. Signs of construction marred the pristine beauty: churned-up mud, drifts of sawdust, and stacks of lumber outside the open wooden frame of an incomplete house.

Parked cars lined the long drive and there were over a hundred people occupying the construction site. Men stood in small groups, defying Prohibition with full glasses, and many women and children sat on picnic blankets which had been spread on the soft green grass.

"That's our house," Alice said, pointing. "Well, it's going to *be* our house." Baby Elizabeth bounced excitedly, then her gurgle turned demanding.

Alice slipped away to the foreman's cottage she and Siegfried had been sharing. She had just finished feeding her daughter and buttoning up her blouse when Maria dashed down the hallway and slammed the bathroom door.

Alice smiled and called, "I remember how that feels!"

"Only three months to go!" Maria said happily when she emerged a few moments later. "At least I'm not confined to bed." She patted the curve of her belly. "And he's still growing."

"I'm so glad you could make it," Alice said as they walked back together toward the party.

"We wouldn't have missed it for the world. Let me know if you need help with anything."

"Absolutely not! You're here as a guest, Mrs. Roye!" Alice said, then spoiled the effect by giggling. They hugged each other, then Maria was carried off by friends who hadn't seen much of her since she had married Hugh and moved to Healdsburg.

Alice surveyed the long trestle table set up in the front yard with a hostess' assessing gaze. It was covered with platters of food: cold fried chicken; deviled eggs; sliced cheeses; potato, macaroni and green salads; breads of all descriptions; and meatballs. Flanking the table were two large barrels, one filled with homemade wine and the other with home-brewed beer.

"Do you fear our guests will starve?" Siegfried came up behind Alice and nuzzled the nape of her neck.

"Not today, they won't." She shivered pleasurably, shifted Bethie to her hip, and turned to kiss him thoroughly.

"Your mother is here," Siegfried said, when she let him up for air. "She wants to see the baby."

"I'd better go," Alice said, but she stood on tip-toes to give him another quick kiss.

A welcoming smile blossomed on her face as she walked quickly to the gate beneath the palm trees, where her mother's sleek car stood. "Mama! I'm so glad you could make it."

"Alice honey, I'm sorry I'm late. I missed the ten o'clock ferry." Florence, elegant in a beige linen traveling dress, reached out to stroke the curve of Bethie's cheek with the back of her finger. "Oooh, and look who's grown!"

She had spent several weeks at Montclair last month, helping Alice after Bethie's birth. Now Florence took up the baby with experienced hands. "What a precious!" She held her granddaughter tenderly and smiled at Siegfried, who had placed a proprietary hand on his wife's shoulder. "She looks just like her daddy."

"And her great-grandfather," Hugh commented as he strolled up. "She's a Roye, all right."

"Thank you for coming today, Mother," Siegfried said to Florence. "Have you met my cousin, Hugh Roye?"

"We're acquainted," Florence replied, with a wink at Hugh. "It's been many years, though. I almost didn't recognize you."

Hugh turned almost purple with embarrassment. "I'm married now," he blurted.

"How nice for you," Florence said, demurely. "I met your wife when Bethie was born. Maria is a very nice girl. I hope you're taking good care of her."

Alice realized where Hugh must known her mother from, and swallowed her horrified laughter with an effort. "Come and meet my neighbors, Mama. The Livernash sisters particularly wanted to meet you. Hugh, will you excuse us?"

She walked away with her chuckling mother, leaving Siegfried alone with his cousin.

"This is a wonderful celebration," Hugh said hastily. "Tell me again why you're doing it?"

"The *Richtsfest* is an old German custom, to honor the builders of a house and wish its family good fortune," Siegfried explained, filling Hugh's glass with a 1906-vintage Montclair claret. "As far as I am concerned, it is a good excuse to have a party."

"Any excuse is a good excuse." Hugh took a sip of the

wine, and smiled beatifically. "Aaahhh. Grandpa had a way with wine."

"And you have a way with selling it," Siegfried toasted him. "To our partnership, and our contract with the Rosenbergs!"

Hugh swallowed again and said, "Speaking of good fortune, not only will we be able to sell kosher wine to the New York market, but I got the response on our application yesterday." He smiled, holding his glass out for another measure.

"We may sell medicinal champagne?" At Hugh's nod, Siegfried wanted to jump for joy and dance with all his neighbors. He settled for grabbing Hugh's hand and shaking it enthusiastically. "That is wonderful news! Alice will be so pleased!" Pinot Noir made an excellent long-lived red, but it made even better white champagne.

"We'll have Paul Masson for competition," Hugh warned, "but I think we can make a profit."

"And Montclair remains a winery, as *Opa* Roye wished."

It had been a gamble, buying cooperage— only the best— from winemakers who were getting out of the business. And Hugh had managed to pick up equipment some fellows were giving away.

Siegfried looked up at the completely rebuilt winery at the crest of the hill. This fall, he would make wine again. He would not have to follow his harvest pickers with tractors, tearing out his vines, as many other wine growers had done.

"Have you heard from Tati?" Hugh turned the glass around in his fingers. "I thought you mentioned she would be here."

"She will not talk to you?" Siegfried shook his head sadly. "What a stubborn old—"

"Roye," Hugh finished.

"She is a foolish old woman, Hugh. She did telephone this morning and apologize that she would be late. Something about her 'old bones.' Perhaps you will have another chance to—"

"I don't think she'll ever change. At least, after hearing Alice tell her side of the story, I understand *why*."

"Well, I hope, for her sake, that she will apologize to you today," Siegfried said, slapping Hugh on the back in comradely fashion.

Hugh gave a short laugh. "I'm glad Alice accepted *my* apology. Maria would have had me sleeping on the sofa forever, otherwise."

Siegfried looked for Alice and saw her talking and laughing with her neighbors. Bethie was safely asleep on

Florence's shoulder, and Maria was smoothing the baby's thin, strawberry blonde hair. He smiled at Hugh and lifted the glass in his hand. "We are so fortunate."

Hugh was about to agree when they were interrupted by a shout from above.

Henry Behrens, the master carpenter for the new house, had climbed into position. He waved his arm, and Siegfried and Hugh went to the cable looped over the rooftree. They pulled steadily and a fir wreath rose slowly above the gathered guests, many of whom called encouragement and advice. Alice and Maria came to stand near as the garland was hoisted onto the long beam.

And then, sitting on top of the roof, Behrens pounded in the final nail in the frame of the still-unshingled roof and addressed the attendees in a loud, American-accented German: *"Es möge Gott dieses Haus und die Bewohner vor Unheil zu schützen."*

Hugh clapped and cheered with the rest, but he looked askance at Siegfried when the noise died down. "So, what did he say?"

Siegfried grinned, grabbed Alice around the waist and kissed her in front of everybody. "And if it pleases God, protect this house and its inhabitants from all misfortune."

"Amen!" said Alice, and kissed him back.

Put me as a seal upon thy heart, as a seal upon thy arm,
for love is strong as death.
Song of Solomon, 8:6